Praise for the Lucy [Kincaid series]
from *New York Times* bestselling author
Allison Brennan

Stolen

"The evolution of Lucy and Sean's relationship has been a critical piece of what makes these novels so compelling. Brennan is a true master at providing byzantine plotlines that keep readers guessing as the danger amplifies."

—*RT Book Reviews* (4½ stars, Top Pick)

"All the excitement and suspense I have come to expect from Allison Brennan."　　　　　　—*Fresh Fiction*

Stalked

"Once again Brennan weaves a complex tale of murder, vengeance, and treachery filled with knife-edged tension and clever twists. The Lucy Kincaid/Sean Rogan novels just keep getting better!"

—*RT Book Reviews* (4½ stars, Top Pick)

"The novels featuring Lucy Kincaid and her cohorts are marked with deep characterizations and details of the workings of investigations by private eyes, the police, and the FBI . . . Catch the latest in this series as Lucy continues to evolve in strength and wisdom."

—*Romance Reviews Today*

"They've certainly got it . . . there's plenty to be a critical page-turner . . . these reviews, so engrossing, beyond . . . the matter is compelling tension, that they will keep readers glued to the pages until the . . ."

— *Publishers Weekly* (starred review), on *Tell No Lies*

"All the . . . monumental suspense . . . I have come to expect from Allison Brennan."

— *Associated Press*, on *Cut and Run*

"Dynamic . . . a smart, satisfying mystery . . ."

— *Kirkus Reviews* (starred review)

"Brennan has once again proven plenty of twists . . . no detail . . . steady throughout, filled with non-stop tension and a fast-paced plot like I love. Kincaid and Rogan are a . . . heroes you won't forget."

— *RT Book Reviews* (4½ stars, Top Pick)

"The . . . is fantastic. Tense, focused and action-packed . . . moving with clever . . . characters . . . only scratches at the surface of mysteries. She captures the reader and never lets go . . . the . . . Find . . . the latest work of her complicated . . . she wants to deliver, this installment . . ."

— *Romantic Review Today*

Silenced

"Brennan throws a lot of story lines into the air and juggles them like a master. The mystery proves to be both compelling and complex . . . [A] chilling and twisty romantic suspense gem."   —Associated Press

"The evolution of Lucy Kincaid from former victim to instinctive and talented agent continues in Brennan's new heart-stopping thriller . . . From first to last, this story grabs hold and never lets go."
                  —*RT Book Reviews* (Top Pick)

"An excellent addition to the Lucy Kincaid series. Lucy and Sean continue to develop as complex, imperfect characters with a passion for justice . . . The suspense [is] can't-put-it-down exciting."   —*Fresh Fiction*

BEST
LAID
PLANS

Allison Brennan

St. Martin's Paperbacks

This is a work of fiction. All of the characters, organizations, and events portrayed in this novel are either products of the author's imagination or are used fictitiously.

BEST LAID PLANS

Copyright © 2015 by Allison Brennan.
"Maximum Exposure" copyright © 2014 by Allison Brennan.
Excerpt from *No Good Deed* copyright © 2015 by Allison Brennan.

All rights reserved.

For information address St. Martin's Press, 175 Fifth Avenue, New York, NY 10010.

ISBN: 978-1-250-06432-5

Printed in the United States of America

St. Martin's Paperbacks edition / August 2015

St. Martin's Paperbacks are published by St. Martin's Press, 175 Fifth Avenue, New York, NY 10010.

10 9 8 7 6 5 4 3 2 1

CHAPTER ONE

Elise Hansen almost puked when she realized the guy was dead.

She bit her thumbnail, dreading what she had to do next.

"Why couldn't you have waited until *after* we screwed before you croaked?" she muttered.

But there was no turning back. She had the pictures she needed—he'd been out of it, but not so much that she couldn't get him into the right position—and now she had to finish it. In a manner of speaking.

Elise unbuckled his pants and pulled them down to his ankles. Then his boxers. He stunk, like he'd peed himself. She knew what she had to do, but it took her a minute to work up the courage.

"He's only going to get deader." She spit into her hand, then rubbed the guy's dick twice.

"Ugh." She ran to the bathroom to scour her hands. There was no soap, but the water got hot enough that she was satisfied there was no dead guy on her palm. She looked into the mirror—her makeup was still intact, but she reapplied the bright red lipstick because most of hers she'd smeared on the mark's neck and mouth.

No way in *hell* was she putting her mouth on his dick

now that he was dead. Why couldn't he have just gone along for the ride from the beginning? She was young and cute and knew exactly what to do and say to get any guy off, even the most prudish prick. How could he say *no*? It made her job that much more difficult. And disgusting.

She'd damn well better get a bonus.

Elise left the bathroom and surveyed the room. Her prints and DNA were where they needed to be, her mark was half-naked, and she'd been in enough cheap motel rooms to know the scene looked exactly how she wanted it to.

She extracted his wallet from his pants and removed his cash—$120—then tossed the empty billfold on the nightstand. She grabbed his cell phone and pocketed it before walking out.

"*Señora!*"

Elise closed the door and froze.

"*Señora*, I'm here for *Señor* Worthington. He say to come back in one hour."

She turned and assessed the intruder. He was in his thirties, Mexican, with a moustache and rumpled clothes. A taxi was parked a few stalls down.

She showed her best seductive expression. "I wore him out." Then she winked. "I can wear you out, too, sugar."

He backed off. "Uh, I'm married." He held up his left hand to show her his ring.

"So was he. It'll be between you and me."

The taxi driver shook his head. "Can, um, you tell *Señor* that I'm here?"

She frowned. "He has the key." She knocked on the door, then shrugged. "Sorry. He sleeps like a rock, I guess." She hesitated, considering what this driver might do or say. Chances are he would leave but she couldn't count on it. She glanced around, saw no one, then bit her lip and said quietly, "You know, I really gotta go or my boss will take it out on my ass. I don't like being knocked around." She jogged away from the motel, keeping her head down.

The taxi driver didn't follow or comment.

At first, Elise thought getting caught outside the door would be trouble, but then she realized it could actually work to her benefit.

Once she was out of sight of the motel, she slowed to a walk and continued three blocks south. She opened the rear door of an idling black Mercedes, and settled back into the soft leather seat. The car pulled into traffic.

"Problems?"

"The guy didn't want to fuck. But I got the pictures, and everything else went as ordered." Sort of.

"Anyone see you?"

"Worthington's taxi driver returned. I hit on him and he scurried away."

Silence.

"What?" she said.

"You were supposed to be a scared whore, running because her john had a heart attack."

She rolled her eyes. "He barely spoke English."

"That doesn't matter! Dammit, Elise, can't you do one thing right?"

"I did it *all* right, and I'm not going to take shit from you. Told the driver that my boss would beat me if I didn't get back. Besides, he probably'll just disappear. He's a fucking taxi driver, not a rocket scientist."

"You're a fucking bitch."

"I learned from the best." She stuck her tongue out at the back of the driver's head. Mona Hill was an old whore; Elise was the next generation. But right now, they needed each other. "They'll find me and I'll play my part. I've already done my research. This is going to be a piece of cake."

"Don't get cocky. There's a lot at stake and we can't afford any screw-ups."

Elise scowled. Like Mona needed to tell *her* that?

Mona drove Elise ten minutes across town and pulled into a hotel roundabout. "Your john is waiting for you in room 606. Make sure you let the security cameras see you. And try to look at least a little scared."

"Nothing scares me." She took the card key from her driver.

"And that's what's going to get you killed, Elise. Fear can be healthy."

Fear? Not her. *Never.* Fear wasn't even in her vocabulary.

"This'll be a rough one," Mona continued, "but that'll play to our benefit."

"Maybe you should go fuck him then."

"Get out, and remember who owns you."

Elise got out of the car and slammed the door. *No one* owned her. She just let them think they did. She took a deep breath and tried to look scared.

It was hard to look scared when you'd been looking out for your own ass most of your life.

Because she had a hotel card key, she was able to access a side door and go up the stairs—not the elevator—to the sixth floor. She made a point to look down the hall both ways—let both security cameras see her, eyes downcast, looking skittish and guilty—then sought out room 606.

She let herself into the room. It was a whole world nicer than the motel she'd just left.

A man in his late forties lay partly clothed on the bed. She didn't know his name and he didn't know hers, but that didn't matter. Mona knew exactly who he was.

He was playing with himself while watching porn on the hotel's television. "You're late." He stood up. He was pudgy around the middle with a sharply receding hairline.

She pouted. "I'm sorry. I'll make it up to you." She looked at X-rated video he was watching. The girl was masturbating while sucking off the guy. "You want me to do that to you?"

"I want a lot of things." He licked his lips. "How old are you?"

"How old do you want me to be?"

"Legal."

She smiled. "I'm legal."

"You look younger."

Because she was, but she wasn't going to blow this job. Too much money at stake. Sure, she was a little nervous. Who wouldn't be? But it wasn't like she hadn't done it before.

Elise walked over to the hotel bar and took out a bottle of vodka. She took a long swig, then put the bottle down. She moved things around a bit, put her purse down. The other mark's phone slid partly out of her bag. She smiled, took another drink, and turned around.

He was right behind her.

"I picked this hotel because the walls are thick, and I want to hear you. Understand?" He grabbed her by the wrists. It hurt, but she didn't react.

"Yes. I need the money first."

He frowned, but gestured toward a white envelope on the desk. He dropped her wrists and went back to the bed, watching her closely. She picked up the envelope, glanced inside, quickly counted. Two hundred dollars.

That, on top of the thousand dollars she was being paid to set the jerk up. With the earlier job, she was pulling in over three thousand dollars tonight.

Not bad. But there was even more money for her down the road. Tonight was just icing on the cake.

She stuffed the envelope into her purse, adjusted the flap, then said, "What do you want me to call you?"

"Call me Daddy. And I'm going to spank you. Hard."

This was getting better by the minute.

"Spank me, Daddy," she said, and he did.

CHAPTER TWO

Sean woke up the moment Lucy climbed out of bed. He glanced at the bedside clock. It was 3:30 A.M.

Lucy slipped out of the room and Sean sat up. It had been months since Lucy had had a full night's sleep. This insomnia of hers was going to wear her out. And him. He'd found himself napping during the day for a couple hours after lunch, and he couldn't blame the heat.

It was more than insomnia. Lucy was physically and emotionally drained and wanted to hide it from everyone. Except, she couldn't hide it from him even if she wanted to.

He'd thought she was fine. After they'd rescued nine abused boys who'd been used as couriers for a drug cartel, Lucy had seemed to be unfazed by the whole operation. She'd saved lives. But to save lives, she'd had to take lives. She'd had to lie about defying orders even though her boss suspected what she'd done. She'd wanted to come clean but couldn't without damaging the careers and reputations of others.

She'd been put on administrative leave for two weeks and didn't blink. They'd spent part of her leave in Sacramento with his brother and newborn niece. While she'd been upset about disappointing her boss, she'd appeared content. She'd spent more time with her brother Jack and Sean's brother Kane than anyone else, but at the time Sean hadn't thought much about it.

That should have been his first clue. When he'd first met Lucy eighteen months ago, she had kept herself closed off from others, icy and distant. It had been a defense mechanism to manage the pain and rage from her past. Constantly training, running for miles, working long hours. She didn't let herself feel anything, and that meant the only time her emotions were free to escape was in sleep. And those emotions became nightmares, violent memories that Sean had helped Lucy overcome.

And for months, he'd thought they were over. After they'd moved to San Antonio in January, she rarely woke before dawn, her insomnia under control. But the nightmares had returned when they came home after her leave. He wanted to pull the truth from her, because he didn't think she was being honest with him. She wasn't lying to him . . . just omitting details. She never wanted to worry him. But what she didn't understand, what Sean hadn't made clear enough, was that holding back made him worry more.

He thought time would fix the problem, as long as he was here for her, and some nights she did sleep soundly. But not tonight. The urge to hit something propelled him out of bed. He'd put in an aggressive workout later. Instead, he followed Lucy downstairs.

He thought she'd be in the kitchen brewing coffee—he smelled the rich coffee beans Lucy liked—but the pool lights were on. He walked outside and saw Lucy swimming laps, her long, curvy body as graceful as a mermaid's as she swam the breaststroke one way, flipped, and did the backstroke going back. He could watch her for hours. She'd swum in high school and college, but now she did it for fun. Or a workout. Or trying to out-swim her personal demons.

The late spring nights were cool, but not cold, and the early morning air was refreshing. It would be another humid scorcher today, but right now the weather was perfect. Maybe there was a benefit to getting up at three thirty in the morning.

Sean liked everything about the Olmos Park house he'd picked out for them, but the pool had sold him. It wasn't as fancy as some of the others—no rock walls or elegant waterfalls or curving design. It was a large, black-bottomed rectangle and the only added touches were custom tiles along the edges and a raised infinity hot tub that dropped water into the pool below. When Lucy first saw the pool she grinned like a kid, then jumped in fully clothed. Such behavior was out of character, but also a testament to her complete and total joy, justifying Sean's decision to purchase the house and surprise her.

Sean wanted that Lucy back. The Lucy he knew was still in there, waiting for the nightmares to run their course.

After twenty laps, Lucy slowed down for a few more, then got out and spotted him. "I woke you up," she said. "I'm sorry."

He handed her a towel and kissed her lightly on the lips. "Do you want to talk about it?"

She shrugged and dried off. "I feel better." She drank from a water bottle. She was out of breath, but there was color in her cheeks.

He wrapped a hand around her neck and kissed her warmly. "I'm here."

"It helps."

"I want to do more."

"You do far more for me than you should. I need to stand on my own two feet. But having you here gives me peace. Know that. I'll get over this funk."

"It's more than a funk, Lucy. We've been back for two months and you've only slept through the night twice."

She frowned. "Are you keeping track?"

"No, not like that, but I love you and I know when you're not sleeping."

"The nightmares aren't so bad," she said. "They just seem real. They startle me, because I wake up at first not knowing that it was a dream. I think that's what's bothering me so much. There's like a minute or two when I don't know where I am, I don't know who I'm with, I think I'm still there."

"Where are you?"

She didn't answer the question, not directly. "It changes." But she didn't look him in the eye, and he feared she was retreating further into the past, beyond the imprisoned boys in Mexico, back to the darkest time of her life, when she'd been held captive by a psychopath and repeatedly raped.

Sean hugged her tightly, because he had to. For him as much as for her. She grabbed him just as tight. She whispered, "Let's go back to bed."

He kissed her. He would have made love to her in the pool, on the lounge chair, *anywhere*, but Lucy would be nervous having sex outside. And he wanted—needed—her to relax and feel how much he loved her. He picked her up and carried her inside.

As soon as he stepped through the door, the house phone rang. Lucy jumped out of his arms. "It's never good news before dawn," she said and answered the closest phone. "Hello?"

Sean watched her face. In two blinks she'd gone from romantic to panicked to professional.

"I'll be there in thirty minutes," she said a few minutes later then hung up. "That was Juan. A VIP is dead. Doesn't appear to be murder, but the circumstances are suspicious, and the dead guy is a government contractor with high-level security clearance. The powers that be want the FBI to take the lead."

The way she spoke surprised Sean. "Do you know him?"

"No, why?"

"Because you generally show more compassion for the dead."

She hesitated then said, "SAPD reports that the guy, fifty-four, was having sex with an underage prostitute when he died. They think heart attack, the girl got scared and ran. The police think the girl robbed him after he died. She was scared that her pimp would beat her senseless if she didn't bring back any money. And yet this pervert is the *victim*? If the police find her, they'll terrify her even more." She started up the stairs. Halfway up she turned around. "I'm sorry, Sean."

"No apologies. It's nice to see that fire back. But I will take a rain check on what you promised."

She smiled at him, warm and genuine with a hint of teasing. "I'm cashing in that rain check tonight." Then she ran up the stairs.

Maybe Lucy was okay. At least she sounded like she was back on track.

Sean went to the kitchen to make her breakfast. If he didn't feed her before she left, he knew she'd go without until lunch, and after that morning swim, she needed fuel.

CHAPTER THREE

The White Knight Motel was near the freeway, on Camp Street, not far from San Antonio PD central headquarters. It could have been cloned from any number of dives in the area—two-story crumbling structures with questionable rental and cleaning policies. Lucy had investigated a murder at a place just like the White Knight when she'd been in D.C. last year. A prostitute had been brutally murdered and Lucy had moved heaven and earth to work that case and find the killer.

This time, the john was dead, and Lucy had no sympathy.

The coroner's van was already on site, along with several SAPD cop cars. It was barely dawn and the on-lookers were mostly drunks or other guests at the motel—keeping their distance, wary of the police.

Juan had given Lucy the bare minimum of information—he'd hardly spoken to her outside of work for the two months she'd been back on duty. She'd hoped her two-week administrative leave had been enough time for her boss to forgive her, but Juan was still angry. Maybe not angry—disappointed. Somehow, that was worse.

Suck it up, Kincaid.

Before she got out of her car, she read over the brief memo Juan had emailed to her and the other agent assigned to the case, a nearly twenty-year veteran named Barry Crawford. She hadn't partnered with Crawford before. In the six months she'd been in San Antonio, she'd noticed that Crawford was one of those agents who did his job and went home. He seemed to be smart and competent, but she couldn't remember him ever working past five or taking an extra assignment.

Juan's memo was brief and to the point. The deceased was Harper Worthington, owner of Harper Worthington International, a global accountancy corporation that primarily handled government contracts and audits. Because he specialized in auditing defense contractors, he had a high-level federal security clearance. In addition, he was married to Congresswoman Adeline Reyes-Worthington.

Worthington had been found dead and partially clothed in a motel room at the White Knight at approximately 1:00 A.M. by the motel manager when a taxi driver retained by Worthington insisted management check the room. The driver had been waiting for over an hour for the deceased, who had requested the pickup, and he'd witnessed a teenaged girl leaving just after midnight. When SAPD arrived and checked the deceased's ID, they recognized the name and contacted their chief, who in turn contacted the FBI.

Juan ended with:

> *This case is need-to-know. I don't have to explain the sensitivities of not only Worthington's position as a government contractor, but the potential media interest because of his congressional ties. I expect this case to be handled with complete discretion and the utmost professionalism.*

Lucy checked her reflection in the rearview mirror. Sean was right, she looked tired. She added more concealer under her eyes and a touch more makeup than she usually wore before she got out of the car.

Lucy recognized Julie Peters, one of the deputy coroners. Lucy had met many of the SAPD and county staff during the two months she'd spent working on Operation Heatwave, which had culminated in hundreds of arrests of wanted fugitives through the combined efforts of all levels of law enforcement.

Julie was leaning against her van talking to one of the cops as Lucy approached. "I heard the feds were taking over," Julie said.

"By mutual agreement," Lucy said. "Good to see you again, Julie."

"VIP," Julie said and rolled her eyes. "Agent Kincaid, meet Officer Garcia. Garcia, Kincaid. She's okay for a fed."

"I'll take that as a compliment." Lucy extended her hand to Garcia.

"You should. Julie doesn't like anyone," Garcia said.

Julie snorted. "Not true. I just prefer dead people. They don't lie."

Lucy didn't know Julie's story, but she was about forty years of age, dressed down almost to the point of being sloppy, wore no makeup, and had a barking laugh. She'd also graduated from the prestigious university Texas A&M with a degree in biology and a minor in chemistry. She was a well-respected forensic pathologist.

Lucy asked, "Is the body still inside?"

Julie nodded. "Waiting on the crime scene techs. I swear, they're a bunch of prima donnas now that they have a gazillion television shows about them. Think they run the world. Well, that body's gonna start stinking to high hell as soon as the sun comes up, so they'd better get a move on." She glared at Garcia.

"I'll make another call." He stepped over to one of the patrol cars and picked up the radio.

"Is Agent Crawford here?"

Julie scowled. "Perfect Hair? Not yet."

Lucy barely refrained from laughing. The moniker fit Crawford.

"Wanna see the body? He was caught with his pants down, literally. That's why I love the dead. They have no secrets."

She did want to see the room, because crime scenes were her specialty. But she'd been on thin ice for two months, and Barry was the lead agent. "I should wait for Barry."

Julie shrugged.

Garcia came over and said, "Five minutes out, they said."

"They mean fifteen," Julia countered. She looked at her watch. "It's quarter after five. They'd better get their asses here or I'm going to chew them a new one. I want the body on my table this morning—and considering who he is, he'll go to the front of the line. If there's anything wonky here, I'll find it."

That perked up Lucy's ears. "Wonky? Prelim said heart attack."

"Right, and patrol cops can tell that just by looking at a corpse. I did an external exam when I got here and sure, it has all the signs of a guy getting his rocks sucked off until his heart gives out, but . . ." She motioned for Lucy to follow her.

Lucy hesitated, glancing around for Barry, but he hadn't yet arrived. Her curiosity won out and she followed Julie. Yellow tape sealed off room 115, but the door was open.

Worthington was flat on his back on top of the stained

brown bedspread. His pants and boxers were around his ankles. His shoes were on his feet. His white dress shirt was unbuttoned and he wore an undershirt. The man was lean and looked like he exercised regularly.

On the dresser was a half-empty bottle of cheap vodka and two plastic cups. Lucy breathed deeply. The room smelled dirty, and there was a sharp liquor aroma as well as the stench of urine. He may have thrown up, though she didn't see any evidence of it from the doorway. His wallet was on the lone nightstand.

"Are you tired, or what?" Julie asked. "You look like you've been up all night."

"Just didn't get enough sleep."

Julie nodded in commiseration, but said, "Look again—you'll see it."

Lucy looked again, taking in first the big picture, then the smaller details. "Okay—it looks too neat. A sudden heart attack isn't instantaneous. He would have bunched up the comforter, tried to get up, maybe knocked over the lamp. Collapsed on the floor, across the bed, not laid out on his back. Called for help, maybe. But if he didn't know he was having an attack, which is possible, he may not have reacted, especially if he was drunk or on drugs. It would be a massive coronary event, though, and the prostitute would certainly have known something was wrong."

"True—too scared to report but not too scared to empty his wallet?"

Lucy didn't comment. She'd worked enough cases with prostitutes to know that their psychology could be complex. The girl was more scared of her pimp than the police.

"Okay, I'm giving you a rough time because you really can't tell unless we inspect the body up close and personal, like I did a frickin' *hour* ago when I got here," Julie said, looking over her shoulder and muttering about entitled nerds. She pointed to Worthington's pants around his ankles. "The deceased peed in his boxers when he croaked. Bladder totally released."

"Which would suggest that he was wearing them when he died."

"Suggest?" Julie laughed. "Cops. All about alleged this and possible that. He *was* wearing them. And his pants, which are also soaked with urine."

"Not sperm?"

"I know the difference between sperm and urine, Kincaid." Julie rolled her eyes. "Of course I'll test to make sure, but I'm not usually wrong." She shrugged. "Maybe there's nothing to it. Maybe the girl didn't realize he was having a heart attack and thought he was just excited to screw her. But I think that a rich guy like Worthington would have found a better place to screw a whore, ya know?"

"It's about power. Secrets. Discretion."

"He could have bought discretion two miles from here at a four-star hotel. And why a street girl? There's a whole business of call girls in town, you pay for discretion and a modicum of class."

"The girl was underage, according to the witness, and that makes him a pervert. Perverts like seedy motels." She was getting angry. Not so much at Julie's flippant conversation, but at how her tone seemed to suggest that she condoned the whole sex business. Or if not condoned, at least tolerated.

But when powerful men like Worthington started using underage prostitutes, it wasn't a new or sudden obsession. He would continue and eventually look at younger girls. Because it was about power and control, the need to dominate, the belief that girls were chattel to be bought and sold like animals. It wasn't the crime scene in front of her that made Lucy's stomach turn over uncomfortably, it was the motivation of the dead guy. She couldn't muster much compassion for him. Maybe his death was divine retribution.

Officer Garcia called over to them. "CSI just pulled up."

"It's about effing time," Julie said.

"And another fed."

"Thank you," Lucy said. She turned to Julie. "I've worked too many cases where prostitutes were beaten and murdered by men like Worthington. I don't have a lot of sympathy."

Julie assessed her. "Well, you're welcome to sit in on the autopsy. Assist if you want—you have the creds. But trust me when I say this: I've worked in San Antonio for thirteen years, have been called to thousands of death scenes, and have performed over three thousand autopsies, everything from stabbings to strokes to heart attacks to sudden infant death syndrome. Some that looked suspicious, but were natural; some that looked natural but weren't. Ninety-seven percent of my cases are routine, nonviolent deaths." She paused to remove the crime scene tape so the two CSIs could go in and process the room. "My gut tells me Worthington falls in the three percent."

Lucy approached Agent Barry Crawford as he was talking to one of the patrol officers. Barry was dressed impeccably, as always—pressed light gray suit, shiny black shoes, crisp white shirt. His blond hair was neatly trimmed and styled—and yes, perfect—and he looked like the stereotypical fed. He was physically fit and always wore a serious expression. Lucy couldn't remember ever seeing him actually smile, and he never laughed. She knew very little about Barry because he rarely participated in casual conversation with the squad and never socialized after work.

Barry glanced at her. "You should have waited for me."

"Excuse me?"

"You went into the room."

"I just looked."

Barry ignored the comment and said, "Officer Nava says the taxi driver wants to leave. We need to interview him before he does. You speak fluent Spanish, right?"

"Yes."

"Mine is rough. Translate for me."

"I can question him if you want to—"

"I need to ask the questions."

Lucy bristled. She might be a rookie, but she was also a psychologist and had extensive training in interrogations and questioning witnesses. She could handle a simple interview. But she kept her mouth shut, remembering that she *was* a rookie, and already on thin ice with her boss. More than anything, she wanted to get back into Juan's good graces, and if that meant taking orders from Crawford, she would do it.

Officer Nava led them across the parking lot to where the motel manager sat with the taxi driver on a worn bench outside of the small office. The office had bars on the windows and no place inside to sit.

The manager said, "Y'all need to get that body out of my motel and let me get back to work. You're ruining my business."

Barry said, "Officer, please take Mr. Valera to retrieve the logbooks and surveillance tapes."

"We don't have any of that," Valera said.

"Then step aside so I can do my job. I'll talk to you next."

Barry nodded at Nava, who took the manager far enough to prevent eavesdropping. Valera lit up a cigarette and paced.

The taxi driver had been identified as Carlos Potrero. He showed his ID and cab license to Barry. He was edgy, but Lucy suspected it was simply because he'd been here for hours—he could have easily left before the police arrived. That told her he wanted to help, even though it had likely cost him half his daily income.

"Mr. Potrero, do you speak English?" Barry asked after identifying them as federal agents.

He moved his hand up and down. "A bit."

"Agent Kincaid will translate if you're more comfortable speaking in Spanish."

"Si. Gracias."

Barry instructed Lucy to ask the driver how he knew Mr. Worthington.

Lucy asked in Spanish, "Mr. Potrero, you told Officer Nava that you dropped Mr. Worthington off here at eleven P.M. and that he asked you to return at midnight, correct?"

"Si, Señora."

"Have you driven Mr. Worthington before? Did he call and request you?"

"No, Señora."

"Where did you pick him up?"

"Airport."

"San Antonio Airport?"

"Si."

Barry cleared his throat. "Agent Kincaid, you need to translate for me."

Barry should have been able to pick up on the simple answers, even with basic Spanish. Was this his way of wielding his authority? "Mr. Potrero never met Mr. Worthington before tonight. He picked him up at San Antonio Airport, left him here at eleven, was asked to return at midnight."

"Which airline?" Barry asked. "Did he pay by cash or credit?"

Lucy frowned and said to Barry, "I know what to ask. I'll translate for you, and let me know if I forgot anything.

This three-way conversation is going to make it difficult on all of us."

Barry gave her a curt nod, but the pulsing vein in his neck showed his irritation.

She asked Mr. Potrero the questions, and translated for Barry. "He picked Worthington up at the United terminal. Worthington paid cash—two hundred dollars up front."

"That's high for a trip from the airport."

Lucy agreed and asked Mr. Potrero why Worthington had paid so much.

In rapid Spanish, he replied, "He's a very nice man. We talked about my family. My wife, my three girls. He said it was for a round trip, he was returning to the airport to catch another flight, and the money was for my waiting time. He told me to take a break and be back in an hour. I didn't want to take so much, but he insisted. I came back in exactly one hour." It seemed important to Potrero that Lucy believe he was honest.

Lucy relayed the information to Barry, then asked Mr. Potrero, "Did he say why he was coming here?"

"A meeting, *Señora*. He had a meeting and it would take no more than an hour."

"But you knew which room he was in."

"I watched him go into room 115"

Barry said, "Ask about the girl."

"Mr. Potrero, you told the other officers that you saw a girl coming out of the room. Can you describe her?"

"*Sí*. Young. Fifteen. Sixteen, no more. But old—you know—street old."

"I understand. Hair color? Eye color? What did she wear?"

"Hair was blond, but from dye, you know? Brown eyes."

"Hispanic?"

"No, white."

"White like me or like Agent Crawford?" Lucy asked

because she was half-Cuban, and while she had the dark hair and eyes, her skin was lighter than most Hispanics'. Crawford was clearly Caucasian.

"Whiter than both of you. Very pale skin."

"That's good. And what did she wear?"

He looked almost embarrassed. "Short shorts. A short T-shirt, you know." He put his hand across his midriff. "Lots of makeup. Too much. I see a lot of girls like her because I drive nights. Sometimes, I give them a ride. Do nothing with them!" he added, as if she would think he was a pervert. "Just a ride. But I've never seen her before."

"Would you recognize her?"

"*Si.*"

"Would you be able to go down to the station and look at some pictures?"

He looked panicked. "Now? I must be home by seven. My wife goes to work then, someone needs to watch my girls."

"Anytime before five this afternoon."

He sighed in relief. "*Si*, after I take my girls to school, I come in."

Lucy looked at Barry, told him what Mr. Potrero said about the prostitute, then asked, "Do you think Detective Mancini can work with him?"

"You know Mancini?"

"From Operation Heatwave." Tia Mancini had been on the joint task force because she was the lead SAPD detective for sex crimes. In her capacity, she also worked with victims of the sex trade—particularly underage prostitutes. She helped at-risk girls get off the streets. If the girl had been on the streets a while, Tia would know who she was.

"I'll call her," Barry said.

Lucy reached into her wallet and handed Mr. Potrero one of Tia's cards. "This detective will show you some pictures."

"You carry her cards with you?" Barry asked.

"We're friends," she said, "and worked together in the past."

Barry said, "Ask him why he waited so long."

Lucy thought on that—Barry's question was a bit hostile, and Potrero had clearly understood him, but opted to feign ignorance.

"Carlos," she said, using his first name to build a better rapport, "not many taxi drivers would wait for a client for so long."

"He paid me. A lot of money. The girl said he was sleeping."

"What else did the girl say to you?"

"I—I can't repeat it." He averted his eyes.

"You don't have to use exact words. Can you give me the basics?"

He looked pained. He looked at Barry and answered in broken English. "She offered her . . . services."

Like many devout Hispanic men, he didn't want to discuss sex in front of a female. Lucy understood—it was a cultural consideration.

Barry nodded. "Did you take her up on her offer?"

Lucy bit her tongue to refrain from saying something to Barry. No way was she going to ask that—it was clear from Potrero's body language that the mere thought disturbed him.

"No, no, no!" Potrero shook his head.

Lucy interrupted. "Where did the girl go? Did she have a car? Did she leave on foot?"

He pointed between the office and the main building. "She ran down that path. Told me she had to go, her boss would beat her." He shook his head. "Where's her family? How do girls do this? So many, too many, and bad men beat them. I don't understand."

"Go home and hug your children," Lucy said and gave

him her card. "We have your contact information, and may be following up with you after you talk to Detective Mancini."

Barry said, "Ask him if Worthington had a bag with him when he picked him up at the airport."

She did, mentally hitting herself that she hadn't thought of it.

"No bag. He said he was flying in for this meeting and flying out tonight. He didn't even have a briefcase." The driver paused. "He made a call. Left a message for someone."

"Do you know what he said?"

"I didn't want to pry. It sounded personal. I heard him say, 'I'll see you at breakfast.' But that's all."

Lucy and Barry approached room 115 as the crime scene techs were telling Julie she could take the body.

"There's not much we're going to get from here," one of them said. "We bagged the vodka and cups, the wallet, printed the door, nightstand, bathroom knobs, dresser. But we're getting dozens of prints. We'll bag up the bedding if you need it."

"Better to be thorough," Barry told them.

Lucy concurred. If this was a suspicious death like Julie thought, they had to treat it as such from the beginning. There was no going back to collect evidence after the fact, especially in a place like this.

"Did you find a cell phone?" Barry asked.

They hadn't and they'd conducted a thorough search. There was nothing in his pockets. His wallet had three receipts tucked away, two from today and one from yesterday, all from Dallas businesses. Barry asked for copies to be emailed to him as soon as they were processed, but he also wrote down the names and addresses from the receipts. There were no flight stubs in his pockets or wallet, and no return ticket. Not unusual if he used a mobile boarding pass. Barry stepped out of the room to take a call.

Lucy watched as Julie and her crew zipped up the body bag, then she followed them to the coroner's van where they loaded the body and slammed the door shut. Julie turned to Lucy. "I'm cutting into the guy at eight A.M. sharp. Come if you want." She climbed into the van and waved good-bye.

Lucy didn't see Barry, so she watched the crime scene techs finish bagging potential evidence. They chatted among themselves while they worked. She'd been where they were. She'd collected evidence and processed scenes. It was methodical and organized, and the routine soothed her.

Harper Worthington had been in Dallas until last night, when he'd flown in late, apparently to have sex with an underage prostitute. Worthington lived in San Antonio, his business was in San Antonio; why would he come to his hometown for sex when it would have been easier for him to find a no-name motel in Dallas?

And Julie was right about the money—Worthington could afford a much nicer place, and considering he'd paid hundreds of dollars for the flight, why not fork over a hundred bucks for a halfway decent dive? There were motels and hotels closer to the airport. This made no sense. Except that it was anonymous. But if he wanted to remain anonymous, why stand out by giving the taxi driver two hundred dollars to return?

Barry approached her. "Let's go."

"We should talk to the manager."

"I did."

She glanced up at him. "I would have joined you."

"It was routine. And you're better with these lab rats than I am."

"I used to be one," she said. "What did he say?"

"Nothing that helps."

She mentally counted to ten so she didn't snap at her partner. "How did Worthington pay for the room?"

"He didn't. Manager didn't even see him. I got a basic description of the girl, but the taxi driver had more detail. Not much to go on, but maybe Mancini has a photo for him to ID."

"Prostitutes don't pay for the room. And if he didn't recognize her, she wasn't a regular."

"These kinds of places thrive on anonymity. I pressed, he couldn't give me anything."

"If she's in the system, we'll ID her," Lucy said. "There were prints on the vodka bottle and his wallet."

"We need to notify his widow before the press gets wind of this," Barry said.

Lucy looked at her watch. It was just after six in the morning. "Julie Peters said I could assist with the autopsy, if you want me to head over there."

"Let Peters do her job, you do yours," Barry said. "Meet me at FBI headquarters. I'll brief Juan and then we'll go to Worthington's house. So far, SAPD has kept everything quiet, but considering we have a couple witnesses, the crime scene techs, and a half dozen cops, I suspect the press is going to be circling like vultures before noon. I don't want the congresswoman hearing about her husband's death, or the circumstances, from anyone but us."

CHAPTER FOUR

Harper and Adeline Worthington lived on a large ranch twenty minutes northwest of town, where working ranches were interspersed among gentleman farms and horse property. Even the smaller tracts of land had to be at least ten acres, Lucy thought. Worthington's property didn't have cattle, but a large barn could be seen in the distance, surrounded by an empty corral.

Barry turned off the two-lane road and drove a hundred yards to a gate. He identified himself and a moment later the metal gate silently slid open. The system wouldn't keep out anyone determined. Two signs proclaimed that the land was monitored 24/7 by hidden cameras. They weren't that well hidden—Lucy spotted several at the gate and along the fence.

A wide expanse of grass separated the sprawling two-story ranch-style house from the perimeter, and towering, neatly trimmed ash trees lined the drive, providing shade and decoration. Though the house was large with a Spanish flair, it wasn't ostentatious.

"The legislature is in session," Lucy said. "Why is Congresswoman Worthington in town?"

"Congresswoman Reyes-Worthington," he said. "She hyphenates her maiden name. You should know that. As far as being home, she made a promise during her first campaign to return to the district on weekends."

Lucy hadn't immersed herself in local politics, and had only read a bit about the congresswoman while waiting for Barry to brief their boss. She'd been elected during a special election seven years ago when the sitting congressman had died while in office, a year after she'd married Harper Worthington. If the media could be believed, this upcoming election was going to be her most hard fought, as her opponent was a military veteran and the district had a sizeable veteran population in addition to displaced civilian employees from military base closures over the past twenty years. Yet she seemed popular and had built a broad coalition, according to the local newspaper's editorial board. They'd written an op-ed when they endorsed her in the first election that opined she was intelligent (graduating cum laude from a prestigious Texas university), successful (running her own real estate development business for two decades), had a popular father (a former six-term mayor), and had married into an old-time, well-respected Texas family (the Worthingtons).

She was Worthington's second wife—she'd married him eight years ago and had no children of her own. Worthington had one daughter from his first marriage, which had ended when his wife died from cancer when his daughter was only five. Now Jolene was twenty-nine and worked for her father at HWI headquarters.

"The spouse is always a suspect in a suspicious death," Lucy commented.

"This is a different situation. Worthington was supposed to be in Dallas."

"I wasn't implying she was guilty of anything, only that married men who use prostitutes tend to be repeat customers, and I'd think a wife would pick up on something like that."

"I may ask her that, but a suspicious death doesn't always mean foul play. We're not here to interrogate the congresswoman. Understood?"

"I wasn't intending to, I just thought—"

"I'm lead, so follow my lead."

Was Barry always such an arrogant jerk or was he this way because he was being forced to work with her? Had Juan said anything to Barry about her record?

Although Juan wouldn't have had to tell him anything. What had happened in Hidalgo and with their colleague Ryan Quiroz was no big secret. Everyone on her squad knew she'd disobeyed orders. Maybe they also suspected that she'd gone to Mexico in breach of a dozen different federal and international laws, but no one—not even Ryan—had said anything to her. Juan knew—not officially or unofficially, but he knew.

Which was why he didn't trust her.

Her head ached. The tension in her office was adding to her insomnia.

Lucy followed Barry to the door, which opened as soon as they knocked. The Hispanic male was dressed impeccably in a dark gray suit, crisp white shirt, and burgundy tie. Conservative and almost formal.

Barry showed his badge. "Special Agents Barry Crawford and Lucy Kincaid to see Congresswoman Reyes-Worthington."

He nodded formally. "I'm Joseph Contreras, her personal assistant. May I tell her what this is regarding?"

"We need to speak with her directly. It's about her husband."

Again, he nodded, then led them into a vaulted foyer with beautiful Spanish tile floors and a large glass chandelier towering above them. Far more opulent than

Lucy had expected and didn't fit in with the Tex-Mex decorations—a large wood-inlayed Texas star on one wall with the Texas flag and the American flag framed on either side.

"Wait here, please. You may have a seat." He gestured toward a long antique bench that Lucy recognized as a restored pew. *What a neat idea*, she thought.

Neither she nor Barry sat, but he studied the house, ignoring her. She'd started off on the wrong foot with him this morning—Barry was a by-the-book FBI agent with a solid record. He'd been in the Violent Crimes Squad in Los Angeles prior to 9/11; when VCMO had been drastically cut back, he'd been assigned to the elite Counterterrorism Squad in New York City. He'd transferred to San Antonio and back into Violent Crimes three years ago. It seemed like an odd move after such a high-profile assignment. If she knew Barry better, she would ask him more about his history and why he changed squads. While it was common for FBI agents to move around to different field offices—particularly after their rookie years—it wasn't as common for an agent to change specialties.

Contreras returned and said, "The congresswoman will be happy to meet you in her home office. She has a full schedule, so I need to ask that you keep this as brief as possible."

He led them down a large, wide hall past large, wide rooms with large, wide—and masculine—furniture. The residence felt like a man's house, and Lucy wondered if Worthington had lived here before he married Adeline.

Adeline's office was across from a spacious library with floor-to-ceiling bookshelves. Her office was smaller in scale, but no less grand. Here there was definitely a feminine touch—the floors were a pale cream, the walls a delicate-print wallpaper, and the furniture a light, intricately carved wood. A wall of windows looked out into a vast rose garden.

The congresswoman rose from her leather desk chair and walked over to them on four-inch heels. She was still shorter than Lucy, who wore low-heeled ankle boots. "I'm Congresswoman Reyes-Worthington. It's a mouthful, I know, so I insist you call me Adeline."

Barry and Lucy both shook her extended hand, and Barry handed her a business card. "FBI Special Agent Barry Crawford, and this is Special Agent Lucy Kincaid. May we sit?"

"Of course." She motioned to a couch and two chairs. Above the couch was a detailed oil painting of a battle Lucy was unfamiliar with. It included a Texas flag and pre–Civil War clothing.

Congresswoman Adeline Reyes-Worthington was an attractive, petite Latina dressed in a crisp, tailored business suit and soft pink silk blouse. She was in her forties and had the air of a businesswoman used to being in charge and getting things done.

"May I ask Joseph to bring coffee? Water?"

"No, thank you," Barry said. "We're here on official business. We regret to inform you that your husband, Harper Worthington, was found dead this morning."

She blinked several times. "Harper?"

"We are sorry for your loss. We won't keep you long, as I know this is a difficult time."

She shook her head. "I don't see how that's possible. I spoke to Harper last night, before I left for a charity dinner. He was fine." Her bottom lip quivered just a bit, and her voice cracked as she asked, "Was there an accident?"

"I need to be blunt with you. Though the FBI will do everything to ensure that no details of Mr. Worthington's death are released publicly, because you're a public official, there may be unscrupulous reporters digging around."

"I don't understand what you're saying." She turned to Lucy, confusion in her dark eyes. "How did he die? It was an accident, right? It had to be an accident."

Lucy didn't say anything, deferring to Barry.

"The Bexar County Medical Examiner's office is performing the autopsy, and we hope to have answers shortly," Barry said, "but you should know that his body was found at the White Knight Motel in downtown San Antonio."

She sighed in relief, though her eyes were still confused and wary. "It's not Harper. There has been a huge mistake. Harper is in Dallas on business. He won't be home until tomorrow morning. And he would never go to a motel."

"We have confirmed that the deceased is Mr. Worthington. He flew into San Antonio last night, arriving at approximately ten thirty P.M. He took a taxi from the airport to the motel, and had a return flight scheduled at one thirty-five A.M. He never made the return flight."

Adeline didn't say anything. She opened her mouth, then closed it. Her jaw quivered, and her left hand fumbled with the simple pearl necklace around her neck, as if touching it would stop the shaking.

Barry asked, "Were you aware that he was flying into town last night?"

She closed her eyes and shook her head.

"When did you last speak to him?"

"Five thirty last night." Her voice was a whisper and she cleared her throat. "He was on his way to a business dinner, and I was on my way to the charity event."

"Do you know who he was dining with?"

She shook her head. "We didn't talk about business."

Barry waited until Adeline was looking at him, then said, "An eyewitness saw a blonde woman who appeared to be a prostitute at the motel with your husband. Are you aware if your husband habitually used prostitutes?"

Lucy winced at the indelicacy of Barry's question.

Adeline shook her head emphatically. "Harper? Absolutely not."

"I'm sorry to be so blunt, Adeline," Barry said, his voice a bit softer, "but Mr. Worthington's body was found in a compromising position and I don't want you to hear about it from the media. We're working closely with the crime scene investigators and the coroner to determine exactly what happened, but it's important that we know everything about your husband's medical conditions. Did he have a heart condition?"

Adeline didn't say anything. Her eyes were wet, but she wasn't crying. She stared at first Barry, then Lucy, and then stood up. "I—I need a minute. Just two minutes. Please."

Barry stood, so Lucy followed. "Of course, take all the time you need."

Adeline walked briskly from the room.

Barry immediately got on his phone. Lucy felt compassion for the woman, who had to learn about her husband's perversion from two FBI agents. It had certainly thrown her, but Adeline seemed to have a spine of steel underneath the Southern charm.

Lucy looked around the room, trying to get a better feel for Adeline Reyes-Worthington.

Her office was immaculate, her desk devoid of clutter. A dainty straight-back chair sat directly on the plush carpet. There was no mat or impressions in the carpet, suggesting that she didn't spend much time working at this desk. No phone, no charger for the computer, and only one slender drawer in the desk. The decorative bookshelves contained a vast collection of leather-bound hardcover books and fancy knick-knacks.

Lucy had the distinct impression that Adeline didn't work in this office, that she used it only to meet with people who came to her home. It didn't necessarily mean anything, but the elected officials who Lucy had known when she lived in D.C. often worked from a home office.

She heard Barry wrap up his conversation. It was clear he was speaking to someone at headquarters, but she couldn't tell who it was from his end.

Adeline walked back into the room five minutes after she'd left. Her eyes were red and her mascara looked a bit smudged. "I called Jolene. She's in Dallas—she was supposed to have breakfast with her father, but he didn't show. She's been calling his cell phone and the hotel . . ." Her voice trailed off. "I had to tell her. I don't want her hearing about it on the news, and she was getting a bit frantic. I hope that's okay."

Without waiting for them to answer, Adeline continued, "Jolene and Harper were very close."

If someone told her over the phone that one of her parents was dead, Lucy would be extremely upset. It seemed very impersonal. It was why law enforcement, whenever possible, did death notifications in person. To make sure the person hearing the news had someone to stay with them. Adeline might have been Harper Worthington's wife, but Jolene was his only child.

"What did you tell Jolene?" Lucy asked.

Barry gave Lucy a sharp look, but Lucy kept her eyes on Adeline.

"I—I just said that Harper was found dead of a heart attack in San Antonio. I didn't tell her about the motel, or anything else. Oh, God, I'm going to have to tell her, aren't I? She worships her father. This is going to break her heart." She brushed away moisture under her eyes with the tips of her fingers.

"We didn't say he died of a heart attack," Lucy said.

"You asked if he had heart problems. I assumed." Adeline sat back down. So did Barry, but Lucy stood next to the sofa and asked, "And did he have heart problems? We'll get a copy of his medical records, but if you can give us the information now, it'll speed up our investigation."

"I—no, he didn't, though he'd seen his doctor last month and had been acting a bit melancholy. I thought perhaps a midlife crisis. Harper was always so grounded, so down-to-earth, I can't imagine . . ." Her voice trailed off and she looked at her manicured hands. "But that would explain the prostitute, wouldn't it?"

Barry cleared his throat and said, "We know this is difficult for you, Mrs. Worthington."

She nodded, glanced at Lucy, then turned back to Barry. "Thank you. I know you're just doing your job, and I appreciate that." She rose from her seat, turned her back to them, and stared out into the garden.

Barry narrowed his eyes at Lucy, then walked over to Adeline and said, "Why don't we sit back down? I only have a few more questions."

Barry steered Adeline back to the couch. Her questions were valid, though perhaps she should have asked them more diplomatically. Maybe Lucy was projecting, because it bothered her more than it should that Adeline had told Jolene about her father's death over the phone. Yet Barry himself had been blunt with Adeline. What had Lucy done wrong?

Barry said, "So you don't know if Mr. Worthington had any major health issues?"

"No. He played golf, rode his horses almost every day when he was in town. He's not that old, he'd have been fifty-five this September."

"Do you know why he flew from Dallas to San Antonio last night?"

"No. He would have told me. If not me, then Jolene.

They worked together. He was grooming her to take over HWI. For me," she added wistfully.

"I don't understand," Barry said.

"I wanted Harper to spend more time with me in D.C. He didn't like the travel, or the socializing—he's an accountant, he preferred numbers to people. But this election has been difficult—my opponent is an air force veteran, well liked, well funded by his party. Harper recognized that us being seen together was good for my career, and he supported me fully. He was the one who urged me to run in the first place when Roy—Roy Travertine—died while in office. Roy and Harper had been very good friends. But Harper was the face of HWI, so he couldn't take much time off. It's much harder for a male spouse in this business, than if our roles were reversed." She pulled a tissue from her small jacket pocket and averted her gaze while she dabbed at her eyes.

"Agent Crawford," she said after a moment of silence, "what really happened to my husband?"

"It appears to be natural causes, but because of the circumstances, we're investigating. Not only because he was married to a federal official, but also because his company has several sensitive federal contracts."

"You said he was with a prostitute . . . I can't even imagine why he'd do such a thing."

Lucy's ears perked up. It was how Adeline had phrased the comment.

"But you believe he could have?"

"Before today, no. I'd never have considered it. Are you certain this witness is reliable? Perhaps he or she was mistaken."

"Did you suspect your husband of having an affair?" Lucy asked, ignoring Barry's sidelong glance.

"Of course not. Harper wouldn't do that to me. He

knows that my career is important, that this election is critical. My party has hired additional campaign staff, allowed me to spend more time in the district to make sure I'm doing what I need to be doing to show my constituents that I'm accessible. Harper was a kind and generous man." But she looked away, as if she was thinking about something specific.

Before Lucy could press her, Barry asked, "Had your husband disappeared before? Taken a spontaneous trip?"

"Never. Not as long as we've been married." She hesitated, then added, "He travels to Dallas monthly for business. HWI has an office there, because so many of his clients are based in Dallas. HWI also has a small office in Arlington, Virginia, just outside of D.C.—because of their military contracts. He goes there two or three times a year."

Mr. Contreras entered the room. "Ma'am, I wouldn't normally interrupt, but Senator Clarkson is on the phone."

She quickly stood and looked both embarrassed and a bit panicked. "I forgot all about our scheduled call."

Barry rose. "We're done for now. I'll be in touch when we have more information about your husband's death. Would you like to release the information to the press or would you like the FBI to do so? We won't be sharing any details of the investigation."

She hesitated, then said, "Can I have a few hours? I need to wrap my mind around what's happening."

Barry nodded. "I would suggest you do so today, in case the press gets wind of it. We'd request you reveal no specific information until we have cause of death."

"Yes, of course. Thank you, Agent Crawford." She shook Barry's hand, then Lucy's. "Agent—I don't remember your name. I'm sorry."

Lucy handed her a card. "Kincaid," she said.

"Right. Kincaid. Thank you. Mr. Contreras will see you

out." Lucy had the distinct impression that the woman was lying about something.

Barry was silent for the first ten minutes of the drive to Harper Worthington's office. Lucy knew he was angry with her, but she didn't make a peep.

"What in the world were you thinking going after a member of Congress like that?"

"I wasn't going after her," Lucy said.

"Your questions were hostile and insensitive. She's in a position to have you removed from this investigation. I don't think you need another black mark on your record."

Lucy bristled. "I don't know what you think you know about me or my record, but I stand by my questions. Without asking, she contacted the deceased's daughter. Over the phone. *That* was insensitive."

"We do not judge how other people handle their personal lives. The congresswoman is not a suspect under interrogation."

"Perhaps."

"I will have you removed myself if you step over the line again."

"I didn't step over a line."

"She's a grieving widow."

"She wasn't surprised about the prostitute."

"She was in denial."

"I don't think so." Two years ago, Lucy would never have challenged anyone verbally, particularly someone with seniority. But she'd learned that her unique experience coupled with years of intensive training gave her insights that not all cops had. Confrontations still weren't easy for her, but she'd become more confident since Quantico.

"Were we even in the same interview?"

"One of the benefits of you asking the questions and me

observing is that I can catch subtle psychological clues that aren't always obvious. She was clearly surprised that he was in San Antonio. But I think she either knew or suspected that he was sleeping around. Maybe she didn't think prostitute, but that he was having an affair. Her reaction was off."

"People don't react in a set way."

"If she had broken down when you first mentioned the prostitute, then I would have believed her. If she had completely denied it from beginning to end, I would have believed her. But she went from *No, my husband never would have* to *Well, I should have seen the signs* without any leading down that path."

"You're reading far too much into this."

Lucy bit her tongue. It was difficult, but she did. "If she knew that her husband had a proclivity for underage prostitutes, that makes her just as guilty as he is."

"Stop. We're not investigating a congresswoman who *may* have known her husband was using hookers to get his thrills. We're investigating the death of a man under suspicious circumstances. The chances are, he died of natural causes. No blood, no external sign of injury, nothing. If it looks like a duck and acts like a duck—"

Lucy interrupted. "It looks like a duck, but we have no proof that it acts like a duck."

"I don't know what the hell you're talking about."

"I'm saying, we need to find out why Harper Worthington spent hundreds of dollars to travel from a big city to his hometown to have sex in a twenty-dollar-an-hour motel with a streetwalker when he planned on attending a breakfast meeting three hours away with his daughter."

Barry opened his mouth, then closed it. "Point taken. But I've been working Violent Crimes long enough to know that sexual deviants don't care how much money they have to spend to fulfill their fantasies."

Lucy's stomach turned over and she glanced away. Barry was right. Perverts would spend anything for their sick fetishes.

She should know.

Sean had picked the house in Olmos Park not only because of the privacy the landscaping afforded, or the attention to detail inside, but because it was located in an established neighborhood filled with trees, quiet streets, and families. The weekends were alive, with kids riding bikes, families walking to the nearby park, and the splashing of water from neighboring pools before the brutal heat of early summer drove everyone inside for the afternoon. With the dangerous and often unpredictable lives he and Lucy led, he'd picked the most normal, traditional neighborhood for their home.

Sean hadn't thought he'd like San Antonio when Lucy was first assigned here, but the city had quickly grown on him, and he and Lucy could be happy here—if he could help her overcome whatever was truly bothering her so deeply that it disrupted her sleep nearly every night.

His cell phone rang while he was finishing his morning workout in the small gym he'd added downstairs. He put a towel over his neck and grabbed his phone. He recognized the number and his heart sank. He could no longer put off this conversation.

"Rogan," he answered.

"Sean, it's Clive Devlin."

"I was expecting your call."

"Funny, I was expecting yours."

"I got your message, but I had to assess a few things." Sean walked down the hall to his office.

"I understand, especially if your answer is yes."

He hesitated. "I can't take the assignment."

Devlin didn't say anything for a minute. "If it's the money, name your price."

"It's not the money, it's the time." He sat down at his desk and booted up his computer. "I can't be gone for the next two weeks."

"I can work around your schedule. I know New York is quite a ways from Texas, but—"

"Dev, I appreciate the offer. Truly, I wish I could say yes, the job would be a challenge and I love a good challenge. But right now, I can't leave. Call my former partner, Patrick Kincaid. He'll be able to help you."

"You're the best at handling this kind of sensitive situation."

"I would drop almost anything for you, Dev. But right now—I have to be home." If Lucy knew that he'd turned down a job because he was worried about her, she would be furious. She'd insist she was fine and try to hide her nightmares from him. He hadn't told her about the offer, so she wouldn't know he'd declined.

Devlin said, "I won't push it, but there's no one I'd want more than you on this project."

"Patrick used to be the e-crimes expert at San Diego PD. He and I founded RCK East a couple years ago, and he's now running the office. He was good before he became my partner, now he's better. I taught him most of my tricks."

Devlin laughed. "From you, high praise."

"I'll let Patrick know you'll call." He sent an email to Patrick with Dev's information.

"Is there something wrong? All you have to do is ask."

"I appreciate that, but it's personal." He cleared his throat and continued. "Patrick will call me if he needs to. I just forwarded you his contact information. You're in good hands."

"I wish they were your hands, but I understand. Take care of yourself, Sean."

"You too, Dev."

Sean hung up. He wished his decision didn't feel so wrong.

He needed to find something to do locally. Money wasn't the issue—he had a flush savings. If he took a couple big jobs a year he'd be fine. But he needed to challenge himself. Lucy had told him that he'd be bored if he didn't have a puzzle to work out, and he'd told her he had plenty of things to keep him occupied. But she was right. He was bored. When he'd been a kid, boredom had gotten him into all sorts of trouble. He liked to think that now that he was thirty, he wouldn't fall into the same bad habits. But he didn't lie to himself: boredom had gotten him suspended from many schools, expelled from Stanford after he hacked into a professor's email, and nearly cost him his freedom when he hacked into a bank while at M.I.T. The challenge of solving complex puzzles coupled with the thrill of straddling—and occasionally going over—the legal edge still excited him.

When he first moved to Texas, he'd put some feelers out to local companies, not only in San Antonio and Austin but all the way in Dallas and Houston. He'd had a couple of temp jobs, but most of the businesses wanted to hire him to run their day-to-day security. He didn't want to work nine-to-five, be responsible for staff, have an in-house office, or wear a suit. It would be fun for a week or two, but once he got the operation up and running, he'd be bored again.

Maybe he needed a new approach. It was an election year, and he was well trained in event security. With his high-security clearance and contacts at the Secret Service as well as the FBI, maybe he could get on with a candidate or venue to run security for debates or speeches or rallies. He really didn't like politics and had never met a politician he trusted with a dime of his money, let alone the national treasury, but such an assignment wouldn't bore him because it would be different each time.

And more important, he would be at home with Lucy every night.

CHAPTER FIVE

The head of HWI's security was a tall, broad-shouldered man by the name of Gregor Smith. Barry had called ahead, and Smith was waiting for them when they arrived. Gregor was fifty, looked and talked like a cop, and was the first private security chief Lucy had ever met who carried a gun on his hip.

Why did an accountancy firm need an armed security chief?

"Let's go to my office," he said. He bypassed the security checkpoint, which included a metal detector.

Smith's office was on the second floor of the six-story building just inside the outer freeway loop. Though spacious, the offices were functional and efficient, neither cheap nor opulent. The atmosphere subtly said, *You can trust us with your money.*

"Thank you for seeing us on short notice," Barry said.

"Harper Worthington was one of the best men I've ever known. I've been here for ten years, been the head of security for the last six. Anything you need, it's yours. I already spoke to Harper's administrative assistant. She's on her way in to help pull any information or files that you need. But first—I need to ask—is this a homicide investigation?"

"Mr. Worthington died under suspicious circumstances, but there's nothing to suggest homicide," Barry said. "We're awaiting the autopsy report, but even though we've expedited this case, lab work could take a few days."

"What happened? Harper was supposed to be in Dallas last night."

Barry didn't answer the question. "The FBI is particularly concerned about any potential security breaches. Mr. Worthington didn't have his cell phone on him when he died, and though his office key card was still in his wallet, we don't know if and when he last used it. Since HWI has several sensitive federal contracts, we need to ensure that no information has been leaked."

"I've already started an internal audit, cancelled Harper's key card, and frozen his access. The last time Harper used his key card in this building was when leaving the parking garage Wednesday afternoon. We require the key card to both enter and exit the garage. We have scanners at all entrances that read the key cards whenever employees walk in and out of the building or into restricted areas."

"Is your work that sensitive?" Barry asked.

Smith nodded. "We have banking information for all of our clients, confidential tax returns, court documents, audit material. While most of the business runs on computers these days—and we have state-of-the-art computer security—we also have hard copies of all our reports archived in a temperature-controlled, fireproof vault. In addition to potential financial fraud, corporate espionage and insider trading are always a threat. Consider if a business had information about a pending court decision or an audit—they could use that information for illegal personal or professional gain."

Smith pressed a few keys and said, "Harper arrived at our Dallas office at seven thirty-seven A.M. Thursday morning. He left there Friday evening just after four." He clicked again. "His schedule has him having dinner with a client and his daughter, Jolene, at six on Friday."

"We'll need the client's contact information," Barry said. "Did you know that Harper Worthington flew into San Antonio last night and planned on returning to Dallas before this morning?"

Smith shook his head. "I would never have believed it if you hadn't told me. It's completely out of character. And it's not on his schedule."

Barry asked, "May we have a copy of his schedule?"

"Of course—his assistant, Ms. Alexander, will print out whatever you need."

"Because of Mr. Worthington's security clearance, and the fact that he was involved with a prostitute, we're concerned about his travel and—"

Smith interrupted Barry. "Harper was not using a prostitute."

"We have a witness."

"Your witness is mistaken," Smith said without hesitation. "Harper would never hire a prostitute. I want to know who this witness is. If that rumor gets out, Harper's reputation will be tarnished. His business—hell, I don't care about his business. I care about what it would do to his daughter. What it would do to his impeccable reputation in the community. It's simply not true."

Lucy's ears perked up. "You seem confident," she said, speaking up for the first time since introductions.

"Because I am confident. It's not something I can put my finger on specifically, but I was an MP in the army for twelve years, then a cop for ten years in Corpus Christi. I trust my gut, and my gut tells me Harper is everything he appears to be. Harper was a religious man. Not a wear-it-on-your-sleeve holier-than-thou hypocrite, but quietly religious. He didn't swear. He rarely drank, and when he did it was usually with a client. He raised his daughter after his wife died of cancer. He didn't even start dating again until Jolene was in college. In fact, before he met Adeline I don't think he saw anyone regularly. His entire life was HWI and Jolene."

"And his wife?"

"He loved Adeline, but when they married, he didn't change much. He still worked from seven in the morning until six in the evening, four days a week. He would attend her local campaign events, but he hated traveling to D.C. and only did it if there was something important to Adeline, like when she received an award from a humanitarian group last year. He supported her career wholeheartedly—he'd encouraged her to run for office in the first place when his friend Roy Travertine died. But Harper is San Antonio born and bred, and he loved it here. Adeline accepted it. They were sweet together. She'd sometimes surprise him and come by the office in the late afternoon with a treat, usually ice cream from Amy's. Harper loved ice cream."

Smith had been all professional and straightforward, but for the first time there was a crack in his demeanor. He averted his eyes for a moment and stared at the computer screen.

Lucy said, "I know this is difficult for you. We are very sorry for your loss."

Smith nodded. "I need to call the staff. When are you releasing the information?"

"The congresswoman asked that we let her do it," Barry said. "We advised her to do it today before the press does it first."

"I'll call Adeline and work with her. And Jolene—does she know yet?"

"Adeline called her," Lucy said.

"On the phone? I guess she's still in Dallas. Does Scott know?"

"Who's Scott?" Barry asked.

"Jolene's husband. He's a surgeon here in town, but if he's not on call he usually travels with Jolene. I'll call him."

"Mr. Worthington's cell phone is also missing," Barry said.

Smith frowned. "That's not good. I changed his password, but I'm more concerned about his emails. I can erase the phone remotely, but they may have already pulled down what they need—" He snapped his fingers. "Was this a robbery? We have GPS on all our phones."

"That would be helpful," Barry said.

Smith typed again on his computer. "I sent a note to our tech chief, he'll take care of any security issues related to the phone and determine its location. It shouldn't take long."

"I appreciate your cooperation," Barry said.

"Then tell me this—why do you think Harper was with a prostitute?"

"I can't share the details of an active investigation," Barry said. "Suffice it to say, there is both a reliable witness and physical evidence that Mr. Worthington was with a prostitute last night."

Smith shook his head. "I understand that you're doing your job, and I will do mine and ensure that no sensitive information has been compromised. But I want to make something perfectly clear: Harper Worthington was a good man who ran a good business. He would never enlist the services of a prostitute. And I sincerely hope you do everything in your power to protect his reputation. Not just for his company, but for his family. If what you say is true, that Harper flew into San Antonio last night, then you need to find out why. Because it sure as hell wasn't to have sex with a hooker."

Debbie Alexander, Harper's administrative assistant, met Lucy and Barry in the outer office of Worthington's suite of offices in the corner of the top floor. Like the rest of the business, the offices were spacious and minimalist, but there was a little more personality here—a large old map of Texas framed on one wall, pictures of Harper with staff and friends, business recognition plaques, and certificates of appreciation. HWI had sponsored a Little League baseball team and a girls' softball team for the past fifteen years and all the team pictures were framed on one wall.

"Let's go to my office," she said. Her office was large and functional with multiple workstations and doors on either side, one labeled *Harper Worthington, CEO.* Instead of looking out to the freeway like the security office, she had a view of a man-made lake and a small park. She sat down at her desk and turned on her computer.

Debbie had made an attempt to put herself together— tailored gray business suit, crisp white shirt, and her black hair pulled tightly back into a bun. But she wore no makeup and her eyes were red and swollen, though dry. Lucy noted that she wore two different-colored pumps, one black and one navy. The only jewelry she wore was a gold wedding band and a small diamond ring.

"Thank you for coming in so quickly," Barry said. He glanced at her wall and said, "You were in the Air Force?"

"Yes, sir. Six years."

"And Texas A&M?"

"Yes—on the GI Bill. I graduated with honors in finance and business administration. Mr. Worthington recruited me right out of college, and I've been with him for five years."

She typed on her computer.

"How far back do you want his schedule?"

Barry didn't answer right away. He sat down, so Lucy took the other chair. "You tell me, Ms. Alexander. Did you know Mr. Worthington had a round-trip ticket to San Antonio from Dallas last night?"

"No, sir," she said.

"Is that odd?"

"Yes. I handle all his travel arrangements. But it's also odd because Mr. Worthington is frugal. He is willing to spend money, but he doesn't waste it. He's efficient."

"Has he done anything like this before?"

"No," she said, then glanced away, her brows furrowed.

"Do you remember something?"

"It's personal."

"It's important that we know everything that relates to Mr. Worthington's life, particularly during the last few weeks," Barry said. "There may be extenuating circumstances. But it's clear from our investigation, even though we're just getting started, that his behavior last night was out of character."

"Behavior?"

When Barry didn't explain, Debbie said, "Three weeks ago, he canceled a lunch with one of his top clients. He never canceled on anyone, unless it was an emergency—and when I say emergency, I mean serious, like when Jolene's appendix ruptured last year. But three weeks ago, he left work early and said he wasn't feeling well." She stopped abruptly, and seemed conflicted about whether to speak.

"Anything you tell us is important to determine his state of mind last night," Lucy said. "Especially if it's out of character."

"It's hearsay." Debbie glanced from Lucy to Barry. "My husband saw Harper entering a dive bar on North Zarzamora. A place you go when you don't want anyone to see you. Donny is a therapist who works with disabled veterans. It was a chance sighting—Donny was working with a vet who is severely scarred and didn't want to leave his apartment."

"Did you ask Mr. Worthington about it?"

"No, of course not—he's entitled to his privacy. It was just out of character. And then, after that, he started working later and on weekends. He often worked late, but rarely worked weekends."

"Print out his schedule for the last four weeks," Barry said, "and we'll also need his phone records, personal and business."

"Of course. Anything that will help."

Lucy asked, "How was the Worthingtons' marriage?"

Barry shot her a glance, but she ignored it.

Debbie said, "If you'd asked me three weeks ago, I would have said idyllic. He was so proud of Adeline and all that she's accomplished."

"And now?"

"Why is this important?" Debbie asked.

"It's not," Barry said. "We're just trying to get a sense of who Harper Worthington was and why he would feel the need to use the services of a prostitute."

She stared at him in stark disbelief. "He wouldn't," she said.

"Evidence suggests differently."

"I don't care what your evidence shows, he's not that kind of man. You can ask anyone who knows him, his friends or even his business competitors, and no one will believe you. They will all agree that he's a man of faith and integrity."

She sounded personally offended. Harper Worthington had instilled a deep loyalty in his staff, Lucy realized. Then why did his wife have a different impression?

Debbie continued. "If there were problems in their marriage, Mr. Worthington wouldn't seek out companionship elsewhere. He would work it out. It's what he did with everything."

"Would he talk to his daughter?"

"No, not about his marriage."

"Why?"

"This isn't relevant."

"Let us be the judge of that," Barry said.

Debbie bristled, but said, "Jolene and Adeline didn't really get along. Jolene was a daddy's girl for a long time, and Harper adores her. It was the two of them. Harper did everything for Jolene, and she has a great respect for her father. Jolene simply didn't have the opportunity to get to know Adeline because she was away in college at the beginning of their relationship, and that caused some friction."

"Between father and daughter?"

"Oh, no. If Jolene had told Harper not to get married, he wouldn't have. She wanted him to be happy. The friction was between Jolene and Adeline. You know how some fathers think their daughter's boyfriend will never be good enough to be a husband? That's how Jolene was with Adeline, that no woman would be good enough for her father. But as far as Harper was concerned, Jolene had no issues. She kept them private. They both were very private people."

"Then how do you know about them?" Lucy asked pointedly.

"I'm observant. And since Jolene married Scott last year, she's mellowed out." Debbie frowned. "That probably isn't a polite thing to say." She pulled a file folder from her drawer and put all the papers she'd printed out inside and handed it to Barry. "Schedule and phone records."

Gregor Smith walked into Debbie's office. He went over to her and squeezed her shoulders. "Why don't you go home?" he suggested.

She shook her head. "Donny is working today. I don't want to be alone."

"If you need anything, let me know." He then turned to Barry and Lucy. "Our tech guy has some information about Harper's phone that I think you should see."

The IT department was in the basement. Their servers were state-of-the-art and they didn't skimp on staff. "Corporate espionage has moved high-tech," Smith said. "It's becoming rare for competitors to come on-site to steal secrets—they're far more likely to use cyberspace."

He knocked on the window of a glass-enclosed office. A young tech in jeans and a polo shirt with the HWI logo on the pocket swiveled in his chair. "This is Todd," Smith said. "He's the one who ran the report. I'll let him share the information."

"Hi," Todd said and cleared his throat. "Um, the cell phone was off from nine oh-five P.M. until ten twenty-seven P.M., likely because Mr. Worthington was on the airplane. He turned it back on while at the airport." He brought up a screen on his computer. It was a map of San Antonio with a yellow line cutting through. "I mapped his route based on cell tower pings—we have tracking software in all our phones." It was clear from the map that Worthington had gone straight from the airport to the White Knight Motel just as the taxi driver had said.

"He made one call at ten fifty, to another company cell phone registered to Jolene Hayden. That's Mr. Worthington's daughter."

Todd enlarged the screen. Lucy leaned over. There was a dot at the White Knight Motel, then a red line leaving the motel. "At twelve fifteen, the phone pinged here." He had a dot at an intersection about three blocks from the motel. "I connected the motel with the location, and this is the most likely route by vehicle to get to that intersection. It would only take a minute."

"What about on foot?" Lucy said. The driver had said the girl had left on foot. "What would it take, five to seven minutes or so?"

"Yeah, about that." He tilted his head.

"And then the red line is thicker, why?" Lucy asked.

"Oh! Well, the phone was pinged at multiple locations between here"—he pointed—"and ended here, two point six miles away, at twelve twenty."

"A car."

"That's most likely."

"What's at that location?" Lucy asked.

"A hotel—a real nice executive hotel." He wrote down the name and address and handed the piece of paper to her. Barry took it out of her hand.

"Where is the phone now?" Barry asked.

"Still at the hotel," Todd said.

Smith said, "I've already locked out the phone, in case anyone attempts to access any of Harper's or HWI's private files. We would need the phone to determine what might have been accessed on it, such as contact information, but Todd verified that the phone hasn't been used to access company files or emails."

"Do you have the phone backed up to a cloud server?"

"No," Smith said. "That kind of security is marginal at best, and we have too much sensitive information. We have an intranet that employees can access from home with a login and password."

Barry excused himself to take a call. Lucy complimented Todd on his program. "This is useful."

"I hope you find out what happened to Mr. Worthington."

"We will," Lucy said with confidence. She had a modicum of guilt over what she'd first thought of Harper Worthington. With this additional information, she didn't know if what appeared to have happened really did happen. But she trusted the evidence wherever it led them. Like Julie Peters said, the dead don't lie.

"Agent Kincaid?" Smith said.

"Yes?"

"Your name is familiar," he said. "You wouldn't be related to the Kincaids at Rogan Caruso Kincaid, would you?"

"My brothers are those Kincaids," she said, not surprised that HWI's head of security knew of RCK. "Jack and Patrick."

"Jack Kincaid. Hot damn." He grinned. "God, I love that man. He saved my ass more times than I can remember. I did have to arrest him once—but that was long ago, and not my choice."

"Arrest him?"

"I was an army MP for twelve years." He snapped his fingers. "Of course, you're Rogan's girlfriend. I tried to hire that kid when I heard he was moving to San Antonio. Turned me down flat."

"Sean only consults."

"That's what he said. He has high-security clearance—I might be able to use him on this forensic audit." Lucy didn't quite know what to say to that—would that be a conflict? She didn't think so, but she didn't give him any push in either direction.

"Didn't I hear that Jack got married or something?"

"Yes—to an FBI agent in Sacramento."

He smiled. "Good for him." He shook his head. "Wow. Jack Kincaid's sister."

There was a bit of hero worship going on, but Lucy wasn't surprised. Her brother had led an amazing life both in the army and then out of it as a mercenary. There was a nearly twenty-year age difference between them—he'd already enlisted in the army by the time she was born—but they'd become close over the last few years. He'd taught her everything she knew about self-defense and getting her life back together after she killed her rapist when she was eighteen. She loved everyone in her family, but there was a special bond between her and Jack and she never wanted to lose it. Maybe that was why she'd bonded so quickly with Sean's oldest brother Kane when she met him two months ago. He reminded her of Jack.

Barry ended his call and gave her a quizzical look. He didn't tell her what the conversation was about, but said instead, "Mr. Smith, thank you for your time. We'll contact you if we need additional information. When you're done with the internal security audit, please let me know."

"Of course," Smith said. "And keep me apprised of your investigation."

"As much as we can." Barry was already walking away.

Lucy thanked Gregor and Todd and quickly followed Barry out of the building. "What happened?" she asked. "Where are we going?"

"Julie Peters called. She wants us at the morgue."

"She has cause of death?"

"She would only say it's suspicious."

Barry glanced over at her as they got into the car. "I would strongly suggest that your boyfriend not insert himself into this investigation."

"What?" She was confused.

"I heard your conversation with Gregor Smith."

"I didn't bring Sean up."

"I know," he conceded, "but it could make things sticky

if someone from HWI is involved in Worthington's death, and the FBI agent investigating the case is sharing a bed with HWI's consultant."

He turned the ignition and got on the phone so Lucy couldn't comment, even if she could have thought of something to say.

CHAPTER SIX

When Lucy walked into the morgue, she relaxed for the first time all day.

She'd interned with the Washington, D.C., Medical Examiner for more than a year while waiting to hear back on her FBI application. The experience had not only been educational, but she'd found she was good at the job. Because she was a certified pathologist, she'd assisted in autopsies and had been so meticulous that her D.C. supervisor wanted her to apply for a full-time position. But Lucy's goal had been to become an FBI agent.

Most deaths were natural, and the Medical Examiner could give answers when no one else could. There was a methodical process that was comforting in its order, from logging the body to the external exam to the actual autopsy. But what Lucy liked the most was the overlaying sense of calm and serenity. There was a deep respect for the dead.

The Bexar County Medical Examiner's office was much larger and busier than she was accustomed to, even in D.C., because it was a teaching facility located at the University of Texas Health Science Center. But the sights and smells were the same, and Lucy felt immediately at ease.

Julie Peters had left their names at the main desk, and they were escorted to Julie's cubicle by a quiet intern.

"I was right," Julie said before Lucy or Barry could say hello. She didn't look at them, but continued filling out a form.

"About what?" Lucy asked.

"Everything."

"You're done already?"

"It's noon. Of course I'm done. I can't give you an official report because I don't have toxicology and a few other tests, and I need my boss to sign off on my findings, but I *can* tell you that he died of asphyxiation."

"He was strangled?" Barry asked.

"Nope," Julie said. "He couldn't breathe."

"Suffocated?" Lucy said.

"Not exactly. There were no signs of bruising around his nose and mouth, and no fibers in his mouth, nose, or throat."

"Asphyxiation is the lack of oxygen," Lucy said. "If he wasn't strangled, drowned, or physically suffocated, it would have to be chemical or natural, like an allergy."

"Hence, my need for toxicology before I can make an official determination. But I have some facts that may help in your investigation. First, the deceased was already dead when his pants were removed. He'd voided his bladder when he died."

"I thought that only happened in a violent death," Barry said.

Julie shook her head. "It can happen to anyone at time of death, particularly if their bladder was full. Blood stops circulating, lungs stop working, muscles relax, et cetera. It really depends on a variety of factors, but it's not uncommon.

"Second, the victim did not have sex near the time of death. There was no semen in the urethra or ducts—which means he wasn't aroused. No pre-cum in his pants, nothing to indicate sexual excitement."

"Some sexual predators can't ejaculate," Lucy said. "I worked a case in D.C. where a rapist brutalized his victims with foreign objects because he couldn't orgasm."

"It happens, but in this case I doubt it—all his equipment is there and appears to be in working order, but some drugs can have an impact on sexual performance, for better or worse," Julie said. "For my next fact, I found saliva on his penis. A quick test determined that it was female, but I've asked for a complete DNA analysis."

"How old was the saliva?" Lucy asked.

Julie snapped her fingers. "Smart girl! There was *no* saliva or female DNA in his underwear. Nada. Our forensic lab examined the underwear extremely meticulously—at my request—using all the tools at our disposal. So I would testify under oath that the saliva wasn't present until after his pants were pulled down."

"Which means that he was dead."

Julie grinned. "Yep."

"That's disgusting," Barry said.

Lucy had investigated worse. Nothing about human nature surprised her anymore.

"And?" she asked Julie.

"You think there's more?"

"You could have told Barry all of that over the phone. Which means you want to show us something."

"You're so right. I could just let you read the report, but I think in a sensitive case like this, you need to see what I saw." Julie stood and motioned for them to follow.

"The crime techs confirmed that there was vodka on his

shirt and neck, but it's clear someone poured it into his mouth," Julie said. "We have a down-and-dirty blood alcohol test, and his BAC was zero. His stomach contents are consistent with having had a meal at approximately six thirty this evening. We're running the contents for common poisons, but he had no external symptoms of natural toxins, such as anaphylactic shock that might occur with a shellfish or peanut allergy. I have his medical records, and he has no known allergies."

They were at the end of the hall and Julie led them into the locker room. "Booties and gloves. Can't have contamination."

Both Lucy and Barry put on the gear Julie handed them, and she led them across the hall to one of the autopsy bays.

One autopsy was currently being performed by three other pathologists. Julie nodded to them as they passed, then on the far side of the room she pulled back a plastic sheet that hung from the ceiling to reveal the body of Harper Worthington laid out on a steel autopsy table. His chest had already been sewn back together.

"I've already talked to the crime techs about this, and they're going to come back with a plausible theory after they play with their computers. Because I absolutely know what this is, I just can't picture how it happened."

Julie turned on the bright overhead light. It made Worthington look even more pale, but every imperfection was visible. Julie tilted his head a bit and Lucy peered at a small red mark that was halfway between the side and the back of his neck.

"It looks like a puncture mark. A needle, perhaps."

"Looks like. Cops." She rolled her eyes. "Yes, it *looks* like a needle mark because it *is* a needle mark."

Barry asked, "What was he injected with?"

"Don't know yet. I took tissue and blood samples and the lab knows this is a priority, but you're going to have to give us a day or two. I know it's nothing common—I can test for most narcotics right here. It would have to be fast acting, because there was no sign of a struggle. No defensive wounds. No skin under his nails. He didn't fall to his knees or hit his head. I can't picture how someone could get close enough to inject him and he didn't at least try to get away. But you saw the room—it was tidy."

Lucy could picture a couple different scenarios, but one seemed the most plausible. She said, "That lends credence to the fact that a prostitute was in the room and Worthington intended to have sex with her. Maybe they were kissing and the girl puts the needle into his neck. He pushes her away, but can't move. Collapses onto the bed. That would have to be an extremely fast-acting drug."

She walked around the table, collecting her thoughts. "But why? What's the motive? Did she kill him for kicks?"

"A Thelma-and-Louise spree," Julie suggested.

"That doesn't feel right. You say he didn't have sex, that he was fully dressed when he died. No evidence that he hurt the prostitute—the taxi driver didn't mention the girl was injured, and he doesn't have any bruises or cuts on his hands. This wasn't random. He was lured from Dallas for one hour of sex with a prostitute."

"If," Barry interjected, "his wife knew about his fetish, she could have hired someone."

Lucy's eyes widened. "I thought you didn't believe she had anything to do with this."

"You got me thinking about the possibility," he said.

She almost smiled. "How would his death, if it was ruled natural causes, benefit her politically?"

"Sympathy votes."

"I'd think she'd get more negative press than sympathy," Lucy said.

"She'd be a widow. Her opponent wouldn't be able to run any real negative ads against her or her record without being made to look like a jerk. Eventually, the circumstances would fade away, leaving behind only the fact that she lost her husband during the campaign. There could be extenuating circumstances—does she gain financially from his death?" Barry was on a roll. "I'm not saying I think she's behind it—I don't know. But it sounds to me like Julie is calling this a homicide."

"I'm right here," Julie said, holding up her hands. "And I haven't made my official determination. I'm calling his death suspicious right now. When I get the lab results on what he was injected with and talk to the ME about my findings, I'll revise that. But unofficially? Hell yeah, someone killed him. Whether the girl did it on her own or was hired to do it, who knows? That's where you two come in."

Barry was thanking Julie when Lucy interrupted. "What did his liver look like?"

"It was a bit enlarged. I took tissue samples, which is standard protocol in a suspicious death like this with no obvious COD."

Liver tests could take a day or a week, depending. But there was something familiar about Worthington's death.

"What are you thinking?" Julie asked her.

"I worked a case when I was on vacation last Christmas—"

Julie interrupted. "Why am I not surprised that you worked while on vacation?"

Lucy rolled her eyes. "Not my choice. I sort of walked into a situation. Anyway, a nurse used a neuromuscular blocker to kill her victims. Reaction time is fast, death usually less than thirty minutes, depending on the dose. Almost impossible to detect unless you know what to test for."

"I'll make sure I checked all the boxes," Julie said. "And give the lab a heads-up."

"Thank you, Julie," Lucy said.

"Just doing my job."

CHAPTER SEVEN

The elegant chain hotel where Worthington's phone was still transmitting was only a few miles from the White Knight, but a world of difference. Grand entrance off a busy street, elegant furniture set out in intimate groupings, a restaurant to the right with a hostess and white linen tablecloths, a bar to the left with businessmen and businesswomen drinking alone or in small groups.

Barry and Lucy talked first to the concierge, then the manager, and finally the head of security got involved. Andreas Jackson was a tall, broad-shouldered black man dressed in an impeccable dark suit, white shirt, and navy tie. An earpiece with the telltale curling cord curved around the back of his ear and under his collar. He escorted them to the security office upstairs. Two people watched a wall of twelve security monitors. Jackson's office was in the corner, and he had one-way windows that looked out to the lobby below.

Barry explained again what they needed and gave Jackson the specs of the phone, a BlackBerry P'9983.

"It's a relatively new model," Barry added.

"There was no such phone turned in from the public areas in the last twenty-four hours," Jackson said. "If he was a guest, housekeeping may not have gotten to his room, or he may not have checked out."

"He wasn't a guest," Lucy said.

Barry said, "A person of interest took his phone after our contractor died. The phone is now here."

Jackson picked up his phone, spoke for a minute, then hung up. "The housekeeping supervisor is checking with her staff and will contact me directly." He sat down behind his desk and motioned for them to take seats in chairs across from him, which they did. "If the phone is in this hotel, we'll find it." He eyed them with interest. "Government secrets? Must be serious if two federal agents are looking for a phone."

Barry glanced at Lucy, though she didn't know what he wanted from her. He then turned back to Jackson and said, "The phone was stolen from a deceased government contractor."

"If you have a GPS log, I can review the security footage from our public areas at the time the phone entered the hotel."

"That would be helpful," Barry said. "Thank you." He wrote down a time frame and tore the page from his notepad. "This is the window we're looking at."

Jackson pressed a button on his phone. "Please cut a copy of security feeds from all entrances from twelve thirty A.M. through one A.M." He turned back to Barry and Lucy. "Only the main entrance is unlocked after ten P.M., but I'll get you feeds from all the entrances in case the individual in question had a hotel room key."

"We appreciate that," Barry said.

Jackson's phone rang and he excused himself. Barry pulled out his phone and responded to a message. "Jolene Hayden called headquarters and wants to meet with us as soon as possible."

Lucy looked at her watch. It was late in the afternoon.

Adeline had told Jolene seven hours ago about her father's death. "When?" Lucy said.

"It's nearly five. We've been going since five this morning."

Lucy was used to working a case until she was exhausted. It helped her sleep, for one. And for two, she couldn't put work out of her mind when she was mulling things over. But it had been a long day.

"Her father just died. She'll be an emotional wreck," Barry added. "It would be better to talk to her after a night to process."

"She may have helpful information. She was in Dallas with her father, she may know why he was coming to San Antonio."

"I thought of that, which is why I had Zach call her and ask her to come in first thing Monday morning." He glanced at her. She couldn't read Barry well. When she thought she understood what he was all about, he agreed with her on something and surprised her, or disagreed and surprised her. She didn't know how his mind worked. "Some advice?"

"Can I avoid it?"

He showed no emotion. "You're not a bad agent, Kincaid. But if you keep going at the pace you've been going since you got here, you'll burn out fast. You don't think I'm ignorant of what people say about me on the squad, do you? Particularly the people you hang with. Nate, who has PTSD and probably doesn't sleep more than two or three hours a night. Ryan, who's going through a nasty divorce and needs to work or he'll fall apart. Even Kenzie, who's admittedly my favorite, can't take a day off—that's why she still puts in time with the National Guard, it gives her the excuse to continually work out and do something on the weekends.

"I work eight to five, five days a week, and take my

on-call weekend once a month," Barry continued. "That's what I'm paid to do. I'll work longer if necessary, like today when we were called in at five in the morning on a Saturday, but I always give one hundred percent when I'm on duty. Then I turn it off when I go home. Go out with friends. A girl, if I have one. Watch a ball game. I coach my nephew's Little League team in the spring—we just finished our season last week and I already miss it. But I've been an FBI agent for nineteen years, and I plan to put in my time, retire at fifty-seven, and not have high blood pressure, a head full of violence, or a drinking problem. So my advice is, find a way to turn it off before it turns you inside out."

Barry hadn't spoken that many words to her all day. In fact, he hadn't said that many words to her in all the months they'd worked in the same office. At first she didn't know what to say. Barry turned back to his BlackBerry.

"You're right," she said momentarily, when he wasn't looking at her. "But it's not easy to turn it off."

"You have a boyfriend. Go do something fun tonight. Take tomorrow and go on a picnic before the heat gets unbearable."

"We're not working tomorrow?"

"It's Sunday. We're not going to get much done. We're not going to get lab results, we're not going to be able to interview anyone potentially involved, and since we don't have a cause of death or a photo of the girl who was with Worthington, what do you suggest we do? We need to give HWI time to put together their files and forensics time to do their job."

He was right. But the problem was, she couldn't just stop. She needed to work, because when she didn't work, she made work. She could research HWI, run a background on Harper Worthington and his wife, learn more about the business, the campaign, how they met—anything that might help her understand why Harper Worthington sought out a young prostitute. If not for sex, why? And who was this girl? Why was she there? Was she working for someone and if so, who? Why did someone want him dead? Why would he fly in just for a meeting? Did he know he was meeting a prostitute or was he expecting someone else? She would be dreaming about the case whether she wanted to or not.

Lucy recognized that she wasn't normal. She hadn't been normal since she was eighteen. Maybe not since she was seven when her nephew was murdered and her family grieved so deeply it changed all of their lives. She'd had a rather idyllic childhood—they weren't rich, but they were close, for the most part. Until her oldest sister moved away after Justin's murder, and Jack enlisted in the army and didn't come home for years because of a major fight with their father. And one by one, her brothers and sisters left home. And then when she was eighteen her own life changed irrevocably. She couldn't go back to the girl she'd been, just like she had never been able to reclaim her innocence. In the back of her mind she felt compelled to save others. To stop those who would prey on the innocent, stop those who recruit young women into the sex trade, stop those who hurt children, who abuse people who can't defend themselves. She didn't know who this young prostitute was, but Lucy wanted to help her.

Maybe Lucy couldn't relax on weekends because she somehow felt she didn't deserve to have fun.

Sean had changed that—he gave her a deep joy she hadn't thought she'd ever experience. But it was like she was waiting for something bad to happen to destroy the one thing that made her happy.

What did that say about her? That she was going to

waste her time with Sean for the fear that she wouldn't have him forever?

She pulled out her phone and sent Sean a text message.

I love you.

Sean was the romantic one in their relationship, and she wished she could be more like him. It didn't come easy for her. But thinking about him now reminded her of how thoughtful and wonderful he was, all the time. He'd learned to cook for her, he'd moved to San Antonio for her, and while he'd left his position at RCK for other reasons, her career had certainly played a part in that decision. She never wanted to forget the sacrifices he made. She had to learn to turn off the job, if not for her, then for Sean.

Jackson finally came back into his office after nearly fifteen minutes. "I'm sorry that took so long, but you need to come in and view the security tapes. I had my team pull additional time stamps and we're making you a copy." He led them through the security office, down a hall, then through a door he accessed with his card key. They crammed into a room filled with equipment, manned by an operator who was working on a computer with the largest monitor Lucy had seen outside of Quantico.

"First, housekeeping found the phone in room six oh six," Jackson said. "The guest checked out early this morning via computer. The room was cleaned at noon today and staff left the phone in the main housekeeping office—Saturdays are busy and the supervisor hasn't had the opportunity to contact the guest. No other personal effects were left behind. I sent one of my security people to retrieve it. But after I spoke to the floor manager, I was curious, so I pulled the sixth-floor security footage as well." Jackson said to the tech, "Run both segments."

The first segment wasn't the main entrance, but a side

entrance. "This is our northeast entrance," the operator said. "It's used by guests after hours—most of the popular restaurants are east of us, as well as River Walk access."

A girl roughly fitting the description given to them by the taxi driver used a key card to access the door. There was no clear shot from that angle. She carried a large, over-sized bag and wore heels with her very short shorts.

"She would have been stopped by security immediately in the lobby," Jackson said. "Asked if she were a guest and in what room. We take a hard line against prostitution. We recognize that some of the more high-priced call girls would get by simply by how they present themselves or because they come in with a registered guest, but we discourage solicitation. The giveaway is not just the clothing—many young girls wear immodest shorts and tops—it's her bag and overall appearance. When you've been in this business as long as I have, you know."

"Have you seen her before?" Lucy asked.

"Never," Jackson said.

"This shot isn't clear," Barry said.

"The elevator footage is on a different feed and black and white. I'm working on getting that copied, but I have a better shot of her on the sixth floor."

The operator pressed a couple buttons and the image changed to a wide-angle lens showing a generic hallway. "This is the sixth floor," he said.

The girl who'd come in through the side entrance walked down the hall slowly, looking at each door number. The quality and lighting was better on these cameras. She turned abruptly and looked one way, as if something startled her, and when she did they were able to get a very clear shot of her face. Then she turned the other way and continued to look at the numbers. She stopped at one door, fumbled with the key, then slid it into the lock. It opened.

"That's her," Barry said. "She matches the description of our person of interest."

"I made you copies. We only have digital files, so the copy is as high quality as the original. I'll put it on a disk, but I can also email it to you."

"That would be terrific. I appreciate your help, Mr. Jackson. I need the name of the guest registered in that room."

"I thought you might. I'm going to need a warrant for that. It's hotel policy. I can share anything that's public—copies of security feeds, for example—but the names and addresses of our guests must remain confidential unless there is an official warrant. I'm sorry."

He actually sounded like he *was* sorry.

Barry nodded. "I understand. I'll have one first thing Monday morning."

"I'll have what you need ready."

Lucy said, "Can you show us the security feeds from this morning? Around the time the guest checked out."

Jackson hesitated, then said, "I don't see why not. Like I said, hotel policy is to cooperate with law enforcement as much as possible, and there are signs posted about the hotel's video surveillance."

Jackson motioned for the operator to fast-forward the tape. It scrolled by quickly. There was little movement, then a lone person, then a couple with suitcases, then—

"Stop," Lucy said.

The tech did.

"Back up a couple minutes. I want to see the girl as she's leaving."

The tech complied. At 4:47 A.M. per the time stamp, the blonde left room 606. She wore the same clothes but was walking like she was in pain. She kept her head down for the most part, and weaved a bit as if drunk. As she neared the elevator she turned her head. She had a cut on her face and bruises on her neck. Then she disappeared into the elevator.

"Bastard," Lucy muttered. He'd had her in that room for four hours. Lucy didn't care if she was a hooker, she didn't deserve to be brutalized. It was clear she was well under eighteen. Certainly no older than sixteen, and Lucy would not have been surprised if she were younger. That's why this john wanted her, not only because she was young but because she looked young.

"Do you need to take a break?" Barry asked Lucy.

She was surprised by the question. "No," she said. "I'm fine." She wanted to skewer whoever hurt the girl.

"Keep going," Barry said, clearing his throat. The tech sped up the recording.

It was nearly three hours later that the guest left the room, dressed business casual. He carried a small overnight bag. He was well over forty.

"I'll get the warrant to make it official," Barry said. "But I know who that is."

CHAPTER EIGHT

Driving back to FBI headquarters from downtown San Antonio took twice as long as usual because of traffic, but Barry used the time productively. He first told Lucy that the man in room 606 was James Everett, a multimillionaire who'd made his money in real estate. "I don't see what the connection is between Everett and Worthington, if there *is* a connection," Barry said. "They could have known each other because they were both wealthy, established families in the city. Probably moved in the same circles, but they weren't business partners. And Worthington is dead and Everett isn't—otherwise I'd think maybe we did have a potential serial killer targeting dirty old men."

He glanced at her. "You're quiet. I expected you to have a theory."

"There is a connection—that girl. She went from Worthington's room to Everett's room. She left Worthington's phone in Everett's hotel."

"You don't know that."

"If she gave the phone to Everett, why would he leave it there? It connects Worthington—a suspicious death—to him."

"Good point."

"The girl must be working for someone who is getting her these jobs," Lucy said. "She had the card key to the hotel room. She went straight up to the room, but the numbers aren't on the cards."

"You got intense back there. Are you okay with this case?"

"Of course," she said. "I'm just mad." And upset, but she had closed down her emotions as soon as Barry had seen her reaction in the security office.

Nothing about human nature surprised Lucy. She was only twenty-six, but had faced evil too many times, in her personal life and on the job. She'd interviewed hookers and johns, pimps and madams. She understood the business of sex better than almost anyone, and that didn't make her happy. She wondered if that was why Juan had wanted her on this case, because she understood this world. An underage prostitute rarely worked for herself. Almost exclusively, they had managers. They were often exploited, especially at the beginning of their careers, but over time they became as hardened as those who recruited them.

There were many paths that led young girls into the life of selling themselves. Childhood abuse. Manipulation by a boyfriend or even a fellow girlfriend. Kidnapping. Runaways. Some went in knowing full well what they were doing; others had no clue. Many became addicted to alcohol and drugs; most died far too young, broken.

The men who used them were more predictable. For most, it was about power and control. To pay a submissive to do what they wanted when they wanted. For some, it was a fantasy; they pretended they weren't paying the girls, that the girl was with them because she wanted to be. But wealthy, influential men like Harper Worthington and James Everett probably convinced themselves that because she was paid, it wasn't child rape. Because she was willing, it wasn't sexual exploitation. They wanted, they took.

Men like Worthington and Everett made her physically ill. She didn't harbor a lot of sympathy for the fact that Worthington was dead and Everett was going to be on the hot seat. She felt true empathy for the girl who'd been used and manipulated. If she did have a hand in Worthington's death, she needed to get help more than punishment. Someone must have set her up to do this. And Lucy needed to convince her to overcome her fear—of law enforcement and her pimp—and talk to the authorities.

But first, they needed to find her.

"Send the photo to Tia Mancini at SAPD and see if she knows the girl," Barry said. "I need to call Juan."

"We're going to talk to Everett, right?"

"Not tonight. It's six o'clock. Neither of us is at the top of our game after thirteen hours in the field. After I talk to Juan, I'll call you and let you know what the plan is."

"I want to be in on it, Barry."

"You want it too much, Lucy."

"I'm pretty certain Juan called me in to work with you on this because of my experience working with victims of the sex trade. I can't help this girl unless I know exactly what's going on, and that means I need to be part of the conversation with James Everett."

Barry didn't say anything for several minutes as they crawled through traffic. Lucy sent the image Jackson had clipped from the video to Tia Mancini with a note that this was the girl they wanted to question about the death of Harper Worthington.

"I know I can be a little intense," Lucy said. "I have a hard time lightening up. I wish I could be more fun like Kenzie or compartmentalize better like Ryan. But I am good at my job. All I want is to be part of this investigation. To contribute and not feel like I can't say something or ask a question."

Barry hesitated, then said, "I'm used to working alone," he said. "When I get a rookie to work with, they usually don't have much experience in the field. That probably wasn't fair to you today."

She hadn't expected an apology, but she appreciated it. "If I mess up, tell me. I'm still learning."

Barry turned into the secure FBI parking lot and shut off the car. "Will do. Go home. Relax. I'll call you tomorrow if anything pops up. Likewise, if Mancini gets back to you about that girl, call me. If it seems best to interview Everett tomorrow instead of Monday, I'll call you in. Fair?"

She nodded. "Thanks, Barry."

Barry finished briefing Juan Casilla on the case. He hadn't been lying to Lucy that he didn't like working weekends. The squad rotated who was on call, and it was his weekend, but he didn't have to like it. It wasn't that he didn't like his job; he did. He liked the authority and power that came with being a federal agent. He was good in the field, and the AUSAs loved him because he gave them prosecutable cases with no potential issues like illegal searches. In fact he worked so well with the AUSAs on cases that Juan usually assigned him to work anything legal. Plus, he did well with public relations. He'd been offered the position of public information officer a few years back, but declined it because it would have meant erratic hours.

He supposed his predilection for a regular eight-to-five schedule was the primary reason SAC Ritz Naygrew had brought in Juan Casilla as the SSA three years ago instead of promoting Barry. For a while, Barry was disgruntled and had considered leaving the Bureau, or at least San Antonio. Especially since Casilla rarely worked weekends because of his large family. Five kids under twelve with another on the way. Yet Juan had a solid management style that Barry respected, firm but flexible.

"What do you think?" Juan asked. "It seems clear that Worthington was murdered."

"It appears that way, but I'm not going to make assumptions, not until the morgue comes back with the test results. The big hiccup here is how this girl connects with Worthington and Everett, and why she was in both hotel rooms on the same night. Aside from the obvious."

"But your report indicated that Worthington hadn't had sex with the girl."

"Honestly, the whole case seems fishy. It appears that Worthington was set up to look like he was in a compromising position, but we still need to interview his daughter and find this prostitute. And I can't shake the fact that he made this unscheduled trip to San Antonio and didn't tell anyone."

"I've fielded two calls from Jolene Hayden—one from her, and one from her husband."

"I had Zach call her to set up a meeting for Monday morning. Kincaid and I have been going nonstop since before dawn. We'll miss something if we talk to her tonight. Other than the taxi driver, she may have been the last person to see her father alive. She also may know why he left Dallas for San Antonio, but she wasn't in town earlier for us to talk to."

"I agree—talk to her fresh. Zach said she was amicable to meeting Monday morning once she knew that we were serious about the investigation and that we wouldn't have any results from the coroner until Monday."

"Is that what you told her?"

"I'm not going to give her the preliminary results over the phone." Juan leaned forward. "Tread lightly with the congresswoman. That's why I wanted you on this case,

Barry. You understand the sensitivities of a potentially political investigation."

"Thank you, sir."

"Which brings up Lucy Kincaid."

"I've been watching her closely like you asked," Barry
said. He hadn't been surprised by Juan's request, and he
didn't feel guilty about it, either. The only way they could
function in the law enforcement role established by Congress was to have good agents under the command of a
strong leadership. He'd often assessed rookie agents, especially since joining the San Antonio office.

"She's focused and has good instincts," Barry said. "She
took my direction, even when I could tell she was frustrated that I wouldn't let her pursue something or ask
questions. Though she's only been here a few months, she's
already built relationships with local law enforcement, including the deputy coroner, Julie Peters, and SAPD detective Tia Mancini which, honestly, made the crime scene
this morning go smoother than I would have expected after
we took over the investigation.

"Lucy is like the Energizer Bunny—she doesn't stop,"
Barry continued. "Not in the same way as Kenzie, who
simply can't sit still, but her mind is continually turning
over evidence and information. She wanted to continue
working tonight, but I sent her home. It's clear to me that
she's going to burn out quickly. She seems to recognize
this in herself, but she doesn't know how to turn off the
job. And—to be honest—I don't think she wants to turn it
off. That would be my number-one concern."

"I knew that when she was assigned to San Antonio,"
Juan said.

"Are you having me assess her because of what happened in Hidalgo?" Barry knew Juan hadn't told the staff
the entire story, and Ryan wasn't talking about it, either.
Lucy had rescued a group of kidnapped boys being used

as drug couriers, but she'd been put on unpaid administrative leave for two weeks for disobeying a direct order. Yet no one seemed to know what that order was, and the punishment seemed extreme considering what she'd accomplished. There were a few rumors going around about whether she'd violated federal law by crossing the border into Mexico while running an op, but there was nothing in the official record and Barry wasn't going to ask. It wasn't his place.

Juan didn't answer his question, which made Barry think the rumors were accurate. Instead, Juan said, "How is she in the field?"

"Like I said, sharp. She was too confrontational with Congresswoman Reyes-Worthington, but I smoothed it over."

"Why confrontational?"

"She didn't think the congresswoman was surprised that her husband was with a prostitute. She thought the woman seemed calculating."

"Maybe she wasn't surprised. And politicians can be very calculating, always looking at poll numbers and how something will appear on the news."

"It just seemed—I don't know, Kincaid focuses on different things than other rookies I've worked with. I'm afraid she projects too much, and sees things that are simply not there."

"She has a master's in criminal psychology."

Barry hadn't known. "That explains a lot." Like how she assessed the situation at the hotel, and how she worked through the possible scenarios from a personal point of view rather than simply making a factual summary. But had he known earlier would he have changed the way he investigated this case? Probably not.

"I need to make sure she's not a danger to herself or others in the field," Juan said. "I want to know if she has tunnel vision, if she takes unnecessary risks. You're the most even-tempered agent on this squad, and you understand the regulations better than anyone. You're also unbiased and the only one I trust with this particular assessment."

"Thank you, sir. I'll do my best."

It was after seven Saturday evening when Lucy walked into her house. She was looking forward to brainstorming with Sean—she enjoyed discussing her cases with him. His insight was always sharp, and he seemed to enjoy walking through the facts with her.

She thought about what Barry Crawford had said, that she needed to learn to turn off the job. Easier said than done.

She stepped into the kitchen and was greeted by a mouth-watering, spicy aroma. "Sean?" she called. He didn't answer.

The kitchen was a mess, with pots and pans in the sink, a couple empty beer bottles on the counter, and remains of chopped veggies on the cutting board.

Her phone vibrated. It was a message from Sean.

Welcome home. Go upstairs and change.

She laughed and responded.

Bossy, aren't you?

He texted back:

Pretty please.

She went upstairs, dumped her briefcase and gun on the dresser, and then noticed that a dress was laid out on the bed. She picked it up. Next to it was a note in Sean's writing.

Remember when you bought this?

They'd been in San Diego, right after Christmas, and drove up to La Jolla where there were lots of boutiques. Sean had admired the dress in the window and she'd teased him that he should buy it for himself. He'd asked her to try it on and she did. It was perfect—casual and comfortable and classy all at once, a free-flowing blue silky thing that hung shorter in the front than the back. She'd bought it but had never worn it.

She changed into the dress, touched up her makeup, and brushed out her long wavy hair, then went back downstairs expecting to see Sean. He wasn't there.

I'm dressed. Where are you? she texted him.

Pool house.

Odd. She went outside. A warm breeze whipped around her, soothing and cooling after the blistering hot day. The pool looked inviting, and Sean had turned on all the outdoor lights—both the pool lights and the tiny white lights weaving throughout the trees that surrounded their property.

The pool house doubled as a guesthouse. It was L shaped with a small kitchenette, bathroom, eating area, and a living area that doubled as a bedroom when they had company.

Sean had set the table with heavy blue dishes she didn't know they had, an assortment of candles, and a bottle of her favorite red wine. Faint music played in the background. But she barely noticed any of that. She stared at Sean in disbelief.

"You're wearing a tux?"

He grinned, revealing his dimples, and bowed. His hair flopped over his eyes and he pushed it back.

She laughed when he took her hand and kissed it. Then he led her to a chair and sat her down. "Thank you," she said.

He poured her some wine, picked up his glass, and toasted her. "To the woman I love."

She held up her glass. "To the man I love."

He took two plates out of the mini refrigerator—salads he'd already prepared. "You spoil me," she said.

"Your wish is my command."

"I'm so hungry, and whatever you cooked smells amazing. And here I thought you could only cook breakfast and spaghetti. Not that I'm complaining—you make the best spaghetti I've ever had. Don't tell my dad that."

"Never. I want to remain on his good side."

"You are. It's Jack you have to worry about."

The brief flash of panic on Sean's face had Lucy laughing. It felt so good to laugh.

"I'm teasing," Lucy said through her giggles.

She ate the salad—Bibb lettuce and blue cheese and walnuts and cranberries. "This is—like a restaurant."

He feigned hurt. "Are you implying I didn't make it myself?"

"Of course not. I saw the mess in the kitchen." She smiled. "It just looks like you took a crash course in food presentation. And it tastes as good as it looks."

When they were done with the salads, Sean retrieved two plates that had been warming in the oven. He took off the lids and presented them.

"You made jambalaya?"

"You loved it when we went to that restaurant in Sacramento. So I researched different recipes and thought this would be spicy enough for you."

She tasted. "Oh my God, I'm in heaven."

Sean was certainly pleased with himself. "I thought it was good, but I've been nibbling all afternoon."

"It's better than any I've had. And I'm not just saying that to stroke your ego."

"More wine?"

She rarely had more than one drink, but smiled and held up her empty glass.

They talked about everything except work. Sean showed Lucy new pictures of his niece Molly. He told her about Patrick taking a temporary job in New York City and Elle going with him. "What kind of trouble is Elle going to get Patrick into now?" Lucy said.

"She's good for him."

"She's a train wreck. But I'll reserve judgment."

Sean laughed. "This is you reserving judgment? I seem to remember Patrick wasn't too pleased when you and I started seeing each other."

She opened her mouth to argue, then said, "You got me." She told Sean about a long, frustrated email from her sister Carina, who was pregnant and due in less than two weeks.

"She's not handling maternity leave well," Lucy said. Carina was a San Diego homicide detective and had been on desk duty for the last three months. She had started her maternity leave last month when the doctor told her to stay off her feet after a false labor episode.

"I don't know a lazy Kincaid," Sean said.

"She said if it's a girl, they're naming her Rosemary— Rose for our mom, Mary is Nick's mom."

"Pretty. And boys?"

"Carina wants Nick, Jr., but Nick apparently put his foot down."

"He'll give in."

"I'm surprised they haven't already peeked at the gender. My sister doesn't like surprises."

"That, too, runs in the family."

"I liked this surprise," she said and sipped her wine. "I'm stuffed."

"What? No room for dessert?"

"Maybe in an hour . . . or three." She leaned back and finished her wine.

Sean smiled. "It's chocolate mousse."

Her weakness was chocolate. "You made chocolate mousse?"

"No. That I bought from Bird Bakery."

She loved that place. "I've never seen chocolate mousse on the menu."

"It's a special order. They like me." He grinned and straightened his bowtie.

"Okay, why all this attention? You made the most amazing dinner. You're dressed in a tux. You bought my favorite dessert. Favorite wine—" For a split second she thought he was going to give her bad news. Her mind went to the dark side, all the things that could go wrong with them or their families. But he wouldn't have done all this if it was bad news.

Sean stood up and took her hand. "I know that look, Lucy." He pulled her up and kissed her. "I want you to feel loved."

"I do. Every day." She wrapped her arms around his neck and put her head on his chest. "You don't have to cook elaborate dinners to make me feel loved."

"I know. But that look on your face when you first walked in . . . I'll do it again and again just to see the joy in your eyes." He tilted her chin up to look at him. "I love you. I will never get tired of saying it, or hearing it."

Lucy kissed him. "I love you," she whispered. She

kissed him again, lightly biting his bottom lip. "I love you," she whispered again. She smiled as she kissed his jawline, his neck, behind his ear.

"You do that again and I'll carry you into the house and have my way with you," Sean said, pulling her to him.

"This is a house," she said. She stepped back and pulled the dress over her head. She stood in front of him in her simple black bra and panties and strappy sandals. Maybe it was the second glass of wine, or the flickering candles, or the intimate pool house, but she didn't feel self-conscious in the slightest. With Sean, she had always felt wholly safe and deeply loved.

She took Sean's hands and backed into the living area where a mound of throw pillows spilled over the wide couch. She pushed half the pillows to the floor, then pulled loose Sean's tie with a smile on her face. She took his hands and backed into the couch, pulling him down with her.

No work, no crime, no murder. Just them, alone and together.

CHAPTER NINE

Sunlight woke Lucy for the first time in months. It streamed through the pool house windows at a low angle. Still early, but much later than she was used to sleeping.

She stretched and rolled over to where Sean was sprawled next to her. They were both naked, a throw blanket covering Lucy. Sean had an internal heater, he was never cold. She kissed his bare chest and he wrapped his arms around her, pulling her close.

"You know when you kiss me in the morning I get exceptionally horny," he said, his voice gruff.

"I know," she whispered and kissed him again.

"If you insist," he said and pulled her on top of him.

They made love again, a smooth and easy love after a rather wild night. At least wild for them. They'd had sex on the couch, fast and furious, then Sean had fed her the chocolate mousse. That led to a long, slow, and excruciatingly seductive lovemaking that left them both exhausted and unable—and unwilling—to clean up and go inside. Being with Sean made Lucy feel not only loved, but blissfully normal. Wonderfully alive.

Morning sex was a different connection, lazy and fun.

Sean held her close when they were both satiated. "We need to shower."

"I know."

"And clean up."

"I know." She snuggled into him. "I don't want to leave."

"Leave? You have to work?"

"No. I don't want to leave this pool house. I feel like we're a million miles away from everything and everyone."

He ran his hand through her tangled mass of hair. "You slept through the night."

"Yes, I did," she said with a smile. "Good food, great sex, I think I passed out from sheer pleasure overload."

"I'm happy to help with that anytime you want, princess."

"It's so quiet."

"There's no phones, no television, no computer out here. Maybe that's a good thing."

She kissed him. "We should do this more often."

"Agreed. I don't know why I didn't think of it before." He sat up and stretched. "But duty calls."

"I don't have to work today."

"No, but tomorrow is pool-groundbreaking day at the boys' house. We still have yard work to take care of before the crew can come in and dig a hole."

"You know you didn't have to buy them a pool."

"The contractor gave me a good deal."

Two months ago, Sean had bought a house for the boys he and Lucy had rescued from the drug cartel, across the street from St. Catherine's Church. Father Mateo Flannigan, the pastor at St. Catherine's, had worked with the diocese to create a much-needed program for boys of convicted felons who had no family to care for them. The foster-care system was overburdened and overworked, and these boys had slipped through the cracks and nearly died because of it. Now they had a home, a school, and people who cared about them. It had been Sean's idea, and he was emotionally invested in the project. Lucy had never loved him more.

He tickled her and jumped up, bringing her with him. He glanced at the clock in the kitchen. "Seven thirty A.M. *You* are a lazy butt."

"Let's go take that shower, and we'll see who's lazy."

After showering so long the hot water turned cold, Sean and Lucy cleaned up the pool house, then went inside to tackle the kitchen.

Lucy saw her briefcase on the table with her phone next to it. There were several text messages from Barry Crawford, confirming that they were meeting with Jolene Hayden at 8:00 A.M. on Monday, and then asking that Lucy come in an hour before the meeting. After Jolene, they'd talk to James Everett.

She confirmed, then saw she had a voice mail.

She listened to it. It had come in at nine last night from Tia Mancini. "I have a lead on your girl. Call me."

"Something wrong?" Sean said.

"No—I'm just glad I left my phone inside."

"Lucy—I know your work is important. I would have understood if something came up."

"I know you would, Sean. Barry Crawford, the agent I'm working with on this case, told me I didn't know how to turn off the job. He's right, you know that, but last night I wanted to turn it off. I didn't know that we'd be spending all night in the pool house, but I'm glad we did."

"You have to work today?"

"I don't think so. Tia called about the girl we're looking for. An underage prostitute who was in the room with Harper Worthington when he died."

"Lucy—I have no idea what you're talking about."

She hadn't told Sean anything about the case, because last night had been all about them. "Maybe you don't want to know. I need to learn to compartmentalize."

He didn't say anything for a moment.

"Sean?"

"Of course I want you to share with me. I don't want you to think you have to keep anything from me. Unless— is talking about your work giving you the nightmares?"

"No, of course not. It's just—last night was incredible. I didn't want to tarnish it with a homicide investigation."

He gave her a half smile. "I am pretty incredible."

"You are." She kissed him, but her mind was elsewhere.

"Lucy? What is it?"

"Sometimes, I bring the darkness home with me. And . . . I wonder if that's all I have inside."

"Don't. It's not true. Inside you are passionate and compassionate, you're everything I want or need. Lucy, I'm here for you, light and dark. Good and bad. It would hurt more if you didn't want to share, because I know how you think, how you work. You immerse yourself in your cases. It's what makes you so good—and what troubles you." He pushed her damp hair off her face and ran his thumbs down her jaw to her neck. He kissed her.

She returned the kiss and smiled. "You make everything easier for me. And I really do like brainstorming with you, your mind thinks through problems better than anyone I know."

"I *am* brilliant, as well as incredible."

She laughed. "Yes, you are."

"Lucy, last night wasn't isolated. We've done pretty good for the last eighteen months balancing the dark with the light."

She sobered up. "But you're the light, Sean. I'm the dark."

"Don't even think that way." He caressed her cheek. "You can tell me anything."

"You want to know, don't you?"

"I want to share everything with you, Lucy. You know that."

After filling Sean in on the Worthington case over breakfast, she realized that she and Barry had covered a lot of ground yesterday. "So Tia is helping us locate the prostitute. Once we talk to her, I think we'll finally know what's going on."

"But you think he was murdered."

She hesitated. "Yes. I just don't know why he was killed. Because he was a pervert? Because of something related to HWI? Because of his wife, the congresswoman? Once we know why he flew to San Antonio on Friday night, I think we'll have the answers. Hopefully tomorrow, when we interview his daughter."

"I don't know if I told you, but HWI offered me a job a few months ago."

"You didn't, but yesterday I met the head of security, Gregor Smith. Small world—he mentioned you, after he found out who I was. He was an MP and arrested Jack once."

"Now *that* would be an interesting story. But I mention the HWI offer because Smith called me again yesterday afternoon. He didn't tell me that you'd been to the office, just that he wanted to hire me to test their security and assist in the forensic audit. I accepted, but I didn't know you were the lead agent. I can back out."

"First, I'm not the lead agent—Barry Crawford is. Second, I'm not going to tell you to take it or not take it. In fact, it would probably be more of a conflict if I'm involved in the decision making, so I'm recusing myself." It would be easier on her at work if Sean wasn't involved with the same cases she was, but at the same time, they worked so well together that she certainly wouldn't complain if he did take the job.

"All right. I'm meeting with him tomorrow morning."

She kissed him. "They couldn't have hired a better consultant."

"That's what I said." Sean winked. "Call Tia, then we'll go to the boys' house. If you need to bail on me, that's fine—but you'll have to find *some* way to make it up to me." He kissed her. "Like, a full body massage after my long day of hard labor."

"You'd like that, wouldn't you?"

"Oh, yeah, I would." He grinned.

Sean went upstairs to change into his grungy clothes while Lucy called Tia.

"Sorry I'm just getting back to you—I just listened to your message," Lucy said.

"It was Saturday night, hope you and Sean had a night out on the town."

"Nope, just stayed in, but he cooked."

"I'd give anything for a man who cooked."

"You can't have him."

"He's a little young for me. I'm going to be forty at the end of the year. Does he have a single older brother?"

She pictured Kane Rogan, who was an older, leaner, meaner version of Sean. "Yes, he does."

"I'll get an intro out of you one of these days. Anyway, I got your message and was surprised I'd never seen the girl before. I know most of the regulars, if not by name then by face. She's not in the system, at least in Bexar County. I'm widening it to all of Texas, but it'll take a little more time without a name or prints."

"SAPD ran all the prints they could get from the motel and nothing popped," Lucy said. "We're running them federally, but there's no criminal. Nothing yet from missing persons." Lucy sipped her coffee. "You said you had a lead?"

"Maybe. I talked to one of my informants, showed her the picture. She recognized her, said she's new in town, but doesn't know anything about her. I have a couple places to check out where she might be. I can do it myself, I don't want to infringe on your Sunday."

"I don't mind."

"No, seriously—the lead may not pan out. How 'bout this—I'll check them out, and if I get eyes on her, I'll call you."

"Fair enough. I'm doing yard work at the church this afternoon, so I *really* hope you get eyes on her for more than one reason."

Tia laughed. "Tell Sean I said hi." She hung up.

Sean came downstairs. "So, do I have you as my slave all day, or does Tia need you?"

"If you put it that way, maybe I should call her back up and tell her I want to tag along."

He smiled. "So you're mine today."

"Every day."

Adeline Reyes-Worthington took visitors all Sunday at the house. Some were friends and family, others just pretended to be. Everyone had the same thing to say.

"We're so sorry for your loss."

"Harper was a wonderful man."

"We just saw him last week. He seemed so healthy."

Everyone loved Harper. That affection was the primary reason Adeline had married him. That, and his money. She needed the money to run her campaign. Her father certainly wouldn't have given it to her. He claimed he didn't have the five million she needed to win her first election. What had he done while being mayor of San

Antonio? He'd helped so many of his friends, why didn't he help himself? He could have mortgaged his ranch, but of course he wouldn't do *that*. He loved his damn horses more than he cared about his daughter's career.

She needed a break. She told Joseph that she was going to her room to lie down and to make apologies for her. What would she have done without Joseph? He had been a rock for her, as her personal assistant and as a friend. He also ran the house—something Harper thought didn't need to be done, but once Joseph came on board Harper appreciated him.

Instead of going to her room, Adeline went to her private office, upstairs in the west wing. She liked the sound of that. She didn't expect to ever be president of the United States—a black *man* could be elected president, but not a Hispanic *woman*. She didn't really care, anyway. She had her own power base right here in the heart of Texas, and it wasn't going anywhere.

She never brought anyone upstairs to this office, where she worked while at home. The downstairs office with the antiques and view was for guests and meetings; this office was functional with a computer, printer, files, and everything she needed to conduct business—even a separate and secure phone line. She sat at her desk and looked through her schedule. Most events she would have to cancel or reschedule. She cared for Harper, but the timing of his death was poor. She had a lot of pokers in the fire right now, and going through the motions of grief was going to distract her. She supposed if she said that out loud, people would think she was callous, but Harper certainly shouldn't have been off screwing a prostitute. The information would eventually get out, so she needed to do damage control before it did and make sure that she came out on top.

She sorted through the in-box on her desk and saw a

manila envelope with her name on it. She almost tossed it aside for her secretary to deal with, but something about it drew her attention.

She picked it up. It was addressed to her by name only—no stamps, no mailing address, no return address. She first thought it was a condolence card, but dismissed the idea—guests weren't allowed upstairs and there was a table in the hall for cards and flowers.

Curious, and a bit suspicious, she opened the envelope and slid out the contents.

There was a photo and a letter.

Her stomach turned. The photo was of Harper, half-naked in a motel room. He appeared to be sleeping. But she knew he was dead.

The letter was short and to the point.

> *Adeline ~*
> *I told you two months ago that if you changed allegiances, you would regret it. I want what you owe me. You have forty-eight hours, or you're next.*
> *I know you won't say anything to the police or FBI, because I have enough evidence to bury you. Not only evidence of our arrangement, but proof that you had your husband killed.*
> *~ Tobias*

Adeline was shaking so hard that she dropped the letter. The words blurred, and her eyes were drawn again to the photo. There was no proof that she had had Harper killed because she hadn't had him killed! What had Tobias done?

This was not happening. It could *not* be happening. She hadn't heard a word from Tobias after she broke off what had once been a mutually beneficial financial arrangement.

He'd been completely destroyed when the DEA shut down his gun-and-drug-smuggling operation. His inside cop had been arrested. Certainly that person would spill the beans eventually, and Adeline had had to cut all ties so she wouldn't be caught up in the fallout. It had been a business decision, and she and Tobias were business people. She thought he'd understood that, his temper tantrum two months ago notwithstanding.

She hadn't taken his threat seriously because he had no more power.

He'd had Harper killed? *That's* what his threat meant?

Adeline paced, her heart racing. This could *not* be happening to her. Not now.

She hated being scared. Why was she scared of that man? He had *nothing*. He'd barely gotten out of Trejo's compound alive, according to her sources. How could he think that anyone would believe she had something to do with Harper's death?

He couldn't possibly frame her for Harper's murder! He couldn't create evidence out of thin air.

Yet . . . maybe it was possible. Two months ago he'd had great power. What if he still had someone inside the police force? Someone to plant evidence? Someone to implicate her?

Dammit! What was she going to do? She couldn't just sit here and take it. And giving him money? She'd had to spend a small fortune to protect herself when Tobias had lost the gun shipment. She'd had to placate people, make sure they understood that it was Tobias, and not her, who had screwed up. It was the cost of doing business, she'd told him, and she stood by it.

She had to fix this. And the only way to fix it was to take out Tobias himself.

Except . . . she had no idea where he was. She didn't

know what he looked like, or if Tobias was his real name. They worked through an intermediary. She'd talked to him on secure phones, but she'd never met with him in person. He was particular about that—she didn't know why. Their arrangement had been working beautifully for years until he'd screwed up.

That was on *him*, not *her*.

If she couldn't take out Tobias, she'd do the next best thing—take out his entire operation. And she knew exactly who to call to have it done. She'd use the rest of Tobias's money to pay for it.

Fitting.

If Tobias thought that she was so weak that she'd cave because he killed her husband, he would learn that he'd screwed with the wrong woman.

She pulled a secure cell phone out of her desk and dialed the private number of Javier Marquez, whom she'd started doing business with exclusively after Tobias nearly got caught by the authorities.

"It's Sunday," Marquez said.

"Tobias had my husband killed and threatened me."

"Why is this my problem?"

"He threatened our new arrangement."

"Tobias knows better than to come after my operation, especially when he's been cut off at the knees. You worry too much, Adeline."

"He's rebuilding."

"Hmm."

"I can tell you who and where. It's Jamie Sanchez's old operation. They moved safe houses. I know where they are."

"It will cost you. This goes beyond our agreement."

"I understand."

"Send Mr. Contreras to me with the information and payment. I will take care of it."

CHAPTER TEN

Once Joseph had left to meet with Marquez, Adeline paced. She nibbled at the food Harper's grieving friends had brought, but she wasn't hungry. She was too nervous. She needed Joseph to return and tell her it was taken care of, that Javier would live up to his agreement and Tobias would no longer be a problem.

She was still stunned that he'd killed Harper. Tobias had surrounded himself with dangerous people, but because he was so elusive and secretive, he'd never threatened anyone directly. He'd lost nearly half the gun shipment two months ago when—according to Tobias—a mercenary seized several of the trucks while they were on their way to the buyer. That had been a major blow to the entire organization. Adeline had had to scramble to replace the money Tobias had used to obtain the guns, because the people who were expecting them wouldn't take the screw-up as an excuse.

Tobias had excuse after excuse, but in the end, Adeline had decided to cut ties with him because he was obviously reckless and weak. She'd built a solid operation without him; she certainly didn't need him now.

He killed Harper.

She shook her head to clear her mind. Maybe it was for the best. Harper had been so withdrawn lately. She'd worried for a while that he was suspicious about some of her land transactions—he'd asked questions about the land she'd sold to cover Tobias's screw-up. So what if she'd sold it for more than market value? That was how the game was played—a lobbyist wanted something from her, she needed money to save her ass. It wasn't like she was compromising her principles—she would have voted for the legislation anyway—so what harm was it that she earned a little extra money on the side?

She'd made up a lie about natural resources on the property and the buyer was betting on future earnings, blah blah. At the time, Harper seemed to accept her explanation and didn't ask about it again, so she put it aside. But what if he'd started digging around? She hadn't wanted him dead, but if anyone knew about her questionable practices, they might think that was a motive.

Shouldn't Joseph be back by now?

Adeline glanced at the clock and saw that only fifteen minutes had passed. She was far too antsy, she needed to calm down. A glass of wine would help.

She went down a curving staircase into the large, finished basement. Half of the basement had been converted into a temperature-controlled wine room with all the bells and whistles. Harper was generally frugal—too frugal at times—and she never understood why he spent so much time with his wines when he never had more than a single glass from any bottle. Such a waste. He always had prided himself on having the perfect bottle with a meal, but never allowed himself to drink to excess.

Adeline had learned a lot about wine from Harper, but she didn't know what the big deal was. She liked her alcohol straight up, preferring tequila to all else. She knew which wines Harper liked the best, and which bottles—in a special rack—he'd told her were for "special occasions." Well, he was dead, and all this wine was just going to waste. She considered opening up the wine cellar for the funeral. There were at least a thousand bottles, not like they'd do Harper any good now. His friends could take one to remember him by. Or maybe she'd give them away as gifts.

She picked up a cabernet with a French name she couldn't pronounce and took it upstairs to the library. Immediately, she heard bells that told her someone had come through the gate. They had the code, which meant it was one of two people on a Sunday afternoon—Joseph Contreras, who couldn't be back this quickly, or Jolene.

Adeline opened the wine and poured herself a glass, waiting. She heard a car speed down the drive, then a door slam. A minute later, the front bell rang, followed by pounding. Adeline looked at the security camera. It was, indeed, Jolene.

Though Adeline hadn't changed the gate code, she had changed the locks last year and kept "forgetting" to give Harper's daughter a key. Served her right for being a stuck-up little daddy's girl.

Adeline sipped the wine. It was pretty good, she supposed, but there were far cheaper bottles of wine that tasted the same to her.

The bell kept ringing and Adeline pressed the panic button hidden in one of the bookshelves. She was so *tired* of coddling the whiny, spoiled child. Jolene needed to grow up.

Adeline took her time walking to the front door.

"Jolene, what's with all the pounding? You scared me."

Jolene burst in. She wore no makeup, her face splotchy from crying. "What did you do to my father?"

"Come, sit down, Jolene. I know you're upset, which is

why I wanted to give you time before we talked about funeral arrangements."

Keep it calm, motherly, Adeline told herself as she started back down the hall. It would set Jolene off.

"No! You will have *nothing* to do with Daddy's funeral. I want you out of this house. Out of my life! I know you did something. Daddy changed, something was bothering him. And I know it was you."

Jolene was right about Harper being preoccupied. That bothered Adeline, but she'd checked all her ventures, and nothing had been compromised. The thing about the land—he hadn't asked again. "Jolene, dear—"

"Don't talk to me like you care!" Jolene followed Adeline to the library, neglecting to shut the front door. "This is *my* house, *my* home. You can't be here."

Jolene stared at the wine bottle. "That—that—that was my mom and Daddy's anniversary wine. You—" Jolene grabbed the bottle. Wine sloshed out of the top. "How dare you! He's dead and you're drinking his wine?"

"Jolene," Adeline said, "can I get you some water? Tea?"

"Get out of my house!"

"This is *my* house, Jolene. And you know it. Harper left the house to me."

Jolene's face scrunched up in pain. She'd of course known about the changes in Harper's will. She'd been upset about the house because this was where she'd grown up, but then she married Dr. Scott Hayden, who had plenty of money and had apparently promised to build her a dream house, so she finally shut up about the changes to Harper's will.

Jolene Ann Worthington Hayden, the prima donna princess who'd been given everything she'd ever wanted her entire life. She was the epitome of everything Adeline despised. She had a father who doted on her. A husband who worshipped her. If Jolene hadn't been around, maybe Adeline and Harper would have had a better relationship. But Jolene was always interfering. Always that disapproving daughter, even when she *said* she was fine with the marriage. Harper had actually *asked* Jolene if it was okay to remarry! His wife had been dead for *fifteen years* and he'd asked his grown daughter if it was *okay?*

"You manipulated him."

"There's nothing you can do about it. Harper always had the best lawyers. There will be no loophole you can wiggle through. If you'd been nicer to me, more supportive of my career and my marriage to your father, maybe I would have sold you this place."

"It's always been about money with you. You think I don't know? That you married my daddy so you could use his money to run for office?"

Adeline was so angry that her eyes watered. She tamped down on the anger but let the tears come. "You never understood that I loved him. That I gave him pleasure. Happiness. He'd given up everything to raise you, and when he finally decided to do something for himself, to start dating again, to marry *me*, you couldn't handle it. Your father *wanted* me to run for office. He encouraged me. And I had a very successful career in real estate. I brought plenty of money into this marriage."

"Don't you dare rewrite history now that Daddy can't defend himself."

Snot ran out of Jolene's nose and she brushed it away with the back of her hand, like a child.

"I think you'd better leave," Adeline said. "Before we both say things we regret."

"I'm planning Daddy's funeral. You can come, only because it'll be expected. But I'm talking to Pastor Melton, and I'm planning the celebration of Daddy's life, and you'll stay the hell out of my way." Jolene turned to leave.

From the corner of her eye, Adeline saw the lights coming down the drive. Of course the sheriff's department would be fast; she was a federal official.

"No," Adeline said. "I spent more time with Harper than you did in the eight years that we've been married. I will not allow you to take this away from me. Away from your father. You could never see beyond your selfish needs that your father was sick and tired of catering to you."

Jolene turned back around at Adeline's accusation. "That's not true! How dare you!"

"Do you know how your father died?"

"A heart attack—which I'm sure you drove him to!"

"A heart attack? Perhaps. But he was screwing around with a prostitute. He was found with his pants down in a cheap motel room."

"I don't believe you!"

"So, the police haven't spoken to you yet? Ask them. Your father wasn't the man you thought he was. He wasn't the man I thought he was."

Jolene shook her head frantically, her jaw slack and trembling. "Daddy would never—"

"Men do, and your daddy was a man, Jolene. Suck it up, because it's going to leak to the press."

Jolene stepped forward. "How dare you—"

Adeline looked up at her stepdaughter. Tilted her head defiantly. "*I* certainly wouldn't leak the information. Do you think I want everyone to know, especially in an election year, that your father was a pervert?"

Jolene raised her hand and noticed that the wine bottle was still in it. She screamed and lunged for Adeline. Adeline sidestepped her and knocked over the small end table. "Jolene! Stop!"

"Ma'am!" a deep male voice said. "Put the bottle down now."

Jolene seemed stunned that two uniformed deputies ran into the room. "Ma'am, please," one of them said.

Jolene looked at the bottle and at Adeline. "I hate you!" she screamed. She threw the bottle against the wall opposite Adeline, and it shattered, spraying wine in all directions. The two deputies immediately grabbed her. One handcuffed her, then ushered her out of the den. The other turned to Adeline. "Ma'am? Do you know that woman?"

She nodded, brushing away tears. "Yes. My stepdaughter. My husband died Friday night and Jolene—she is upset with me, with him." She took a deep breath. "It's about money. It's always about money, isn't it?" She feigned a dizzy spell and the deputy caught her and helped her sit in one of the plush armchairs. "Thank you, deputy," she said with a half smile.

He said, "We'll need a statement. Are you pressing charges?"

"I don't know—I don't want to. Can you call her husband? Or take her home? She's grieving. I'm sure tomorrow she'll regret everything."

"Of course. We'll make sure she gets home. I would suggest you have the codes and locks changed on the house, and make sure your security system is on, even when you're home."

"Yes. I hate to see Jolene come to this. I wanted us to be friends, that's all I wanted after I married Harper, and she hates me." Adeline put her head in her arms and sobbed.

The deputy took a few minutes to write up a statement, then called his supervisor with a report. Adeline smiled to herself when he characterized Jolene as hysterical. When he was finished, she thanked him for his prompt response and walked the deputy to the door. His partner was standing next to their car with Jolene in the backseat. Adeline closed the door and whispered, "Don't mess with me, Jolene. I always win."

As soon as the deputy's drove off with Jolene, Adeline rushed over to her phone and called her campaign manager, Rob Garza. Other than Joseph, there was no one else she trusted, no one else who understood the many layers of her life.

"Rob, Jolene just attacked me at the house. Two Bexar County Sheriff deputies were here, saw everything, and are taking her home. Make sure the press gets a picture of her when she gets there. You have less than fifteen minutes to set this up. I want her completely discredited. I don't think she knows anything about our side business—if she did, she would have spilled it tonight, because Lord knows I baited her—but if she does suspect anything, I don't want anyone to believe her."

"Consider it done," Rob said.

As soon as blogger Gary Ackerman read that Harper Worthington was dead, he started to pack.

Somehow, they'd found out.

And they'd killed him to keep their secret.

Gary wasn't certain who *they* were, but one of *them* was Harper's wife, Adeline Reyes-Worthington.

Gary had tried to tell voters seven years ago that Adeline Reyes-Worthington was bad news, but they voted her in anyway. For a while, he'd become obsessed with proving that she had rigged her election, to the point where Adeline had gotten a restraining order against him.

He didn't know *how* she did it, but she'd done it.

He'd stayed away from her because he didn't want to go to prison. He'd be killed inside, because he knew too much. The Chinese were buying up the country with Obama's blessing—and probably his help—and the Bushes had put their blue-blooded cronies in every corporation in the country. The unions benefitted their leadership more than the workers and Wall Street controlled the financial system to benefit the few. Someone high up in the government had assassinated Kennedy, and someone else high up in the government had tried to assassinate Reagan. Oswald and Hinckley were just scapegoats—part of the conspiracy, but not the leaders of the conspiracy.

Everything was tied together, a sick and twisted fist tightening its control over the hearts and minds of Americans. He told the truth on his blog every day, and he didn't flinch from the hate mail. He got it from everyone—so-called conservatives who thought he was wrong about their golden child; so-called liberals who thought he was a racist because he didn't praise the president; racists who thought all the problems were because of blacks/Hispanics/Jews. He despised them all. They didn't understand that the root of all the evil in the world was the corruption of government on all levels. It was insidious. It was everywhere. And *they* would do everything they could to preserve their power and control.

He had proof. Harper Worthington was dead. The one respectable person who had actually *listened* to him was dead.

Gary hadn't believed Harper when he first came to Gary two months ago. He thought Adeline had sent her husband to trick Gary into violating the restraining order so they could put him in prison where he would be killed. But Harper agreed to all of Gary's rules: no Internet or cell phone communication (it was all monitored by the government); no meeting at Gary's apartment (he had rented it under a false name); correspondence only through a mail drop. When they finally did meet, it was at a dive bar in a neighborhood without surveillance cameras.

Harper didn't call him paranoid or weird like most people did. He listened to everything Gary had to say.

Some of it, Gary could tell Harper didn't believe, but he never once made Gary feel foolish. And when Gary told him about the history of suspicious land deals that his wife had been part of, Harper was very interested.

Except Gary had no proof. His strength was seeing patterns, and there was a pattern of land that had been bought and sold at above and below market prices. He didn't know what it all meant. He'd written out a sheet of numbers and Harper had understood.

Finally, someone believed him. Harper said he would get to the bottom of what was going on.

And now Harper Worthington was dead.

Which meant *he* would be next.

For about two seconds he considered calling the FBI and telling them what he knew. Except the FBI was part of the government, and the government was all corrupt. How would he know if he got one of the good agents and not one of the bad agents? He'd read about the DEA agent who was working with the drug cartels. There were more. He didn't know who they were. He didn't want to die.

He had a safe place, out in the middle of nowhere. A one-room cabin completely off the grid with a year's supply of water, food, and ammunition. That's the only place he would be safe. He'd forget about Harper Worthington, forget about Adeline, and just survive.

Gary grabbed his bag and opened his door.

Almost before he could register that there was a man standing in the doorway, three bullets hit him in the chest.

CHAPTER ELEVEN

DEA Agent Brad Donnelly hated desk duty, but his doctor hadn't cleared him for the field. He was lucky to have been allowed to work at all considering he'd been tortured and nearly killed by a high-ranking member of a small but violent drug cartel. Most of the crew was dead and Brad had survived, so he'd take the pain and move on with his life.

He was ready to go back full-time, but his body wasn't cooperating. His knee had been shattered. Surgery had replaced the knee, but running was still difficult, and after a full day working, he limped. His physical therapist told him he was making great progress, but it didn't feel like it to him. It had been nine weeks.

But he came in early every day because he met with his trainer at 5:00 A.M., five days a week, in the hopes that diligence and hard work would bring his body back to top form. By seven Monday morning he was showered, dressed, and sitting at his desk reviewing the work of his field agents, itching to join them. Today, his direct line was ringing before he even sat down.

"Donnelly," he answered.

"Kane Rogan."

He'd kept in touch with Kane Rogan after he'd helped take down Vasco Trejo's cartel in Mexico. In addition to using young boys as drug mules, the gang had been part of a larger conspiracy to steal guns from the US military. Or, rather, Kane had kept in touch with him when he had information. Kane had been following Trejo's remaining gang in the hopes of shutting them down before anyone took over Trejo's enterprise. What he'd learned was that someone was still pulling strings and Trejo's people were still unified under an unknown leader.

Donnelly had learned early on that Kane didn't do small talk, so he said, "You have something?"

"The last members of Trejo's core group were taken out last night in San Antonio."

"I haven't heard of a major op. Are you sure it was us?"

"They're dead. Possibly a rival gang; I don't know who yet. Word is retaliation, but there's nothing on my radar that would warrant such a splash. It's got to be a rival gang cleaning house when Trejo's people didn't join up. You?"

"I got nothing. I've been digging into known associates and they're in prison or dead. Except—" He hesitated.

"Spill."

"Tobias."

"Shit."

Brad's thoughts exactly. Tobias was a shadow. He had been on no one's radar until nine weeks ago. He'd been seen entering Trejo's compound in Mexico minutes before an explosion took it down, but that didn't mean he hadn't escaped.

The disturbing thing was that neither Kane Rogan's vast connections south of the border nor the DEA had heard of Tobias before that day. They didn't even know if Tobias was his real name. Lucy Kincaid, one of two people who had seen the man, had poured over photographs and hadn't been able to identify him. She and one of the boys she rescued had worked with a private sketch artist, but the image was too generic. They'd only seen him at night under poor lighting.

"If he made it out," Brad said, "he could have the connections to keep Trejo's group together."

"Find out what's going on with that attack. SAPD has the scene, but because of the known connection to the cartels, you'll be called."

"I'll jump on it. Are you in town?"

"No." Kane hung up.

Brad lowered his receiver and shook his head. Kane was a hard guy to talk to, but his intel had always been solid.

Brad called his DEA liaison with SAPD, Jerome Fielding. "Jerry, it's Brad."

"How'd you hear so fast?"

"About the hit on Trejo's people? I have my sources." Kane never ceased to amaze Brad.

"Are you coming down?"

"I literally just heard. I don't even know where, when, how many, or why."

"I'll send you the address. It's off Mission Road."

One of the worst crime areas in the city, run by the gangs.

Jerry said, "Are you back on duty?"

"I can go to a damn crime scene."

"Wear your vest. We're not wanted down there."

"Got it. What else?"

"I know the when—last night at seven thirty P.M.—and the how many—nine. But not the why. Yet. Maybe you can help there."

"I might. Nine dead? Any survivors?"

"None at the scene. We found drugs and guns. Every victim was shot at least three times, all with at least one head shot. Not just the gangbangers, but two women and a kid."

"It's a fucking execution."

"If this is the first shot, there's going to be a bloody war down here."

"My source says it was retaliation."

Jerry was silent for a minute. "If it was, then it's out of my jurisdiction. There's been nothing of this magnitude for a long time, nothing on the wire. It's an abandoned strip mall that had been taken over by a gang with ties to Sanchez and Trejo—who you took care of. Honestly, it's been quiet the last two months since those bastards were put in the ground."

"Someone must have seen something."

"And they're not going to talk to us."

Jerry was right. No one talked to the police down there. They didn't trust cops. Didn't matter if they were first, fifth, or tenth generation; it was cultural. Even those who did trust law enforcement feared retaliation by the drug cartels if they said anything. Fear was a powerful silencer.

"I'll be there in an hour," Brad said.

Sean dragged himself into HWI headquarters at eight Monday morning. Lucy had woken before dawn with another nightmare, even after they were both exhausted from a full day doing yard work in the heat.

She wouldn't talk about it, and that bothered him, too. She kept saying she was fine. Then she did something she rarely did—distracted him with sex. He hadn't noticed it at the time, but once she'd showered and left for FBI headquarters, he'd realized she'd changed the subject about her bad dream by kissing him and taking him back to bed.

They would be talking about that tonight. He was angry—and he didn't want to be angry with Lucy. Which made him doubly frustrated.

Sean checked in with HWI's front desk and was immediately sent up to Gregor Smith's office. "Sean Rogan, it's good to finally meet you."

"Likewise. I'm sorry to hear about your boss."

Gregor nodded. "It's been hard on the staff. And Jolene, Harper's daughter. Please sit." Gregor had a large desk completely devoid of clutter. A computer monitor and phone were the only items on the desktop. "I don't know how much you know about the FBI investigation into Harper's death."

"Some," Sean said. Lucy had told him what she knew, but Gregor didn't have to know that.

"Because he died under suspicious circumstances, we need to run a full forensic audit. We've already started the process, but we also need to verify that our systems haven't been breached from the outside. Our IT department is good, but I would feel better having someone from the outside review our system. When it comes to computer systems, I'm a bit out of my depth."

"Most people are," Sean said. "You have this office, Dallas, and a small office outside D.C., correct?"

"Yes."

"And your internal logs show nothing suspicious? When did you last run them?"

"Every night at midnight the system runs a security check and produces a report. The IT department determines if there have been any problems and alerts me immediately. So far, there've been no successful cyber attacks. Attempts, like usual, but no one has gotten close. But as you know, if someone is good, they can get through any barriers. Because you have a high government clearance, I can give you access."

"I don't need access."

"But I thought you agreed to take the job. If it's money, I can go to the board—"

"You agreed to my standard rate. I don't need access because I already hacked into your system." Sean slid a folder over to Gregor Smith. "Truthfully, you're not that exposed. I couldn't easily get into this office or the Dallas office. If I wasn't concerned about being detected, I could have breached your firewall, however. I can fix that vulnerability. Your main problem is D.C."

"Why? They use our intranet, they shouldn't have any different system."

"True, but any server—even an intranet housed privately—is potentially vulnerable if it can be accessed remotely. The Dallas office has their own server, but the D.C. office dials in, so to speak. I can recommend a few simple fixes. Overall, though, your computer security is better than most companies'. I'll look at the log files for the last quarter to verify that you haven't had any breaches, but since I know how it would have been done, it won't take me long. I can easily explain it to one of your people. What I need to do now is going to be more difficult."

"Which is what?"

"Investigate potential internal breaches."

Smith didn't say anything for a moment. "You mean corporate espionage."

"If I wanted to get into a secure system, I would do it from the inside. With the level of security most companies have these days, that's the best way to access information."

"How?"

"I assume your employees all sign a confidentiality statement which includes permission for HWI to run a background check."

"Of course."

"Then I need access to all employee files. It would be best if I could use an office here. I also need a list of any computers that aren't tied directly to the network, including employee laptops and company cell phones."

"We're a family here," Smith said. "No one would betray us."

That, coming from a former cop, bothered Sean. Loyalty was a strength in any business, but blind faith could be HWI's Achilles' heel. Betrayal wasn't always voluntary.

But he said none of that to Smith. Instead he said, "Then there will be nothing to find."

CHAPTER TWELVE

Lucy arrived at the office early and, armed with a large coffee, read an email Detective Tia Mancini had sent last night. Tia had checked with all her sources and no one knew the girl, except for the one tenuous lead she'd mentioned the day before.

I have a hunch my source is right—your girl is from out of town or new to the business, Tia wrote. *I've reached out to everyone, and no one knows anything. To me it's odd, especially with the level of sophistication your girl seems to have in the business. I'll keep working it—I have one more idea.*

Tia didn't give Lucy a clue as to what other idea she was pursuing, but the detective was right—the whole situation seemed odd.

Lucy forwarded the email to Barry and suggested they go wider looking for the girl. She also had a hunch, and added to her message:

Considering the two men we know she was with, Worthington and Everett, are both powerful businessmen, what if this girl is working a

blackmail angle? I worked a case in D.C. where a
call girl recorded her liaisons for a third party.

Zach approached as she sent off her message. "Have
you seen the news?" he asked.

Lucy hated the little flutter of worry in her stomach. Not
all news was bad news, right? "What happened?"

He dropped a print newspaper on her desk. "It came out
this morning and was all over the morning news and the
Internet."

Congresswoman Reyes-Worthington Attacked by
Stepdaughter
  Congresswoman shaken but uninjured after
Jolene Worthington Hayden threw a wine bottle
at her.

Beneath the headlines was a photo of Jolene Hayden being escorted from a patrol car, in handcuffs, by two police
officers. The photo description read:

Jolene Worthington Hayden, the only daughter of
recently deceased Harper Worthington, CEO of HWI,
escorted home in cuffs Sunday night by sheriff
deputies after she attacked her stepmother, Con-
gresswoman Adeline Reyes-Worthington, at the
Worthington estate outside San Antonio.

"Thanks, Zach," Lucy murmured as she read the
article.

Jolene had gone to her father's house Sunday night.
Witnesses—unidentified—said that she was upset about
the will. According to other sources, Worthington's assets
were split evenly between his wife and stepdaughter, and
in addition his wife would get the house and Jolene the

business. Jolene and her husband, Dr. Scott Hayden, were unavailable for comment. The congresswoman had released a brief statement.

Jolene is distraught over Harper's death, which is completely understandable given the circumstances. Sometimes, the people we think we know best disappoint us. I will, of course, not be pressing charges. I'm sure in the morning Jolene will be aghast at what transpired, and I hope to mend fences.

The article ended with:

Harper Worthington, CEO of HWI, a respected San Antonio CPA firm that specializes in corporate and government audits, was found dead early Saturday morning in a San Antonio motel known to be a downtown hub of prostitution. The cause of his death is unknown, but the Federal Bureau of Investigation is working closely with the San Antonio Police Department. Neither the FBI nor the SAPD responded to questions regarding the circumstances of Worthington's death, but a source close to the investigation said, on condition of anonymity, "Worthington's death has been unofficially ruled a homicide and the FBI has taken over the investigation."

Someone at SAPD had talked to the press. Maybe it shouldn't come as a surprise, but Lucy was angry—not just because there were a few details that would be better to keep out of the media, but because it put the FBI in a negative light. Only a local cop would say the FBI had "taken over" the investigation.

But it couldn't have been someone high up or directly

involved with the investigation—the responding officers knew that their chief had requested FBI assistance.

Barry walked through the squad room and dumped his briefcase and keys on his desk. "Kincaid, Jolene Hayden is here early. I assume you read the article?" He motioned to the newspaper on her desk.

"Yes. Is she upset?"

"Understatement. Let's go, interview room two."

Lucy reached into her bottom desk drawer and pulled out a minibag of peanut M&M's. As she passed Zach's desk, she tossed the bag to him. "Thanks," she whispered.

He grinned without comment and immediately opened the bag.

"Who talked to the press?" Lucy asked Barry.

"Don't know. I'll find out, but dealing with it is Juan's problem. To keep the peace, he'll probably let it pass. I'm very interested in what happened last night between the daughter and the congresswoman. It puts another spin on the case."

"We should talk to Mrs. Worthington again."

Barry stopped outside the door. "Why?"

"She called the police on her stepdaughter. That doesn't say happy family to me."

Two people were waiting in the interview room—Jolene and her husband, Scott Hayden. Barry introduced himself and Lucy and slid over a set of business cards to each of them. "Thank you for coming down," Barry said.

Jolene had made an effort to pull herself together in a businesslike way, but her blond hair was limp and her face pale, even under the makeup. Her husband was dressed in a suit, sans tie, and held her hand.

"Tell me what happened to my father," Jolene said. "I have to know."

"We're sorry for your loss," Barry said.

Her eyes teared, but her jaw clenched. "You told Adeline, but didn't tell me."

"It's policy to tell the next of kin, which in your father's case was his spouse."

"I'm his daughter."

"Honey," Scott said quietly. He didn't need to say anything else. Jolene nodded, her bottom lip quivering. Scott said, "Harper and Jolene were very close. Harper raised her after her mom died. The last forty-eight hours have been extremely difficult."

Barry said, "I'll share everything we know, but in turn, I need you to be completely honest when answering our questions."

"Of course—why wouldn't I be? I need to know what happened. It's not what she said, I know it. And the paper—they said he was murdered."

"That isn't public information," Barry said. "We don't have a definitive cause of death, but we are treating the investigation as a homicide."

Jolene sucked in a breath and squeezed her husband's hand.

"San Antonio PD called the FBI into the investigation, and we're working closely with them to find out exactly what happened." Barry glanced at Lucy and gave her a brief nod. At first she wasn't certain what he wanted, but decided he was asking for a gentle touch with Jolene.

Lucy assessed the woman and determined that Jolene was stronger than she'd first appeared. Her posture was straight, and she was working hard to keep her emotions in check. She was a professional businesswoman, and her husband was there for support, so Lucy decided to be as blunt as possible, but also to walk Jolene through the facts as they knew them.

"I want to give you the big picture first," Lucy said,

"because there are several things we don't know about the events prior to your father's death."

Jolene nodded. "I can take it. I just want the truth."

"Here are the facts. Harper Worthington bought a round-trip plane ticket from Dallas to San Antonio on Friday night. The tickets were purchased last minute—only hours before the plane left. It appeared he only planned on staying in San Antonio for a few hours before returning to Dallas. He told the taxi driver that he had a meeting at the White Knight Motel and requested that the man return for him one hour after being dropped off. The flight times confirm the timeline.

"When the driver returned and suspected something was wrong, the manager opened the room and found your father deceased. The police were called, and when his identity was learned, the police chief contacted the FBI."

"Adeline said he had been with a prostitute. She's lying," Jolene said.

"The taxi driver saw a young woman dressed immodestly leaving the motel room. Because the girl propositioned the driver, he determined that she was a prostitute—we have a surveillance tape with her picture and concur with the assessment. We're looking for her now."

"No," Jolene said. "You think that I can't see the truth, but I know my dad, and he would *never* hire a prostitute. You don't know him like I do. Ask anyone—anyone who knows him, and they'll say the same thing. There has to be another reason my daddy was there."

"Did you know he planned on flying to San Antonio Friday night?" Barry asked.

"N-no," Jolene said, her voice cracking. "We had dinner with clients earlier. Daddy was a little preoccupied, said he was tired. He called me around ten thirty, said he was sorry about cutting dinner short, but we'd have breakfast together and he wanted to talk to me about something important. I thought—" But she cut herself off, and didn't finish the sentence.

"Thought what?" Lucy asked.

"We were very close, Agent Kincaid, but Daddy is a southern gentleman. He didn't like troubling me with personal problems. If it was business, he'd tell me. I started working for him when I was in high school, and I came on full-time after college. I'm not a numbers person like my dad, but I understand people and public relations, and work with our clients one-on-one. So it had to be something personal. And—" She hesitated again.

"Jolene, you need to be open with us," Lucy said. "We're trying to find out not only how your father died, but why he was in San Antonio in the first place. No one at HWI knew about the spontaneous flight, there is no record of the meeting at the White Knight, and his wife didn't know."

"After what happened last night, if I say it's personal and had to do with Adeline, you'd tell me it was sour grapes. And it's not," Jolene said.

"Everything is relevant," Barry said, "until we rule it out."

"First, I want to make it clear that I did not attack Adeline last night. She made it seem that way, but I *did not*."

"Jolene, you need to be completely honest with these agents," Scott spoke up for the first time. "Tell them exactly what happened."

Jolene drank from her water bottle with unsteady hands. "I should never have gone over there."

"You're right," Scott said. He turned to Lucy and Barry. "I had to go to the hospital to check on a patient who was in post-op. There had been complications, otherwise I would never have left Jolene alone last night."

Jolene patted his hand. "Of course you needed to go. It's

my fault. I pretended to be asleep." To Lucy and Barry she said, "Scott is a pediatric surgeon. His patient was a toddler; he saved her life." Even through her grief, she beamed pride at her husband.

Jolene continued. "I heard from a friend that Adeline had had people over to the house all day, receiving them, playing the grieving wife. She hadn't told me anything about it. I didn't care, at first, until I heard that she was planning the funeral. She emailed me—emailed!—that I should come to the house to approve her arrangements. I just . . . lost it. She was married to my dad for eight years— and I knew Daddy wasn't enamored with her anymore. He used to glow about Adeline. How smart she was, how proud he was of her for running for office, how thoughtful she was. But lately—he didn't talk about her at all. And he wouldn't tell me because, well, I wasn't really that supportive of him getting married in the first place." She took a deep breath and shook her head. "You don't care about that."

"What happened last night?" Lucy prompted.

"I went in and she was drinking a bottle of my parents' anniversary wine. It was a special collection Daddy had bought for my mom, and after she died, he would open a bottle on their anniversary to remember her. And she was drinking it and Daddy was dead and I was crying. It makes no sense to anyone else, but to me it was the worst betrayal. She told me that . . . that he was with a prostitute, she said that I didn't know my dad at all, that he—he—he was a *pervert*." She pounded her fist on the table as her eyes moistened again. "I will not let her destroy my father's name. I won't."

Scott said, "The sheriff's deputies told me that the alarm had been tripped and they responded. Adeline baited Jolene into throwing that bottle. But she didn't throw it *at* her. She aimed at a wall."

"But you weren't there," Barry said.

"No, but I believe my wife. I don't know how the press found out about it. They were at our house when the police brought Jolene home."

"Because Adeline called them," Jolene said emphatically. "You know, I don't care about the house. It's just a house. It's what's inside that I want. My memories. Photographs. My parents' wedding album. I can't stand that Adeline will have her hands on it."

Scott said, "You said you're investigating Harper's death as a homicide. Please, be honest with us, was he with a prostitute?"

Lucy didn't say anything mostly because she wasn't certain what she truly believed anymore. Barry said, "Our investigation is ongoing. We don't know why your father went to that motel room or what that girl was doing there. We have evidence that she is a prostitute, but no evidence that your father had sexual relations with her."

"How did he die?" Scott asked. "Adeline originally told Jolene that it was a heart attack."

"We're waiting for toxicology."

"What does that mean?" Jolene asked, turning to her husband.

Scott said, "Blood and tissue samples. To see if he'd been drinking or on drugs."

"Daddy didn't drink much, and he absolutely didn't do drugs," she said.

"We've already determined that he had no alcohol in his system and none of the common illicit drugs were found in his blood or in his possession," Barry said. "We're waiting on additional tests. It appears that he was injected in the back of his neck."

Both Jolene and Scott stared at them, confused.

Barry said, "Technically, he died of asphyxiation—he couldn't breathe. But there was no evidence of strangulation

or suffocation. That's why the coroner is pursuing a chemical reason. But we haven't released that information, because we don't have a final report from the ME's office. So
I'd appreciate if you kept that to yourselves until the official word."

Lucy said, "Go back to something you said earlier,
Jolene. That your father had been preoccupied for the last
few weeks. Why don't you think it was related to his business?"

"Because he would have told me. We talked business
all the time. Maybe not so much last week, but . . . it's hard
to explain *why*. I just know my dad. I guess—we'd talk
about HWI and what audits were pending, what clients we
were taking on or dropping, things like that. We met officially, with the staff, once a week, but I used to talk to
him nearly every day about this or that. Not just business,
but about Scott, or the house Scott and I are building, or
horses—I keep several show horses. We'd catch up on
friends, my cousins—personal stuff. But that all stopped
a couple weeks ago. Maybe a month? He seemed rushed
every time we spoke, like he needed to get to something
else, so we talked about business and then he'd find an excuse to hang up. HWI wasn't having any problems—I
would know. So whatever was bothering him wasn't about
HWI. If that makes sense."

Lucy understood. It was subtle, but Jolene had the most
intimate relationship with Harper, other than Adeline. She
would know if something was occupying his mind. And
her observations matched both Adeline's comments about
Harper visiting the doctor and seeming preoccupied, and
Debbie Alexander's comments about Harper acting out of
character by canceling a meeting.

Barry asked, "Do you know a real estate developer
named James Everett?"

"Of course. Everyone knows Everett," Scott said. "But I don't think we've ever met him."

"I did, a couple times," Jolene said. "He wanted Daddy to go in with him on this land purchase outside of Mc-Allen, but Daddy said no. He felt it was a conflict of interest to get into a business deal with one of Adeline's biggest supporters. Mr. Everett and Adeline were in business together, a real estate development company, before she ran for office. I was in the meeting where he pitched the idea to Daddy. Mr. Everett was not happy my dad refused, and suggested Daddy give me the money to go in on the deal to avoid a potential conflict, but that made my dad even more furious. He told him to leave."

"Do you remember when this conversation took place?"

"A couple of years ago. Before Scott and I got married. I don't even think we were engaged. If it's important, I can find the exact date. We met at HWI, they keep permanent records of all scheduled appointments."

"I'll let you know," Barry said. "Would you say that your father was friends with Mr. Everett?"

"No," Jolene said. "Friendly, maybe, but not friends, especially after that meeting. Why?"

"His name came up during our investigation," Barry said vaguely. "We're doing everything we can to find out exactly what happened to your father. If you have any additional information about why he might have been in San Antonio Friday night, it would help."

Jolene hesitated, then reached into her large purse and pulled out a computer tablet. "I wasn't sure I should give this to you."

"Jolene," Scott said with a warning tone.

"Well, I wasn't, Scott! Not after what Adeline said. I don't want to give her any ammunition to destroy my daddy's reputation. He was proud of his name, his business.

And now it's *my* business, and I'm going to carry on his legacy. He would want that."

She slid the tablet across the table. "Saturday morning, when Adeline called me and said that Daddy was dead, I packed up his hotel room. I didn't think anything of it then, because I was really upset, and I didn't know how or when or anything. This tablet was in his briefcase, which he'd left in his hotel room. I've never seen it before. Last night, I turned it on, but it's password protected. I tried all Daddy's usual passwords, none of them worked, and it locked me out. I was going to give it to the security consultant HWI hired to assist with the forensic audit, but maybe you should have it."

Barry said, "You did the right thing." He rose and shook their hands. "Thank you for coming down, and we'll be in touch." He opened the door. "By the way, who did you hire?"

Lucy's stomach fell. She should have told Barry immediately about Sean, but she didn't think of it when she saw him.

"Sean Rogan. He came highly recommended, and Gregor—our security chief—says he's the best in the business. I can give you his contact information if you need it."

Barry glanced at Lucy. She couldn't read his expression, but the blank face couldn't be a good sign. "We have it."

CHAPTER THIRTEEN

As soon as Jolene and Scott left, Barry pulled Lucy back into the conference room and closed the door. "You should have told me."

"I didn't know until yesterday when Sean told me. I didn't suggest to Smith that he hire Sean. And I didn't give Sean any direction. It's his decision, not mine."

"You should have told Sean to turn it down. This is a huge conflict."

"It's not a conflict. Sean is a security consultant. He has consulted with the FBI on numerous occasions. Having him on the inside will only help us. And honestly, it's not my place to tell Sean what contracts he takes or doesn't take. Besides, if they didn't hire Sean, he would have recommended someone from RCK. They're one of the top private security firms in the country with high government clearance. The 'K' stands for Kincaid."

"I don't like it."

"I'm sorry, Barry, but this is Sean's business." She *was* sorry that there was a conflict with Barry, but she wasn't sorry Sean had taken the job. "Why don't you meet with Sean? Maybe if you get to know him, you'll understand that when it comes to security, he's all business."

"I'm going to have to tell Juan."

"I would have told you, but when you came in we immediately met with Jolene."

"All right."

She was confused. "What?"

"You tell Juan. Now, not later. And I'm going to find out where James Everett is so we can interview him." He held up the tablet. "I'm going to give this to Zach to work on cracking the code and extracting data."

Lucy nodded and left the conference room. Barry didn't follow her, but sat down at the table and pulled out his phone.

She walked back to her squad room and knocked on Juan's doorframe, even though his door was open and he was typing at the computer. He had an open-door policy, but ever since she'd been suspended, she'd avoided him. She hated the tension and suspected it contributed to her insomnia.

But if she was truthful with herself, she knew there was far more to it than tension in the office. Seeing Michael and the other boys yesterday had reminded her that there were more children like them out there. It was her overwhelming feeling of helplessness that disrupted her sleep. Intellectually, she knew she couldn't save everyone. That children would be murdered and women raped and predators freed. But when her defenses were down and her mind was at rest, her emotions took over and all she could dream about were those she couldn't save.

And sometimes, in her nightmares, she couldn't save herself.

Juan looked up. "Come in, Lucy. Close the door."

She sat on the edge of a chair. "On the case Barry and I are working, the victim's company hired Sean to assist with the security audit. Sean told me yesterday. I don't think there's a conflict, I didn't recommend him, but Barry wanted to make sure you knew."

Juan nodded. "Sean called me."

"Oh. Okay." She stood.

"Sit back down."

She did, her heart pounding. She hadn't done anything wrong since she'd returned. She'd done everything she'd been asked, gone above and beyond, worked extra hours—yes, to make amends for what happened in Mexico, but also because she loved her job and wanted to get back in Juan's good graces.

Juan finished typing something on his computer, then turned his attention to her. "Agent Donnelly called this morning. He asked me to loan you to him on a case he's working. The last-known associates of Jaime Sanchez and Vasco Trejo were murdered last night. Nine people dead, including a child."

Her stomach turned. "What happened?"

"I don't have the details yet. Brad was heading to the crime scene when he called. I can't let you work the case. You're in the middle of an important investigation."

"Yes, sir."

"You're welcome to talk to him and share information, but I need you working the Worthington case with your undivided attention."

"Absolutely."

"However, Brad's concerned about your safety and frankly, so am I. You and Brad were instrumental in taking down Trejo's smuggling operation and Sanchez's local gang. While most of their people are dead, that doesn't necessarily mean you and Brad are not on the cartel's radar. I already talked to Ryan, and he's going to liaison with the DEA's office until we figure out what's going on with this situation."

"Thank you for letting me know. Is that all?"

"Yes."

She got up and put her hand on the doorknob.

"One more thing, Lucy," he said.

She turned, still apprehensive.

"Don't think I haven't noticed that you've been putting in extra hours. You don't need to do that."

"I know," she said, then added, "I love my job."

Juan didn't say anything else, so she walked out, uncertain if she'd helped or hurt her case.

Barry approached. "Everett's in his office, let's go."

She grabbed her gun and credentials from her desk drawer, then rushed to follow Barry out to the parking lot. They ran into Ryan Quiroz getting into a pool car. "Luce," he said, "did you talk to Juan?"

She nodded. "He filled me in."

"Make sure you watch your back."

"If Trejo's entire network was taken out, that should be good news."

"Unless there's a more dangerous player involved. I'll let you know what I learn, I'm meeting Donnelly at the crime scene."

"Thanks, Ryan. Tell Brad I said hi."

Ryan drove off. Though he'd been angry with her for a few weeks after she came back from her suspension, they'd recently started talking and things were almost back to where they had been. She liked Ryan a lot—he was a great cop and they'd worked well together during Operation Heatwave. She wanted that back. Maybe she should plan a dinner or something at the house this weekend. Sean enjoyed socializing more than she did, so he'd probably be amicable to the idea.

"What's going on?" Barry asked as he drove away.

"Remember Operation Heatwave?"

"Of course."

"Fallout from that. Nine people from the Trejo/Sanchez gang were murdered last night. Ryan's working with the DEA on it."

"Is your attention going to be divided?"

"No—I'm committed to the Worthington case."

"Good."

She wasn't lying. While she would do anything for Brad Donnelly, a man she liked and respected, she didn't like working drug cases. What Brad and his people did was difficult, dangerous, and largely unrewarding. Because of their proximity to the border, the DEA had additional concerns and worked closely with all federal and local law enforcement agencies. Gun running, human trafficking, drugs—sometimes Lucy wondered why they had to have multiple agencies when the problems overlapped so much.

"I learned something interesting while you were talking to Juan," Barry said. "James Everett has been a big supporter of Adeline Reyes-Worthington from the beginning—until last month when he endorsed her opponent."

"How does that connect with him calling in a prostitute?"

"It doesn't, but it's an odd coincidence that Worthington's phone ends up in Everett's hotel room."

"How do you want to handle this?"

"Don't bring up the prostitute, at least at first," Barry said. "I want to see what he says when I tell him about the phone. We have no proof that the girl is underage, or that he had sex with her. And truly, no judge is going to put him in prison because he paid for sex—even if we can prove it. I want to see how fast he calls in one of his lawyers. Then, when I give you a signal, flip over your note pad and show him the photo of the girl."

Lucy was listening to Barry, but she was also thinking about why Jane Doe would take Worthington's phone and leave it in Everett's hotel room. "What if Everett hired her to steal the phone? Maybe she had nothing to do with Worthington's death—he could have been dead when she got there. She grabs the phone and delivers it."

Except, why set up the scene to make it look like Worthington had sex before he died?

"Why would he leave it in a room where it could be traced back to him?" Barry asked. "Let's pretend we didn't see the security tapes. We traced the phone's GPS to James Everett's hotel room. Let him tell us how it got there." Barry changed the subject. "Did you tell Juan about your boyfriend?"

"He already knew. Sean called him."

Barry didn't say anything. If he expected Lucy to say something more, she had no idea what it was, so she kept quiet.

Barry reached into his pocket and tossed her a folded sheet of paper. "That's the information from the warrant we served on the hotel this morning—Kenzie took care of it while we were interviewing Jolene Hayden. Confirms everything we knew from the security footage, plus the time he registered and when he was in his room."

Lucy read over the information while Barry drove in silence.

Ten minutes later, they arrived at the sprawling complex where James Everett's development company took up one four-story building in the multi-building, square-block office park on the outskirts of San Antonio.

Everett made them wait for twenty minutes before his secretary led them to his private office. She closed the doors behind her. Everett continued to sit behind his desk looking through a stack of papers. He was in his late forties, thick around the middle, had thinning gray hair, and wore an expensive suit. He barely glanced at them. "I have a meeting in ten minutes. I don't see how I can help you. I knew Harper Worthington, but we weren't close friends."

Barry said, "When did you last see Mr. Worthington?"

"Months ago. I don't remember when."

"And his wife, Congresswoman Reyes-Worthington?"

Everett didn't say anything for a second and looked up from his papers. "A few weeks ago. Maybe a month or so. Why is this relevant?"

"We're retracing Harper Worthington's last few days."

"And as I said, I haven't seen him lately."

"Were you registered at the Del Rio Hotel this weekend?"

Everett didn't answer the question. He rolled his gold pen back and forth between his fingers. "Why do you need to know?"

"Just following up on a lead."

"I really don't see why it's important for you to know where *I've* been."

Barry said, "Harper Worthington's cell phone was found on Saturday in a room at that hotel. The last registered guest was you."

"Impossible," he said.

"According to hotel records, you checked in Friday afternoon and checked out Saturday morning."

"So?"

"Housekeeping found the phone. How did it get in your room?"

"I have no idea."

"According to the GPS logs, it arrived at the hotel at approximately twelve thirty Saturday morning. An hour after Mr. Worthington died."

Everett didn't say anything for a long minute. He then said, "I don't know what you're talking about, but I'm not going to answer any more questions without my lawyer present."

Lucy flipped open her notebook and held up the photo of the unidentified girl in the hallway outside room 606. "Would you be able to give us the name of your girlfriend? Maybe she has additional information for us."

James Everett couldn't hide his shock. He stared at the picture, his face pale, an involuntary twitch making his head jerk almost imperceptibly. "I have nothing more to say," he said quietly.

"Are you sure?" Barry asked.

"I asked for my attorney."

"We haven't placed you under arrest."

"I don't have to talk to you without an attorney."

"Would you like to call him? We can wait. Or, I can arrest you for obstruction of justice, bring you in front of a judge, then once all the preliminary paperwork is done, interview you formally."

His eyes widened. "You can't arrest me! I haven't done anything."

Lucy said, "Obstruction of justice is when someone who may or may not have committed a crime impedes the investigation into a crime, whether or not said individual is a suspect."

"I'm not impeding anything! You haven't even told me what this is about."

Barry said, "We did, twice. Harper Worthington's phone was found in your hotel room. This girl is wanted for questioning as a potential witness. She was seen in the area where Mr. Worthington was found dead, and she was seen an hour later going into your hotel room. Feel free to call your attorney. We'll wait."

Everett cleared his throat and shook his head. "No. Absolutely not. I'll contact my attorney and then arrange a meeting later this week. I'm not going to be bullied by a couple of feds."

Barry tensed beside Lucy. Barry was a serious, even-tempered agent. The fact that he was getting angry showed just how much Everett was getting to him. But his voice was calm when he said, "If Agent Kincaid and I walk out of this office without the information that we want, I will require you to submit to questioning by five P.M. today at FBI headquarters, or I will get an arrest warrant for obstruction of justice and compel you to speak under oath in a public court of law."

Everett's face reddened. "You can't do that." But he wasn't looking at them.

Barry didn't say another word. The longer Barry remained silent, the more Everett squirmed.

Finally, Everett said, "I need five minutes."

"We'll wait here."

Everett couldn't get out of his office fast enough.

Lucy was impressed. "I just had the best lesson in field interrogations ever."

"He pissed me off." He glanced at her. "You kept your cool. It's easy to get rattled with people like him."

"The only sign that you were angry was that your lower jaw shifted forward and your neck muscles tightened."

"You can see that?"

"One of my psych classes dealt solely with physical reactions to emotional stress. It's easy with a guy like Everett who uses his bravado and pomp to steamroll over people, harder when someone is calm and even tempered like you."

"Can you tell when people are lying?"

"Usually. Some people are really good at it, though. They tell half truths and use emotion to work for them rather than against them. The best liars are those who are telling mostly the truth, or who have a sociopathy where they believe their own lies to the point that they themselves can't distinguish between truth and fiction. They're harder to pinpoint unless I have solid evidence I can use to rattle them."

"People probably don't like playing poker with you."

She laughed, then covered her mouth. "Actually, I'm a really bad liar."

"Our goal here is to find out who that girl is," Barry said. "She's the one who took the phone from Worthington and left it in Everett's room. Do you think he knew about the phone?"

"No," Lucy said. "I don't even think that he cared about the hotel, until you mentioned when the phone was left there. That's when he started to worry about why we were here."

Everett returned ten minutes later, along with his attorney—a tall, lean brunette named Miriam Shaw.

"I'm Mr. Everett's corporate attorney," Shaw said, "and if I feel that this conversation is treading too far into criminal law, I'll halt the interview and we'll make arrangements for Mr. Everett to meet with you once he retains another lawyer."

"This should have been simple," Barry said. "Mr. Everett is the one who made it complicated."

"And you're the one who threatened him with arrest."

"Only if he breaks the law," Barry said. He nodded to Lucy.

She pulled a photo of their Jane Doe from her folder. "We need to find this girl. We know she was in your hotel room Friday night. We need her name and phone number."

Everett stared at the picture, lips in a tight line.

"Mr. Everett," Lucy prompted.

"I don't know," he said.

"You don't know what?" Lucy asked.

Shaw said, "My client has just said he didn't know this girl."

"Then what was she doing in his hotel room from twelve

thirty A.M. until four forty-five A.M. Saturday morning?" Lucy asked.

"I don't know," Everett said.

"Lying to a federal agent is a felony," Lucy said. She pulled out additional surveillance photos. "This is you registering at the hotel at four thirty-six Friday night." She slapped down another surveillance photo. "This is you having dinner alone in the hotel bar at seven-ten." Another photo. "This is you entering your room at nine-seventeen Friday night. You didn't leave. You purchased two adult videos from the hotel's streaming service." She pulled out the photo of Jane Doe. "This girl entered at twelve thirty that night and left at four forty-seven in the morning. You left at seven forty-five Saturday morning after checking out via the hotel's automated service. Are you still saying that you didn't know that this girl was in your hotel room at the same time you were?"

"I mean—of course I-I-I knew she was there," James fumbled. "B-but sex between two consenting adults isn't a crime."

Lucy had to bite her tongue to avoid mentioning that paying for sex was still a crime. She couldn't prove that Jane Doe was underage, or that money had been exchanged. "Then what is her name?"

"Why do you need to know?" Shaw asked. "My client is a married man, and he doesn't want any publicity about an extramarital affair."

"Then he shouldn't have one," Lucy snapped. She immediately regretted it. It was completely unprofessional.

Barry picked up the questioning immediately. "We need the information because this woman is a witness in a major criminal investigation, and if Mr. Everett does not give us her name, I will arrest him for obstruction of justice until he agrees to give us her name and contact information. And *that* will go on the public record."

"Elise," Everett said. "Her name is Elise."

"Elise what?" Barry asked.

"I don't know."

"How did you meet her?"

"A mutual friend."

"A mutual friend sent her up to your hotel room?"

Everett wiped sweat off his forehead with the back of his hand. "It doesn't work that way."

"How does it work?"

"It's complicated."

Lucy leaned forward. She was familiar with how a variety of prostitution rings were run. "Let me guess," she said, trying to speak as calmly as Barry did. "You call a number. You tell them what you want, deliver a hotel key and money to a specified location, then wait at the hotel for the girl to show. Am I warm?"

He nodded.

"Give us the number."

He pulled a piece of paper from his desk note pad and quickly wrote it down. His hand was shaking when he handed it to Lucy.

"That's it?" he said.

"For now," Barry said.

"One more question," Lucy said. "Had you ever met with Elise before Friday night?"

"No. I, um, my regular girlfriend is Bella."

"Did you ask for someone different?"

He shook his head. "Bella was sick. I don't want to get her in trouble. You're not going to get her in trouble, are you?"

His concern for his hooker was odd, but it was clear he was equally as concerned about his own hide.

"No," she said, and meant it.

On her way out, she saw a picture of Everett with his wife, a young boy, and a younger girl. Picture perfect. She picked it up, then looked at Everett. "You have a beautiful family. Why would you jeopardize your relationship with them?"

"You wouldn't understand." He refused to look at her.

"How can you have sex with teenagers when your daughter is about to become one?"

"You're sick," he said, fuming.

"I'm not the one who's sick."

Lucy put the picture down and walked out.

Barry immediately called Zach and asked him to research the phone number.

"You should also call Tia," Lucy said. "She may have a database, or the names Elise and Bella might mean something to her. I suspect Bella has the same basic appearance as Elise. These men rarely deviate from their preferred type."

"Go ahead and call her," Barry said. "It was a good question. Except for that little judgmental slip, you did well."

"I shouldn't have let his attitude bother me."

"And when I say judgmental, I'm not saying I condone his behavior."

"I know. It's the get-more-flies-with-honey argument."

"Honey wouldn't have worked on him."

Lucy almost smiled, then he said, "You shouldn't have mentioned his family. That was over the top."

"Men like him will justify anything. Sometimes they need to be called out on it. He likes young girls. He'll want them younger." Barry was going to argue, but Lucy said, "Unfortunately, I know a lot about sexual perverts. He's borderline violent. He controls it now, but soon it won't be enough to spank the girls, he'll hurt them. He'll find out that hurting them turns him on, and he won't be able to stop. He's sick, he needs help, but society doesn't have a redress for perverts like him. Not until he kills one of the prostitutes or goes after his own daughter."

Before Barry could comment, she called Tia and put her on speaker. "Hi, Tia, it's Lucy. You're on speaker with me and Barry Crawford."

"Hi, Barry. It's been a long time."

"Yes, it has," Barry said.

"I have some info on the girl we're looking for."

"So do I. She goes by the name Elise. One of her johns said he usually uses a girl named Bella, but Bella was sick and the service sent him Elise. I have a number if you need it."

"I know who you're talking about. Not Elise, but Bella Jones. She works for Mona Hill. I'll send you Mona's file—it's thick. The woman is a piece of work. I've tried taking her down a couple of times, but she has friends in high places. I can't make anything stick, and she walks after paying a fine or time served. If Elise is working for her, Mona won't flip her."

"Is Bella underage?" Lucy asked.

"Probably, but I have no way of proving it. Solid fake IDs. You know how it is, Lucy. We only have so much time and resources."

"Help those who want help," Lucy said. There were so many young girls exploited in the sex industry that the older girls—over fourteen—were often beyond help. Younger girls, whether they wanted the help or not, were given priority, then came the older girls who sought help. Usually they were arrested for solicitation or drugs and if they showed signs of wanting to get out of the business, Tia would connect them with the right halfway house, get them into school or a GED program, or develop opportunities for them to go home, if feasible.

"If you can nail Mona, I'll help you wield the hammer. I keep an open file on her, just in case she gets wrapped up in something bigger."

"What do you have on Elise?" Barry asked.

"I didn't have her name, but I showed her picture to one of my CIs. He recognized her, said she's new and not from Texas. Didn't think she was working for anyone but herself, and definitely didn't work the streets. I was thinking she was a special order—she's young, probably fifteen. These girls rarely work for themselves, and none of the girls are chattering about an interloper."

"Would Mona Hill know about her?"

"Mona keeps her finger on the entire sex trade in southern Texas. If there's a new girl in town, she knows."

"That number I have—would you be able to confirm it belongs to Mona?"

"Probably, but I couldn't say for certain. She uses different numbers for different johns. When she wants to cut someone off, she disconnects the number. But send it to me, I'll run it."

"Thanks, Tia."

"Be careful with Mona. She'll do anything to protect her organization."

"What is she scared of?"

"Nothing."

"Everyone is scared of something," Lucy said.

"Not true. Read Mona's file before you talk to her. I just emailed it to you. If you can find a weakness, more power to you. This woman has seen more violence than you and me combined. Prison doesn't scare her. Death doesn't scare her. She's worked herself up from the bottom multiple times. If her business is destroyed, she'll re-create it elsewhere. San Antonio isn't her first town. And absolutely don't let her get in your head."

"If she's not scared of anything, then we simply have to shut her down."

"That might be all you can do. Call me if you need

anything else. I'm not afraid to go after her, but I need something solid before my boss will let me take another run. She's already slipped out of my hands twice."

Lucy hung up. Her phone beeped with the email Tia had sent her containing Mona Hill's file. She said to Barry, "I need an hour to read this."

"If we go down this path, we're going to be stirring up a hornet's nest," Barry said.

Tia didn't have to be explicit for Barry and Lucy to know that if Mona consistently walked on criminal charges, that meant she had someone in law enforcement or the judicial system on her payroll—either as clients she blackmailed or people she bribed. While law-enforcement agencies at all levels tried to keep their houses clean, there were a few bad apples in every barrel. "We have to do it," Lucy said. "Elise is new in town, gets tied up with Mona Hill, is at the Worthington crime scene, then leaves Worthington's phone with her next client—one she's never been with before?"

"We have no evidence that Elise is affiliated with Mona," Barry said. "And how would she benefit from killing Worthington and trying to frame Everett? His alibi is solid, we confirmed it through hotel security that he was in his room during the time of death."

"He could have hired her."

"Why? And if he was involved in any way, why would Everett leave Worthington's phone in a hotel room registered in his name?"

"Maybe she intended to kill them both."

"Again, why?"

Barry was right in all his questions—and not having answers meant all they could do was speculate. At this point, nothing made sense. There was no motive, and while there was no doubt that a teenager could kill someone in cold blood, the way this all unfolded seemed too well planned.

"Maybe Elise is as much a pawn in this as Everett," Lucy mumbled.

"What do you mean?"

"The taxi driver saw Elise leave, but that doesn't mean she was the only one in the room with Worthington. And we still have no idea why Worthington went to the motel. There was nothing on his calendar, in his emails, or phone records that tells us why the spontaneous trip to San Antonio—Zach would have called us if anything popped up. And I keep wondering, why did Elise take his phone in the first place? She must know that cell phones can be tracked."

"It could be that she or someone else wanted information on the phone," Barry suggested. "But according to HWI, nothing on the phone had been downloaded, and the phone wasn't used to make a call or go online after Worthington's call to his daughter."

"But what if she simply looked at information? Would the techs be able to know that?"

"I don't understand what you mean."

"I keep notes on my phone. If I download them to my computer or update the note or send it to someone, there is a record. But what if I just read the note?"

"I have no idea. I'm pretty tech savvy, but I don't know what logs are kept. I'll ask our tech team about it."

"We need to find Elise," Lucy said. "She has the answers."

Lucy feared for the girl. Whether she was a willing participant in Worthington's death or forced to do it by someone who threatened her, or simply a witness to murder, Elise was in danger. It would be much easier to kill her than to trust her not to talk.

In fact, Elise might already be dead.

CHAPTER FOURTEEN

Sean often lost track of time when he was working on something challenging. He'd already gone through his checklist—no one had hacked the HWI system, no one had used the HWI system to send suspicious documents, and no staff email raised any other red flags. One guy in the mail room stayed late every night to look at porn sites— Sean flagged his computer so Gregor could decide what to do about him—and one of the admins spent an unusual amount of time playing online games. Again, Sean flagged the person, but didn't find anything in their behavior that said corporate espionage. He ran full diagnostics through- out the system to make sure there was no malware down- loaded through third-party sites—porn sites were notorious for that—but the virus protection software that HWI ran was state of the art.

It could be that there was nothing to find—it wouldn't be the first time that Sean had encountered a clean busi- ness. But he would go through each possible avenue of po- tential exploitation before he put his stamp of approval on HWI.

Once he determined that there was no overtly suspi- cious behavior, he dug down to the next level. He first

verified that employees were only accessing the files their
clearances gave them access to. Next, he looked at employees who had been there for less than a year. There were
six, but only two with high-level access. While he ran full
backgrounds on each of them, he looked at long-term patterns.

Most people who looked at computer data saw only
numbers and words with no context. Sean saw patterns
where others saw chaos. He first looked at the business as
a whole—whether productivity was consistent within each
month, quarter, and year. As would be expected in a CPA
firm, activity peaked in April and October—tax-filing
periods—with smaller peaks at quarterly intervals. Year-
to-year productivity was consistent, once Sean allotted for
increases in staff and clients. HWI had been growing
steadily since Harper Worthington opened the business
thirty-one years ago. He'd started as a corporate CPA and
taken his first small government client two years later.
After his firm was awarded a court-mandated audit of a
state government program twenty-two years ago, he'd
branched out into working more audits and government
contracts than private. The breakdown was still pretty
good—60 percent government, 40 percent private, en-
abling him to withstand any lulls in business from either
sector.

Looking at how Harper Worthington ran his business,
Sean grew to respect him. Harper was a smart businessman, if a bit more conservative than Sean would have
been. He didn't take risks, didn't overspend, and had moderate costs. He provided employees with slightly above-
industry-average income-and-benefits packages, including
retirement plans, but no one person was paid out of line
with anyone else in a similar position.

After a short break, Sean ran a custom program that
would highlight changes in computer behavior over

time—basically, if someone was using their computer in a different way now than they had in the past. The types of programs accessed, time spent online, the Web sites visited, printing or viewing documents, downloads. Changes in computer usage could mean a variety of things from innocuous, such as getting a promotion or change of software, to criminal, such as spending more time with certain files than an employee's job should warrant.

One thing jumped out at him immediately.

Harper Worthington had almost completely stopped using the computer at his desk over the last four weeks. His login and password hadn't changed, so Sean crossreferenced the computer IP addresses with the log that Gregor had given him, and determined that Harper—or someone with his password—was using a computer in another office.

Sean tracked Gregor down in his office. "Why wasn't Harper using his computer?"

Gregor looked at him blankly. "What do you mean?"

"He was using a computer in a vacant office. Or gave someone his password."

"That doesn't make sense." Gregor rose and followed Sean down to Harper's office. Sean had met Debbie Alexander, Harper's admin, that morning. She was at her desk. "Debbie, Mr. Rogan seems to think that Harper wasn't using the computer in his office. Was there a problem with it?"

"Is something wrong?" she asked, obviously confused.

"It's an anomaly," Sean said.

"Three or four weeks ago he took over the BLM audit—"

"BLM?" Sean asked.

"Bureau of Land Management. There were several boxes of files, and Terry—that's our accountant who usually handles the BLM—is on maternity leave. Terry told him to use her computer because she had all the relevant documents in her office." Debbie's eyebrows scrunched together. "You know, Terry thought something was off with one of the boxes BLM sent. She wanted to come in and help Harper sort through it, but he told her to stay home with the baby."

"Did Harper usually take over clients when someone went on leave?" Sean asked.

"Sometimes."

"And use their office?"

Debbie was surprised by the question. "No, not since I've been here."

"I need to see his computer, then Terry's."

"All the files, except for physical documentation, are on the intranet," Debbie said. "They can be accessed from any computer."

Sean ignored her because he wasn't looking for the obvious.

He sat at Harper's desk, ignoring both Debbie and Gregor, who watched him with blatant curiosity.

Why would Harper not use his own computer? Did he think something was wrong with it? That it had been compromised? Why wouldn't he have said something to Gregor or the tech department?

Sean booted up the computer and used the admin code he'd created that morning so there would be a record of everything he did—important if anything he uncovered led to a civil or criminal trial or employee termination. He had already run system-wide diagnostics, but he ran diagnostics on a deeper level on Harper's computer. Nothing popped—no viruses, no malware, no piggybacking of data. He checked the logs and found a deleted memo from Terry to Harper. It was a long email listing all the projects she was working on and who she'd assigned them to while she was on leave. At the end she wrote:

*BLM has continued to send over documents,
past our deadline, and there are a couple of
discrepancies that I can't seem to reconcile. I've
asked for specific files—the memos are in the
master file—but they claim they've already sent
them. Maybe this pregnancy has made me more
tired than I thought. Ian has been working with
me on this, and can take it over while I'm gone.
However, you might want to work with him
because he hasn't handled something of this
magnitude alone. Everything is in my office—
I pulled the questionable files from the storage
room last week to give them another look through.
Call me at home if you have any questions. I'm
sure you'll find the problem. ~Terry*

"Debbie," Sean said, "why didn't Harper bring the boxes into his office? Or the conference room?"

"I never asked," Debbie said. "Since my office is between Terry's and Harper's, I didn't think anything of it. But I told the FBI agents who were here that Harper wasn't quite himself for the last couple of weeks. He was distant, like he had a lot on his mind, but he didn't say anything to me. Maybe I missed something."

Sean walked back through Debbie's office and into Terry's much smaller office. It was crowded but immaculate. The boxes were neatly lined up and labeled, three high, under the solitary picture window. The desk was clear of work. "Debbie," Sean said, "I need to talk to Ian."

"I'll call him in," Debbie said and left.

Sean went back to Harper's office. It was twice the size, with a second workstation in the corner and an adjoining conference room. There were photos of Harper and his wife, Harper and his daughter, Harper and horses, awards, his degrees, as well as a comfortable couch. The room was warm and inviting, but also said conservative and professional. Why hadn't he moved all the files into the larger, more comfortable space? Why work at a colleague's desk?

Sean skimmed through Harper's emails. He'd exchanged several emails with Terry related to the files, mostly asking questions about what she'd done. Nothing that pointed to a crime or even a suspicion of a crime.

Sean leaned back in Harper's chair and closed his eyes, ignoring Gregor's unspoken questions.

Harper hadn't wanted to work in this office. He'd changed his habits and worked in Terry's office, at the same time that his behavior had changed, according to his admin. Sean wished he could call Lucy and ask if she had confirmed with his family or friends that Harper's personal behavior had changed at the same time as his office behavior.

Clear change in behavior. Preoccupied. Didn't use his own computer. Which meant he didn't use his phone . . .

Sean sat up and typed rapidly on Harper's computer.

"What?" Gregor asked.

Sean didn't answer right away. He accessed HWI internal phone records and located Harper's phone number.

Harper hadn't taken any calls at his desk for four weeks. No ingoing or outgoing. Sean checked Terry's extension— it had been used consistently during the time Harper was using her office. Which meant that even when he wasn't working on the BLM audit he wasn't using his phone or his computer.

Sean unplugged the phone from the wall. He then took his tool set from his computer case, unscrewed the handset, and carefully pulled it apart.

He turned it around so Gregor could see the bug in the mouthpiece. "He knew this was here," Sean said. "That's why he used Terry's office."

Sean inspected the bug carefully because he didn't want

to damage it. "Expensive. Completely undetectable unless it's activated, and it's activated only when he's on the phone. This is high quality. Used by governments or well-financed criminals."

"Can you trace it?"

"They may have turned off the receiver, which means there's no way to trace it. And depending on how it was initially set up, I don't know that it's traceable at all. Unless we can get prints off the bug or trace the serial number. If I were the one bugging an office, they'd never trace the number back to me. Still—if it's possible, I can do it. I need to get some equipment, and then I want your permission to bring in the FBI."

"Of course. They're investigating Harper's murder. This may be connected."

There were a couple of reasons Sean wanted the FBI involved, though he'd never consider bringing them in if Lucy wasn't an agent. He wanted to leak information and give whoever had bugged Harper's phone actionable intelligence—but nothing that would jeopardize the case.

He said to Gregor, "This only works if there are no other bugs in here, otherwise they already know our plan."

"I already sent a message to the head of IT to sweep the entire building," Gregor said. "Why didn't Harper tell me about the bug?" He was both angry and hurt that his boss hadn't trusted him, and not a little furious that someone had bugged the phone.

Sean was wondering the same thing. Why had Harper been so secretive? Did he think someone inside HWI had betrayed him? The first person Sean had cleared was Gregor Smith himself—as head of security, he would have the most access. But so far, he was clean. Sean would dig deeper into his finances, but Sean didn't think Gregor was corrupt.

Sean said, "The big question for me is—how did Harper know the bug was here in the first place? And even if he didn't want anyone to know, why didn't he destroy it himself?"

CHAPTER FIFTEEN

Brad Donnelly stood with his SAPD liaison, Sergeant Jerry Fielding, next to the tactical van outside the crime scene. The dilapidated strip mall had once housed a video rental store, a small grocery, and a Mexican restaurant. Now it was completely boarded up. The fence that had once surrounded the long, narrow building had been torn down. Heaps of jagged chain-link fencing and barbed wire lay tangled on the broken cement. Weeds grew through the holes in the metal, a testament to how long it had been abandoned. Gang graffiti covered the sagging structure.

He'd been here for hours, walked through the scene before the bodies had been removed, and imparted what knowledge he had about the victims to Jerry and his team. Brad recognized three as known associates of Jaime Sanchez, which meant that they were affiliated with Vasco Trejo. It held to reason the rest of the victims were also part of Trejo's group—possibly new recruits after others had been killed or imprisoned.

"I haven't heard of anything this big in a long time," Jerry said, not for the first time. He was antsy and it showed. Brad kept his nerves to himself. A hit of this

magnitude put everyone in law enforcement on high
alert.

FBI Agent Ryan Quiroz had arrived shortly after Brad,
but went off with one of the SAPD detectives to canvass
the neighborhood. So far, no one would talk, but Brad
hoped that Ryan could convince someone to step forward.
Ryan, a sixth-generation Hispanic Texan, spoke fluent
Spanish with a keen ear for different dialects. Ryan had
been helpful in past joint operations because of his linguis-
tic skills and non-cop-like demeanor, but Brad wasn't as
confident this time around. Getting drugs out of neighbor-
hoods was one thing—many of the residents, while completely distrustful of law enforcement, didn't like the
proliferation of drugs in their schools and communities.
Turning in a mass murderer with gang or cartel affiliations
was a far more dangerous ball game.

"Fielding," one of the senior crime scene techs called
over to them.

Brad followed Jerry to where the crime techs were cataloging evidence.

"Have something?"

"A whole lot of weird something." He looked at Brad.
"I'm Ash Dominguez. Donnelly, right?"

"Brad. You processed the Sanchez storage facility a
couple months ago."

"Yep. So, we've counted two hundred shots fired, which
is a rough estimate."

"Shit. Do you know what type of weapons?"

"M4. There were several rounds that were ejected or
dropped. They didn't police their brass. We'll process
everything—might get some prints. These gang bangers
don't usually wear gloves. Not that prints are going to help
us find these bastards."

"M4s are primarily military issue."

"Yep. But you know as well as I do that the US government has sent them far and wide, not to mention that shipments have been stolen."

Two months ago, the DEA had recovered part of a stolen shipment of military rifles down in Mexico that had been stolen by Trejo's operation. Had someone in Trejo's organization sold the rest of the guns? Was this an exchange gone bad? Or a completely different set of weapons?

"You have an idea?" Jerry asked Brad.

"I might. But I need more intel. We're certain the dead men were all Sanchez/Trejo's group?"

"No doubt on three of them. Working on the others," Jerry said.

"Want more weird?" Ash asked. "The killers didn't take the drugs. We're still processing, but there's approximately twelve pounds of heroin, thirty-six packages. Of course, we need to test it at the lab. How much is that worth?"

"Depending on the quality, that's probably a street value of a million bucks." Definitely a hefty score. "Was it hidden?"

Ash shook his head. "And if there'd been money, the shooters took it."

"Did you get any electronics?"

"Yeah, bagged and tagged and photographed. There was a computer system in the drug room, all shot up. Don't know if we can get anything from it, but we'll try."

"Vigilante?" Jerry asked.

"God, I hope not," Brad said. But leaving the drugs behind didn't scream that this was a gang hit. A rival gang would take the drugs.

Ash said, "Just a gut feeling looking at the evidence, I still need to talk to my team and recreate the scene, but here's my take. Minimum of four shooters. Looks like the building was taken from all points of entry. These guys didn't have a chance. Half of them couldn't even draw their own guns. They were all carrying, even the girls. The killers opened fire until everyone was down, then they went around and put a bullet in everyone's head, to guarantee they were dead. I have some possibly helpful news. We collected blood by one of the rear doors, with a trail leading to the road. A sufficient amount to suggest one of the attackers got hit."

"Good—we'll alert hospitals and clinics," Jerry said.

"Already done," Ash said, "but some clinics won't report."

Brad had some ideas on where someone would go who didn't want the shooting to get back to the police. Brad would be persona non grata there, but he could get Ryan to do it, if he grunged down a bit.

"With four or more shooters, we're probably not looking at vigilante," Brad said. "Why not take the drugs?"

"To make a statement? Punishment?" Jerry suggested. "But damn, they wouldn't leave a million dollars, so why leave a million in drugs?"

Brad had no answer. Kane Rogan had said the hit was retaliation. But for what? And how had Rogan learned about it only hours after it went down?

Ryan approached them. "Almost a complete waste of the last three hours."

"Almost?"

He held up a small videotape. "No one said a word other than admitting to hearing the shots, and the time was consistent with the nine-one-one calls that came in. However, I got a hint that one of the homeowners wouldn't care if I took this tape out of a camera he had mounted on the corner of his garage. If the getaway car went south, it's here. If it didn't, we have nothing."

"Fifty-fifty chance? I'll take it," Brad said to Ryan. "Anything else, Ash?"

"Naw. We'll be here another hour or two. It's going to take a few days for the coroner's report, but from the amount of blood, they all died from gunshot wounds. If there's anything odd, Jerry'll let you know."

"I'm particularly interested in the bullets and if you can determine how many shooters, vehicles, and prints."

"That shouldn't be a problem, give me a little time and I'll have the answers. I'll run all prints through AFIS. We have already identified most of the deceased, and the others we should have by tomorrow."

"We might be able to get more information from the families," Ryan said.

"Maybe." Brad wasn't optimistic. "Let's focus on IDing the female victims and child. Those families might be more willing to talk to us."

"The female victims were Julianna Romero and Maria Romero," Ash said, looking down at his notes. "They both had purses with photo identification." He shook his head. "Sisters. I feel bad for that family."

"I'll bet the kid belonged to one of them," Brad said. "Find the family and go from there."

"I'm going to finish up here then send ya'll my report." Ash waved his hand as he departed and went back inside the strip mall.

"Thanks for coming out," Jerry said to Brad and Ryan. "SAPD appreciates your assistance."

"Anytime, Jerry," Brad said. "Keep me in the loop, and if I learn anything I'll pass it on."

"Do you want to talk to the girl's family?" Jerry asked.

"You take a run at them, this is still an SAPD case," Brad said. "If you get any wonky vibes, call me."

"Are you back on duty?" Ryan asked.

"Desk duty," Brad said. "But I'll clear it with Archer." Samantha Archer, his boss, had been a stickler for him staying at his damn desk, but Brad had a feeling she was reacting more emotionally than professionally. He just needed to get his doctor to give him the official all clear. "And I'll get that damn doctor's note," he added.

Brad and Ryan walked back to where they'd parked in an open field across the street.

Brad asked, "You want to come to my office and look at the tape?"

"I can't. I have my boys this week and need to pick them up at my mom's."

"How are they?"

"Good, thanks. I miss them. Divorce sucks."

"It's why I never married."

Brad opened his car door. Before he could leave, Ryan asked, "You asked Juan for Lucy. Why?"

"It wasn't personal."

"That doesn't answer my question."

"I don't know what you want me to say."

"What happened in Hidalgo?"

Brad couldn't give Lucy up—not only would she get in trouble, but he would be suspended for lying in a report. She'd already told him that Juan suspected she'd gone down to Mexico to help rescue him from Sanchez and Trejo, but she hadn't admitted it, and Juan hadn't said a word. Sam Archer had no clue what had really happened at Trejo's compound, and Brad had no desire to fill her in on the details. He would only get reprimanded, but Lucy could lose her job.

"All I can say, Ryan, is that if it weren't for Lucy, I'd be dead. So would those boys. Whatever she did or didn't do, her motives were pure. The last two months have been rough on her."

"I know," Ryan said. "I'm partly to blame, I was hard on her. But, Brad—it's hard to trust your partner when she isn't honest with you."

"Believe me, after what happened in my own operation,

I get it." One of his own people, someone he trusted explicitly, had been working with the cartel and was party to the murder of a band of Marines who were transporting recovered weapons back to the States. Nicole Rollins was now in jail pending trial, though word was that she wanted to make a deal. If Brad had his way, there would be no deal: Nicole would be tried for treason and murder and executed.

There was really nothing left to say on the subject. Ryan would come around—Brad thought he already had, it was just his ego that was still wounded.

"Speaking of your former partner," Ryan said. "She might know something about this attack. She was high up in the Trejo/Sanchez organization. She might talk to you."

"I hate that woman," Brad said. "There's no guarantee that she knows anything and, if she does, that she'll tell us. The DOJ is still playing games with her, and I wish they'd just locked her up. Instead, she's sitting in the county jail."

"She's not high up on my list of beer buddies, either." Ryan frowned and glanced back at the crime scene. "If there's a new player in town taking out the rest of Trejo's gang, they could go for her."

"And that would be a bad thing?"

"Murder is always a bad thing. They killed a kid, Brad. Don't let your hatred for Rollins cloud your judgment."

Ryan was right. But Brad didn't have to like it.

CHAPTER SIXTEEN

Lucy had worked several cases related to the sex trade, but she wasn't prepared for Mona Hill.

Rather, she was partly prepared because of the files Tia had sent over. She knew, for example, that Mona's childhood was sketchy. She'd been raised by a single mom in Houston who'd been in and out of prison for prostitution and drugs. Mona appeared to have raised herself or lived with relatives during her mother's imprisonment, because there was no record of her going into foster care. In fact, there was no documentation on Mona until she was eighteen. Everything Tia wrote was conjecture she'd picked up over the years, though Tia noted that there was no juvenile record, sealed or otherwise.

When Mona was nineteen, she'd pled guilty to attempted murder and had spent eighteen months in a California prison. There was no explanation as to why the sentence was so short, and Lucy made a note to look into it. There might be something there that would give her insight into the woman.

Mona had been arrested multiple times since her release from prison: California, Nevada and Texas all had arrest records. But she'd never served more than a night in jail—all the cases had been dismissed or pled out with a fine. She'd starred in legal pornography for years before moving to San Antonio four years ago, where she took over part of the sex trade. According to Tia, at least a third of the "working girls" in San Antonio worked for Mona at least part of the time. A client called a special phone number, told her what he wanted, and she got it for him—charging a premium. The johns paid Mona for the "referral" and paid the girls directly, so no girl ever gave Mona money.

Tia had listed Mona's known associates, and in her notes wrote that she suspected at least one judge had been compromised—but if Tia knew who, she hadn't put the name in the file.

The question Lucy most wanted answered was why Mona had sent Elise to James Everett. There had to be a specific reason, over and above that his regular girl Bella was sick. *If* she had been sick.

"Barry," Lucy said as they were driving to Mona Hill's residence, "I think we should talk to Bella first."

"Why?"

"Because this whole thing feels wrong. Bella gets sick and Elise is sent to Everett instead—after she either killed Harper Worthington or witnessed his murder."

"You're jumping to a conclusion."

"Am I? A witness put Elise at the motel at Worthington's time of death; she then goes to Everett and that's where we find Worthington's phone. It's like someone is dropping breadcrumbs for us to follow. I feel like we're being led from point A to point B because that's where someone wants us to go."

"The evidence hasn't been that easy to obtain," Barry countered. "We're good investigators, and we have access to a lot of information and resources. Plus, young prostitutes aren't the smartest girls on the street."

"I know what you're thinking—Elise took the phone,

probably wanted to sell it or get information off it, and accidentally left it in Everett's room not realizing that tracking the phone would be so easy." Lucy just didn't believe it. It felt off to her, and she couldn't explain why. "It seems too coincidental."

"Let's assume that Elise was involved in Worthington's death," Barry said.

"That's an easy assumption."

"What if she was ordered last-minute to take over Bella's client?"

"Okay," Lucy said.

"Okay? You're giving in too easily."

"I'm not giving in. I think it's possible. But that's why I want to talk to Bella before Mona Hill knows what we want. If this woman is as dangerous as Tia thinks, she may intimidate Bella into silence."

Lucy looked up Bella's address from Tia's records. "Well, dammit," she said. "Mona Hill owns and lives in a twelve-unit apartment building west of downtown. Bella rents an apartment from her. Bella isn't going to talk to us, especially at her apartment."

"Because someone will rat on her."

Lucy nodded. "Tia might be able to track her down and talk to her off-site. Can I send her a message?"

"You don't have to ask me."

Lucy hesitated, then said, "I don't really know what my role is in this investigation." There. She'd said it.

"What does that mean?"

"Sometimes, you keep me out of the loop, on a need-to-know basis. Or you get irritated when I ask questions. Or completely dismiss a theory. Then other times, you seem to want a dialogue, or seem surprised when I don't automatically do something—like email Tia."

He didn't say anything and Lucy hit herself for being so damn needy. No, it wasn't that. It was that she wanted to know exactly where she stood. Was there something wrong in that?

"I'm a rookie, and I took your conversation to heart on Saturday night. I had a wonderful dinner with Sean, we spent all day Sunday doing yard work at St. Catherine's Boys Home, and I barely *thought* about the case. I know that I'm obsessive and a workaholic. But I also have an impression that you're waiting for me to slip up."

"I'm not," Barry said. "I'm not used to working with a rookie like you. The last rookie we had on the squad was a guy who never should have been in Violent Crimes. He couldn't handle half the cases we deal with and had no instincts to speak of—in what he said or did. He left the month before you got here—went into an analysis unit at headquarters, because he should never have been around people—so maybe you're bearing the brunt of my leftover frustration with him."

Lucy didn't think that was the complete story, but it satisfied her for the time being. She turned her attention to her phone and sent Tia a message.

Barry pulled up in front of Mona Hill's apartment building a few minutes later.

It wasn't what either of them expected.

While the neighborhood wasn't particularly nice, the apartment complex was well maintained. Two brick buildings faced each over a tidy green courtyard. Each building had a main entrance, so no one had a door that went directly outside, which helped with security. There were blinds on the windows, not the sheets or newspaper that were often the décor of necessity in some slums.

Barry looked at the address again. "Hill is in unit one, the building on the right."

They crossed the street and walked through the courtyard. The front door was solid wood with thick, etched glass in the center. Barry rang the bell for Mona Hill's apartment. Lucy felt eyes on her. She glanced behind her, but didn't see anyone. All the blinds were closed.

"What can I do for the FBI today?" A voice came out of the speaker.

Barry frowned and glanced at Lucy. Obviously there was a camera, and they must look like federal agents on the surface, though Lucy thought they also could have passed for SAPD detectives.

Barry said, "Mona Hill?"

"Yes?"

"Agents Crawford and Kincaid with the FBI. We have a few questions. It won't take long."

"I don't care to speak to the FBI."

"You're not in any trouble, we just—"

"I know I'm not in any trouble, sugar," Mona said.

"Ma'am, this is an official federal investigation, and if you don't talk to us here, we'll need to bring you in for questioning."

"Really?" Mona said. "After you just told me I'm not in any trouble?" She laughed. The speaker made her voice sound tinny.

Barry was tense and muttered something under his breath that Lucy couldn't make out.

Lucy said, "Ms. Hill, you know how this works. We can do this dance indefinitely, but in the end, you'll either talk to us here, or talk to us at FBI headquarters."

"That's not how it works in *my* world."

"Or Agent Crawford and I can make your life miserable. Follow your employees—for lack of a better word—when they go out to work. Arrest them, arrest their clients, cause you a few sleepless nights. Indefinitely. That's my idea of fun."

"You must not have much of a life, Agent Kincaid." Her

words were meant to be insulting, but her tone had changed
from playful to all business. "I would then sue you for harassment."

"That would cost you time and money before you could
get us off your case. Considering evidence that you have
information pertinent to our investigation is pretty damn
good, we'll get a warrant and compel you to talk. Or you
can talk to us now."

Silence. Lucy held her breath, kept her expression blank
and her chin up. She felt Mona Hill watching them, though
Lucy resisted looking around for the camera.

"Good luck getting your fucking warrant," Mona
said.

"Thank you for your time," Lucy said. "We'll just wait
here and speak to your employees until the warrant comes
through."

Barry opened his mouth, then didn't say anything.

The door buzzed and Lucy pushed it open before Mona
changed her mind.

"Ballsy," Barry said under his breath.

Lucy didn't respond—couldn't respond—because her
heart was pounding. There was something about Mona's
tone that had her on edge.

The first door on the right opened and Mona stepped
out. She closed the door behind her. "That's far enough,
sugar," she said.

Lucy had miscalculated. Mona wasn't scared of them,
she was curious. Suspicious. Shrewd. Wanted them to
show their hand.

Mona was in her mid-thirties with wise eyes and a self-
assured confidence that wasn't just bravado. She was of
mixed race, so Lucy couldn't tell which ethnicity she might
identify with, if any—she could have blended with almost
any culture with relative ease. Her skin was slightly darker
than Lucy's half-Cuban complexion, but her eyes were

green and her hair was a curly light brown. She was alluring and sharp, as if every bone in her body could cut someone in half.

Lucy wished she could warn Barry that they'd stepped into Mona's sandbox, and Mona was in charge.

"Thank you for speaking with us, Ms. Hill," Barry said.

"Your girl threatened me," Mona said, sounding wholly unthreatened. "I don't really have a choice, do I?" Every word out of her mouth was a contradiction. She damn well knew she had a choice, and her choice was to listen, not speak, unless she wanted to tell them something.

"It wasn't a threat, Ms. Hill. We're looking for a girl named Elise. We heard she works for you."

"I don't know anyone by the name of Elise," she said.

She was lying.

"We know you sent her to meet with at least one of your clients," Barry said.

"No, you don't," Mona countered. She was answering Barry, but looking straight at Lucy.

"We're not here to arrest you for solicitation," Barry said.

Mona laughed.

"But we can make your life difficult if you don't cooperate."

"Sugar, you don't know the pile of shit you're stepping in."

"Elise is a suspect in a murder investigation," Barry said, "and I have enough evidence to get a warrant for your phone records, property records, employee records, rental records, and bank records—and whatever else I can think of between here and the AUSA's office."

Mona tightened her jaw but didn't say a word. That threat seemed to hold a bit of water. She was used to dealing with SAPD and the San Antonio criminal justice system; the federal system was not only different, but carried a mightier hammer.

Lucy spoke. "We know that Elise is new in town. Why would you protect her?"

"Who says I am?"

Mona was good. She didn't reveal anything in her expression or body language. She was assessing them, but Lucy knew Mona would never give them any information if it didn't directly benefit her. And Mona didn't get to where she was by turning on her girls at the first sign of trouble.

"I'm new in town, too," Lucy said. "I have no loyalties, no friends, no baggage. I will make it my life's mission to make your life miserable. Or I can forget you completely."

She hoped her expression was as serious as her voice.

Silence descended in the small entry for a good minute. No one moved.

"There's nothing to this story you're pulling out of thin air," Mona said. "It's simple. Last week a girl who called herself Elise asked for some work. She seemed to know the ropes. When one of my regulars got sick, I called her. That's it."

"How many clients did you send her to?" Barry asked.

"I'm not answering that."

"What's her phone number?" Barry asked.

Mona rattled off a number and Barry wrote it down.

"You wouldn't take a stranger into your operation without vetting her," Lucy said. "You're not that stupid. Who referred Elise?"

Mona laughed humorlessly but didn't answer.

"Agent Kincaid asked you a question."

"Get a fucking warrant, and I still won't tell you."

"I think you will," Barry said, irritated.

No, she wouldn't. Lucy was certain this was the extent of the information Mona would share. Enough to give them

a lead, not enough to put Mona or this Elise in any direct
harm from the authorities. In fact, it was too easy. She gave
them one thing—a way to track Elise. Why? Why even
give them that? She could have lied, said she didn't have a
number. She could have told them to pound sand. But she
gave them a lead.

Mona stared at Barry without blinking. "Arrest me, or
leave my property."

"We'll be back," Barry said. "We have more questions,
and like I said, it'll be here or at headquarters."

He turned to the main door and opened it. As he stepped
out, Lucy followed. Mona said, "Agent Kincaid?"

Lucy turned. Mona had a half smile on her lips, but
there was nothing friendly about her expression.

Mona said, "I never forget a face."

Lucy's head spun and if Barry hadn't touched her arm
just then, she might have collapsed. She turned and walked
out with tunnel vision. She didn't really remember how she
got to the car, only that she was in the passenger seat sitting on her hands to keep them from shaking.

Barry asked, "What happened back there? You look
like you've seen a ghost."

"Nothing," Lucy said.

Everything.

"Talk to me."

"There's nothing to say."

"Hill was just trying to get under your skin. You got us
in, that's the first step. We'll come back and push harder."
He glanced at Lucy, then turned the ignition and pulled
out of the parking space. "I thought you had a thicker skin
than this."

She straightened her spine. "I'm fine. She just caught
me off guard."

"We don't have that luxury," Barry said. "She's savvy.
She'll hold us at bay for as long as she can. But we'll run

the phone number, see what we can get. Probably a burner, but it's a local area code. We might get lucky and track down where it was purchased, see if we can get more info about this girl. It's nearly five, we need to head back to headquarters."

Lucy just wanted to go home.

Mona Hill couldn't possibly know about Lucy. Other than Operation Heatwave, she hadn't been involved in any major cases or investigations in the five months she'd been in San Antonio. Lucy had irritated the woman, so Mona turned around to issue an idle threat. It couldn't be because she recognized Lucy; it was simply a threat that she'd never forget or forgive the intrusion. At least, that's what Lucy wanted to believe. It wouldn't be the first time a suspect had tried to intimidate her.

Mona had been in the porn industry. Legal porn was big business, but illegal porn was bigger. The chances that Mona knew about or had seen the video of Lucy's rape eight years ago were slim to none. And while nothing online was ever truly gone, the FBI—and Lucy's family—had gone to extraordinary lengths to suppress copies of the video. In this day and age, porn was higher quality and far more prevalent, the quantity growing exponentially. On one popular porn site users uploaded more than one thousand new clips *daily*. The chances that Lucy's rape video would be readily available—without digging deep for it— were slim to none.

But in the back of her mind, Lucy's fear grew. That her past would always be with her, that she'd never be able to escape what she'd done . . . or what had been done to her.

By the time they got back to FBI headquarters, it was after five. Barry handed Zach the phone number he'd gotten from Mona, and Lucy sat down at her desk. She responded to a bunch of emails so she could leave with a clear plate.

Barry asked Zach, "Where are we on the tablet Jolene Hayden gave us?"

"It's not only password protected, but has a fail-safe. I didn't want to risk erasing the data, so passed it off to the tech unit. They know it's a priority."

Lucy almost offered Sean's services to crack it, but decided she wasn't going to further irritate Barry. They'd been making progress in this partnership until her near panic over Mona's threat, and she didn't want to give him any reason to pull her from the case. She thought she'd recovered well, but now he thought she had a thin skin.

If he only knew just how thick her skin really was.

Ryan rolled his chair over to Lucy. Their cubicles were kitty-corner from each other. "Hey," he said.

"Hey," she said.

"Donnelly said to say hi."

"How's he doing?"

"Physically he seems fine. He said when he gets tired his knee gives out. He's in physical therapy, but is hoping to be cleared this week."

"Desk duty is probably driving him up the wall. What happened out there?"

"Nasty business. Nine dead. Three with known ties to Sanchez, so it reasons that they either were the remnants of the Trejo/Sanchez enterprise, or the remaining few were trying to rebuild the organization. Could have trampled over someone else's territory. And remember, Sanchez had been involved in recruiting or killing off smaller gangs. Could easily be old-school retaliation. One shooter was injured, SAPD and the DEA are trying to track him down. It might help ID who targeted the group. But get this—they left the drugs."

"That's . . . odd."

"Understatement. A million dollars in heroin. Who

targets a gang and leaves the drugs? It was a hit, pure and simple."

Juan's door opened at the head of the squad room where the agent cubicles were crammed. "Crawford, Kincaid, I need you."

Ryan rolled to his desk. "Watch your back, Luce."

"You, too."

Lucy got up and followed Barry into Juan's small office. She was surprised to see Sean sitting in one of Juan's chairs. He winked at her.

Juan closed the door and sat down. "Barry Crawford, Sean Rogan. Sean has some information that might be pertinent to your investigation."

There were only two visitor chairs in Juan's small office so Lucy leaned against the door. Whatever information Sean had, Barry was the lead detective. He sat in the chair next to Sean and said, "I'm all ears."

"I've been hired by HWI to run full diagnostics on their network. They have a few small holes, but they're clean, at least as far as anyone hacking into their system. But I learned that Worthington hadn't been using his own desk for the last month. He took over another office from an employee who was on maternity leave. He used her computer and phone. He was working on a complex Bureau of Land Management audit that had been flagged by the employee as having problems. I don't know yet if he found something suspicious in the files—HWI is taking point on the audit. But it was odd that he wouldn't work from his own office. That's when I uncovered a bug in his phone."

"Corporate espionage? Insider trading? What kind of device?" Barry asked.

"I don't know the why, but it's an extremely sophisticated transmitter. I suspect the relay is outside of the building, a literal phone tap. Which means that whoever is bugging him not only is committing a federal crime, but they probably have people and resources to monitor the tap. It's only active when there's a phone conversation, and I checked all HWI phones—only Worthington's is tapped and the security team found no other bugs in the office. They're hiring another consultant to sweep their Dallas and Virginia offices as well. But the key point is that the bug is impossible to trace unless it's actually running."

"Did you think about calling us to check for prints?" Barry asked. "Or having us trace the serial number?"

Sean, to his credit, remained calm. He didn't like working with the FBI on projects. Even though Lucy was an agent, and Sean had worked with other agents over the years, he still harbored a deep hostility toward law enforcement. But Lucy recognized, particularly since they'd moved to San Antonio, that Sean had learned to temper his distrust.

"There is no serial number on the outside of the device, which means we'd have to take it apart," Sean said. "Which I'm more than capable of doing, but wanted to put forth another option that might yield quicker results."

"There's no indication that the bug has anything to do with Worthington's murder," Barry said.

Sean's jaw tightened. In a calm voice he said, "No, but it's an outlier in his life. According to his admin, he started acting preoccupied three to four weeks ago. That's about the time he stopped using his phone. He must have known the bug was there."

"Did he tell his staff? His security chief?"

"No, which is also suspicious. But I've been running deep backgrounds on everyone, and nothing has popped. Gregor Smith is more than competent in his field, but I'm digging around in his background as well."

"With what authority?" Barry asked.

"The authority that HWI gave me when they hired me

as an independent consultant," Sean said through clenched teeth.

Lucy glanced at Juan; he was watching the two of them as if this was some kind of test. And maybe it was—not just for Sean, but for her. She had to stay out of this.

Juan said, "Sean has an idea to draw them out, but the decision is up to you, Barry."

"What's the idea?" Barry asked Juan.

Sean answered. "At this point, whoever planted the device knows that Harper knew he was being bugged— Harper's office extension hasn't been used in nearly four weeks. They also know that he's dead, even if they had nothing to do with his murder. I'd like to stage a call to leak specific information, partly true, partly false. I would monitor activity from HWI to see if someone internal is involved; you would monitor the people in Worthington's private life."

Lucy was afraid that Barry would just shut Sean down right there. It was a good idea, but there was no guarantee that it'd yield results.

Barry asked, "How exactly would you do this without the party involved being suspicious that it was a set up?"

"Since HWI hired me, it's reasonable that I would be working from Worthington's office. It'll be in the evening, I'll be running late and call Lucy at home."

"And not use your cell phone?"

"Dead battery. But I don't think anyone would think about it. The purpose is twofold. One, to get controlled information out there to determine who might be listening, and two, to trace the receiver. The bug is only a transmitter. The tap has to be in one of three places—the phone system in the router building next to the office, the relay station, or the main phone company. If it's the latter, that means it's a federal wiretap."

Juan said, "We don't have any ops with wiretaps right now within our jurisdiction."

"There's a slim chance that it's completely off system, that the transmitter is going to a nearby recorder—in a van or building. But that would be a short distance, and I doubt that a van could be monitoring twenty-four-seven over the last month. There is one other office building close enough that could pick up the transmission, but my bet is a wiretap."

"That makes sense," Barry said.

Lucy breathed slightly easier.

Sean leaned forward. "I have software that can trace the bug as soon as it starts transmitting. I just piggyback my call through the computer and it's instant tracking. We'll find out where it's relaying the information almost immediately, and then your people can take it from there. The tap will have coding as to where it's sending the data."

"Why not do it now, without this elaborate plan?"

"Because if these people are good—and their tech tells me they're good—it won't be easy to find them. Giving them intel they may act on gives you two avenues to pursue."

Barry glanced at Juan. "You're okay with this?"

"I don't have a problem with the plan. But it's up to you. And you need to control the information."

"When?"

"Tonight, if possible," Sean said.

Barry looked at Lucy. "You're onboard?"

"Yes," she said.

"Juan, do we have a team that can retrieve the wiretap when Rogan traces it?"

"Not a problem."

"So the big question is, what do we tell these unknown people?" Barry said.

Sean leaned back in his chair. "The BLM files are interesting only in that Worthington was obsessed with them. He was working primarily on that audit, so it reasons that if someone was concerned about what he might find, they'll want to know if he found it. I'd like to leak something true but innocuous—that Worthington was obsessed with the case, that he had pages of notes but no one in the office really understood why. Then I would ask about the tablet his daughter gave the FBI."

"How do you know about that?"

Sean finally snapped. "Why does everything that comes out of your mouth sound like you're accusing me of something?"

"I need to know who knows what about my operation." Barry glanced at Lucy. Lucy wished he hadn't done that. Sean was very sensitive about how his job might impact her career, and she constantly reassured him that it wasn't an issue. With one glance, Barry had confirmed that it was a problem.

Sean said, "Jolene told me this afternoon. And I'll bet I have higher security clearance than you, so Lucy can tell me whatever she damn well pleases."

Juan cleared his throat. "Has the tech team broken the code?"

"They're working on it," Barry said.

"Then that's what we leak, whether or not they break it tonight."

"I could break it," Sean said.

"It's evidence. Chain of custody," Barry said.

"I could do it here."

"My people will do it," Juan said. "If they can't, it goes to the FBI lab."

That was the final word on the tablet.

"If this is personal," Lucy said, trying to diffuse the tension, "I should tell Sean I think someone is lying. Specifically, Adeline Reyes-Worthington."

Juan shook his head. "If someone is illegally gathering information, and something one of my agents said gets out and is used during a political campaign, all of our heads will roll. Is there something forensic that hasn't been released but won't damage a future prosecution if we do release it?"

"His death has been ruled suspicious," Barry said, "but not officially a homicide. Lucy thinks he was poisoned with a neuromuscular blocker and the coroner is running additional tests. We don't have confirmation yet."

"I could simply say that," Lucy said. "Remind Sean about the case I worked in San Diego where a nurse used a drug that caused similar symptoms. If it ends up being what happened to Worthington, it will be released with the ME's report. If it's not what happened, I'm just talking about a theory and then the report would simply prove me wrong."

Barry nodded. "I like it. And I can get the ME to suppress the report for a couple of days either way, until we wrap this angle up."

"Okay," Juan said. "You three, work it out. I'll call in our tech team to work with Sean on the trace. They'll be ready to go in an hour."

CHAPTER SEVENTEEN

Sean used his key card to get into HWI. Gregor Smith had given him full access, which made it easier, particularly after hours. Sean asked him to make sure all employees were gone by six thirty. Smith was the only one who knew about the bug or that Sean was bringing in a federal agent, and Sean wanted to keep it that way.

Sean would have preferred to do this alone, but Barry insisted on coming. To make Lucy's life easier, Sean agreed without argument, but he didn't have to like it. He wasn't certain he liked Barry Crawford, though Lucy didn't seem to have any problems with Barry. The guy was a bit too by the book for Sean, but more, he looked, talked, and acted like a stick-up-the-ass federal agent.

But even Sean had to admit Barry had a good track record. Sean had called Kate Donovan, Lucy's sister-in-law, earlier that day just to get her two cents on Lucy's temporary partner. Kate, who taught at Quantico, had been an agent for eighteen years and knew Bureau business better than most anyone. Kate said there were no blemishes on Crawford's record; he'd asked to transfer to San Antonio to be closer to his family when his father became ill. Crawford's family lived half an hour outside of town.

Barry wasn't a chatty cop, either, which was fine with Sean. Sean motioned for him to sit in the chair across from Worthington's desk. When he had booted up Worthington's computer and made sure everything was how it should be, he sent the FBI techs in the van outside a text message asking if they were ready. As soon as the bug detected a live call, it would start transmitting. They would then use software Sean had designed to track it. Sean planned on keeping the call going as long as it took to nail down the location.

A few seconds later the techs confirmed they were in position. "Show time," he said to Barry.

He picked up Worthington's phone and dialed Lucy on the house phone. Two rings later Lucy answered. "Hey, princess, you're home."

"Just walked in a few minutes ago. Where are you?"

"Still at HWI." Sean monitored the transmitting bug from his tablet, which showed that the bug was still active. Good. The techs outside should be able to pinpoint the location of the receiver quickly.

"I thought you'd be done by now. I picked up barbecue from your favorite place."

"The Rib House? You're killing me. I'm starving."

"I'll keep it warm."

"Give me another hour or so."

"Find something odd?"

"Their systems are in good shape, but Harper seemed to be obsessed with these files that came over from the BLM a few weeks ago. I'm trying to figure out his arcane note system. Why can't everyone use computers?"

"Not everyone is as good as you."

"No one is as good as me," Sean teased. "You sound tired. Tough day?"

"Long day."

"Everyone's asking me about how he died. His employees all seemed to like him. I haven't heard one negative comment."

"The coroner hasn't issued a report yet. It's still ruled suspicious. They're running an expanded tox screen since the initial screen came back negative."

"They must have seen something."

"His liver was slightly enlarged. Remember the nurse in San Diego?"

"You mean the nurse who was killing her cancer patients? Who almost killed you?"

"Almost is an overstatement, sweetheart," Lucy said. "She used a neuromuscular blocker on her victims. Almost impossible to detect unless you're looking for it. That's why she got away with so many murders."

He got a text message that the FBI techs had a location for the receiver. It wasn't in the phone box outside the building, but it wasn't far. He responded that he'd wrap up the conversation.

"Thanks to you, she's locked up for life. You think the same type of drug was used to kill Harper? So you really think it was a homicide?"

"What I think and what I can prove are two different things. But yeah, I think he was poisoned. We won't know for a couple of days."

Sean heard the doorbell ring in the background. He leaned forward, tense. He wasn't expecting anyone.

"Who's there?" he asked her.

"Just a sec."

He refrained from telling her to be careful, especially in front of Barry Crawford, who was hanging on every word while pretending to be disinterested.

"It's Brad Donnelly," she said. "Hold on, I'm going to let him in."

The phone was muffled for a second, then he heard Lucy greet Brad.

"Sean?" she said into the phone.

"What's Donnelly doing there?" He realized he probably shouldn't have said that, considering the phone was tapped.

Lucy, fortunately, covered. "Just stopping by to say hi."

"I'll get home as soon as I can," Sean said. "Love you."

"Love you, too."

Sean hung up.

Barry said, "Donnelly from the DEA?"

Sean didn't answer. Instead, he picked up his cell phone and dialed the lead tech. "Where is it?" he asked.

"The routing station, about a mile down the road."

"Can you get to it tonight?"

"We don't have a warrant. Casilla said if we can talk our way in to grab it, but if we can't, we'll have to wait until tomorrow morning."

Typical. Sean could get in and out without being detected, but he didn't say anything. He didn't completely trust Barry Crawford, and since he was now semiofficially involved in this FBI op, there could be issues if this ever came to trial and he had skirted the law to obtain evidence.

"Thanks," he said. "You can leave my equipment with Lucy tomorrow."

"Always fun to work with you, Rogan."

"Likewise." Sean hung up. He loved working with tech people. He understood them far better than cops.

"He's probably briefing her about the gang shooting," Barry said.

It was an obvious ploy to get Sean to talk, and it almost worked.

"Donnelly is a friend," Sean said. He wanted to ask what shooting, but stopped himself. He would find out soon enough what Crawford was talking about.

"I figured he was, since he wanted Lucy to work the case with him." Crawford stood and stretched. "We're not on opposite sides here, Rogan."

"I didn't think we were."

"Good."

Sean didn't know what Barry's game was, if any. Maybe he wasn't being calculating, but he was acting like the all-powerful fed, which irritated Sean. He recognized that it was his own biases that sometimes rubbed cops the wrong way. He'd had a few run-ins over the years, particularly in his youth. He'd seen cops abuse their authority more than once.

But he wasn't going to say anything to jeopardize the respect that Lucy had earned in her office, or to risk the job she loved. So he kept his mouth shut.

They walked out together and Sean, against his better judgment, said, "Do you want to come over to the house? It's not too far from here, in Olmos Park."

Barry looked marginally surprised. "No, but thanks. Maybe next time. It's already eight and tomorrow is going to be another early day."

Sean walked into his kitchen fifteen minutes later. He dumped his laptop on the counter and breathed in the smell of barbecue coming from the warming oven.

"Sean," Lucy called, "we're in the living room."

He walked down the wide hall and into the large, sunken living room. The pool lights automatically turned on at eight, and the setting sun cast an array of brilliant colors across the evening sky.

Brad rose and shook Sean's hand. "Good to see you, Rogan."

"Likewise. You look a million times better than the last time I saw you."

"I'd feel even better if I can convince my doc to look at me tomorrow rather than Friday. He just needs to sign the damn papers so I can go back into the field."

Sean leaned over and kissed Lucy, then motioned for them to follow him to the kitchen. "I'm starving, and I know Lucy probably hasn't eaten since lunch. Have you eaten?"

"Cold pizza in the break room," Brad said.

"Then join us."

Sean and Lucy liked eating at the big island in the kitchen. There were six stools and plenty of room, so while Sean took out the food, Lucy distributed plates and utensils. Sean handed Brad a beer and took one for himself. After light conversation, Sean asked, "So what really brings you by tonight?"

"There was a shooting last night," Lucy said. "Ryan's working with Brad on it."

Brad said, "Nine people, several with a direct connection to Sanchez, were murdered late last night. The killers left drugs worth a million behind. Ryan found a surveillance tape with an image of the escape van, but the quality sucks and the license plate is filthy. There are some distinguishing characteristics, so we're putting out a BOLO and working on an enhancement."

"Who's going after Sanchez?" Sean asked. "He's dead. His operation is toast."

"Actually, your brother thinks Tobias took over the remnants of the Sanchez/Trejo operation."

"You talked to Kane?"

"He gave me the heads up this morning," Brad said. "It could be that Tobias was always the one in charge and Trejo worked for him. The conversation Lucy overheard two months ago at Trejo's compound suggested that Tobias was either equal to or in the hierarchy above Trejo. If that's accurate, someone else could be going after Tobias since he's now in a weak position."

"Or," Sean countered, "Tobias is taking out the rest of Sanchez's people after Sanchez screwed up his operation. If they hadn't kidnapped you, Brad, we wouldn't have raided his compound. We might never have found the guns. That's all Sanchez's doing."

"We still would have gone after the boys," Lucy said quietly.

Sean took her hand. "Yes, we would have."

"Kane thinks the hit was retaliation. I half expected him to call me back to find out what I learned, but I haven't heard from him, and I don't know how to reach him." Brad drained his beer. Sean got up to fetch another, but Brad shook his head. "I'm good."

Sean grabbed himself another beer and leaned against the counter. "Who are the other players?"

"That's the thing—there's no chatter on this. Nothing. I need to talk to Kane. Do you know how to reach him?"

"I can leave him a message. No guarantee he'll call me or you back. He's annoying that way."

"Then leave a message. Tomorrow I'm talking to Nicole Rollins. I wish you could come with me, Luce. You're good in interrogations."

"Trust me, she wouldn't talk with me in the room," Lucy said. "She would be far too defensive. With you—you understand her."

"I don't fucking understand her!" Brad exclaimed. "That's the thing. How could she not only betray everything our job stands for, but set up Marines to be murdered? And what for? Guns for the drug cartels? And money. A shit-load of money. Our forensic accounting department found accounts totaling over two million dollars. Nicole told

Sam Archer that she would have disappeared when she got to five million. Just walked away. In the meantime, she was responsible for many deaths, directly or indirectly."

"She doesn't think that way," Lucy said. "She justified everything. Convinced herself that the war on drugs will never be won and why not take a slice of the pie? The boys the cartel used, just collateral damage—besides, they were the kids of violent criminals, statistics suggest they'd grow up to be the same. It's cyclical."

Brad looked at her oddly. "You don't think—"

Lucy shook her head. "No, of course not—I'm trying to think like Nicole. You have to understand why she did this if you're ever going to get her to share information. Go in knowing what you want, but don't ask for it. If she sees any sign of desperation on your face, she'll be overjoyed in keeping the information from you. You need to manipulate it out of her, but don't let her see you manipulating her. Remember—you know this woman better than everyone else."

"Do I? I didn't know she was a traitor."

"But you worked with her. Even if you don't think you know her, you do. Granted, she was an exceptional liar. What is it you want to know?"

"We need information on Tobias. He's a ghost. No last name. You and the kid, Michael, were the only two who saw him well enough to give a description, and even so, it's not very detailed. Either he had Sanchez's gang killed, or he's the next target. If he retaliates, there'll be extensive collateral damage. We can't let that happen. Innocent blood has already spilled—a kid of one of the gangbangers was killed in the raid."

Lucy frowned and rubbed her eyes. "I'd know Tobias if I saw him." She really was tired, Sean noted, and probably not just from work. The thought of another child dying because of these cartels angered Sean, and it tore Lucy up inside. He walked over and rubbed her back.

"Between the DEA and Kane, we'll find him," Sean said.

"She's not going to give up Tobias unless it benefits her," Lucy added.

Brad shook his head. "She's not getting out in her lifetime, no matter what or who she gives up."

"Find out what she wants, other than her freedom," Sean said. "Then you might have something to negotiate."

Brad shrugged. "And that's the crux of my problem—what does she want?" He got up and motioned to the refrigerator. "Maybe I do need another beer."

"Help yourself," Sean said. "Do you really think Nicole knows something about the attack last night?"

"Hell if I know. But I need information. Anything I can get at this point. I don't know *what* is going on, but it's out of the norm. And I don't like anything I don't understand. Give me a drive-by shooting, or a retaliation kill, or a drug theft . . . but this? It's like someone is moving in and taking out everyone on the opposing team. They'll start with one, then move to the next group that doesn't capitulate. A power grab like this? We have to stop them. And if we don't know who the fuck they are, how the hell do we find them?"

Brad left at ten and Sean tried to call Kane. Of course he didn't answer so Sean left a brief message. "Call Donnelly. Then call me."

Sean was partly bothered by the fact that his brother was involved in this situation at all. Why was Kane keeping tabs on the elusive Tobias? Why would he call Donnelly? Kane rarely worked with law enforcement. He would share information, usually through RCK because

Kane didn't have a tolerance for bureaucracy. Which made Sean think there was something else going on.

He would find out what it was.

Sean sat down next to Lucy on the couch. She leaned over and rested her head on his chest. "I assume you got what you needed from our conversation?" she said.

"Yes. The tech guys Juan sent were good."

"High praise."

"Barry's a jerk."

"Sean—"

"He may be a good cop, but he's still a jerk."

"Okay."

"You're giving in easily."

"I thought the same thing about him at first."

"And now?"

"I understand him better. He's not like us. Or, rather, me. He doesn't obsess or let his work consume him, but he's sharp. He gives one hundred percent when he's on duty, and when he's off, he's off. It's healthier that way. I sometimes wish . . ." Her voice trailed off.

Sean turned her head so he could kiss her. "I know exactly what you're thinking, and stop. You're thickheaded, you know that? How many times do I have to tell you I love you exactly the way you are?"

"Maybe I just like hearing you say it."

That wasn't it. She was doing it again, feeling like something was wrong with her. "What happened today?"

"It was just a long day."

"Lucy." He wasn't going to let her avoid the conversation.

She didn't say anything for several minutes. But she was too tense to be sleeping.

"We interviewed this woman named Mona Hill. She has a long and sordid past—and she's hard. Shrewd and calculating. I got the distinct impression that, if given the choice, she would continue down the same path. That she actually enjoys what she's doing."

"Which is?"

"Running call girls. She owns an apartment building—a nice place in a so-so area. The girls all rent from her. It won't be easy getting to them."

"And this girl you're looking for works for her?"

"Elise," Lucy said. "Don't have a last name yet. But I don't think Elise works for Hill. Elise is from out of town. According to Hill, Elise called her up looking for work and Hill sent her to cover for a girl who'd gotten sick. Sounds so plausible, but . . ."

"You don't believe her."

"I don't know. Except, according to Tia, Elise *is* new to town, so there's a ring of truth. It just feels . . . Okay, this new girl comes in, kills Worthington, and then drops Worthington's phone in another john's hotel room? Why? There's so much we don't know."

"Backtrack. You think this girl killed Harper Worthington?"

"I don't know!" Lucy tensed. Sean tried to rub out the tension, but Lucy pulled away. She said, "Elise had to have been involved in some way, right? She came out of the motel room—the taxi driver only saw her. There are no security cameras, so the killer could have left before Elise. I can see her not calling the police, but the evidence suggests that someone staged Worthington's body after he was dead. And truth is—while I originally thought that he was a pervert and maybe, subconsciously, thought he deserved what he got—we've found nothing that suggests he planned on meeting a prostitute. I think he planned on meeting an informant, or someone who had information for him, or a blackmailer, or *anyone* other than a prostitute. Then you find a bug in his office and we know he's changed his patterns over the last month. That tells me he was either doing something illegal or trying to figure out if someone else was doing something illegal. But if it was someone else, why didn't he talk to Smith? Or law enforcement? There's nothing in his background that suggests he was doing anything illegal, but white collar crimes are out of my specialty area."

"That's more my area of expertise." Sean considered what he'd learned about Worthington's business today. And Worthington himself. "I haven't uncovered anything, even a hint that he was doing anything illegal, but the fact that he kept a separate computer—the tablet—suggests he was definitely hiding something."

"And he was killed for it. Whatever *it* is. And whoever killed him wanted to embarrass him, even in death."

"And this Mona Hill knows who this girl is."

Lucy shivered. Sean wouldn't have noticed except that he was touching her.

"What else happened today?"

"Nothing."

"You're tense. When you were talking about Mona Hill, and now when I said her name. What is it?"

"Nothing," Lucy said. But she wasn't looking at him. "Maybe because she's running underage prostitutes? And this one, this *Elise*, is missing? Every cop is looking for her and she's nowhere. Maybe in hiding. Maybe dead. And she has all the answers."

Lucy was avoiding something. Sean shifted on the couch and turned Lucy to face him. "What aren't you telling me?"

"What do you mean? You want me to recount my entire day for you?" Her voice rose as she spoke.

"I want to know what happened with Mona Hill that scared you."

"I'm not scared."

"Do not lie to me, Lucy. Never lie to me."

She stared at him with pain in her eyes, but her mouth was set in anger. "I'm not lying. About anything. I'm just tired, and frustrated, and you're reading something into this conversation that just isn't there." She rose from the couch. Sean reached for her—he didn't want to argue with Lucy, he wanted answers—but she pulled away.

That infuriated him.

"You did exactly this when I asked about your nightmare this morning."

"Maybe I just don't want to talk about it."

"That's not acceptable." Not with him.

"You can't fix everything, Sean." Her eyes watered. "I'm going to bed." She turned and started for the stairs.

"Don't walk away, Lucy. We need to discuss this."

She hesitated, but didn't look at him.

He held his breath, waiting for her to explain. Waiting to hear why she was scared. Because he'd felt it in her body, and he knew her better than anyone. Better than she knew herself.

Then she walked away without another word.

Sean didn't move for several minutes. He couldn't think. He could scarcely breathe. How could Lucy walk out like that? Without talking it out? He wanted to go after her, but he was too angry. And hurt. Like she'd stabbed him in the gut. Because if Lucy didn't trust him with her fears, she didn't trust him at all. And if she didn't trust him, she didn't love him.

He buried his face in his hands. He would do anything for Lucy. He would kill for her. He would die for her. He would follow her to the ends of the earth and back again. For years, before Lucy, he'd lived a purposeless life. Parties. Women. Fun. Making money and spending it, on cars and electronics and other toys. He'd helped his brothers when they needed it, but mostly, he lived to please himself.

It was a shallow, meaningless existence.

Until Lucy.

She gave him a purpose in life he'd never had before. Her compassion and vision, her drive and determination . . . they empowered him. She made him a better person. He looked at her and melted.

He'd known from the beginning that it wasn't going to be easy to pull Lucy out of her icy shell and show her the world beyond her work. But he had—very successfully. She laughed and enjoyed the small things that she'd never noticed when they first met. Like ice skating and Disney movies and eating ice cream on cold winter days.

Keep my girl smiling.

It was the voice of Lucy's father, when he'd given his blessing upon learning they were moving in together.

That's what had been missing for the last two months. Lucy hadn't smiled as often. She hadn't laughed as much. She'd retreated inside again, the nightmares drowning her. And she wouldn't talk to him about it. She talked around it, or distracted him, but she never really told him what they were about.

And then today . . . something had happened with this Mona Hill.

Sean stood and walked down the hall to his office. He hesitated briefly at the bottom of the stairs, wanting to go to Lucy, to kiss her, to tell her he didn't want to go to sleep with this hanging over them.

But instead, he went into his office, shut the door, and started a very deep—probably illegal—background check on Mona Hill.

Mona Hill had built her career around one thing: people. No one could keep a secret from her. No one could lie to her. She always found out. Those who knew her feared her, starting from when she was a young teenager playing cons, running drugs, and selling girls. She'd learned to use that fear to maintain complete control of every situation.

It pleased her that she'd been right about this one. The feds were a little faster than she'd expected, but they came asking the right questions.

She called her contact. His name was Jay. That was all she knew—his first name and how to reach him. She'd met him once. He was all muscle and did what he was told. But that didn't mean he was stupid.

Mona did not underestimate the people she took jobs from. That would be the fastest way to the grave.

"Tell your boss that the feds came knocking today," she said.

"And?"

"They have her name but nothing else. Should I move forward with the plan?"

"Do it tonight."

"We'd originally agreed tomorrow night. Why the change?"

"That is none of your business, Ms. Hill."

She bristled, but didn't say a word. She didn't want to admit that she was scared of these people; rather, she'd simply say that she had a healthy respect for their methods. She knew more about their plans than they realized, but not enough about their plans to be confident she knew everything. And she wasn't quite sure who was in charge.

All she knew about the boss was that he had a particularly sick fetish. She'd procured girls for him on several occasions, and they'd never been seen again. She wasn't particularly concerned . . . She gave him girls who wouldn't be missed. If she'd had a conscience, it would bother her.

But he paid extremely well, and when one of her girls got out of line . . . Well, she needed to be punished. Apparently, the boss was extremely proficient in the art of punishment.

And one thing that Mona had learned in her business was that men with an insatiable obsession—any obsession—were rarely in charge.

There were, of course, exceptions. Which was why Mona danced the waltz with Jay. She'd let him have the pick of her litter, so to speak, and he liked one girl particularly well. He didn't hurt her, so Teresa was happy to give away a freebie every week in exchange for a reduction in rent. Besides, Mona could not afford to make an enemy of anyone with power. Judging from the way they'd taken out Harper Worthington and set the dominos in motion, she thought that their plan might actually work. If it did . . . she'd know for certain whose good side to remain on.

She almost didn't tell Jay what she had, but at the last moment, before he hung up, she said, "I have some information that may be valuable."

"We've already paid you for your assistance." He was angry. No one liked getting a bill for services they'd already paid for.

"This is something completely new. I'll send you a sample. You can let me know what you want me to do with it."

"You had better not be wasting my time, Ms. Hill."

"I assure you, this will be worth every second."

She hung up with a smile. She sent Jay a ten-second video clip and waited. Almost immediately, he called her back.

"Is that doctored?"

"No."

"Is that all you have?"

"I told you, it's just a taste. I have a full seven minutes."

"I'll let you know what to do with it."

"It'll cost you."

"How much?"

"It's negotiable. Think about it while you replay that clip." She hung up again and laughed.

CHAPTER EIGHTEEN

Lucy was angry—at herself, at Sean, at the world. Though Sean was downstairs, she felt alone and isolated in their bedroom.

She took a long, hot shower and wanted to cry. But she didn't. She rarely cried. Another deficiency in her psyche, another scar left over from her forty-eight hours of hell. That her life could change completely, irrevocably, over such a short time . . .

Stop.

She was feeling sorry for herself. Yet again. For the past year she'd thought that she was truly over her rape. Not *over* it in the sense that she could forget it completely, but that she'd compartmentalized it in such a way that the past could no longer hurt her. She'd come a long way toward healing and acceptance before Sean, but it was Sean—proving to her that she was lovable—who closed the book on the past.

Yet here it was. Again. It had been haunting her for the past two months and she didn't know *why*.

Some cases did that to her. Some cases brought on a panic attack, but her last one had been nearly a year ago, and she'd managed it. Not perfectly, but she'd controlled it enough that she calmed herself down. Some cases reminded her of being tied up, like when she'd found the young women in cages on a farm in Virginia. Some cases reminded her of the humiliation, like the serial killer in New York who'd nearly killed Sean's cousin. And some cases brought back the pain, a phantom ache that felt all too real—like the brutal murder of a prostitute in D.C. It was like she could feel the knife cutting into her flesh, in all the places it had cut through the victim.

As her brother Jack had told her in Sacramento when they'd gone to visit Sean's baby niece, maybe rescuing the boys as well as seeing the dead had triggered grief she needed to purge.

"Like you, Lucy, they were innocents who were held captive and brutalized."

"It was worse for them. They were children. Little boys. They suffered for months. None of it was their fault."

"Look at me," Jack said.

She did.

"I thought so."

"What?"

"You think you deserved it."

She slapped him. "Fuck you, Jack."

She rarely swore. She certainly didn't use the F word. But Jack didn't flinch. He'd just stared at her until she turned away. Because he was partially right.

She didn't think she deserved to be gang raped. But it had certainly been her fault.

She'd thought she was so smart, so clever, to meet her online "friend" at a public place. But her "friend" wasn't who she thought he was. He wasn't his picture, or his name, or his background. He was an imposter, and she'd never seen it coming . . .

"What are you too scared to face, Lucia?" Jack whispered.

"I'm not scared."

"You're scared."

"I don't know," she finally said.

Jack relaxed. "Honey, that's the first step."

"What?" She almost cried. Almost.

"Admitting the fear is inside. You're strong, Lucy. We'll figure it out."

But they hadn't figured it out the week she was in Sacramento, and when she'd returned to San Antonio, the nightmares had come back, too.

She hadn't been lying to Sean completely. She really didn't remember most of her dreams. They were flashes of the past, confusing and disconnected, mixed with things that never happened but seemed all too real. Of her past, of dead bodies, of Sean almost dying, of her brother's coma, of the boys they'd found in Mexico, of Brad being tortured and Michael Rodriguez killing Trejo. So many acts of violence, so many victims. All those truths interspersed with vivid images, twisting everything around, so that the people she loved were dead and those who preyed on innocents celebrated.

She almost went downstairs to apologize for walking out, but she wasn't ready to talk. And Sean wouldn't let her just say *I'm sorry* and go on as if nothing had happened. That's what she desperately wanted to do, turn back the clock and find a way to lock down her emotions before she'd talked to Sean about the case. Then he would never have known.

Maybe.

She rubbed her aching head. Sean had always been good at reading her, at knowing what she was thinking and feeling, even when she didn't want anyone inside her head. It was wonderful and intimidating at the same time.

Instead of talking to Sean, Lucy crawled into bed and

snuggled under the blankets even though the house was warm. She didn't expect to fall asleep.

Lucy was naked. And cold. Very, very cold.

"Open your eyes, Lucy," the voice said. The voice that haunted her in sleep. Trask.

"No."

"Do it."

"You're dead. I killed you."

He laughed. "I'm alive, Lucy. I'm alive because you think about me every day. Even when you're not, I'm here, an itch you can't scratch."

Hands on her, everywhere. Touching her. Hurting her. And Trask laughing through it all. He knew he was dead, but so was she. She was dead inside. She had no life in her. She was a shell, a phony.

She would never forget. She would never be whole again. He'd torn her up, gutted her.

I wish he'd killed me.

No, no, no! *She didn't want to die.* Fight back, survive. It's only your body, he'll never have your mind. He'll never take your soul.

"I have a reward for you because you're doing so well. Open your eyes, see your prize."

She didn't want to open her eyes, but they opened anyway. All around her were computer screens, reflecting the violence that had been done to her. And flashes of the disclaimer.

Fantasy rape role playing. All participants are actors.

No! Don't believe it! It's not true.

Then she saw him watching.

Sean.

He was standing there, not looking at her, but watching the multitude of videos all around the room. He saw everything. Her pain and suffering, her humiliation. How could he ever see her as she was? Maybe because this was who she was. A victim. Maybe this was why he stayed, too scared to let her go. She was broken, she was beaten, she would never be able to give Sean what he deserved. A home. A family. Happiness.

Mona Hill walked into the room. She laughed at Lucy. "Really? Tears? It's just sex. Do you know how much money I make selling sex? Who do you think is in control? Not the men. It's us, sweetheart. You and me. Well, me. Because I know how the game is played. And you're just pathetic."

She laughed and laughed and then there was silence.

There were no lights, no sounds, only Lucy shaking on the cold, filthy mattress. The door opened and she saw him.

"Please, no."

"Your fans have voted." Trask lifted his hand. A knife glittered in a spotlight. Because this was a show. It was Trask's show. "You must die so I can live."

"No!"

"Look at the audience, Lucy. Look at your biggest fan."

She closed her eyes, but they were pried open. She was on a stage and in the audience was one person. Sean. His hands were strapped to the seats. He was forced to watch her die. And there was nothing either of them could do about it.

"Why, Lucy?" Sean cried.

Because she'd failed everyone. And here she was.

Trask took off his clothes and came toward her. "Only you can help me, Lucy. Only you."

The sharp blade cut into her neck and blood dripped onto stained satin sheets . . .

She opened her mouth and screamed.

Sean jumped out of the chair before he was fully awake. Lucy's screams echoed in the large house. He'd fallen asleep in his office, and as he ran up the stairs two at a time, he vaguely realized that it was three in the morning, that the house was quiet but the lights were still on.

He flung open the door of their bedroom.

Lucy was sitting on the edge of the bed, her body convulsing in violent sobs but no tears.

His chest hurt seeing Lucy in such pain. He sat next to her and held her tight. Her body shook, every muscle frozen, and she was icy to the touch. She crawled into his lap like a child and clung to him.

Guilt washed over him. He should have been here, in bed with her. She needed him, even if she hadn't admitted it. His research into Mona Hill had told him why the woman had gotten to Lucy. But he'd been hurt and angry that she'd shut him out. He didn't want to think that staying downstairs was his way of punishing Lucy. That he'd just been working when he decided to rest. It was his own damn insecurities that drove him to such pettiness.

"Lucy," he whispered as he stroked her hair.

"I'm sorry, I'm sorry," she repeated.

"Shh. There's nothing for you to be sorry about."

"I don't want you to see." Her face was buried in his chest. Her arms were so tight around his neck that he couldn't move.

"Honey, it's okay."

"It's not okay! Don't say it's okay, I never wanted you to see me like that."

He didn't know what she was talking about.

"It's just a nightmare, princess. Just a nightmare."

And then the flood of tears came with a guttural cry that tore Sean apart. He held Lucy tight, but he didn't know what to do. He didn't know how to take away this pain. Had she been suppressing this anguish every night when she woke up, unable to sleep? Because she didn't want him to see her suffer? How had she done it? What was inside her head? He would do anything to help her.

He pulled at a blanket until he freed it from the bed and wrapped it around Lucy, holding her close. He held her, rocking her in his arms, because he didn't know what else to do. He held her because he loved her and her pain was his pain. There had been times when Lucy had been upset or woken from a bad dream when he wanted to hit someone. Beat senseless the people who'd hurt her. Anger helped him cope with her suffering.

Now, all he wanted was to make things better for Lucy. Forget those who hurt her—they were all dead anyway—and focus on the present. Something had happened to trigger these nightmares in Lucy after more than a year of peace.

The first step was for him to address what she was scared about. He had an idea about what it was. It pained him to talk about what happened eight years ago, so they never really talked about it. They talked *around* the events. Because he'd worked so closely with her brother Patrick, he knew the truth. He hadn't been a part of her life then, so it was easy to avoid the conversation. They'd first met after one of her rapists had been murdered by a vigilante. They'd never had to talk about what had happened because she knew he knew. He'd thought it would be better that way. Was he wrong?

When he'd first met Lucy, she had a hard, icy exterior that not only prevented anyone from getting too close, but also kept her emotions buried. He'd recognized that she needed him from the very beginning, to ground her, to give her a wall of protection so that she could let down the shields and relax.

He didn't remember when he'd realized that Lucy and his brother Kane were so much alike. They were driven to

right wrongs, to protect innocents, and with everything
they'd done and seen in their lives—and the cruelties that
had been done to them—they kept the shell to protect them
as much as to give them the ability to keep up the fight.
Sean had made it his mission to give Lucy a home, a place
of peace, a security that she would never doubt, not even
for a second. And she had been happy.

Until the boys.

He'd known that the mission would be hard for her—
not the mission itself, because like Kane, Lucy could
compartmentalize and shut out emotion. But the aftermath.
Because Lucy sometimes couldn't pull her feelings back
out of the box, as if she'd buried them too deep and she
couldn't find them.

That's why the nightmares were back, Sean realized.
Maybe the dreams represented emotions she'd buried so
deep she couldn't think about them, didn't want to feel
them, in the light of day. He had to shine a light on her
fear, or she'd never sleep through the night. He had to know
what she was scared of, or the nightmares would kill her.
No one could survive this every night.

"Talk to me, princess," he said. She'd stopped crying.
His shirt was wet from her tears, but all that remained was
her shaking.

"Hold me." Her voice was so quiet he almost couldn't
hear her.

"Always."

He wanted to pull her back into bed and hold her closely
until she slept. But then, in the morning, she would have
her guard back up and not tell him the truth. Maybe she
hadn't deliberately lied to him. Maybe she'd so compartmentalized her emotions that she didn't even remember
why she was upset, the only remnants of her angst being
fatigue.

He gave her a few more minutes. He kissed her forehead, brushed her damp hair back with his free hand. Then he picked her up and carried her to the oversized chair in the corner of their bedroom. She liked to read in this chair, and while it wasn't quite big enough for two people, with Lucy on his lap they fit perfectly. He readjusted the blanket to cover her.

"What are you scared about? What do you fear?"

She swallowed. With a rough voice she said, "Jack asked me the same thing."

"And what did you say?"

"I don't know. That's what I told him."

"And now?"

She didn't say anything and tried to shift away from him, but he held her tight.

"Lucy, tell me. You know, don't you?"

A small cry escaped from her throat and she turned her face into his chest.

I never wanted you to see me like that.

It was what she'd said when she was hysterical. And then it clicked.

"Oh, God, Lucy, no."

He pulled her head up to look at her face. Her eyes were red and swollen. Her face flushed. And still she was shaking.

"Lucy, listen to me. I've never watched it. Never. Not even one second. We both know what happened to you. And dammit, I will never let it come between us. I love you. *I love you.* We're going to figure this out."

"You make me feel. And sometimes, I don't want to."

"I know, sweetheart."

"This last year, the nightmares were gone. I thought forever. I no longer felt like I was teetering on the brink of the abyss. Before you, the only thing that mattered to me was justice. Fighting for others. When I helped people, when I saved victims, I was on the right side of sanity.

I don't think anyone knew how . . . tightly I was wound. Maybe you did . . ." Her voice trailed off.

"Lucy—"

She continued. "But the nightmares are back, and they're worse. I feel so helpless again, because there is still so much pain and suffering and I can't stop it."

"Of course you can't. To put that weight on your shoulders will suffocate you. You've done more in a few years than most people do in their lifetime. Michael is alive because of you. Toby. The other boys."

"Not all of them."

"That's not on you!" He didn't want to yell, but how could she blame herself for not saving everyone? That was insane.

"I know, but . . ." Her voice trailed off. Lucy, the expert in holding back her emotions, was truly one of the most compassionate and empathic people he'd ever met. But the intensity of her emotions made what she suffered so much worse, hence the need to shut everything down. The battle inside tore her apart. Sean ached for her.

Sean let her head fall back to his chest and she started to relax. It was what had happened in Mexico two months ago that had instigated the nightmares, but it wasn't because of the boys that she had them. It was because she feared that Sean would see her as a victim.

He'd never watched the video that the bastard Trask had live-streamed for the perverts who paid to watch Lucy be raped repeatedly. Her brothers had seen parts of it while they'd searched for her, and maybe that contributed to Lucy's anguish. She'd gone through therapy, but someone like Lucy was good at playing the therapy game, giving the counselor what she needed to hear.

But tonight she'd told him the truth. She didn't have to go into the details; neither of them needed to hear them. It was the conclusion that mattered: that Lucy's fear was about how Sean saw her.

"Mona Hill knows about the video," Lucy suddenly said.

Sean tensed. He tried not to, but he couldn't control his reaction. Lucy froze in his arms. "What happened?"

"She didn't know, not until she saw me. *I never forget a face*, she said. And I knew. The truth was in her eyes."

That Sean could remain calm was a testament to his maturity. Because he wanted to kill Mona Hill. And after what he'd learned while digging into her past, she deserved to die.

"I won't let that woman—I won't let anyone—hurt you."

"I have to face the truth."

He didn't like the monotone in her voice. "What truth?"

"That people who know me will see it. And when they do, they won't be able to hide the truth in their eyes."

"Lucy," he said, planting a kiss on the top of her head. "We'll cross that bridge *if* we come to it. Together. You are not in this alone."

CHAPTER NINETEEN

The last thing Brad Donnelly wanted to do was visit his former partner, but Ryan and Lucy were right: if anyone other than the killers knew about the mass slaughter of Trejo's remaining gang, it was Nicole. He needed to get it out of the way, so he arrived at the jail before eight Tuesday morning.

Former DEA Agent Nicole Rollins was being held at the Central Texas Detention Facility while her lawyers and the AUSA negotiated the terms of her guilty plea. It had been an arduous process because initially the Department of Justice had wanted the death penalty, and that would require a trial. Nicole was being charged with multiple counts of accessory to murder, bribery, abuse of authority, attempted murder of a federal law enforcement agent, conspiracy, facilitation of drug trafficking, and more. They still hadn't uncovered every crime Nicole Rollins had committed during her fifteen-year career with the DEA.

The last time Brad had seen Nicole was the day he was kidnapped by Sanchez nine weeks ago. When he'd called his boss last night and asked for permission to talk to Nicole about his current case, the first thing Samantha Archer said—even before reminding him he wasn't cleared for field duty—was "You really don't want to see that cold bitch."

Nicole had been part of Brad's team. He was the SSA, he was responsible for his people. When Nicole had transferred into his unit three years ago, he'd liked that she was seasoned, calm, and sharp. She was also unemotional, which Brad appreciated because he sometimes became too involved in his cases. So he found himself asking for her backup more than other agents'.

He'd trusted her. And she'd handed him over to Jaime Sanchez on a silver platter, knowing that Jaime intended to torture and kill him.

Fortunately, it didn't take Brad long to convince Sam that Nicole might have valuable information. Sam concurred that Nicole probably wouldn't talk to anyone else. She wasn't doing much talking now, which was also holding up the process. Still, the DEA wanted her close to home, so to speak, because cops in prison never fared well—even when they were corrupt DEA agents working for known drug lords. She was also being kept isolated, because she knew far too much about undercover operations. They were extracting assets and changing procedures on every operation of which Nicole might have had knowledge. It took time, especially in a government bureaucracy.

A guard escorted Nicole into the small meeting room in handcuffs. She'd attempted to escape shortly after being transferred to CTD and, because she was well trained in hand-to-hand combat, the prison had determined that she would only be allowed out of her cell in cuffs.

Prison could change people quickly, but Nicole hadn't changed much at all. Aside from no makeup, shorter hair, and the orange prison jumpsuit, her blue eyes were still intelligent and she still looked physically fit. Maybe even more so.

Brad stared at her, refusing to break eye contact first. The pain of his torture, of Nicole's betrayal, ate at him, but he still held her eyes. It was a testament to her mental fortitude—and lack of remorse—that she didn't look away.

The guard sat her down and locked her cuffs into the ring on the table. "If you need anything, Agent Donnelly, just let me know. I'll be right outside the door."

"Thank you," he said with a brief nod.

When the guard had left, Brad said, "The last known associates of Jaime Sanchez were murdered two nights ago. Who did it?"

Nicole gave him a half grin. "No. We don't start with what you want. We start with what I want."

His jaw tensed. "And what would that be?"

"Conversation."

"No."

"Then I'll go back to my cell."

"You have no rights."

"Last I checked, prisoners have a lot of rights."

"Not you. You'll sit there until I tell the guard to take you away."

She laughed. "So dramatic, Brad. Really. Ask me something else."

"I have nothing else to ask."

"The first time you've come to visit me and you don't have any other questions? All business? I don't think so."

"This isn't a visit, Nicole."

She tilted her head. "You want to know why."

"There is no justifiable reason for what you did. People died, Nicole. Agents. Children."

Her face was blank. Sam was right. Nicole was a cold bitch. She'd pushed Brad and he reacted, reminding him that Nicole understood him better than he understood her.

"I guess I have a hard time believing you did it for the money," Brad said, his voice a low growl. "But unless you tell me otherwise, it was all done out of greed. You're a fucking sociopath."

Her lips turned up ever so slightly. "So, you know why I did it. The money. The thrill. The adrenaline rush! Mostly, the money. That's not what I was talking about. You want to know why you didn't see it coming. How you could be so blind. So *stupid*. So it'll never happen again. Trust me, Brad, it will. You think your house is clean? It'll never be clean."

Nicole glanced down at his hands, which were clenched on the table. She smiled and leaned back, victory shining in her cold eyes.

She was deliberately baiting him. And it worked. He felt the anger burning inside him, and he wanted to hit her. God help him, he wanted to beat that smirk off her face.

"There is absolutely no incentive for me to tell you anything," Nicole said. "I'll never see the outside of a prison—unless, of course, I manage to escape."

"You won't."

She shrugged. "I'm not scared of the DEA or the DOJ. You can't hurt me."

"Whoever took out the rest of Sanchez's gang killed a kid. An eight-year-old boy."

"There's no future for these children. You have such a bleeding heart, you think that anyone can be saved. Haven't you learned better by now?" She laughed. She was enjoying this, whatever *this* was. A conversation? An interrogation? A game? That's what it felt like to Brad—that Nicole was playing games with him, with everyone. He was a pawn, she was the master chess player.

"Wake up, Brad," she continued. "The war on drugs? It's over. They won. You either join them, or keep tilting at windmills until one of their bullets pierces your skull. Don't you realize that our focus on stopping them raises the price of drugs and increases the violence? But they will continue to bring in heroin and cocaine and marijuana and pseudoephedrine, and for every shipment you stop, every gang you shut down, three more spring up. Grow the fuck up, Donnelly. Get out while you're still breathing."

Brad had to stop letting Nicole steer the conversation. "I suspect," he said slowly, "that with Sanchez and Trejo dead, Tobias was attempting to solidify his organization. Because he was weakened, another player went after him. He's done. Every one of Sanchez's associates is dead or in prison."

"You will never understand because you have no vision, Brad."

"Then explain it to me, Nicole! What don't I understand?"

She stared at him for a long minute. He was losing it. He'd planned on being completely calm, in complete control, but she'd goaded him, and he'd let her. He forced himself to breathe slowly to calm his pounding heart.

"Only because I actually feel sorry for you, I'm going to explain one thing. Tobias isn't scared of you. If someone took out Sanchez's people, Tobias let it happen. Two nights ago? If Tobias was at all angry about it, you would have already seen a bigger bloodbath."

"Who is Tobias?"

She smiled. "So that's what you really want. You want Tobias. I'm certainly not giving him up to you—even if I could." From her tone, Brad realized she knew far more about Tobias and his operation than anyone else. She might imply she didn't, but it was clear she enjoyed keeping the information to herself. "I'm not loyal to you or the fucking DEA. You go ahead and charge at those windmills, but watch your back while you're sitting on your high horse. You fuck with Tobias, he'll fuck you back twice as hard. You might want to tell that rookie you have the hots for to watch her back, because she pissed off the wrong person."

For a minute, Brad didn't know what Nicole was talking about.

"Lucy?" he asked.

"You want to screw her so badly."

"You're insane."

"I know you, Brad. I know you better than you think I do. That rookie five years ago who Jamie Sanchez iced? Don't think I don't know that you were sleeping with her. That's why you went all psycho anti-rookie. Guilt. Guilt is a powerful motivator, isn't it?"

Brad didn't say a word. The past haunted him, the mistakes he'd made, the people who had gotten hurt because of it.

How does she know about Rebecca? We weren't even working in the same city.

But he didn't ask. She knew a lot of things, and that made him wonder if she was corrupt long before Vasco Trejo caught her on camera killing a drug dealer and stealing his cash.

"And I'm pretty sure you'll feel just as guilty if serious, sad, pretty little Lucy Kincaid gets whacked because of your obsession with going after a man who has more power behind him than you can possibly know. And that's all you're going to get, Brad." She stared at him. "Of course, if you can convince the powers that be to put me into witness protection—on *my* terms—I'll give you everything you want, and more. But Sam Archer put her foot down. She thinks I know nothing of value." Nicole smiled widely. "She is so very wrong."

CHAPTER TWENTY

Sean drove Lucy to work Tuesday morning. He hadn't asked her to stay home, though she could see in his expression that he didn't want her working after last night. And for about two minutes, she'd considered calling in sick. She had no energy and the makeup she'd layered on couldn't completely hide the dark circles under her eyes.

But she'd made a promise to herself long ago that she'd never let what had happened to her—or the fallout—stop her from doing her job. Whether it was when she was in college or grad school or working for search and rescue or the morgue . . . and now the FBI . . . she couldn't let her emotional turmoil keep her from her responsibilities.

Sean pulled into a parking spot and turned off the car. "Are you sure you don't want to go back home? I can make double chocolate chip brownies and we can watch *Guardians of the Galaxy* for the hundredth time."

She smiled, genuinely smiled. "You exaggerate. We've only seen it fifty-six times."

Sean touched her face. "Be safe, Lucy. Call me if you need anything."

"I will. Are you going to HWI?"

"At some point. I have a few things to check on, then I'll give Gregor my report."

Lucy wanted to tell him to forget last night, but of course Sean would never be able to, just like it would be burned in her memory forever. She didn't know if telling Sean about her nightmare was going to help, and she certainly didn't know if discussing the dreams would stop them, but it had been cathartic. Difficult beyond nearly anything she'd had to do, but when she was done, it was like every drop of blood had been drained from her body. She couldn't move, couldn't think, and had allowed Sean to put her back to bed and hold her. Needed him to hold her. Neither of them had slept, but that was okay.

"I love you," she said.

He kissed her. "Catch a bad guy today, princess."

She waved good-bye and walked into FBI headquarters. She was late—she was never late—but fortunately, Juan wasn't a stickler about tardiness. Most of them worked longer than the eight-to-five shift required of them.

She passed Ryan on her way to her desk. "You look like shit."

"Now I know why you got divorced," she snapped. She put her hand to her mouth. "I'm sorry. That was uncalled for."

"It wasn't. Just unexpected." He followed her to her cubicle. She sat down and booted up her computer. "What's wrong?"

"I'm fine."

The response was automatic, and Ryan knew it was a lie.

"As long as you're not sick. I don't have any sick time left—took it when my boys had the chicken pox. One right after the other."

"I'm just tired." She hesitated, then added, "Insomnia. Some nights it's worse than others."

"If you need anything, let me know."

"I talked to Brad last night about the gang shooting. Anything new?"

Ryan shook his head. "Not much. We haven't found the van. Haven't ID'd two of the victims, and no one's talking. I had a message when I got in that SAPD talked to the kid's family. The kid was there with his mother and aunt—we confirmed that the baby daddy was one of the gangbangers. They family was hysterical, but gave us nothing useful. Did Brad tell you he's talking to Nicole Rollins today?"

She nodded. "He's having a hard time with it, but he's the only one she'll talk to."

"She said that?"

"No—it's my gut feeling."

Barry walked past the Violent Crimes Squad cubicles and spotted Lucy. "Good, you're here." He handed her a packet of paper. "The tech team finally extracted the data off Harper Worthington's tablet. Unfortunately, it's mostly raw numbers and spreadsheets with no key as to what it all means. I had them email the data to our cyber experts at Quantico."

Lucy looked at the thin packet he'd handed her. "What's this?"

"Other than the spreadsheets, he kept some notes. I printed them out, made a few copies."

Ryan said, "I'll let you two get to work."

She turned back to Barry. He said, "The tablet has an automatic logging system, so we know that it was first used on May ninth."

"Almost four weeks ago."

"The same time his daughter, wife, and assistant thought he was acting preoccupied. And when he stopped using his office phone."

"We need to retrace his steps leading up to the ninth."

"Zach and the tech teams are working on it. HWI gave us his schedule for the last three months, so we can compare that with what we find and see if there are discrepancies." Barry gestured to the thin packet of paper in Lucy's hand. "Look at the first page."

She looked down.

Meet G.A. @ 11—Camp Street #115

The White Knight Motel was on Camp Street. Worthington had died in room 115.

"That note was created Friday afternoon. Only minutes before he made his flight arrangements," Barry said. "The notes are collated from most recent to oldest."

"Does it correspond to an email or a phone call?"

"Yes. He received a call from a blocked number on his cell phone at the same time that he created the note. Juan is getting a warrant to get the number from the provider. We'll have it before the end of the day, but my guess is it'll be a burner phone."

"It could match one of the other numbers we have. Like Elise or Mona Hill."

"Could, but we'll have to confirm that when we get it. Don't jump to conclusions."

"I'm not, I'm theorizing. So basically, he set up a one-hour meeting with someone on a Friday night hours from where he was staying. That would suggest that he knew his attacker. And—again a theory—it suggests that whatever was on this tablet was somehow connected to this meeting."

"Then why didn't he bring it?"

"Maybe he was suspicious of the meeting. Or maybe it wasn't about the information he had, but information he was going to add to it."

She turned the page. A list of dates—with no context—that went back nearly eight years. None of them meant anything to Lucy, but she went through them a second time and frowned at the very first listing.

"Barry—isn't this the day Adeline Reyes-Worthington was elected to office in the special election?"

He looked over her shoulder. "Yes. But none of these other dates relate to elections. It might mean nothing."

"But this is the first date on this list."

"What are you thinking?"

"I don't know—just that Worthington thought this information was important enough to not only keep on a tablet that no one knew he had, but to put extra security on it *and* create unlabeled spreadsheets so no one would understand what the data meant."

She turned the page. A list of numbers caught her eye. "What are these?" she asked Barry.

"I'm not one hundred percent certain, but I think they're land parcel numbers. Zach is researching them."

There were a couple dozen numbers, some in sequential order, some not.

"Do you think there's a connection between these numbers and the BLM files that Harper was obsessed with at his office?"

"Yes. We're working with HWI to give us access to those files. We could get a warrant, but because they've cooperated, we're giving them time to work through some contractual issues of either giving us copies or letting us access them. Flip to the last page."

Lucy did. There was one name.

G.A.—Roy Travertine.

"Is that important?" It sounded familiar, but she didn't know why.

"That was the first note on the tablet. Roy Travertine was the congressman who died in office—the person who Adeline Reyes-Worthington replaced. According to both Adeline and Worthington's daughter, Travertine and

Worthington were longtime friends. I don't know how that relates to what else is on the tablet, except that the initials 'G.A.' appear a couple of times."

"We should show Adeline the dates and ask her if she knows what they mean."

"I've been going back and forth about that. If it were any other case, I'd do it."

"But she's a federal official so you can't?" Lucy was having a difficult time treating this case as different from any other case.

"It's not that I can't, it's that we have an obligation not to do anything that could be seen as impacting an election. It's sensitive."

"Then we go to her house. It's reasonable that we would want to talk to her about her husband's murder."

"We still haven't had it confirmed."

Zach stepped in. "Yes, you have. This just came over the fax machine."

It was a preliminary coroner's report. The cover memo was addressed to Agents Crawford and Kincaid, from Julie Peters.

Barry & Lucy ~ Attached is the preliminary coroner's report. I'm still waiting on some test results, and I need to review this with my boss, but I'm confident that COD for Harper Worthington was an injection of curare, a poison. The lab eliminated commercial availability—meaning, this strain isn't from a pharmaceutical drug that might have medicinal purposes. This is a plant-based, homemade version from plants found in Central and South America. I've called in an expert to narrow this down—he should not only be able to tell us what plant was used and where it's most likely found, but also be able to isolate the

*genetic markers to see if there are any unsolved
cases with this strain.*

*You should have the final report by the end of
the day. But COD is asphyxiation due to poison
injected into the bloodstream. I'm ruling his death
a homicide.*

"Lucy, call Julie and ask her if she can suppress this report for a day or two. I need to talk to Juan."

Barry left the squad room and Lucy called Julie. She
answered on the first ring, and said no problem, she could
hold the report in house until Friday if they wanted.

Now that Lucy had something to focus on, she began
to feel better. The coffee that Ryan kindly brought to her
desk helped as well.

Lucy looked through the pages from the tablet again.
Harper had typed data into a simple note application. Each
note was only a few lines, if that, except for the list of numbers that Barry thought were land parcel numbers.

There were two other meetings with the unknown
"G.A." listed in the notes. One on May 11 and one on June
1, both Mondays. June 1 was five days before he was killed.
Both meetings were at different locations with no street address, just a street name.

The June 1 meeting was at two thirty at St. P—Lucy
didn't know if that was a street name, a business, a church,
or what. She looked at the corresponding day in his office
calendar. There was nothing scheduled on the calendar.

The May 11 meeting was at one at N. Zarzamora.

The latter was definitely a street, but it was miles long.

She looked at the calendar again. That was the day he'd
cancelled a meeting. His admin had remembered because
it was out of character. And her husband had seen him.

She immediately called Debbie Alexander on her cell
phone.

"Hello?" the admin answered.

"Debbie, this is Special Agent Lucy Kincaid. Do you know what bar your husband saw Harper leaving?"

"No, but I can ask him."

"Would you? And call me right back."

"What's wrong?"

"Nothing, just following up." She hung up and circled the meeting. This was important, she could feel it.

Now if only they could find out what the initials G.A. stood for.

Barry hadn't returned, so Lucy did an Internet search for *Roy Travertine, congressman* plus *Harper Worthington* to narrow the list to articles that referenced both of them.

Most of the information she read in Travertine's obituary and an extensive article on Travertine after his death. Travertine and Worthington had known each other since childhood. Travertine was godfather to Jolene Hayden, and Harper was godfather to Travertine's firstborn son. They had had completely different careers—Travertine was an architect. When he died, he left behind a wife and three children, the youngest of whom was now in college. After Travertine's death, Harper had donated a large sum of money to renovate an old library in San Antonio and rename it the Roy H. Travertine Memorial Public Library.

Travertine himself had been in office for five years. He was only forty-eight when he died. He wasn't a career politician and still kept his business. He ran for office primarily because of business issues, but had quickly adopted a tough-on-crime stance—particularly federal drug crimes. His crowning achievement was to make it easier for federal, state, and local authorities to pool resources in border states to combat smuggling—drugs, weapons, humans.

Why was Worthington thinking about his old friend

now? Did the information on the tablet have anything to do with Travertine?

Barry came back into the room. "Let's go. Juan gave us the green light to talk to Adeline, give her the cause of death, ask her about the information on the tablet. First I want to talk to Jolene."

"Did you look up Harper's schedule the week he bought the tablet?"

Barry nodded. "His office has him marked down as being on vacation from May fourth through the ninth, but he changed it last minute to fly back on the eighth—to Dallas instead of San Antonio. He then spent a few days there before coming back to San Antonio the morning of the eleventh."

"Was Adeline in D.C. with him?"

"It appears so—we'll ask her about the trip. But what I really want to know is what happened on the seventh or eighth that prompted this change of schedule? We'll ask Jolene and Harper's admin."

Lucy slid over her notes about the two other meetings with "G.A."

"June first—that's only days before he died. And the one on May eleventh? You said he returned to San Antonio that morning. That's also the day his admin said he cancelled an important business meeting. I called and asked her to check with her husband, who saw Harper's car in an unusual area, where he saw it. What if it was near North Zarzamora?"

Barry looked over Lucy's notes and compared the days and times on the schedule, just as she had done. "It's worth following up on," he said.

It didn't take long to drive to HWI since the morning rush was over. Jolene was in her office—a small, cluttered office with many homey touches, including a pillow-covered couch, a hand-knit afghan, and lots of pictures of her and her dad and husband, or her and a horse. She seemed less angry and more heartbroken this morning than she had yesterday. "I'm glad you're here—I have some information for you."

She picked up a thick file folder from her desk. "I made a copy for you. This is my father's will. He had a living trust, so the settlement process shouldn't take too long, but Adeline is going to contest it."

Barry took the folder, but didn't open it. "Is it important that we have this?"

She shrugged. "My father's attorney didn't see anything wrong with giving you a copy. A few weeks ago, my father contacted his attorney about changing his will. It was finalized three days before he died. I didn't know anything about it. When my father married Adeline, he changed his will so that, essentially, she and I would split his estate, plus a trust fund to keep open the library he helped rebuild and a few other bequests. Now, everything Adeline was going to receive has gone to me, including the house. He didn't tell me. He didn't tell Adeline—at least, that's what she says."

"You don't believe her?" Barry asked.

"I don't know." Jolene rubbed her eyes. "She appeared shocked when the lawyers told us yesterday afternoon. Completely stunned. Scott doesn't think she was faking it. But what if she knew he planned on cutting her out? What if she killed him?"

"It's a serious accusation," he said, "but there is no proof that she had anything to do with your father's death. We're still investigating his death as suspicious, but there is nothing that points to Adeline."

Lucy wondered why Barry didn't tell Jolene that they'd confirmed homicide.

"Elected officials get a pass all the time," Jolene said bitterly. "On corruption, adultery, any number of things. When Uncle Roy was alive, he had these stories about people, both Republicans and Democrats, who were so corrupt in taking money for this and that and passing legislation to help their friends, and no one did anything about it. Aren't you guys supposed to stop that?"

Barry said, "Are you referring to Roy Travertine, the former congressman?"

"Yes, I'd known him since I was born. I've always called him Uncle Roy, and his wife Aunt June. Uncle Roy was my daddy's closest friend."

Barry slid over the list of numbers. "We accessed the tablet you gave us. On it were a bunch of spreadsheets and this list of numbers. Do you know what this is?"

She studied them. "These are land tracts, these"—she pointed to a group in the middle with the same beginning numbers—"are in Bexar County, but the others are a variety of different counties. I don't know which ones offhand."

"Were these your father's properties?"

"No. He only owns his house and a couple commercial buildings, including the HWI buildings here and in Dallas. Maybe this is related to one of his clients. Do you want me to run it through our system?"

"No—not yet. We'll let you know if we need your help there, but we're still pursuing a couple of angles. One other thing—we were going over your father's schedule for the last month. He was in D.C. the first week of May. His office indicated that he was on vacation. He had a change of travel arrangements."

Jolene seemed confused by the question. "I vaguely remember that. He went to D.C. with Adeline because she was being recognized at some award dinner. He really didn't like going to D.C. Daddy was a homebody." She smiled wistfully and looked out the window, lost in thought.

Lucy gently prodded. "He flew in a day early, to Dallas, not San Antonio."

"Yeah—it was strange. Maybe—that was about the time he became preoccupied. I should have asked him more questions. Pushed him. Maybe I was too selfish to see that something was bothering him."

"Maybe he hid it from you," Lucy suggested. "Fathers do that when they don't want their children to know something. My dad was in the hospital after a heart attack over Christmas, and none of us kids knew he had been having heart trouble because he and Mom didn't want us to worry."

Jolene nodded. "Maybe you're right. My dad didn't like me to worry about him."

"On that weekend he was in Dallas, there was nothing on his calendar, but he didn't return to San Antonio until the eleventh."

"I really don't remember. I wasn't in Dallas with him. Our office manager, Beth Holloway, might know what he was doing. You're welcome to contact her. Her information should be in the employee files Gregor sent over."

Barry wrote down the information. "We'll do that. One more thing—can you think of a friend or colleague of your father's who has the initials G.A.?"

Jolene looked at the ceiling, her brows furrowed. "No," she said slowly. "I can look through his personal files. It could be a client. HWI has hundreds of clients."

"If you could, that would be great."

"What does it mean?"

"We don't know yet, but if you come up with a list, it would be helpful."

Barry thanked Jolene, and he and Lucy went down the hall to Debbie Alexander's office. She was on the phone, so they waited.

A minute later she hung up. "Agent Kincaid, I was just going to call you. That was my husband." She tore off the top sheet of a note pad. "This is the street where he saw Harper's car parked. There were only three businesses on that side of the street—a bar, a tattoo place, and an auto body shop. It's not a great area. Across the street is low-income housing."

Lucy asked, "Could he have been meeting someone at the apartments?"

"Doubtful, but then I wouldn't think he'd drive out there in his Lincoln."

"Call Beth Holloway," Barry said as he drove toward Adeline's house west of the city.

Lucy called the HWI Dallas number and identified herself, and shortly Beth Holloway came on the line.

"Ms. Holloway, I'm Special Agent Lucy Kincaid from the San Antonio FBI. Jolene Hayden suggested you might have some information pertinent to our investigation into Harper Worthington's death."

"Anything I can do to help. Jolene is just heartbroken, bless her heart. I saw her right after she found out, poor thing. She loved her daddy, they were very close. He raised her, you know, after his wife died."

"Yes," Lucy said. "I'm calling specifically about a change in Mr. Worthington's schedule on May eighth. He wasn't planning on being in Dallas then, but flew from D.C. to Dallas on the eighth and stayed for three days. His San Antonio office doesn't know what he was doing there, he had no scheduled meetings, and he didn't usually work out of the Dallas office."

"I remember, but let me just pull up my own calendar." She clicked on the keyboard. "That was a weekend. Then on that Monday, he came into the office in the morning.

I was surprised, it was the first I'd known he was in town. He said he was just taking a bit of time to himself."

"Did he do that often?"

"No. But he was the boss, and he looked tired. His favorite golf course is in Dallas, and when he comes here for work—maybe once a month—he always takes at least half a day to golf."

"How long was he in the office?"

"Not long at all. He left by ten, told me he already had booked a flight back to San Antonio. I didn't see him again, not until he came back to Dallas last week."

"Did you know about his spontaneous trip to San Antonio on Friday night?"

"No, I would have told Jolene immediately after I heard what happened. I was certain it wasn't him, but then he didn't answer his phone, he wasn't in his hotel room— Jolene was frantic looking for him."

"Thank you for your time. We'll be in touch if we have any other questions."

"Anything I can do to help, anything at all, please call me. I love Jolene like a daughter, and Harper like a brother. They are a wonderful family, and this is at its heart a family business."

CHAPTER TWENTY-ONE

After dropping Lucy off at work, Sean went back to their house. He'd told Lucy he was running errands, mostly because he didn't want her driving when she was still so emotionally and physically worn out after last night. The entire drive he wondered if he should have pushed her into staying home. She would have, if he'd pressured her hard enough. But she was fragile, and he didn't want her to resent him later. The last thing he wanted to do was bully her into taking care of herself.

Plus, working would clear her head. Give her something to focus on other than reliving last night.

That didn't mean he was going to sit back and do nothing about Mona Hill.

He sat down at his desk and booted up his computer. He'd been thinking all night about how he wanted to handle this. He couldn't exactly turn over the information about Mona Hill that he'd uncovered because he hadn't obtained all of it legally.

He considered calling Lucy's sister-in-law, Kate Donovan. Though Kate was a fed, she was one of the few people Sean trusted when it came to Lucy—outside of Lucy's brothers. But Jack would come down and kill Mona Hill,

Patrick would want plan a sting operation, and Dillon would reprimand Sean for breaking the law and jeopardizing Lucy's career. Kate, however, had a history of breaking the rules for justice. Plus, as a fed, she could find a way for the FBI to obtain the information Sean had obtained, but through legal channels.

And while Sean kept the idea of working with Kate in the back of his mind, he got to work doing what he did best.

First, he had to put aside his emotions. His overwhelming love for Lucy, and the protective instinct that came with that love, meant he might miss something or misinterpret information. He couldn't afford to screw this up.

"This is a job," he told himself. "Just a job. Focus, Sean."

Putting himself in his professional mindset, he skimmed the file that Tia had sent to Lucy. He felt a bit guilty about reading Lucy's emails—Lucy had all her files copied over to her personal computer, which was networked with his office. If he'd asked, she would have said yes. She might have asked why, though, and he didn't want to lie to Lucy.

He needed to know what the cops had on Mona Hill and why they hadn't been able to arrest her. It was clear from Tia's personal notes that she believed Mona Hill had someone high up in the criminal justice system in her pocket. She didn't give details—but it didn't take much imagination to read between the lines. Either she was blackmailing someone or bribing someone—or a combination of both. Maybe more than one person. No government agency was 100 percent clean, as evident from the DEA's recent problem with Agent Nicole Rollins.

And truth be told, law enforcement didn't concern themselves with the sex trade. They had stings here and there, but when facing serious problems like human trafficking, drug cartels, violent crimes—hookers were the least of their concerns. And a group like Mona Hill's? Tia's

notes said that Hill kept her girls under tight control and
didn't beat or abuse them. She paid them fairly, but controlled their lives through where they lived and what jobs
they took. A benevolent dictator.

But Tia's notes were borderline hostile—she certainly
didn't like Mona Hill or find anything benevolent about
her. There had to be something more that wasn't in Tia's
notes, maybe personal. An old case? A cold case? History.
He made a note to dig around. It would take talking to a
contact at SAPD. Unfortunately, he hadn't lived in San Antonio long enough to have cultivated sources who weren't
directly tied to Lucy.

Next he reviewed the information he'd retrieved last
night while running a deeper background check on Mona
Hill. He learned quickly that Mona Hill wasn't her real
name. Why Tia didn't know that, Sean couldn't figure out.
The information had been buried, but not impossible to
find. Mona Hill was born Ramona Jefferson to a prostitute by the name of Carla Jefferson. No father was listed
on the birth certificate. While Mona was a common nickname for Ramona, why had Mona changed her last name?
He couldn't find any records that she'd legally changed her
name or got married. But, she had a social security card,
driver's license, and bank accounts all under the name
Mona Hill—going back to when she was eighteen. Relevant? Possibly. She could have changed her name legally
in another state, but she hadn't done so in the four states
he had record of her living in.

He'd also pulled her credit report and a list of all the
property she owned, and had started to run down her
known associates. She owned the apartment building free
and clear in her own name. A car—again, completely paid
for—and a boat that was docked at Canyon Lake.

He ran businesses and other entities and almost shut
down that avenue of approach. Then he ran businesses on

Ramona Jefferson. The connection between Hill and Jefferson was extremely thin. Most people would assume they were different people. In fact, the chances anyone would connect the two were slim to none because—as a person—Ramona Jefferson had ceased to exist after the age of eighteen.

Ramona Jefferson existed on paper. It wasn't easy to find, and Sean wondered if Mona Hill herself had created this paper trail, or if she had had someone do it for her. It was pretty damn good.

But he was better. Unfortunately, not all the records he wanted were online.

Still, he found an extensive trail of small entities that led him down a path to a company that held one property in Houston. The company was listed as a consulting company and had filed all the appropriate tax forms with a small income, but Sean immediately saw it for what it was.

Companies set up like this were generally laundering money. They took in reasonable fees, paid taxes, and reported properly, but would often have one large account that would buy property and other tangible items to hold and retain until the cash was needed. Then they'd liquidate, report, shut down the business, and have clean money.

But . . . there were no large accounts. The only large purchase was for a house in Houston that was worth just over half a million and bought eight years ago for less than half that.

The company paid a consulting fee to another paper company in the amount of five thousand dollars a month—almost identical to the fees the company took in. If Sean didn't know better, he'd think that this was set up to keep a mistress. Buy her a house, give her an allowance, keep her beholden to her lover who was unwilling or unable to leave his wife.

Mona Hill was a girl. Didn't mean she wasn't keeping a guy—or a girl—but that would be unusual.

There were only minimal records on Mona Hill in Houston, and nothing before the age of eighteen. Ramona Jefferson was also difficult to track, and tracking juveniles was a lot harder—they usually didn't have a paper trail, especially if they were on their own.

He considered the house in Houston. If he had the time, he would fly up there and check it out himself, but it would take all day, and he needed to finish his assignment with HWI and pick up Lucy later. Searching his contact file, he pulled the number for Renee Mackey, a longtime PI out of Houston. She was semiretired and Sean hoped she was around, because he didn't have anyone else he could call locally.

"Yep," Renee answered. Over the phone, Sean heard the long drag of a cigarette.

"Renee, it's Sean Rogan."

Renee barked out a laugh. Her rough, deep voice responded warmly. "How's my favorite computer hacker doing these days? I heard you'd relocated to Texas. Following a girl. Way I remember it, the girls were always following you."

"I've grown up."

"She better be treatin' you right."

"More than right."

"So I guess you're not callin' me to run a background check on the woman." Another drag on the cigarette, or maybe it was Sean's imagination. The woman was seventy and smoked a pack or three a day. Sean had met her years ago, while he was still in college at MIT, and his brother Duke had asked him to spend his summer setting up a complete security system—physical and computer—for a high tech company. Renee had been hired to do background checks. She was old school, Sean was new school, but they'd hit it off immediately.

"Though," Renee continued, "I'm none too happy you're livin' a couple hours from Houston and you didn't pop over to visit."

"My loss."

"It certainly is."

He smiled. "You'll never change."

"God, I hope not. So this ain't a social call. You want something."

"I do."

"I should be offended and hang up, but I love your voice."

"At least I have something going for me."

She laughed, a deep, genuine laugh. "You know I'm retired."

"You'll never retire."

"Whadya want?"

"A house. Occupants. Anything you can dig up on them."

"Sounds boring."

"You know I pay well."

"I don't need the money."

"Yes, you do."

"I don't need the money so bad I'm willin' to take a boring job. Tell me why."

"Will you take it if I do?"

"If you tell me the truth."

"Always."

She snorted out a laugh. "What's so important about the house?"

"I don't know. A known prostitute—a madam, I guess you'd call her—owns it free and clear. It's worth half a million."

"Shit, I went into the wrong business."

"I want to know who lives there, how long, what they do, a full rectal exam—without letting anyone know you're looking."

"You could do it from your computer," Renee said.

"I tried. Everything is in this woman's name. Mona Hill. That's not even her real name, it was Ramona Jefferson. Mona Hill has a different social, but I know they're the same person."

"I trust your instincts, Sean. You know I'd do anything for you, sugar."

"Likewise."

She laughed again, then started coughing.

"Are you sick?"

"Naw, just smokin'. Shouldn't laugh when I'm puffin' away."

He wondered about that. Seventy years old, fifty plus of those years a smoker, her lungs were probably black as night. But one thing he'd learned about Renee was that she did what she wanted when she wanted and damned be anyone who didn't like it.

"You'll do it."

"You know I will. Send me what you have. I'll get back to you in a day or two."

"Thank you."

"You'll thank me by hauling your ass up here and introducing me to your girl."

"Hell, no. One night with you telling stories about me and she might run away."

"Any girl who runs from you is a fucking idiot."

"Love ya, Renee."

"Right back at you." She hung up.

Sean sent off the information he had on the property, then turned his attention to Mona Hill's current residence. She didn't have a large digital footprint—she was smart, he'd give her that—but she had a small one. And all it took was basic information for him to get what he wanted. He found her email address through one of her creditors, then backtraced it to find her internet service provider.

Now he needed to cross from the gray area into the black.

He pulled out his secure laptop. It took him nearly an hour to tweak a virus he'd written long ago so that it could worm its way into Mona Hill's computer and phone— wherever she checked her email. He had to be extremely careful so as not to alert the ISP that he was planting a virus. But one thing he'd learned in his years as a hacker was that businesses were looking for the big hack—the people and foreign governments who were looking to extract vast quantities of information like secrets, credit card information, political dirt. A small, targeted virus was far less likely to be detected. And if Sean's was detected, it would send the ISP all over the world in search of a ghost. It wouldn't be worth their time because nothing was being stolen.

He just needed to access Mona Hill's computer. He'd much prefer to simply break into her apartment, but he couldn't afford to get caught. This way would take longer, but it was much safer.

When he was satisfied that his virus would work as modified, he uploaded it through the ISP's own web form. If they even noticed, they wouldn't trace it to him.

Once Mona Hill checked her email from her computer, he would be able to remotely access her hard drive.

If she really did have the video of Lucy's rape, he would destroy it.

Then he would destroy her.

CHAPTER TWENTY-TWO

Lucy and Barry arrived at Adeline Reyes-Worthington's house just after ten that morning. Barry had called ahead to make sure she was there, and while her house manager or personal assistant or whatever she called Joseph Contreras had tried to put them off until later, Barry was firm.

When they were admitted through the gates, Lucy had the distinct impression that she was being watched. Though years ago she had thought the feeling, originally born out of violence, was paranoia, she'd grown to appreciate the instinct. She certainly didn't dismiss it, so eyed the surroundings carefully.

"What are you doing?" Barry asked.

"There are armed guards all over this place."

"Where?"

"Right inside the gate was the first one I saw, watching our car from behind the small grove of ash trees. Then two are by the house, they slipped around back when we pulled through. There'll be another one, to the left, but I haven't spotted him yet."

Barry glanced in the rearview mirror and nodded. "I see the one by the gate. How do you know there's another to the left?"

"I have good instincts when it comes to people watching me." She didn't care if he believed her, and she wasn't going to explain why. Even she didn't fully understand why—she was just relieved that she didn't panic anymore when the sensation of being watched washed over her.

There was a car in the circular drive when they arrived. They parked behind it, and knocked on the front door.

Joseph Contreras, opened the door. "As the congresswoman said earlier, this is not a good time to talk."

"And as I told you over the phone," Barry said, "we need to speak with her now. We have news about her husband's death."

"You could have said that when you called."

"I didn't think that there would be a problem seeing her."

Barry didn't blink or defer, and Lucy had to admire his ability to command a situation.

Mr. Contreras hesitated only a fraction of a second before opening the door and motioning for them to enter. "The congresswoman is in a meeting. I'll let her know that you are waiting."

Lucy looked casually around, then whispered to Barry, "There's another guard inside, dressed in a dark suit. He slipped down the hall when Contreras opened the door."

"I caught that, too. Is that five?"

"That I've seen." Or sensed. "Not government, because they would have answered the door if there was a legitimate threat."

"And we would know. Congressional protection in the district falls under our jurisdiction."

"Why does she feel she needs a private security force?"

"I intend to ask her."

Mr. Contreras came through the foyer with two men, both dressed in lightweight suits without ties, appropriate for the warm, humid weather.

The shorter man was an attractive Hispanic male in his late thirties. The taller man looked very familiar to Lucy, but she couldn't place him. She stared, trying to remember where she'd seen him. Six feet, sandy blond hair, light eyes—a bit husky, but not overweight. He worked out. No one introduced them, and both men left quickly.

Dammit, where had she seen him? It wasn't recent, but she was usually very good with faces. Maybe he just seemed familiar because he reminded her of someone else.

Contreras didn't say a word, but escorted Barry and Lucy back to the office with the large picture window overlooking the rose garden.

"Mr. Contreras told you that today isn't a good day." Adeline looked both tired and frustrated.

Barry said, "We have news about your husband's death, and as a courtesy, we're informing you first. However, if you would prefer to hear about it on the news, Agent Kincaid and I will leave."

Lucy was surprised at the sharp tactic. Barry's voice was calm and reasoned, but his words were certainly confrontational. It was a terrific approach, and she'd originally had him pegged as a less subtle agent. Which proved that you really didn't know someone until you'd worked with them.

Adeline frowned, but sat at her glass desk. Interesting, considering that their first meeting had been less formal, on the couch.

Barry remained standing, so Lucy followed his example. Barry said, "As you know, your husband's death was initially ruled as suspicious. The coroner's office has confirmed that we're now investigating a homicide."

There was no reaction from Adeline. Either she was in complete shock or denial, or she already knew Harper Worthington had been murdered.

"Have you received any threats?"

"The Capitol Police investigate such matters. They haven't found anything viable."

"Then why do you have so many private security guards on your property?"

"I'm a federally elected official who has taken some unpopular stands. Just a precaution."

"They weren't here on Saturday."

"Perhaps you didn't see them."

Adeline's entire body was a band of tension. If she was wound any tighter, Lucy thought, she might snap and bounce off the walls.

"I thank you for taking the time out of your busy investigation to inform me that my husband was murdered. Now, go find his killer. That is your job, correct?"

"We need to confirm some information, Mrs. Reyes-Worthington," Barry said. He pulled out his note pad, slowly and deliberately, and with equally deliberate fashion flipped through multiple pages, obviously skimming his notes. Lucy knew he read much faster than that, so this was another tactic. Something Adeline had done had set off Barry's instincts as well as hers. What?

She didn't ask how he was murdered.

Barry said, "According to our investigation, your husband flew to D.C. with you on May fourth and spent four nights at your residence there."

"Yes."

"He was going to return on the ninth with you, but instead returned a day earlier and went to his office in Dallas."

"He told me he had work to catch up on, something unexpected. I didn't question him. Both of us have demanding jobs."

Barry turned back in his notebook. "When we first met,

you indicated that he had a doctor's appointment in early May, and had been preoccupied since. We spoke with his doctor, and Mr. Worthington was last in for a checkup last fall."

"I told you that *Harper* said he had a doctor's appointment."

"Do you remember what day?"

"No." She paused. "It was after he came back from D.C. Maybe he has another doctor. Maybe that's why he went to Dallas. He was obviously keeping something from me."

Adeline wasn't agitated or rattled. At the most, she was frustrated that they were asking her questions. She straightened her spine—even more than it was—and said, "I have a funeral to plan. I have a meeting with my lawyer. I have government business to attend to and a campaign to run. Let me know when you find out who killed my husband."

Barry nodded to Lucy. She pulled out a piece of paper—the one with the dates—and placed it on Adeline's desk. "Do you know what these dates mean?"

Adeline didn't touch the paper, but looked down at the list. "No. Some are familiar—the first one is the day I won my election. The others don't hold any significance for me."

Next Lucy put the parcel number list in front of Adeline. "What about these numbers?"

"I have no idea what those are. What is going on?"

Lucy didn't respond. She picked up the papers and put them back in her folder. Adeline was lying, but Lucy didn't call her on it. Her phone vibrated in her pocket, but she ignored it.

Barry said, "Your husband had this information in a password-protected file and we're trying to determine if the dates or numbers had something to do with his death."

"Then why ask me? I'm his wife. You should be asking his employees. Or his daughter."

"We are," Barry said. "Agent Kincaid, do you have the photo?" He held out his hand for it.

Lucy pulled out the image of Elise that had been captured on camera at the Del Rio Hotel. She handed it to Barry and he gave her a subtle nod toward Adeline. She turned her attention to the woman as Barry placed the photo in front of her. "Do you recognize this girl?"

Adeline didn't move. She stared at the photo for a long minute. Too long. She didn't touch it. In fact, her hands were in her lap. If the desktop hadn't been made of glass, Lucy wouldn't have noticed that her slender hands were so tightly clasped together that her fingers were white. The tendons in her arms stood out, all the way to her neck.

"No, I do not," she said, her voice hard and clipped. "Is this the prostitute Harper was with? Did she kill him?"

Barry didn't answer the question. Instead, he picked up the photo and put it in his own folder.

"Do you recall a friend by the initials of G.A.?"

"Really? I have so many acquaintances and colleagues, I can't possibly know who you're talking about. There's Congresswoman Georgia Abernathy, for example, out of Chicago. A good friend of mine. And Senator Grant Anderson from Maine. Should I go on?"

She was defensive. Overdefensive.

Barry asked, "Did you or your husband receive any threats that you didn't report to the Capitol Police?"

"Of course not. There are a lot of kooks out there, not all of them announce their intentions." She narrowed her eyes. "Are you saying that my husband was murdered on purpose?"

"Most murders are on purpose," Lucy said.

"Then I suggest you find out what happened, and you

certainly won't be able to do that standing here in my office."

Barry nodded. "We'll be in touch."

Mr. Contreras was standing outside the open office door. He'd either been eavesdropping or waiting for them during the interview. He silently escorted them to the front door, shutting it as soon as Barry and Lucy stepped out.

Barry walked around to the driver's side and pulled his phone from his pocket. "Tia Mancini left a message."

Lucy looked at her phone. "Me too. She also sent a text. It says, *Found Elise at the hospital. Two GSWs, call me ASAP.*"

"What hospital?"

Lucy dialed Tia's number. "I'll find out."

Adeline stared at the rose garden and for the first time in her life, she didn't know what to do.

Why was that little whore here? In San Antonio? Had she really killed Harper?

This could *not* be happening. Her whole world was crumbling around her—again—and she didn't know how to stop it.

The last time she'd felt this way—two months ago— Adeline had been in D.C. She had to stay because Congress was in session, when she'd really wanted to be home because her entire world was falling apart.

Adeline slammed down the phone, then hoped no one in her office heard her brief tantrum. James Everett had pulled his endorsement.

Was it her fault that Tobias lost the guns? No, but she was still responsible. She was the one who had to pay back the people who'd bought them. Liquidating money was difficult, especially when most of her money was tied up in property. Thirty days? No problem. Tomorrow? Impossible.

*Yesterday she'd been on the phone with James for over
an hour. The whiny bastard was scared. Scared! She'd told
him she would take care of the buyers, but she needed to
sell a prime parcel of land immediately, and he'd better
find a way to do it and get her the cash. He had, but then
he'd told her they were done. She didn't believe him . . .
but just now her press secretary told her he'd endorsed her
opponent.*

Asshole!

*She tried calling Rob Garza—again. Where the hell
was he? Her campaign manager traveled with her everywhere now, because she needed him both in D.C. and in
the district. He managed more than just her campaign. He
needed to help her appease the buyers and find out what
happened so it wouldn't happen again. And help her punish James Everett, that prick.*

*She maintained a small, one-room office near the Cap-
itol so she could make fundraising calls, and that's where
Rob should be. Why wasn't he answering his damn phone?
He'd better be on the phone with a big donor bringing in
the money because her number-one rule was to pick up
the phone when she called.*

*She walked briskly to the campaign office which was
only a few blocks away. She needed to breathe. What was
she going to tell the press about James? What could she
possibly say? That he was a scared little boy who ran at
the first sign of trouble? He was going to regret his decision.*

*The campaign office was locked. She unlocked the
door, not expecting to see anyone.*

*The smell of sex assaulted her senses, followed by
animal-like grunts. For a split second she thought Rob
was watching porn on the television, but then she saw
them.*

Rob, completely naked, had a woman bent over

Adeline's desk, screwing her from behind. By the disarray on the conference table, the cushions from the couch on the floor, and the smears on the glass partition, this obviously wasn't the first time they'd gone at it. Adeline watched as Rob pushed into the girl, his body jerking in orgasm.

"What the hell!*" Adeline exclaimed.*

Rob looked over at her, breathing heavily. He didn't even look embarrassed. Or guilty. He said, "I thought your meeting with Senator Dutton would go on until nine."

"Get her out of here."

Rob pulled his dick out of the girl, then slapped her on the ass. "You heard the boss," he said. "Sorry we have to cut this short." He stood over the trash can and rolled off his condom. Adeline wanted to puke.

The girl got up. She was young. Much too young to be having sex in Adeline's office. She was flushed, with bleached hair and too much makeup.

"You brought a hooker into my office? Are you trying to cost me the election?"

Rob pulled on his pants. "Lighten up, Adeline. You think I don't know you're screwing Joseph in San Antonio and Dennis here?"

The girl dressed in a short skirt, tank top, and jean jacket. She picked up her shoes. "Oh, Robert," she said as she took an envelope out of her purse. "I think you wanted this?" She winked at Adeline, then walked out.

"You're fired," Adeline said.

Rob laughed. "Fired?" He handed Adeline the envelope. "This is the key to your victory."

Adeline frowned and opened the paper—carefully, because that girl had touched it after touching God knows what on herself and Rob. Inside were photographs of the female senator from Texas who was about to come out with an endorsement of her opponent, if the rumors were true.

The senator was naked and in bed with someone who wasn't her husband. In fact, the someone was a woman. A woman Adeline also knew, because she was a high-ranking staffer on the budget committee.

"How did you get these?"

"You should thank Elise. She's not cheap, but she de-livers."

Adeline didn't say anything for a minute. "You screwed her on my desk!"

"Get over it."

She wanted to throttle Rob, but these photos were way too good. No way would the senator endorse her oppo-nent now . . . and if she didn't run for reelection, all the better . . . Adeline had been eyeing the Senate seat even before she ran for the House.

"We have a problem. Tobias lost nearly half the guns. I don't have the details, but the word is that some rogue military group or mercenary gang came in and took them. I'm scrambling to pay back the buyers."

"I told you long ago not to go into business with him. Never trust a business partner you've never seen. Cut your losses and move on."

"I need protection from someone else first. Tobias can be ruthless."

"Can he? No one's seen him. No one knows who he is. Honestly, he's probably a wimp and the first time we push back he'll run away. There are other people we can work with. Marquez, for example. We did that deal last year with him, and everyone was happy all around. I say we do more with him and cut all ties with Tobias and his people. Though losing those guns—he'll probably be dead within a week."

"James is endorsing my opponent."

"Then James can go to hell. I have more dirt on him than anyone else. It won't help before the election, but after the election I'll destroy him. Okay?"

"He knows things about our operation."

"I'll make sure he doesn't say a word." Rob buttoned up his shirt and grinned. *"I've always solved all your problems, haven't I, Adeline?"*

She started to relax. *"Yes, you have. But that girl—"*

"Is just a whore."

She bristled. *"If you ever have sex in this office again, I will fire you."*

He raised an eyebrow and said in a low voice, *"You're the one who wanted me to seduce Jessica and keep her close. Which I did. And that means either she stops traveling with us to D.C. so I can fuck whoever I want in my own apartment, or you get me a second place."*

"You can't just refrain? Or find a girl with her own place?"

"Why should I?" He sat down at her desk and started making fundraising calls.

That girl. That *whore* was here in San Antonio. Had Rob . . . No. He couldn't have had Harper killed. What a ridiculous thought! Yet . . . *that whore* was here, had been with Harper in the motel, and now Harper was dead.

Rob walked into her office. He looked irritated. "I'd just gotten back to the office when Joseph called and said it was an emergency. What's going on?"

Adeline whirled around. "Shut the door." He complied, without mouthing off this time. She must look like a fury. "Your young whore from D.C.? What is she doing in San Antonio?"

He blinked in confusion. "I don't know what you're talking about."

"That hooker I caught you screwing on my desk!"

It took him a second. "Elise? She's not here. You're seeing things."

"Like hell I am. The FBI came in with her photograph. She was in Harper's room when he died. When he was *murdered*. He was murdered. By your whore. Tell me you didn't do it—when I told you that Harper was acting strange, you had that look—"

"Shut up. Hell no. I had nothing to do with Harper's murder. Oh my God, Adeline, I would never . . . I just don't get it . . . Elise is in D.C. She couldn't possibly be here."

"She is. And the FBI is looking for her. It just can't possibly get worse than this."

"I'll find out what's going on. I promise, Adeline, I will get at the truth."

She believed him. She didn't know why that mattered to her, but she did. He seemed just as confused and worried as she was.

"Everything is falling apart!"

"It's not. You have to be strong now more than ever."

She shook her head and said in a low voice, "Tobias sent me a picture of Harper, dead. Told me he would frame me for his murder unless I paid him back the money I kept when he lost the guns. I needed that money to pay back the buyers—why he didn't just accept the loss—when it was his fault!—I'll never know."

"Pay him."

"I tried to reach his people after the FBI left, but every number I have is dead. He's going to destroy me."

"He can't." But Rob didn't sound confident. Now he was beginning to look as scared as she felt.

"I have to leave. Until this dies down."

"You leave, that's it. You'll never win the election."

"And I won't win if I'm in prison or dead."

"Give me forty-eight hours to figure this out."

She was nervous, but she nodded. "Okay. But be careful."

Rob left, and she turned back to the rose garden. She didn't know if she could wait forty-eight hours.

The time that Tobias had given her to pay him back was almost up . . . and he wasn't returning her calls.

CHAPTER TWENTY-THREE

After Lucy talked to Tia, she repeated the conversation to Barry. "Elise was found with two gunshot wounds near Guadalupe and South Laredo late last night. She's still in recovery, we won't be able to talk to her for a few hours. Tia said she'd let us know when Elise is awake."

"Then let's check out that area where Harper's car was spotted the week he cancelled his business meeting."

It was a good plan, though Lucy itched to go to the hospital. Elise was the key and she desperately wanted to talk to her. But they'd simply be standing around waiting, and Tia was already there.

As Barry drove, Lucy closed her eyes. "I thought you looked tired," Barry said.

"I am, but that's not it. I'm replaying the conversation with Adeline over in my head. She was lying about something, but now I can't remember what it was."

"She was lying about everything. She didn't ask how Worthington was murdered. She didn't seem surprised. She didn't have a good reason for having so much security, and she was scared and angry."

He was right about everything. Lucy said, "It was something else. Just give me a second, I'll figure it out."

Fortunately, Barry didn't say anything. Lucy mentally reviewed the case in her head, at least the parts that directly related to Adeline Reyes-Worthington. History, marriage, being cut out of the will . . .

Jolene's Southern drawl popped into her head. *Those are parcel numbers.*

Lucy jumped. Barry had parallel parked on a wide street in central San Antonio.

"I thought you'd fallen asleep. We're here."

"Adeline said she didn't know what the numbers were."

"And that means something?"

"She was in real estate for twenty-some years. She must have recognized that they were parcel numbers. Jolene did."

Barry hit the steering wheel with his fist. "Dammit, I should have caught that. Remind me to let you have a cat nap more often."

"I wasn't asleep."

"You snore."

She stared at him wide-eyed, and Barry laughed. "Power naps work," he said. "Definitely something going on with Adeline. But we need to tread very carefully. We need evidence, because there's no way that the Bureau is going to let us formally question a sitting congresswoman without a pile of proof."

"We may not be able to find the proof without getting a search warrant for her phone, computer, house—"

"Don't say it. Because we don't have enough evidence to get a search warrant. Not even if she wasn't an elected official."

The system sometimes frustrated Lucy, but Barry was right. They had nothing except the fact that Adeline had lied. And proving that she'd lied? Impossible. She could claim that she was distraught after hearing her husband had been murdered and hadn't paid attention to the papers Lucy and Barry had shown her.

They needed more. Like a statement from Elise.

Barry and Lucy got out of the car. The narrow, squat strip mall certainly didn't look like a place that someone of means would visit. Bars on the windows, graffiti painted over with several shades of beige or white paint. At least the businesses made an effort to paint over the graffiti. The tired apartment building across the street looked worse.

"Debbie's husband must have been visiting his patient there," Barry said. "Saw Harper's car in front of this strip mall."

"Bar," Lucy said. "My guess is he met G.A. in the bar. But it could be the individual lived across the street, which is why they met here."

"We'll check both."

Walking into the bar from the bright sunlight outside blackened Lucy's vision, even though she'd been wearing sunglasses. She put her glasses on the top of her head and followed Barry to the counter as her sight adjusted to the dim light.

Though it was not yet noon, there were six men sitting at the bar. One guy slouched in the corner watching a baseball game on one of two small televisions. All seven men, plus the bartender, turned to stare at the two agents.

Barry showed his badge to the bartender. "We hope you can help us, Mister—?"

"Call me Al." Al was the size of a linebacker, large and meaty with tattooed arms.

"Al, I'm Agent Crawford, this is Agent Kincaid. We're trying to track down a patron who was in here about four weeks ago, on a Monday afternoon. Were you working on May eleventh?"

Al snorted. "I'm here every day. This is my bar."

Lucy noted that the two men at the far side of the bar got up and left. Guilty of something? Or simply didn't trust cops?

"The person we're trying to find was with this man." Barry showed Al a picture of Harper Worthington. "Well dressed, drove a dark Lincoln."

"Yep. We don't get many people in suits in here. I don't remember the exact day, but it was a few weeks ago. He'd never been in before, and hasn't been in since."

"What about the man he was with? His initials are G.A."

"Gary. He's a semiregular."

"Do you know his last name?"

"Nope."

"Can you give a description?"

"Midfifties, but he looked older. Skinny, balding white guy. Pasty white. Had a scar on his head from here to here." Al made a motion with his finger from his temple to behind his ear. "Might have been longer, the hair covered some. He limped from an accident he was in, he once said."

"How often does he come in?"

"Once, twice a month. Has for a few years. Doesn't talk much, but when he does, it's about some wild-ass conspiracy theory after he's had a few. You know, like Kennedy was assassinated by the Cubans or Hinckley was paid off by the Russians to kill Reagan and the government just used his obsession with Jodie Foster as a cover. Didn't have a cell phone because he thought the government could track him. Shit like that."

Al refilled one of his patron's drinks, then returned to Barry. "He always drank from a bottle—and insisted he open the bottle himself. Afraid someone would slip something in. A kook, but a harmless kook."

"Does he live around here?"

"Don't know. He comes in on the bus, though. I know the schedule well, it drops off at the corner eight times a day. He's usually inside a minute or two later. Always leaves before the last pickup, on the six forty-five or eight ten."

"So you can confirm that this man"—Barry tapped Harper's photo—"met with Gary here one time a few weeks ago?"

"Yeah. Gary was here first. The guy comes in, looks around, totally out of place and he knew it. He came to me, ordered a bottle, tipped me ten bucks. Ten. Bucks. No one here tips ten bucks on a four-dollar bottle. Took a table over there"—Al gestured to the corner where the old guy was watching the game—"and waited. Gary was at the bar a good five minutes before he went over to talk to him. I don't think your suit had known Gary, didn't recognize him. They had their heads together for twenty, thirty minutes. The suit didn't even finish his beer."

"And that was it?" Lucy asked. "Anything else about their conversation that stands out? Even if you don't think it's important."

"Why?" Al asked. He was simply curious, Lucy realized.

Barry said, "We can't tell you, this is a federal investigation. We really need to find this guy."

"Well, I can tell ya two more things. First, Gary hasn't been in since that day. He wasn't really regular, but I'd see him every two or three weeks for the past couple years. Second, I didn't hear any of the conversation. But Gary handed the suit a folder. That caught my eye, 'cause Gary had the folder hidden under his shirt. Oh—and Gary left out the back door, not the front. That was odd. He said he was using the bathroom, and then he just walked out."

Barry gave Al his business card. "If Gary comes in, call me, anytime. My cell phone number is on the back."

Al didn't take the card. "You know, I don't mind talking to you guys, I'm all for doing my civic duty, but I'm not going to rat out my customers if I don't know what they're wanted for."

"He's just wanted for questioning," Barry said.

Al snorted. "I don't get a lot of cops in here, and never once a fed. My business is slow but steady, I have no employees, I'm here every day. I run a good business, honest, no drugs, no whores. Just guys who need a beer or two because they can't get a job or work twelve hours for minimum wage or less. These guys need to believe I'm not gonna sell them down the river on some petty shit. Unless you tell me that Gary is a fucking pedophile, I'm not gonna be your snitch."

Barry tensed and looked like he was ready to argue, but Lucy sensed that Al was done. She said, "Thank you for your time, Al. We appreciate it. By the way, is that the bus schedule?" She gestured to a bulletin board behind the bar. It was crammed with flyers and receipts, maybe months or years old.

"It's my only copy."

"Could I look at it?"

He eyed her suspiciously, but handed it over.

He had the bus route closest to the bar highlighted. She made note of the route number and the times, then handed it back to him. "Thank you."

Barry followed her out. He was pissed. "You interrupted my interrogation."

"He wasn't going to give us anything else."

"You don't know that."

"He told us everything he knew about Gary, including a first name, which we didn't have before. You think the owner of a dive bar is going to let his regulars know that he's snitching to the feds? Al doesn't want trouble from us, or lost revenue. It could be a day, a week, a month before Gary swings back this way."

Barry was still angry, but he didn't comment.

"The regular bus driver might remember this guy, especially since he has a scar and limp. If he takes the bus everywhere, we may be able to find out where he gets picked up, and take it from there."

"That's a long shot."

"Not as long as waiting for Gary to come back here."

Both of their phones vibrated at the same time. Tia Mancini had sent them a group message:

> *Doc says we can talk to Elise for five minutes. Get your butt to the hospital before he changes his mind.*

CHAPTER TWENTY-FOUR

Tia met Lucy and Barry outside the hospital. "It's easier to talk here," she said. "They're moving Elise out of recovery into a private room, so we have a few minutes."

"You didn't tell us what happened," Lucy said.

"Too long to text." She pulled out her note pad. "This is from the primary witness, Mr. Peter Rabb, twenty-five, resident of San Antonio. I interviewed him earlier. His story holds, but I'll send you his contact info. Last night, just after midnight, this girl—Elise—runs across Guadalupe and is nearly hit by a car driven by Rabb. He didn't see a shooter, but heard two gunshots and when he gets out of the car to check on the girl, he sees that she's been shot. He immediately calls nine-one-one and had competent enough first-aid skills that he slowed the bleeding. Two officers arrive, then the ambulance. They call out the crime scene techs because one officer notices the driver's door has a nice big bullet hole.

"It's not until the detective arrives at the hospital, has to wait out surgery—she was shot twice, once in the arm, and once in the upper shoulder, right in the back, that he recognizes the girl from my BOLO. Calls me, I come down to confirm, then call you."

"Has she said anything?"

"She got out of surgery early this morning. They had her in recovery, and I texted you as soon as I cleared with the doc that we could talk to her. But then they decided to move her, so we have to wait. I ordered a cop on the door— since we don't know exactly what or who we're dealing with. All I know is she didn't give the medics any information except her name is Elise Hansen."

"You've run it?"

Tia nodded. "No pops on the name, might not even be real and she has no identification on her, but I'm going wider on it. My contacts at NCMEC are working on it, going through all missing girls with the first name of Elise who would now be between the ages of fourteen and eighteen, regardless of when they were reported missing. But my gut feeling is she's been on her own for a long time."

"She was on Guadalupe?" Barry asked. "That's a long avenue."

Tia pulled out her notes. "South Laredo and Guadalupe. Only a couple blocks from the White Knight Motel. Rabb was driving west on Guadalupe and Elise was running north on South Laredo. The cops canvassed the scene and found blood along a walkway between a closed business and a motel a block from the White Knight. I sent my guys back out looking for more evidence, because the first team found shit at night."

"And the driver didn't see anyone?" Lucy asked.

"No, but he admitted he wasn't looking. He pulled her body around to the other side of the car because he was scared and didn't know where the shooter was. Several other cars stopped, and her attacker fled. My guys are still out there, but so far nothing."

"Evidence?"

"Not much. A partial shoe print, no bullet casings.

Likely a revolver. I'll let you know what else we find." She looked pointedly at Barry. "Unless you want to take over?"

"No, Tia, just keep me in the loop," Barry said.

"The first wound was superficial—a lot of blood, but not fatal. The second bullet went through the meaty part of her upper right shoulder. I saw the x-ray—it didn't fragment, we should be able to get ballistics from it. Plus we have the bullet from the car. My guys already took both into evidence. Anyway, if that bullet was an inch lower, it would have hit her lung, two inches to the left and it would have lodged in her spine. But shooting her in the back? That's just fucked."

They went inside the hospital and Tia took them to the third floor. She met up with the head nurse. "Elise Hansen. The gunshot victim. Her surgeon said we could talk to her as soon as she was settled in her room."

The nurse nodded curtly. "Two only. And if she gets agitated or upset, I'll remove you. Understood?"

"Yes." Tia looked from Lucy to Barry. "I'm going in there," she said. "Which of you is joining me?"

"I'll observe," Barry said. He looked at Lucy. "This is why Juan wanted you on this case, right? Your work with victims."

"Thanks, Barry," she said. She recognized his tone—he didn't want to regret letting her take the lead on this interrogation.

Lucy followed Tia into a private hospital room, past the SAPD officer manning the door.

Elise was drawn and pale in the hospital bed, her limp blond hair against the white sheets making her look even more ghostly. She was reclined at an angle, and her right arm was in a full sling.

It was hard to pin down her age, because her injuries made her look younger. If Lucy had to make a guess, she'd say fifteen. She was of average height, underweight, and her face still held a faint bruise from where James Everett had hit her. *Allegedly* hit her on Friday night. There were other scrapes and cuts, but those were fresh enough to be from the events last night.

Elise glared at them. Though both Lucy and Tia were in plain clothes, Elise clearly had them pegged as law enforcement.

Tia spoke. "I'm Detective Tia Mancini with the San Antonio Police Department. This is my colleague, FBI Special Agent Lucy Kincaid. We'd like to know what happened last night. Do you know who shot you?"

Elise stared at them. "I'm not talking."

"Okay. That's your right, but someone shot you in the back. It would help us find him if you cooperate."

"Go away."

"We're not going away," Tia said. "We've been looking for you."

"I didn't do anything. I was the one who was shot."

"And we want to find the person who did this to you."

Elise snorted. "Right. Like you care."

"I care," Tia said. She sat in the lone chair. Lucy sat at the end of the bed, on the corner. Tia said, "Let me explain my job. I specialize in special victims."

"Special? Like retards? I'm not stupid."

"Special, like women and children who have been abused."

"Just because I'm shot you think I'm abused?"

"How old are you?"

"None of your fucking business."

"It really doesn't matter, because you're underage and we have evidence that you've been soliciting."

"Meaning, I'm a hooker." She laughed weakly. "Fine me. So what?"

"I can help you. It's what I do. Just tell me you want out, and I'll make it happen. It won't be easy, because you'll have to change your lifestyle. But it's possible. School. Graduation. A safe job."

"Look," Elise said, "thanks, but no thanks. I'm happy with my life just the way it is. I'll bet I make more money in a week than you do in a month."

"You might. But I'll bet, even being a cop, my lifespan is longer than yours."

"You can't arrest me for prostitution because you have no proof. And even if you did, I'd be out like this." She snapped her fingers, then winced. She reached for her water. Her hand was shaking as she brought the straw to her lips. "Why can't you just leave me alone?" She closed her eyes.

Tia took the glass when Elise was done and put it on the nightstand. She nodded to Lucy.

"We can't leave you alone because you're wanted for questioning in a murder investigation."

Elise's eyes flew open. She stared at Lucy. Defiance and fear, all mixed together. Tia was right: this girl had been on her own for a long time. She trusted no one.

"Bullshit," Elise said. "You're setting me up."

Lucy said, "We have a witness who places you at the White Knight Motel exiting a room where a dead man was found. How did that happen, Elise?"

She shook her head. "No. No, no, no. I'm not talking. You have no proof of anything, I'm not saying a word." She turned her head and closed her eyes as if that would make them go away.

The machine next to her bed started beeping. The nurse came in and gave Tia and Lucy a dirty look. She checked Elise's vitals and had her drink more water. Then she checked her bandages under the sling.

"I warned you both about this. She needs rest."

"Five more minutes," Tia said.

"If you upset her again, you will leave."

"Yes, ma'am," Tia said.

When the nurse left, Tia said to Elise with a tone that was both firm and kind, "Elise, you have two options. You come clean now, and we'll help you. Cooperation goes a long way with prosecutors. I give you my word, Elise. You tell the truth, and I'll be by your side for the entire process."

She didn't say anything at first, didn't look at them. Then a little squeak came out. "They'll kill me."

"We can protect you."

Tears leaked from her eyes. "No one can protect me."

"Who shot you?"

She shook her head.

Tia looked at Lucy. Lucy realized what Tia was doing—Tia was being the good cop, she wanted Lucy to be the big bad federal cop. Lucy didn't like that role at all—she didn't want to browbeat this poor girl. But she said in a stern, calm voice, "Elise, we have more than enough evidence to turn over to the prosecution for a first-degree murder charge. You will be tried as an adult. Even if you were granted leniency because of your age and mitigating factors, you wouldn't see the outside of a jail cell for at least twenty years."

"It doesn't matter. They'll get to me in jail." She stared at Lucy. "The only way I'll be safe is if you let me go. I can disappear and they'll never find me."

"We can and will protect you if you tell us the truth," Lucy said.

"You can't!"

"Then I'll have to charge you with first-degree, premeditated murder."

"No, no! It was an accident, he wasn't—"

She stopped talking. Her eyes darted back and forth between Tia and Lucy. She reached for her water again with shaking hands.

"What was an accident?" Lucy asked.

Elise put the water down and stared at the ceiling, tears streaming down her face. With the back of her free hand she wiped them way. She bit her lip and was obviously weighing her fears—was she more terrified of the people she worked for or the police?

"Okay—just this. It was an accident. It was supposed to be easy. Just—go in, seduce this old guy, take pictures. And if I couldn't seduce him, well, shoot him up with a little happy juice. He wouldn't remember anything, and I'd still get the pictures. I didn't know he would die! I didn't know, I just thought it was, you know, something that would make him sleepy and forgetful. I didn't even know he was dead until yesterday, when—" She stopped herself. "Anyway, it was an accident."

"It's still murder."

"It was an accident," she whispered.

"Did you take pictures?"

She nodded.

"You took pictures of Harper Worthington," Lucy said specifically.

"Y-yes."

"Where are they?"

"I gave everything to the person who hired me."

Everything? That sounded like more than just porno-graphic photos of Harper Worthington.

"Were you hired to take pictures of anyone else? Anyone other than Mr. Worthington?" Lucy asked. Tia shot a con-fused glance at her, but Lucy focused on Elise's reaction.

"I—I—you don't understand."

"You'd be surprised at what I understand," Lucy said. "Who hired you?"

She shook her head. "I can't."

"Yes, you can."

"He's the one who shot me. And he's just a middleman, I don't know who really wanted them."

"Who is he?" Lucy pushed again.

"I don't know!"

"We know you got this job through Mona Hill."

She frowned but didn't say anything.

"Mona told us that you are new in town and called her up looking for work." Lucy turned to Tia. Tia nodded. "We have enough to get a warrant to search Mona's apartment and bring her in for questioning."

"She doesn't know anything. I just called Mona because I was bored, and I had to wait around until they told me this guy would be at the motel. They just wanted the porn shots. Probably to blackmail him, I don't know, I don't care! I did my part and got paid and that's all, but—" She stopped talking.

"But?"

"I fucked up, okay? I grabbed his phone because I thought I could sell it, but then I lost it and they were so angry. That's why they shot me, okay? That's why I have to disappear."

"Who."

"I. Can't. Tell. You! Leave me alone! Just leave me alone, please?"

The machines started beeping again and the nurse walked in and told Tia and Lucy to get out. "If I see you here again tonight, I'll have security remove you."

Tia said to the nurse, "Try it. If we need to talk to her, we will, and I'll get a warrant to transfer her to a prison hospital."

Tia turned back to Elise. "Everything I said still holds. Think about it tonight, and we'll talk in the morning."

She and Lucy walked out.

Barry approached them. "I listened from the nurses'

station," he said. "Good job, I think you both got more out of her than anyone else could have."

Tia winked. "High praise coming from you, Crawford."

The nurse walked back. "Take the conversation elsewhere, please. Now."

"No one goes in that room except for your nurses and her doctor," Tia said. "An officer will be on the door at all times. If she needs to be moved, the officer goes with her. If she goes for a scan or x-rays, the officer will be outside her door."

"Is she a prisoner or under protection?"

"Both."

"If she's a prisoner, you need to cuff her."

Tia glanced at Barry. "We haven't placed her under arrest yet," she said to the nurse.

"Then I'll consider the officer her protection. But if she's dangerous—"

"Call us if you have any concerns." Tia handed the nurse her card. She excused herself to talk to the officer at the door.

Barry and Lucy walked to the end of the corridor, to the side of the nurse's station where they wouldn't get in anyone's way as well as have some privacy. Barry said, "Do you think she took photos of James Everett as well?"

That was exactly what Lucy had been thinking, though Elise hadn't explicitly said it. "I can get her to talk," Lucy said. She didn't like browbeating the girl. Elise wasn't cooperating, but she was scared and Lucy understood what these girls had to do to survive. Survival often made them hard and prickly, and often the only way to crack them was to be just as hard.

"There's no doubt," Barry said. "But in the meantime, maybe we should take another run at Mona Hill."

"She's not going to give us anything unless we have something on her—something to trade, like her freedom."

"The solicitation charges won't stick, and she knows it," Barry said.

"Any way you can get a warrant to search her apartment?"

"All we have is her sending a prostitute to a john—if that. She said, she said."

"Elise is underage."

"She's over fourteen. There's a different line."

Lucy hated that line. Girls fourteen and under were special victims. Over fourteen and while prostitution was still illegal, the penalties weren't as extensive. There were fewer resources to get the older girls out of the life. One cop had told Lucy that by the time the girls were fourteen, they were lost causes.

And sometimes they're lost at a much earlier age.

Lucy didn't believe that. Most of the girls in prostitution as teenagers had been abused by their families or manipulated by much older boyfriends into a life in the sex trade. Some had made one bad decision and felt they couldn't come back from that. They often felt they didn't deserve to go back to their families, or that their families wouldn't want them back after they knew what they'd done. And some families were like that. But many welcomed their daughters back with open hearts. She didn't know where Elise fell on that spectrum, but it was clear from her street smarts and her attitude that she'd been on her own a long, long time. Was there even anyone for her to go home to?

"What if," Lucy said, "we work Mona to give us the name of the person who vouched for Elise? Give her a pass on everything if she gives that up."

"We have to find something on her first."

"Between us and Tia, we could pull together enough for a search warrant. Specifically to look for the photos Elise claims she took and the drug used to kill Worthington."

"Do you believe her? That she didn't know that she'd killed him?"

Lucy considered the conversation. "Yes and no. She's a habitual liar, so everything she said we need to verify. There was a lot of truth there, but some misdirection. I believe she went in thinking she was going to take compromising pictures. But I think she knew he was dead when she left the room. But based on her reaction—I don't think she knew the drugs would kill him. Someone gave her the syringe. Mona admitted that she sent her out on the Everett job, and while Elise didn't explicitly say Mona sent her to Worthington, I think we can make the case that Mona was involved. With the right judge, we can get a warrant to search Mona's place for drugs, syringes, photographs, and computers."

"Computers?"

"If they were digital photos, she would have downloaded them. So we'll need any camera or recording equipment, phones—maybe we'll get lucky and find out who arranged the meeting with Worthington. Because I'll bet money that he wasn't expecting a prostitute."

"Slow down, Kincaid," Barry said. "Elise didn't say that Mona sent her to Worthington. She said she was here in San Antonio *because* of Worthington, but called Mona for more work. We might be able to tie Mona to James Everett, but we can't tie her to Worthington."

"But it's plausible. Not only that, it's the only thing that makes sense."

"We have no proof. No evidence. The problem with organizations like Mona Hill's is that she knows a lot of secrets about a lot of people, many of those people with a lot to lose. We need to convince the AUSA that we have probable cause for a warrant and not just a fishing expedition. I don't think we're even close. I'll take it to Juan, it's his call."

Tia returned. "Okay, we're set on the guard." She glanced over at the nurse's desk to where a young man stood waiting. "Mr. Rabb?" she said.

He turned, obviously surprised to see the three of them conversing. "Detective. I just want to make sure that the girl I brought in last night was okay."

"She's resting," Tia said. "She'll make a full recovery."

He approached them with a shy smile. "I guess I wouldn't be able to see her?"

"Not now," Tia said. "I'll give her your contact information if she wants to reach out to you."

"You don't have to. She just reminded me of my little sister. I feel better knowing she's okay."

"We'll walk you out," Tia said, leading the way. "Ignore the two grumpy feds." She glanced back at Lucy and Barry with a grin. "They're probably as hungry as I am."

Rabb thanked Tia and they parted ways in the lobby.

Tia said, "He was a good Samaritan. Not everyone would stop for a gunshot victim, I'm sad to say. But I wasn't lying—I'm starved. It's nearly two. Let's go to Mi Tierra. It's not far, and it's my favorite place. Good food and cheap. Too bad we're on duty, because they make a wicked margarita."

Brad Donnelly picked up Ryan Quiroz at FBI headquarters that afternoon.

"What's the story?" Ryan asked as Brad pulled out of the parking lot.

"Body found in Atascosa County. Two gunshot wounds in the leg, one in the back of the head. Blood type AB positive—the same as the shooter who got away at our crime scene."

"ID?"

"No, but the M.E. said there were gang tats, and the

estimated time-of-death fits." Brad tossed Ryan a file. "Ballistics from the crime scene."

Ryan opened the file. "They confirmed the guns were from the stolen shipment based on the ammo?"

"Yep. The shipment of guns that Vasco Trejo sold to Tobias. At least, that's what we think was going on based on a partial conversation."

"Something you overheard when they captured you?"

Brad hesitated, then nodded. Lucy had overheard the conversation, but he couldn't say that. "Basically, Tobias was furious that Trejo had lost part of the gun shipment to Kane Rogan's mercenaries. He wanted his money back."

"How many guns are still out there?"

"A lot. Rogan was only able to retrieve two trucks but suspected that twice as many disappeared with Tobias or his people."

"And some of the guns that Trejo controlled—ostensibly to sell to Tobias—killed Tobias's people."

"If Sanchez's team joined Tobias."

Ryan said, "Why would Tobias sell guns to one of his rivals? And since Trejo is dead and Rogan thinks Tobias had the guns, why would he kill his own gang?"

"Maybe he sold them to a rival group, who then turned on Tobias."

"But there's been no retaliation. This case is giving me a headache."

"It's too fucking quiet. It's making me itchy." Brad paused, then added, "ATF is taking over as primary. They say since it's an international gun incident, it's theirs."

"That really sucks. A million dollars in drugs and they walk in? None of the guns were found on scene."

"They're wrong, and it's going to get in the way. This isn't about guns, this is about the cartels and their growing foothold in southern Texas. It's a power play, pure and simple. I think they took it because the DOJ doesn't trust us after Nicole. We've had bureaucrats up our ass for two months."

"Did you talk to Rollins?"

Brad's hands clutched the steering wheel until his knuckles turned white. "Sam told me she was a cold bitch, but she goes beyond cold. She wants witness protection. I just can't figure out if she really has valuable intel, or if she's just playing us."

"What did she say?"

"If the remainder of the Trejo/Sanchez gang was taken out, Tobias allowed it or did it himself."

"Do you believe her?"

"I don't know."

"Why would Tobias want to take out his own gang? And leave the drugs?"

"Distrust, skimming, loyalty issues."

"They were Sanchez's people. We know next to nothing about Tobias. We don't know where he calls home base and have only a vague description. And," Ryan continued, "if we think that Tobias has been neutered, we focus our attention on the shooters—not Tobias himself."

Brad's knee began to tighten, and he shifted in the driver's seat. He had a doctor's appointment at the end of the day; he'd moved it up from Friday. He needed to be officially cleared for duty. The only reason Sam had let him work this case was because it was mostly a passive investigation at this point, he was officially "consulting" with the SAPD, and Ryan was assisting in the field.

He really despised being babied.

Brad said, "I really hate that the director and DOJ are considering Nicole's request for witness protection, but Sam made a plea that she didn't deserve to breathe free air. Nicole mentioned it to me again. She said our house isn't clean."

"Did you tell your boss?"

"I tried, but Sam cut me off. She said we can't believe anything she says. That she'll say and do anything to get out of prison."

"What do you think?"

"I think Nicole knows more than she's said, but not as much as she claims."

"She could have been goading you. If you think you can't trust your team, you're all at risk."

And that bothered Brad on a deep, indescribable level.

His phone rang. It was Ash from the SAPD investigative unit. Brad had left three messages for him. "Donnelly," he said. "It's about time you got back to me."

"Don't start with me. The ATF has been having me rerun every fucking test, including ballistics, then they took all the bullets we extracted. Then, I had to walk them through the entire scene at two this afternoon. Do you know how fucking hot it was at two? Hotter than hell. And they kept me for *two hours* when I have a shitload of work piled."

"You need a beer."

"Damn straight."

"Did ATF take the heroin?"

"No."

"Have you tested it? Ryan and I are here, and we can't figure out why the drugs were left behind."

"It's still in evidence. We did the field test on one sample, confirmed for heroin, but I need to sample each brick, determine the purity, input the data, run it through the system to see where it came from—you know the drill."

"Let me know when you have the report. I promise— I'm not nagging you. We have a line on the injured shooter."

"Is he talking?"

"He's dead. But we still may get something out of him yet."

Brad hung up and turned off the highway.

The Atascosa County morgue was housed in the basement of the lone county hospital. If the county had a complex homicide, they'd send the body to Bexar County and
their state-of-the-art facilities. Brad might still ask them
to do so once he and Ryan examined the evidence.

The coroner, Frank Hernandez, doubled as a staff
doctor. He was a small, wiry older man with sharp eyes
behind thick glasses.

"Thought this might be one of yours," Dr. Hernandez
said after Brad showed his DEA identification. "This
smacks of drugs and gangs."

"Thank you for contacting our office so quickly," Brad
said. "The body was found this morning?"

"At dawn, a trucker pulled off the highway to take a
leak. Found the victim in the ravine. Two days later, there'd
have been nothing left but bones. As it was, the only reason the trucker saw anything was because a couple coyotes were chomping down on the corpse. Hope you haven't
eaten, 'cause it ain't pretty. I'm not planning to do the autopsy 'til morning—I just came off a twenty-four-hour
shift, stayed late to meet you boys."

"We appreciate it," Ryan said.

"But you examined the body?" Brad asked.

"Course I did." He pulled open one of the drawers and
unzipped the body bag. The victim hadn't been cleaned,
prepped, or undressed. "I need an assistant to help prepare
the body and preserve the evidence, 'cause this is a homicide. Know you need everything you can get."

The victim was a Hispanic male approximately twenty
years of age. His face was beaten and swollen. The doctor
pulled on gloves and motioned toward the box for Brad and
Ryan to do the same. Then he turned the victim's head.
"First, the swelling is from decomp, though you can probably see he'd been beaten pretty bad."

Hernandez gestured to the dried blood on the back of the head, then he pulled at the matted hair to reveal a hole.

"Gunshot. The bullet's still in there—I did a full body x-ray when he came in. Looks fragmented, though. Don't know if you'll be able to match it with anything."

"Caliber?"

He shrugged. "Small caliber—probably a nine millimeter, maybe a thirty-eight. The left leg had, I believe, two gunshot wounds."

"You can't tell?"

"There's one bullet still inside, a higher caliber round, that's lodged in his bone. The other is gone—and with the coyote bite marks, it's hard to tell, but I think there was a second lower on the leg. Could have been a clean shot, through and through, or the coyotes swallowed it. I should know after the autopsy." He looked up from the mangled leg. "Unless you want me to send the body up to Bexar."

"We don't want to step on your toes, doctor."

He waved them off. "No interagency bull crap from me, boys. Our sheriff thought you might want everything, already signed the paperwork so as I don't interrupt his poker night."

"Did you search his body? Any ID?"

"Pulled out a wallet. No ID inside, but there are cards and photos, you might be able to find out who it is. We pulled prints from his fingers, they're with the sheriff's department. Probably be scanned tonight."

"Anything else?" Brad asked. "Identifying marks? You mentioned tattoos over the phone."

"Got a couple of tats. I photographed the visible ones, but like I said, we haven't stripped and cleaned the body." He zipped up the bag and pushed the drawer back in. "I'll call Bexar and tell them to expect the body tonight."

"Thank you."

The doctor walked over to his desk and opened the bottom drawer. He took out a sealed plastic bag and handed it to Brad. "That's everything that was in the victim's pockets," he said. He handed a folder to Ryan. "Those are copies of the x-rays of the bullets, and the tats on his arms."

Brad signed for the evidence, then unsealed the bag and examined the wallet.

Photos of the dead kid with what Brad assumed was his family—multigenerational, like many of the Hispanic families in the area. Grandparents, parents, siblings. This kid wasn't that old. Twenty, tops. Brad hated that so many young men turned to gangs. Many blamed it on poverty, and that certainly had something to do with it—the allure of drug money was hard to resist. If Nicole Rollins, an educated, middle-class federal agent was attracted to it, why did he expect a kid with nothing and a family to support would turn his back?

But it was more than simple poverty that turned these kids into drug runners. The thrill. The violence. The gang that became their family. Threats. The idea that they would somehow be bigger, more powerful. It was depressing, and Brad had long since put aside trying to reason it out.

Ryan tapped on the photo of a tat from the victim's right forearm. "Know what that is?"

The skull, crossbones, and rosary were clear and well done. Not a cheap tat.

"The San Antonio Saints," Brad said. "Well, shit."

The SAS were run by a thug named Reynardo Reynoso, a wily little prick who'd been in and out of prison. Reynoso had been on Brad's target list during Operation Heatwave two months ago. They'd never found him to haul his ass back to prison—he was wanted on multiple charges including drug distribution, attempted murder, and grand theft auto. Word on the street was that Reynoso now answered to Marquez, a rising star in the drug underworld—bigger now with Sanchez out of the picture.

"Marquez's pet gang took out Sanchez's people," Brad said.

"Reynoso wouldn't act on his own?" Ryan asked.

"Not from what I've heard, but I should talk to Jerry with SAPD. He knows more about the local gangs." Brad stared at the photo, but wasn't seeing anything as he tried to put the puzzle pieces together. "It doesn't make sense, unless Marquez thought Tobias was rebuilding and wanted to wipe him out for good. Power grab, not retaliation like Rogan thought."

"Maybe Rogan was wrong," Ryan said. "No one is right all the time."

But in the short time Brad had known Kane, he'd never been wrong. What was he missing?

CHAPTER TWENTY-FIVE

Lucy always felt at home in a crime lab, just like she felt comfortable in the morgue. There was an organization and science to everything; evidence turned clinical. There were no victims in the crime lab, only pieces of a puzzle to put together.

There'd been a time when Lucy thought she'd be better working behind the anonymity of the forensic sciences, where she didn't have to face the victim or the criminal. Her fourteen months interning for the Medical Examiner in D.C. had been both challenging and satisfying; she could have seen herself working there for the rest of her life. It wouldn't have been difficult, with her college degree and a master's in criminal psychology, to continue in school, get a doctorate or a third degree in biology, and become a senior pathologist, or even go to medical school and become a medical examiner.

But ultimately, she continued down the law enforcement career path. Her unique skill set enabled her to assess crime scenes with the eye of an experienced cop instead of the rookie she was, and her background in psychology added another layer to her abilities. Crime scene investigators collected and analyzed evidence, but they didn't extrapolate or assign the human factor. They took facts and presented them; it was up to agents like Lucy and detectives like Tia to look at the evidence and add in the human equation.

While she loved her job, she sometimes missed the lab environment, so when Tia asked if she and Barry could stop by the lab after their late lunch to look at the evidence from the Elise Hansen shooting, Lucy agreed before Barry could comment.

The evidence was still in the main lab room being processed. They all donned gloves, gowns, and booties, then approached the table where a tech named Stuart was cataloging each item. Everything had been sealed and labeled in either paper bags—if there was biological material like blood—or plastic bags.

Elise's clothes were hanging in a special drying chamber in the corner both to dry the blood and preserve the evidence.

Stu said, "The cell phone is a burn phone. We pulled down the data from the SIM card." He handed a printout to Tia. Lucy looked over her shoulder. There wasn't a lot there.

"Can you shoot a copy of this to my computer and the FBI?"

"Already done," Stu said. "Your second canvass turned up a backpack in a ditch near the shooting site. Inside was a wallet, multiple IDs, makeup, a change of clothes, condoms, a flask of vodka." He gestured to a series of plastic bags that had been sealed and labeled. "She had over five thousand dollars in cash on her. We also found an airplane ticket stub in the wallet."

Lucy picked up that envelope. Barry took a picture on his phone of the information.

"She flew in to San Antonio from Dallas on May thirteenth. Under the name Elise Hamilton."

"Dallas is a major hub," Tia said. "She could have transferred from another flight."

"But now that we have a name and date," Barry said, "we can contact TSA and see where she originated."

"Did she have an ID in this name?" Lucy asked.

Stu nodded. "She had several IDs. I made copies. A Nevada ID under Elise Hansen, age eighteen; a Nevada driver's license under Elise Hamilton, age twenty-one; an ID from Virginia under Elise Harrison, age eighteen; another ID under Elise Hansen but from Texas, age eighteen."

"Fake?" Tia asked.

"All authentic—but there are people who specialize in creating identities. But four authentic identifications? That's odd—at least to me."

"Which ID was issued first?"

"Elise Hansen in Nevada is a state ID that's three years old. The newest is Elise Hansen in Texas—it was issued three weeks ago, the day after the airline stub."

"She got the card in three weeks?" Tia asked. "That fast?"

"One day—the day after she arrived," Stu corrected. "I don't know how she did it or where she bought it. It has all the marks of being a God-honest Texas ID card, but the address is fake—they couldn't have mailed it there."

"Meaning, someone has the ability to create authentic but fake identifications," Brad said.

"Bingo," Stu said. "We're going to run tests on it, but I ran the number—that is real. She's in the system, under that address, posted on May fourteenth."

"Then wouldn't there be a record of who created the ID?" Tia asked.

"Yes and no. If it was created at a DMV, we can trace which one, and we can investigate further. There was a big scandal a few years back where one of the DMVs had a ring of employees who created false identification for illegal immigrants. The state clamped down on them, but that doesn't mean that others couldn't slip through. It's a lucrative business. But it could still be a perfect forgery, especially if they use the same equipment and raw material."

"She's from Nevada," Lucy said.

"Because that's the oldest ID?"

"That, and because she had a second ID with her being over twenty-one. Important if you're hooking in bars or clubs. Nevada also has legalized prostitution," Lucy said. "She could have started there."

"But she's underage," Barry said. "Legalized means regulated."

"And she had false identification," Lucy repeated. "You don't think she could be eighteen, do you, Tia?"

"Slim to no chance. I talked to the doctor—based on x-rays, he put her age at sixteen, and he says that's within six months."

Lucy tapped the Elise Hansen ID card. "I don't know if that's her real name, but I'll bet that's her birthday, plus two years. All these cards have her birthday on April fourteenth." She also thought it was her real name because it was the first card issued.

Tia said, "I'll talk to my pal at NCMEC and run with that. We can focus on Nevada and the West. It gives us a place to start. Plus, I'll narrow the missing-persons search to Nevada and surrounding states."

"She lied to us," Lucy said.

Barry and Tia turned to her.

Lucy continued. "She said she'd been here a week before meeting with Worthington. But she came in *three* weeks earlier."

"Maybe," Tia said.

"Maybe?"

"It could be she didn't specifically lie, she was just being vague. These girls don't like details. They don't want to get pinned down on anything, so if they keep it vague, they can simply say we misunderstood, or they were being general."

Lucy wasn't certain that was the case here, but considering that Elise had been shot and had just gone through surgery—with the requisite pain-killers—maybe she should give her the benefit of the doubt.

"What's this?" Barry held up a plastic envelope with a sheet of stationery. On the paper was an address, date, and time. "This street is near where she was shot."

Stu said, "That's not the girl's handwriting. We found a black book in her bag. We're making a copy because there may be information in there for your investigation—dates and times and clients. Assuming the black book is hers—and I'm pretty certain it is—I can definitely say she didn't write down this address."

"So whoever gave her this note set her up," Barry said.

"Is it Mona Hill's handwriting?" Lucy asked Tia.

"I don't know. But I have a statement she wrote at the office on an unrelated matter. I'll check."

Stu added, "It's expensive stationery—watermarked as well. We have a database of paper samples, and we're running through it now. I should know at least what brand by the end of the day. If it's as expensive as I think it is, there'll be very few places that sell it. There's also an interesting threading in the paper, which tells me that it's a special order of some sort."

"Good job, Stu," Tia said. "Anything else we need to know before you finish up your report?"

"I'm waiting for the ballistics report, but we should have that by the end of the day as well. I did a fingerprint comparison, and her prints match the prints found at the Worthington crime scene. We're running her prints wide now, but so far, nothing else in the criminal database."

Barry glanced at his phone and excused himself. He left the room to take the call.

"There's something missing," Lucy said.

"No, this is everything," Stu said, looking at the log.

"Keys. There's no key. No hotel key card, apartment key, car key. Nothing. We don't know where she was staying. This isn't all her stuff—she was seen in different clothes Friday night, and those clothes aren't here or in the dryer."

"Think she was staying with Mona?" Tia asked.

"Or with one of her girls. Gives us another cause for the warrant." But Barry was right—it was going to be hard to convince the AUSA that they needed a warrant when their probable cause was so thin.

Barry opened the door. "Kincaid, we have to go. Now."

He looked worried, and Barry had the straightest face of any of the agents Lucy had worked with. Something was wrong.

She thanked Tia and Stu, then followed Barry out of the building. "What happened?" Lucy asked.

"Shit if I know, but we've been summoned to headquarters immediately for a meeting with Naygrew and Juan. Zach's the one who called, he didn't know what it was about. Said it was urgent and to drop everything."

Lucy's phone vibrated. It was a message from Sean. She immediately showed the text to Barry.

The FBI planted the bug in Worthington's office.

CHAPTER TWENTY-SIX

As soon as they stepped into the headquarters they were directed to go immediately to SAC Ritz Naygrew's office. If the meeting was connected to the bug that Sean had found—and the FBI techs had identified it as one of their own—then she wasn't worried. Juan had approved the operation and would cover for them if they inadvertently had stepped on another agent's case.

But when she walked through Naygrew's door and saw one of the men who had been at Adeline's house that morning, the one she thought she'd seen before, she knew that this was something else entirely.

"Agents Crawford, Kincaid, thank you for coming in so quickly," SAC Naygrew said. "Please sit."

There were two chairs on the left side of Naygrew's large desk. Lucy took the one farthest from Adeline's staffer, which afforded her the best angle to watch him. Barry sat next to her. Juan was already seated directly across from Naygrew, like a mediator between the two sides.

Naygrew waited until Lucy and Barry had both sat before he started. "Introductions—my agents, Barry Crawford and Lucy Kincaid, who have been working on the murder of HWI CEO Harper Worthington. Crawford, Kincaid, meet SSA Logan Dunbar out of our Washington, D.C., office. I learned late this morning that two separate investigations, out of two different offices, have collided. I've asked Agent Dunbar to come in to brief you, and then hopefully we'll come out of this meeting with a mutually agreeable game plan."

Dunbar. D.C. office. That's why she recognized him. They'd never met, and she didn't recognize his name, but she must have seen him during the few months she'd worked out of the D.C. regional office before she left for Quantico last year.

Lucy began to piece together what was happening. Dunbar worked out of the D.C. office, which often took the lead on cases of political corruption in Congress. He'd been at Adeline's house; he must be investigating Adeline Worthington for political corruption.

"You're undercover," Lucy said.

"I was afraid you'd blown my cover, Kincaid. You don't lie well."

"Excuse me?" Why was he so hostile?

"When you saw me at Adeline's house, you gave me a look and I thought for certain you were going to out me."

She straightened her spine. "If I had recognized you, I would have figured it out immediately. I'm pretty good on my feet."

"Let me make one thing clear: Adeline Worthington did not kill her husband."

Barry said, "We haven't said that she did. We simply asked for permission to pursue a line of questioning with her because there are inconsistencies in her initial statement, as well as our follow-up this morning."

"The night Worthington died, Adeline went to a charity event, then spent hours in a meeting with her campaign team, which included me. I drove her back to her house at one thirty in the morning."

"We don't believe that she personally killed her husband, but she may have a motive to have had him killed," Lucy said.

Dunbar shook his head. "We have access to all her phone records and emails. I have staff in D.C. rechecking everything we've gathered, and nothing suggests that she hired a hit man. So, respectfully, I'm asking you to back off. I am very close to taking this woman down on political corruption and bribery, and your investigation is hampering mine. She's naturally paranoid; your constant questioning is making her more so."

"If our investigation is having an impact," Barry said, "that should tell you she might have something more to hide."

"I've been working on this case for more than a year. It didn't start last weekend," Dunbar snapped. "It's not just me—I have several UCs working in different areas, and I can't have you jeopardizing them, either."

"A man was murdered," Lucy said. "Murder trumps bribery."

Dunbar glared at her. "If it was anyone but you pushing this, I wouldn't even be here."

"Excuse me?"

"Don't pretend you don't know."

Lucy had no idea what he was talking about.

Juan cleared his throat. "This isn't productive. Agent Dunbar, please explain to my team what you told Ritz and me earlier."

Logan Dunbar took a breath, then nodded. Formally, he said, "Sixteen months ago, an informant in the Congressional Interior Committee alerted my office about suspicious activity involving a staff member and a potentially illegal land transaction. A large parcel of land in southern Texas was purchased by the government for three times the market rate because of a supposed environmental protection consideration. Upon further review, the report had been doctored, so we looked deeper and learned that the seller of the land then bought another parcel from Adeline Reyes-Worthington at an inflated price. Under federal campaign law, individuals are strictly limited in political contributions that they can give to a candidate, but candidates can spend their own money with no limit."

Dunbar leaned forward in his chair. "It took us months, but we found several other similar transactions. For a while we thought that her husband was involved because he has the technical skill to bury these types of financial crimes, but when we began our undercover operation, it became clear that the two of them keep their finances almost completely separate. Still, I wasn't positive—he could have been helping her."

"Which is why you bugged his office," Lucy said.

"Your boyfriend tampered with a legal federal wiretap."

How did Dunbar know that Sean was her boyfriend? Or that he was even involved?

"You listened to our call," Lucy said, putting it together. Dunbar had the wiretap, it made sense that he would get a transcript or tape of all calls.

Juan interjected, "As I explained to you, Agent Dunbar, Mr. Rogan was hired by HWI and since we had no knowledge of your investigation, we agreed to track and remove the bug to determine if that had something to do with Mr. Worthington's murder."

"But you don't even know that he was murdered!" Dunbar said.

"He was," Barry said. "The ME held the report so we could pursue a line of inquiry, but now that we've informed

Mrs. Worthington, it'll be released tomorrow. He was poisoned with curare."

"That's ridiculous."

"You're welcome to contact the Medical Examiner yourself," Barry said coolly.

"I mean, if Adeline killed her husband, don't you think that there are a dozen easier ways to kill him than using an exotic drug?"

"Are you aware that the subject of your investigation has hired a private security detail at her house? A half dozen armed men?"

Dunbar hesitated. "I saw an increase in security. But that doesn't necessarily mean anything. If she had been threatened, I would have known about it. She would have contacted Capitol Police, or told her staff."

"She's not acting innocent."

"Because she's not innocent! She's a corrupt public official, not a killer. We're developing an iron-clad case against her. She probably thinks you'll uncover something about her illegal campaign activity while investigating her husband's murder."

Dunbar made a good point, Lucy thought, but maybe Adeline's white collar crimes led to her husband's murder, even if she didn't order a hit.

"If you have all this evidence, why haven't you indicted her?" Barry asked.

"At first, it was conjecture, and we didn't have enough to make what we had stick. We needed to get inside, get her to incriminate herself. Once I got in, six months ago, I started getting close to everyone on her campaign and congressional staff. Her campaign manager, Rob Garza, is neck-deep in everything—he's a piece of work. Not only does Adeline help her friends get rich at taxpayer expense through these inflated land deals, but she punishes her enemies by having the committee she controls seize private land at pennies on the dollar, or declare a parcel environmentally sensitive, which can cost the landowner hundreds of thousands of dollars in legal fees and fines. Often, they'll sell the land on the cheap to one of Adeline's friends and then—surprise!—the environmental protections are lifted."

"That's an elaborate corruption scheme," Naygrew said. "She would need multiple people to pull it off, and conspiracies are hard to maintain the more people involved."

"Yes, sir," Dunbar concurred. "She needs people in different agencies to pull this off, and it's going to be her downfall. But to her credit, no one—except maybe Garza—knows anyone else who's involved, or the extent of the scheme. I have a UC in the EPA and am *this close* to flipping someone else to turn state's evidence. She's up to something bigger than the land deals, but *your* investigation has made her nervous. I didn't want to come here because I feared she'd have me followed. Fortunately, I'm good at being discreet."

Dunbar looked from Lucy to Barry. "What I want you to do is tell the congresswoman that you're pursuing another line of investigation and stop talking to her. Just go away."

Lucy stared at him. She didn't know where to start. But Barry spoke first. "Juan? This is really your call."

Lucy cringed. She didn't want to give up this case, but Barry was right. Neither she nor Barry had any real authority in this room.

Juan said, "Barry, tell us what you know about Harper Worthington's murder."

"An underage prostitute by the name of Elise Hansen was in the room with Worthington when he died," Barry said. "We know he was killed with curare, a paralyzing agent that essentially suffocates the victim. The ME has determined that it was injected into Worthington's system and he died almost immediately. While the room was set up to make it look as if he died while having sex, the ME and crime scene techs have determined that it was staged. He was undressed after he died."

"So clearly," Dunbar said, "the hooker killed him."

"Why?" Lucy said.

"Maybe she's a psychopath," Dunbar said. "Isn't that your specialty, Kincaid?"

She bristled. It was his tone, which told her he didn't like her. And she didn't even know him! "Or she was hired by Adeline to kill Worthington," she snapped. "Because the one thing we don't know is why Worthington went out of his way to be in that motel at that time."

"Because he's a pervert?" Dunbar suggested with a snide tone.

"We believe he had a meeting with someone with the initials G.A.," Barry said. "We've identified him as 'Gary,' no last name, a white male between the ages of fifty and sixty who was in a serious accident that left him scarred and with a limp. We're trying to track him down now. But our witness didn't see anyone matching that description in or around the motel."

"It could be," Lucy said to Barry, "that he only thought he was meeting with Gary."

"And he was surprised by the girl?" Barry nodded. "Could be, but wouldn't Worthington be suspicious?"

"Not if Gary and Harper did everything via email."

"But there was a phone call—we have the phone records before Worthington made the flight arrangements."

"Maybe Gary set him up."

Dunbar watched the conversation between Barry and Lucy. "And I've *said* Adeline has done nothing to make me think she had anything to do with her husband's death. She was surprised when she found out she'd been cut out of the will—and that's the only motive you could possibly have."

"Or she's a good actress," Barry said.

"Elise was shot by whoever hired her to set up Worthington," Lucy said. "She claimed that she thought she was giving Worthington a knockout drug so that she could take explicit photos of him having sex with a prostitute, which she assumed were to blackmail him."

"This is getting wilder and wilder," Dunbar said, as if he didn't believe their story. Lucy was already irritated with his attitude, but he was getting worse. As if his investigation was worthy and theirs wasn't.

"On the contrary," Barry said, backing Lucy up, "in the course of our investigation, we've learned several things that we believe are connected to Worthington's death. For example, four weeks ago—around the time you planted the bug in Worthington's phone—he stopped using his desk phone and his computer. He used another office. He had a tablet that no one knew about, and on it were spreadsheets and notes that appear to be related to land transactions."

"You need to turn that over to me now," Dunbar said.

Naygrew spoke up. "Juan will see to it that you get a copy of all our documents. Go on, Agent Crawford."

"According to multiple sources, Worthington began to act preoccupied four weeks ago—about the time he returned early from a four-day trip to Washington with his wife."

"What if," Lucy said, "Harper realized what his wife was doing? He's an accountant, one of the best in the business from what we've learned. Maybe she said something, or he saw a financial statement that made him think his wife was doing something illegal? And the fact that he was obsessed with the BLM audit suggests that he *did* know something, but maybe couldn't prove it."

"If he accidentally tipped his hand, that would have given her motive," Barry concurred.

"That still doesn't explain why he traveled out of his way to a seedy motel for a meeting," Lucy said.

"Maybe Gary was his informant," Barry said. "There were three meetings that we know of, all in equally seedy places."

"And Adeline found out about the meeting and sent a prostitute to kill him?" Lucy shook her head. "There's something more to it than that. And Gary is a real person. He has to factor in somehow."

"Juan," Barry said, "we're in the middle of our investigation. We have Elise Hansen under guard at the hospital. SAPD Detective Tia Mancini is lead, and she's a good cop who knows about the sex trade. We have extensive evidence that we're in the middle of analyzing, and several people we need to interview or re-interview. Hansen admitted that she took pictures of herself with Worthington, as well as implied she might have taken photos of another client, a developer named James Everett. We want to re-interview him to see if he's being blackmailed. That could point us to Worthington's killer."

Dunbar reacted to the name Everett, but didn't say anything.

Was Lucy the only one who saw it? Barry was about to continue, but Lucy said, "Dunbar, what do you know about James Everett?"

"It's not relevant."

"We're sharing everything we know, it would help if you did the same."

Dunbar snorted and looked away.

Naygrew looked pointedly at Lucy, then at Dunbar.

"Agent Dunbar, has the name James Everett come up in your investigation into Adeline Worthington?"

It was clear he didn't want to answer, but because this

was the SAC asking, he did. "He is a person of interest in
several of the illegal land deals."

"So he was working with Congresswoman Worthington?"

"Everett and Adeline were partners before she married
Worthington. She left the partnership before she ran for
public office, but Everett handled many of these suspicious
transactions. However, they appear to have had a falling
out recently—over the last couple of months—and he endorsed her opponent."

"Do you know why?" Naygrew pushed.

"No, sir."

But he wasn't looking directly at Naygrew. Lucy's instincts twitched. "He's one of your informants, isn't he?"

Dunbar reddened. "I'm not at liberty to discuss any of
our confidential informants."

Which meant yes. Everett was an informant and he
didn't want his reputation to be tarnished when Adeline
went down for bribery and political corruption.

"Why did you bug Worthington's phone only four
weeks ago?" Lucy asked. "Especially since you've been
here for six months. That was right when he came back
from D.C., right about the time he started acting out of
character . . . Did Worthington talk to someone on your
team?"

"I can't—"

Naygrew leaned forward. "Logan, I understand you've
put a lot of time and effort into this investigation, but my
team is investigating the homicide of a federal contractor
who had access to confidential financial information that
involved national security. It helps us to know what he was
doing during his last weeks of life."

"Yes," Dunbar said shortly. He glanced at Lucy, anger
etched in his face, then turned away. "Mr. Worthington
came into the D.C. office on May seventh and spoke to my

boss. He came with information that we already knew, but we didn't know his motive, and we had far more information about his wife's activities than he did. We determined that we could not bring him into the investigation because of spousal privilege—we didn't want to give Adeline any leverage against us when we bring down the hammer. So we put him off. Told him we'd look into it."

"Then you tapped his phone," Barry said.

"So we could keep tabs on him. It was done legally." He glanced at his watch. "I really need to get back to the campaign. I've already been gone nearly two hours."

Juan said, "Barry, Lucy, I think you're on to something with Worthington. But there is no evidence that the congresswoman was involved in his murder. And honestly, there would be easier ways to kill him than to set up a scene that is potentially embarrassing to her and her re-election. However, Harper Worthington could have found something in one of his audits that got him killed, and the manner of his death was simply to embarrass him or divert attention. And it wasn't very professional—DNA and the other evidence at the scene all led you to the prostitute. You need to work her, find out who hired her, and then we'll see where that goes. You have my permission to continue pursuing the investigation wherever it may lead."

"Juan, with all due respect—" Dunbar began.

Juan put his hand up. "But do not approach Adeline Worthington or anyone on her staff without consulting with me first. Logan and his team have a good case against her, and I don't want to risk losing that conviction on the thin chance she may have been involved with her husband's murder. Logan and I will work out a way to communicate, should we uncover evidence that directly links the congresswoman to murder."

"Thank you, Juan," Dunbar said.

Ritz smiled. "I knew if I put you all in the room together, you'd work out a reasonable agreement. Logan, when are you expecting to wrap up your investigation?"

"Sir, the final decision will be with the AUSA and Assistant Director Rick Stockton. Director Stockton is the one who approved this op. Because it's an election year, we don't want to be perceived as being political by exposing her without an absolute clear, irrefutable case; at the same time, Stockton doesn't want anything that could be perceived as an October Surprise, so we're hoping to wrap everything up by the end of June and issue the indictments." He hesitated, then turned to Lucy and Barry. "An olive branch—if I uncover anything that suggests Adeline was involved in her husband's death, I'll let Juan know. Likewise, if you learn anything about Adeline or her staff that might help in my investigation?"

"Of course," Barry said. "Juan will know everything we know."

"Good," Ritz said. "I'll call Stockton with a report of this meeting and our agreement. Thank you for coming down, Logan. If you need any help from my office, call me directly."

"Thank you, sir."

Barry followed Lucy to her cubicle after the meeting. "What did Logan mean about you pushing this investigation?"

"I don't know," Lucy said. But she had her suspicions.

Barry pulled a chair over from Kenzie's empty desk and sat. "Lucy, this is the first time we've worked as partners since you've been here. I have my way of doing things, you have yours. So far, your instincts have been sharp. But I watched your expression in that room, and you were holding something back. What?"

"I'm not keeping anything relevant from you," she said.

"What don't you think is relevant?"

"Logan Dunbar is from D.C. I worked out of the D.C. office for a couple of months as an analyst before I started at Quantico. I butted heads with Dunbar's boss on a case I worked."

"That's not it."

"Then I don't know what." But she did. Only, she didn't want to share with Barry. Or anyone.

"When he mentioned Assistant Director Rick Stockton, you reacted."

"I did?"

"Don't play poker with me." He smiled. It was the first time since they'd started working this case together that Barry seemed to be relaxed around her. As if they were actual partners, not just colleagues.

She caught herself biting her bottom lip, a nervous habit she'd thought she'd lost. "I don't like to name drop."

"You didn't."

She hesitated, because she really didn't want to make it seem like she'd enjoyed any favoritism. It had been difficult enough when she'd learned that her mentor, Dr. Hans Vigo, had pulled strings to get her into Quantico after her application had been denied. But if Barry called the right people, he could learn about her friendship with Rick and she didn't want him to think that she was keeping anything from him. And trust was a two-way street.

"It's really not anything," she said, "but I worked on some projects for Rick Stockton while I was at Quantico. There's a family connection."

"You're related to Stockton?"

"No—nothing like that. Rick is good friends with my brother and sister-in-law." That was the simplest explanation, and completely true. She didn't need to go into Rick's connection to RCK or the Rogan family or talk about what specifically she'd worked on.

"Which brother?"

What did Barry know about her family? She said, "Dillon, mostly. He's a forensic psychiatrist. And Jack, because of Jack's work with RCK." As she said it she realized she was connected to Rick on many levels. He'd also been in the Marines with Kane—at least Lucy thought he had.

"Aren't your brothers both married to FBI agents?"

"Yes." She frowned. "How do you know that?"

"I just heard it somewhere," he said vaguely. Great, Lucy thought, her personal life was a discussion point in the office. "So you've known Stockton for a while."

"A couple of years. Logan thinks it's a bigger deal than it is. I haven't even talked to Rick since I graduated."

"Most of us aren't on a first-name basis with an assistant director of the FBI."

Then Lucy was definitely not going to tell him she was on a first-name basis with *two* of the ADs.

"This is why I don't talk about this stuff," Lucy said. "Yes, I have connections. I have family in the FBI. My brother is a civilian consultant to the FBI. But I just want to do my job."

Barry leaned back. "I understand."

She hoped he did.

"Don't worry about Logan Dunbar," Barry said. "He has his case, we have ours."

"So, where do we go from here?"

"We need to get Elise Hansen to tell us everything she knows. As soon as the doctor clears her for release, we arrest her. It's time to play hardball."

CHAPTER TWENTY-SEVEN

Lucy arrived home before Sean. She showered, then changed into her cut-off sweatpants and one of Sean's T-shirts. She'd never told Sean why she liked to wear his T-shirts, because she thought it would sound silly, but they smelled like him and made her feel safe and loved, even when he was working.

Sean said he'd be home by eight, and it was quarter to that now. She was exhausted, the late night coming back to haunt her. She'd gotten her second wind that afternoon after lunch, but now if she sat down anywhere, she'd fall asleep. Instead, she walked through the house and watered their plants, then stood in the kitchen thinking about what to eat. Nothing sounded appetizing, and she didn't feel hungry. She padded down the hall to the living room and curled into the corner of the sofa. She flipped through her satchel where she kept the files from the case, and pulled out the packet of notes that Harper Worthington had left on his tablet. She wished she knew what the dates meant. So far, no one in the lab had any idea what they were, but they were running a multitude of programs against local and national events to see if anything popped.

Her eyes were drooping, but then her phone beeped. She

thought it was a message from Sean. Instead, it was a personal email from her sister Carina, with a photo attached—an ultrasound of her baby at thirty-eight weeks.

> *The kid will be here any day the doctor says. I'm ready. I feel like I'm carrying a giant pumpkin in my stomach. I have to pee every hour, on the hour, day and night. I hope you can visit when the baby comes. Nick totally rejected Nick, Jr. He suggested John Patrick, after his father and Dad. I think I'll give in to Nick on the boy's name. But we both agree on Rosemary for a girl. Rosie is just a joyful name. Rosemary Thomas. Like it? Connor and Julia are giving us a bad time for wanting to be surprised about the gender. But there're not enough true surprises in the world anymore, and this is one of them.*
>
> *Call me sometime. I'm going stir-crazy. I can live vicariously through you!*

Lucy smiled. Carina was a workaholic, but being pregnant had certainly changed her. She'd been trying to conceive for two years, and suffered three miscarriages. She hadn't thought she'd be able to carry a baby to term, and this little guy—or gal—was a miracle. Lucy was happy for her. Carina planned on going back to work eventually, but since her husband's PI business with Connor, their brother, was finally in the black, Lucy wondered if she would.

Lucy hoped she could get away after the baby was born, even for a weekend, but she was also apprehensive. When she'd been a teenager, the idea of falling in love, getting married, and having a family was a distant dream—far in the future, but pretty much guaranteed. She'd never given it much thought.

Until she was eighteen.

Her rape and the brutality she'd endured for nearly two days resulted in extensive damage, and her uterus had been removed. The surgery had saved her life, but she'd never have children. She couldn't even think about what ifs or maybe whens, because she had no choice. It had been stolen from her, and for a long time she'd been depressed. She hated visiting her counselor after the rape—she didn't want to talk about it, she didn't want to discuss her feelings or her anger or her fear. But the one thing the counselor said that stuck with her was that losing children she hadn't known she'd wanted left her in a state of perpetual mourning.

It had gotten better over time. Sean had been a rock. He said when they were ready to have a family, they'd adopt. She liked that idea, because there were so many kids who needed a stable home. But that was far down the road. She was twenty-six, Sean thirty. They had time. They weren't even married.

Yet . . . spending a week with Sean's brother Duke, his wife, Nora, and their newborn, Molly, had brought back all those feelings of loss, and a deep sense of mourning for something intangible. Lucy couldn't articulate it, and she didn't want to talk about it with Sean. He'd do everything to understand her feelings. He'd listen and hold her and tell her he loved her.

But he'd never have a baby with her. Sean would make a wonderful father, and she feared by loving her, he was missing an amazing opportunity. That she was denying him a child of his own. Watching Sean with Molly reminded her that she wasn't whole, she'd never have a child that was half her, half Sean. Then she'd feel guilty, thinking about all the other women who couldn't have children. Why couldn't she just accept it and get on with her life? Why did this overwhelming sense of loss keep coming back? Why did she feel like she was still broken?

She sighed and closed her eyes. Tears burned behind her lids, but she didn't cry.

She hated feeling sorry for herself.

"Lucy," a voice said. "Lucy, I'm home."

She blinked and stretched. "I guess I fell asleep. What time is it?"

"Nearly ten. I'm sorry I'm so late. I got wrapped up in the files at HWI."

She yawned. "I think I've been asleep for a couple of hours."

"You needed it." He sat next to her and kissed her. Looked her in the eyes as he rubbed her neck. "You still look tired. Did you eat?"

"I had a late lunch."

He frowned. "That's not sufficient. Sit, relax, I'll make you a sandwich."

"I'm not an invalid. I don't want a sandwich. Are there any leftovers from last night?"

"I might be able to whip something up in the microwave. Stay. I'll be right back."

Sean seemed to like waiting on her. She appreciated it, but didn't expect it. She stood and fully stretched, hearing her bones crack and pop. The couch was comfortable, but not good for sleeping.

Five minutes later, Sean returned with two plates of barbecue leftovers. "You gotta love microwaves," he said when he set them down on the coffee table. He reached into each pocket of his pants and pulled out two beers.

"Wow. Anything else in there?" she teased.

"You'll have to find out later." He winked. "Eat. Tell me what all this is." He picked up the package of paper from Harper's tablet.

She was glad to talk about work. It distracted her from all the emotions she didn't want. She explained that the files had been on Harper Worthington's tablet, that they suspected the list of numbers were land parcels, but admitted she was a bit lost on the dates.

"I know exactly what this is," he said.

"Really?"

"I'm guessing. But I've been going over the BLM audit all day, trying to figure out what had Harper so obsessed with it. Now I think I know—it wasn't the audit numbers, it was the transactions. I think these dates match up with these parcel numbers, and I think these parcel numbers are properties that the government sold or purchased over the last seven years."

"Since Adeline Worthington was elected."

Sean glanced at her. "You think she's corrupt?"

"I know she is. There's an undercover FBI investigation ongoing right now. Barry and I almost got pulled from the murder investigation because the UC thought we had exposed him."

"You met with the undercover agent?"

She told Sean about Logan Dunbar and his fear that she would blow his cover.

"He wanted us off the case because we're making Adeline nervous."

"Do you think she's guilty of murder?"

"If she knew her husband was investigating her—forget the FBI—then yes, I think she could have done it. She has a spine of steel, and it's much easier to hire someone than to do it yourself. But the method? It's . . . bizarre. Poison him and have the room set up like he'd been with a prostitute? Why would she do it that way?"

"Because the spouse is always suspected. Such an embarrassing situation would immediately put her lower on the list."

"Maybe. I don't like her."

"I can tell."

"If I were planning a murder, especially if I would be a

suspect, I wouldn't create something so elaborate. I would find a way to make it look like an accident."

"And I'm sure you would get away with it."

She glanced at him and almost laughed. "Hardly. I don't lie very well."

"Maybe."

She ignored Sean's comment because it bugged her. She didn't want to become a good liar. The few lies she'd told weighed heavily on her.

"We found the prostitute," she said. "Whoever hired her shot her last night."

"Is she okay?"

"She will be. She's in the hospital, but Tia sent me a message earlier that the doctor is releasing her at noon tomorrow, provided there are no complications. We're going to arrest her."

"For murder?"

Lucy nodded and sipped her beer. "She's scared and defiant. She's been on her own for a long time, and she doesn't trust anyone. But when we pushed her on the murder, she swore up and down that she thought she was giving him a knockout drug. She said a 'happy' drug—maybe XTC or ketamine or a combo drug. She claims that she was hired to take dirty pictures of him, not to kill him, that she didn't even know him. She was sent to the room and told to wait for Harper to arrive, then drug him and take sex pictures."

"And did she?"

"She said she turned over the photos. She met her contact to get the rest of her payment, and he shot her, twice. She ran into a busy street at midnight and the shooter disappeared."

"Poor kid."

"I hate playing the bad cop."

Sean leaned back and frowned. "Where'd that come from?"

"Tia. She's the one who knows the programs, how to help Elise, halfway houses, school, whatever. I was forced to be the hard-nosed cop who is pushing for a murder charge. I really felt uncomfortable doing that."

He rubbed her arm. "I'm sorry, sweetheart. But you got the information, right?"

"Some, not everything. We don't know who hired her, and she's scared of him."

"He shot her—I'd be scared, too, if I were in her shoes."

"She wants to run, doesn't trust us to protect her. We have a cop sitting on her door—to keep her in as well as the shooter out. But tomorrow—I don't know what we're going to do. Juvie, I suppose, if she doesn't give us his name."

"If anyone can convince her to do the right thing, it's you and Tia."

"Aw, thanks."

"I'm serious." Sean kissed her. "Are you done for tonight?"

"Yes. I'll clean up."

"Later. Now, I want to take you to bed. I've missed you, Lucy. It's been a long day without you." He kissed her again.

She raised her eyebrow. "So can I see what else you have in your pants?"

He grinned. "Be my guest."

Brad didn't get home until late Tuesday night, but he had nothing to complain about. His doctor had officially cleared him for duty.

He'd grabbed takeout and for a split second considered calling Sam and seeing if he could come over. He missed her. Seeing Sean and Lucy last night reminded him how alone he was. Nicole was wrong; he wasn't attracted to Lucy. She was pretty and smart, but it was clear that she had something special going with Sean. He liked her, though. Not only because she'd saved his life, but because she was a good cop who bent the rules when necessary.

Instead of calling Sam, he went home alone. Trying to rekindle anything with his ex-girlfriend would be a mistake. She was his boss now. When they were equals it was frowned on but not forbidden, and they had been discreet. Now as his supervisor, she'd get in serious trouble. One of them would be transferred. Sam was dedicated to her job. Brad liked San Antonio and had built a network here stronger than the networks in the two other offices he'd worked in.

Some people were born to lead, like Sam. Others, like him, were born to act.

He grabbed a beer and sat down in front of the television with his food. He flipped through until he found a baseball game, but didn't pay much attention to it. He had the forensics report from the shooting, and a follow-up report from Jerry Fielding. He'd read through it earlier, but wanted to give it more attention.

His cell phone rang. The number was unlisted. "Donnelly."

"It's Kane. Do you have time?"

"Sure."

"Open your door."

The call disconnected. Brad walked to his front door and looked through the security hole. Kane Rogan stood there, slightly to the side as if watching both the entrance and the street. Brad unbolted and opened the door. "How did you know where I live?"

Kane didn't answer. He walked in and closed the door. "I heard you found one of the shooters. Dead."

"How the hell did you hear that? We didn't release the information."

Kane gave him a half smile that didn't reach his dark blue eyes. "Marquez? This isn't Marquez's style."

"Then his gangbangers are going rogue."

"Or someone else is giving them orders."

"That sounds like bad news."

"We need more information. The balance of power is shifting, and that's bad for this city and for my unit. I have multiple ops in play right now, and if we don't know who's making a power play, my people will be in danger."

"The weapons they used are M4s. The same type of weapon stolen from the Marines that you recovered. We verified the ammo was military issue."

"We only recovered some of the guns. Two-thirds of them disappeared before I could make it back to Mexico after the rescue."

"So who got the guns?"

"That's the million-dollar question. From what I could piece together, Trejo is the one who sold them to Tobias. Except . . . I've gone over Lucy's report multiple times, and there could be another scenario. Tobias could have funded the operation in the first place. He's been this elusive ghost for years. He wasn't on my radar because his name never came up in connection with one of my operations, and he isn't involved in human trafficking. Yet . . . I've learned more during the last two months. I think he's far more powerful than we gave him credit for."

"With Trejo and Sanchez dead, Tobias was the only one in a position to take possession of the weapons."

"That's what my intel suggests."

"Would he have sold them to Marquez?"

"Yes," Kane said without hesitation. "But why would Marquez go after Tobias? Did Tobias do something to piss him off?"

"Based on the crime scene, I'd say yes."

"Or those victims weren't Tobias's people at all and Marquez was taking care of loose ends."

Kane normally didn't talk much, but he was downright chatty tonight.

Without asking if he wanted a beer, Brad grabbed two bottles from the refrigerator and handed one to Kane. "I saw Nicole Rollins today."

"Did you kill her?"

He asked the question seriously. That almost scared Brad.

"She says my house isn't clean."

"I'm sure it's not."

"Who?"

"I don't know."

"But you could find out."

Kane drank half his beer, watching Brad, assessing. "You really want to know?"

"Yes. I can't work there if I don't trust my team."

"If I hear anything, you'll be the first to know."

"I appreciate it."

"Remember that." Kane didn't believe him. But Brad didn't want another Nicole Rollins under his roof. "What else did Rollins say?"

"That Tobias wanted those men taken out. Either he planned it, or simply didn't stop it. She said the same as you—that he's more powerful than we thought."

"I haven't underestimated him. For a man like that not to be on my radar tells me he's either not important or extremely important. I ruled out the former. We took his helicopter, blew up Trejo's house, disabled the Jeeps, and retrieved part of the gun shipment—and still he had a backup escape plan. I haven't been able to locate him. I had one possible sighting a few weeks ago, in San Antonio, but it was a bust. Either it wasn't him or he moved fast."

"So he's in the States?"

"Honestly, I don't know." Kane drained his beer. "He's everywhere, and nowhere." He put the bottle down on the counter. "One more thing. I can't find anyone—I mean *no one*—who has laid eyes on him."

"That can't be possible."

"It tells me he has another name, or he rarely comes out to play." Kane stared at him. "You need to watch yourself."

"I didn't see him."

"But in your official report, you wrote that you did, and you included the description that Lucy gave."

Brad realized the potential danger. "I'll be careful."

"Tobias doesn't know that Lucy saw him, but he knows she was in Mexico," Kane continued. "No one can know what Lucy saw and heard. It makes her extremely vulnerable. I tried to convince Sean to move—Nicole Rollins knows where they live, therefore anyone could know where they live—but my brother is a stubborn bastard."

"We've done a good job keeping her name out of it. Her boss suspects, but we've never confirmed his suspicions. Ryan Quiroz—he suspects as well."

"I've already done a thorough background check on Quiroz. He's clean."

Again, Brad wasn't surprised.

Kane walked to the door. "Thanks for the beer. I'll be in touch."

"Is there any way I can contact you without having to go through your brother?"

For a second, Brad thought he'd give him his number. Then Kane shook his head. "It's for your protection, Donnelly. And mine."

Sean's cell phone vibrated on the nightstand. He opened his eyes. It was still dark. A nightlight in the bathroom cast shadows around the room. He grabbed his phone. One in the morning.

It wasn't a message or phone call, it was his security system alerting him to movement in the pool house. His security alarm hadn't gone off, but someone had broken in. He pressed a button for the camera angle, but it came up black.

Not good.

He glanced over at Lucy and considered waking her up, but she was finally sleeping soundly, and so far she hadn't been disturbed by dreams. He slipped out of bed, grabbed his nine millimeter as well as a butterfly knife, and crept out of their bedroom.

He didn't turn on any lights, but left by the side door, reengaging the system in case this was a trick to get him out of the house in order to get inside to Lucy. Some people might think his system was overkill, but considering Lucy's job—and some of the people both Lucy and Sean had pissed off over the years—he wasn't taking any chances.

He stayed in the shadows. The pool house lights weren't on and the blinds were closed, so he couldn't tell where the person was.

Sean walked up to the French doors and looked at the keypad that controlled entry. The alarm had been disabled. He typed in a code—if he didn't disable the code in ninety seconds, SAPD and the FBI would be notified.

He opened the door and listened. Water ran in the bathroom. He crossed to the bathroom door just as the water turned off and the door opened. He stayed out of arms' reach of whoever was in there.

"Move and I shoot," he said to the dark figure.

"It's me," Kane said.

"Fuck, Kane!" Sean hit the light switch. Kane blinked in the brightness.

Furious, Sean walked out, disabled the code, and came back in. "Why didn't you call me first?"

"You put in motion sensors. Smart."

"Don't fuck with my equipment again."

Kane smirked and helped himself to a beer. "I didn't want to wake you up."

"Instead, you risked being shot."

"You're too good to shoot blindly."

"Don't be so sure of that."

Sean reached into a cabinet and pulled out a bottle of Royal Lochnagar and two glasses. He poured shots for both of them.

"Where the hell did you get this?" Kane asked, looking at the light amber Scotch.

The twelve-year-old single malt was rare and hard to come by, especially in the States. "Eden sent it to me for a housewarming present."

Kane scowled and sipped. Liam and Eden Rogan, the twins, lived in Europe and weren't on the good side of RCK right now. Sean tried to stay out of it—he still talked to them, while Kane and Duke had all but cut the two out of their lives.

Sean asked, "You just get in?"

"A couple hours ago. Paid Donnelly a visit first, then needed a place to crash."

"What's going on?"

Kane sat and downed the shot. Sean followed suit, poured them each another, and waited. Kane would talk only if he wanted to. It could be annoying, but Sean was used to it.

"Donnelly's working a case that's bigger than he knows."

"You alerted him?"

"I don't know enough to help, but not for lack of trying. Tobias is a fucking ghost. He is so far under the radar

I wouldn't even think he existed except that Lucy saw him and overheard his conversation with Trejo. And that's what's really bothering me."

"He doesn't know Lucy saw him."

"But Donnelly had her look at photos. He's kept it quiet, he put in the report that he had eyes on Tobias, but if they have yet another traitor inside, Lucy could be at risk."

"I'll protect her," Sean said.

Kane didn't say anything.

"You look worried," Sean said. "You don't get worried."

"Worry is a useless emotion," Kane said. "It fucks with logic. I'm *bothered* that I can't get a line on this Tobias."

"Is that why you broke into my house?"

"I didn't break anything. And no. I was on an assignment in Colorado and after I got your message decided to stop here on my way back south."

"Colorado? What sent you there?"

Kane didn't like talking about his jobs, partly because what he did wasn't always legal, but partly because he didn't want people thinking he was a hero when he thought of himself as simply doing a job that needed doing. He said, "A buddy needed help getting his little sister out of some serious trouble." He didn't say anything more about it. "I'll be out of here early in the morning to meet with a snitch down south."

"Stay for breakfast."

"You're not letting Lucy cook, are you?"

Sean grinned. "I'm not going to tell her you said that."

CHAPTER TWENTY-EIGHT

Lucy was surprised to find Kane eating breakfast with Sean when she came downstairs Wednesday morning. She kissed his cheek. "Nice surprise."

"Passing through."

"Almost got himself shot last night," Sean said.

Kane snorted and sipped black coffee.

Lucy poured herself a cup of coffee and added sugar. Sean dished up a plate of scrambled eggs, ham, and cheese for her. She sat down at the island and said, "Are you here because of the shooting Brad is investigating?" She liberally sprinkled hot sauce on her eggs and ignored Sean's distressed expression. She liked spicy.

"Partly," he said.

She waited for more, but Kane didn't add to his answer. She'd grown accustomed to his brief communication style. "Ryan Quiroz has been working with him on it, he's kept me up to speed."

"Good." Kane stood, drained his coffee, and said, "I need to head out. Thanks for the room and board."

"Next time, don't touch my security."

Kane turned to Lucy with a half smile. "Sean hates that I'm as good as he is."

"You're not," Sean said.

"You did nail me with the motion detectors. They weren't in the pool house two months ago."

Lucy watched the exchange, intrigued about what had happened last night while she was sleeping. "I'm heading to headquarters," she said. "Do you need a ride?"

"No, thanks. I borrowed a truck." He glanced at Sean, then said to Lucy, "Watch your back."

She didn't like his serious tone. "Okay. Any specific reason why?"

"Sean will fill you in." Kane walked out.

"Sean?" She looked at him.

"He's concerned that you're the only one who's seen Tobias."

"Me and Michael."

"But you're the one who looked at photos."

"So? No one knows I was there."

"Kane's being cautious. He always is, but this time I think he's justified."

There had to be more to it than Kane's natural vigilance. "Why?"

"Because Kane came here last night."

"And?"

"And I don't need another reason. You don't know Kane like I do. He doesn't just stop by to talk. He went to see Brad Donnelly as well. Kane likes federal agents less than I do. A call would have sufficed, but he wanted to be here. I don't think he's going far. What do you know about this gang hit the other day?"

"Only what Brad told us the other night. Ryan said they'd ID'd one of the shooters as belonging to a different gang, possibly a rival of Trejo. I'll be careful, I always am. And I'm partnered up with Barry. He's good."

"I'd rather you were with Nate or Ryan or MacKenzie."

"Why? Because Nate and Kenzie were in the military and Ryan was a street cop?"

"Partly. But mostly because I know them. I don't know Barry Crawford from Adam, and I didn't like him when I met him."

Lucy understood Sean's protectiveness, but this was going a bit far. "Then trust me. Barry's a smart guy. Yes, a little by the book and a stickler for protocol, but he's good."

"Of course I trust you. I just don't want to see you get hurt."

"It's Brad who needs to be careful. He's DEA. He's the one they wanted dead."

"But Brad didn't see Tobias."

"And Tobias doesn't know I saw him." They were going around and around on this and would never come to an agreement. "Sean. Please. I know you worry, but I'm a trained federal agent. Better, Jack trained me before I even joined the FBI. I take precautions. I'm not even working with Brad anymore. I'm working an old-fashioned murder investigation."

"There's nothing simple about this murder investigation."

"That we can agree on." She leaned up and kissed him. "I love you. I'll see you tonight, if not sooner."

As soon as Lucy left, Sean went to his office and took his special laptop out of the safe. Overkill, perhaps, but this laptop could get him into a lot of trouble.

He booted it up using his own secure server and ran a program to search out the worm he'd installed yesterday in Mona Hill's computer. His cell phone rang a minute later and for a split second he thought he'd screwed up and this was Nate telling him that the FBI was on their way to arrest him.

Of course it wasn't. First, he didn't screw up. Second, the FBI didn't work that fast.

It was his old friend, PI Renee Mackey.

"You're fast and wonderful, as usual," Sean said when he picked up his cell phone.

"Don't forget it, sugar," Renee said. "I just sent you a report, with pictures, but thought I'd call and give you the four-one-one."

He put his secure laptop aside and pulled up his email on his primary computer. As Renee spoke, he flipped through the pictures of an upper-middle-class home on a large parcel just outside of the city. There were also pictures of a woman and a boy. The woman was pretty in a simple way—long dark hair, balanced face, good bone structure. She was young—mid to late twenties.

"The woman is Darlene Hatcher, twenty-six. The boy is hers, Bobby. He'll be eight this summer. No father in the picture—no marriage license, no court-ordered child support, no custody agreement on record. I sent you his birth certificate. No father was listed. But, I did a little digging. The residence Darlene put on the birth certificate doesn't exist."

"She's in hiding."

"Possibly."

"But look at the certificate."

Sean scrolled through the documents. Renee had taken a picture of the birth certificate. Name, address, mother's maiden name . . .

"Jefferson."

"Bingo."

Darlene hadn't put her father down on the birth certificate, either. Was she Mona's younger sister? It made sense in a strange way.

He looked back at Darlene's picture. She was Caucasian, like Mona's mother. But as he studied the bone structure, he saw that even though Mona was of mixed race, they had the same basic facial shape and the same green eyes.

"What does Darlene do for a living?"

"She's a teacher. Went to college a little late, graduated last year with a master's in early childhood education. Teaches kindergarten."

Sean tried to process all the information. Mona had a half sister. She was paying for her to live well, while Mona, a former porn star, ran a prostitution ring in San Antonio. There had to be more to it.

"And I know exactly what you're thinking, Sean. So I went there."

"Went where?"

"To the school. Sniffed around. I can act the sweet little ole granny when I need to."

He laughed. "I'd like to see that."

"You'll have to pay me extra. Well, there's more to this story. Darlene listed on her employment forms that she has no family, that her parents are deceased and she has no living siblings. I then thought . . . how did Ramona Jefferson just disappear?"

"Mona stopped using her real identity and created a new one."

"Yes—but eight years ago, a month before the house was purchased, Ramona Jefferson died."

Sean's heart skipped a beat. "For real?"

"No. On paper only. I swear, you owe me big-time because I could have lost my PI license."

"You're retired."

"Well, I still have my license. It doesn't expire until the end of the year."

"So?"

"There's a death certificate filed in Los Angeles County, California, for Ramona Jefferson. But it's a forgery."

It took Sean a minute to process that. "You mean that

Mona inserted a death certificate into the system? How the hell?"

"Oh, I'm sure you could find a way."

"That's me."

"If someone pulled it, it wouldn't hold scrutiny. There was no body, no police report, no burial. But on the surface, it seems legit. So I went to Darlene's neighborhood this morning, after she left with her son, and through one of her nosy neighbors I learned that Darlene's older sister died and left her a trust, which paid for the house and her college education."

Very interesting.

"There's one more thing you should know."

"I'm still processing everything you've already told me."

"Everything you told me about Mona's family was true—her mother was a drug addict, petty theft, drug sales. A real waste case. In and out of prison. The kids, Ramona and Darlene, were often left on their own for days or weeks, but when their mother went to prison for three years, when Darlene was four, Darlene was put into foster care and had a rough time. Records are closed, but I have my ways. Ramona, then thirteen, disappeared. The mom got out, reclaimed Darlene, and proceeded to go down the same path. Ramona may or may not have been around—I'd have to dig a little more. But a friend of mine, a retired cop who worked that beat, said the mom was a piece of work. Used the kid as a mule. The mom overdosed a couple years later—and it was nasty, from what the reports show. I can't get you a copy because my contact at HPD was squeamish about sharing. But Darlene was then sent back to foster care. Lucky for her, she got in with a good family, the Hatchers. She legally changed her name when she was eighteen."

"And what about the boy's father?"

"Nothing. I could probably dig around some more, but she was eighteen when she had him. That makes me think that it was a high school romance."

"Don't dig. Yet. But if you can send me what you know about the Hatchers, I'll consider following up if I need to."

"The girl had it rough growing up, but she seems to have her life in order now. It's not easy being a single mom, but she's never had to worry about money or a place to live, which makes it a whole lot easier. She goes to church on Sunday and the kid plays baseball and has friends. They seem very normal."

Sean didn't want to disrupt their lives.

But Mona Hill had threatened Lucy.

"What are you going to do?"

"I don't know," he lied. He thanked Renee and disconnected the call.

Of course he knew what he needed to do. Sean aimed to find out just how much of a soft spot Mona Hill had for her half sister.

He turned back to his secure laptop. Mona Hill had checked her email last night. His worm had traveled through her system, and he mirrored her hard drive on his own computer. He was searching only for one file.

It didn't take him long to find it. It was the last video file that had been viewed. In fact, a short clip had been copied and saved two days ago. He hesitated, then viewed it.

His heart nearly stopped. It was Lucy. Naked and chained to the floor.

He shut it down.

Rage exploded. He jumped out of his chair. It tipped backward and knocked over the books stacked on the shelf behind him. He barely noticed. He stormed out of the room, slamming his door so hard the wood cracked. Down the hall to his gym, where he hit the punching bag over and over until his fists were sore. A groan escaped his throat and he wanted to kill Mona Hill in the worst way. He wanted to hurt her. What she did for her sister—with her illegal money—might be considered noble to some, but she'd stepped on many, many people to do it.

She'd fucked with the wrong person.

A fraction calmer, but no less angry, Sean went back to his office. He deleted all the video files from her computer. He was about to install a nasty virus when he hesitated.

Why had she created that clip?

Sean searched her emails. The clip was attached to an email that had gone to a blind account that Mona Hill had sent on Monday afternoon—the same day that Lucy and her partner had spoken to her. Lucy's gut instinct about Mona had been right, and Mona had then parlayed her knowledge . . . for what? To whom?

Sean pulled down all the routing information on the blind account. Everything was traceable given enough time and equipment. And desire.

He certainly had the desire.

Then he installed a nasty virus that would obliterate Mona's hard drive and any device that connected to it. But even if he destroyed the virtual files, she might have a copy of the video on a disk. He needed to find and destroy it, too.

He erased his cache, reformatted his hard drive, shut everything down, and locked his laptop back in the safe. He'd rebuild the computer later.

Sean formulated a plan. By the time he was done with her, Mona Hill would do anything he wanted her to.

CHAPTER TWENTY-NINE

Barry was waiting for Lucy as soon as she walked into FBI headquarters. "Let's go."

She didn't even have time to go to her desk. She followed Barry to one of the pool cars. "What happened?" she asked as they pulled out.

"Your idea about the bus route panned out. I had a couple analysts making calls to drivers and we found the stop our Gary used more often than all the others. I was about to send a couple agents out in the field to canvass, see if they could get a positive ID on the guy before we go out there, when Zach found him based on our description and neighborhood."

"Zach is the best."

"Gary is Gary Ackerman. He's dead. Shot to death Sunday night in his studio apartment. I got it cleared by SAPD and we're going there now." Barry tapped a file that was on the seat between them. "That's the report."

Lucy opened it. Gary Ackerman was fifty-five, the same age as Harper Worthington. He had been born and raised in San Antonio. He'd been in the military for twelve years, retiring after serving two tours during Desert Storm. Returned, had trouble finding steady work, until he landed a job as a long-haul truck driver. His career was cut short when—while walking across the street—he was hit by a car. The driver was never found, and Gary woke up with brain damage and blindness in one eye. He lived on disability and a small military pension, had no credit cards, paid cash for everything, and the only thing he used his bank account for was to receive his disability checks—which he promptly withdrew the day they were deposited, never going into the same branch twice in a row.

He was shot twice in the chest Sunday night. Motive unknown, possibly theft. A small laptop that his neighbor said he was never without was missing, but nothing else.

"This isn't a coincidence," Lucy said.

"No, it's not. Did you get to the last page?"

She flipped to the back and read a note Zach had written.

Gary Ackerman graduated high school with both Harper Worthington and former congressman Roy Travertine. Worthington and Travertine went on to college and Ackerman joined the air force. He has a pseudonymous Web site, The Truth Files, which is all about conspiracies, mostly government and military related. Before Travertine's death, Ackerman was a regular volunteer on his campaign and served in a nonpaying role as the head of a group called Veterans for Travertine. It's the only political activity Ackerman has on record. His accident was five years ago, he was lucky to survive. Most of his rants on his Web site appear to be harmless. But some of his insights were proven accurate over the years by subsequent events. For example, three years ago he wrote about a governor in another state and claimed that he had embezzled money out of a fund he created, based on one line in an obscure

newspaper article. Last year, the governor was
indicted for embezzling—not from that specific
fund, but from the prison system, conspiring with
his brother-in-law who worked for the bureau of
prisons.

But the big thing? Adeline Reyes-Worthington
got a restraining order against him seven years
ago, during her first election campaign. Don't
have the details—it was filed in D.C.

"Gary Ackerman must be the guy Harper met with,"
Lucy said. "It explains the note about Travertine on the
tablet. Maybe that's how Ackerman got in to see him."

"What it doesn't explain is what they talked about or
why Ackerman set him up at the motel."

"If Ackerman set him up."

"What other logical explanation is there? There was a
restraining order against him—"

"To stay away from Adeline."

"Still. Would her husband trust him?"

"It seems that way."

"Or Ackerman came up with a way to punish Adeline
by killing her husband." Even as Barry said it, his tone suggested he didn't believe it.

"He doesn't have the resources, and he's a paranoid conspiracy theorist," Lucy said. "Someone could have known
that Harper was meeting with Ackerman."

"It's more likely that Ackerman was hired to set Harper
up—or possibly threatened to set him up—and then killed
to keep him quiet."

Certainly possible, Lucy thought.

Barry didn't speak for the rest of the short drive. He was
preoccupied and more serious than usual.

They showed their badges to the apartment manager,
who let them into Ackerman's studio.

The one-room facility was clean but cluttered. The twin bed was made military neat; the kitchenette was in perfect order with no dishes in the sink. But there was little space to move around. Each wall was covered with floor-to-ceiling bookshelves. They were packed with books, binders, and file folders. On a desk, under the lone window which looked out onto the street, was a power cord. It went with a Toshiba laptop that was no longer on the desk. While the desk was completely clear, there were stacks of files under the desk, all labeled.

"Other than the laptop, we can't possibly know if anything was taken," Lucy said.

"Don't be so sure of that," Barry said. "I've known guys like Ackerman. Once we figure out his logic, we'll know if anything is missing."

Lucy slipped on gloves and opened the desk drawers. "I think I found it."

"That was fast." Barry looked inside the bottom drawer. There were hanging files, all neatly labeled. The contents from one hanging file were missing. The identifying tab had been torn off.

The files on either side of the missing file were dated: *April, June.*

"This must have been what he was working on," Lucy said. "And whatever he was doing in May, that's now gone."

She pulled the two files and glanced through them. Nothing jumped out at her. She was about to sit down and go through them more carefully when she heard Barry on his cell phone. "Juan, can you send Zach with an agent to Gary Ackerman's studio? There's potential evidence here, and we need someone with an analytical mind to weed through the irrelevant files to find the important items."

When Barry was done, Lucy said, "We're not doing this?"

"We have another appointment. I wasn't sure what we

would find here, and I didn't want to send Zach on a wild-goose chase. Juan's going to send Nate with him." Zach Charles was an analyst, not a field agent, and therefore couldn't work in the field without being accompanied by an agent. And in a case like this, an agent would be added protection.

Lucy glanced around before they left. She felt compassion for the veteran she'd never met. A good, honest life damaged by a reckless driver. Living with paranoia and fears he might not even understand. The brain was the most complex organ in the human body. Even neuroscientists knew less about the brain than what they suspected they could learn. But what was the trigger? What event or article or image had Gary Ackerman seeking out Harper Worthington?

Or was it the other way around?

Back in the car, she said to Barry, "What if Harper was the one who sought out Gary's help? They went to school together, and Harper must have known Gary had volunteered for Travertine. It stands to reason he at least knew about his accident and Web site. Harper became suspicious about Adeline's activities and went to the FBI. The FBI put him off because they didn't want him trampling on their ongoing investigation. Harper then contacted Gary—maybe because of something he wrote?—and they put their resources together."

"Zach and his people are going through each of Ackerman's articles—if there's something there, they'll find it."

"It might not be obvious."

"They know how to do their job."

Of course they did. Zach was exceptionally smart. His thought process was similar to Sean's—they both saw not only the big picture, but how all the little pieces fit in. It's why Zach made a good analyst, and Sean a good security expert.

"Where are we headed now?"

"James Everett."

"Agent Dunbar isn't going to like it."

"I don't care."

This was a new side of Barry.

"Did something happen last night that I wasn't involved with?"

"I don't like bringing work home with me, Lucy, and yet I couldn't get this case out of my head." He sounded angry about it, too. "Everett and Adeline were partners. They split up when she ran for Congress, but remained friends. He's feeding information to the FBI. Then two months ago he cuts all ties with Adeline and endorses her opponent. Why not last year when Dunbar first started this investigation? Or why not keep the façade up, considering he could probably gather more information if he remained close to her? And Dunbar . . . his reaction was odd to me. I've been mulling it over and over in my head. Then I thought back to Elise Hansen."

"The prostitute."

"She claimed she was hired to take photos of Worthington, which she believed were to blackmail him. It has a ring of truth. Then why not Everett? He's worth a small fortune. And the one thing that connects the two of them is Adeline."

"So she has her husband killed and blackmails Everett . . . Why?"

"What if she knows about the FBI investigation?"

"Then Dunbar is at risk. We need to warn him." That wouldn't go over well.

"Maybe she doesn't think it's Dunbar. Maybe she doesn't even think that it's someone on staff—but that it was her husband. Or her former partner. So she has Worthington killed but sets it up to look like an accident or natural causes. It's complex because in her head, she'd think that no one would look at her because she wouldn't do something so outrageous that might embarrass her or jeopardize her campaign." He paused, as if realizing how convoluted the reasoning was, but it still sounded plausible. "She then sends the hooker to Everett . . . to get pictures to blackmail him. Maybe he tipped her off that he was working with the feds when he cut ties with her. It made her suspicious. And maybe that's what made Harper suspicious as well."

It made sense, in a twisted way. "We need Elise's statement. She said a man shot her—implied," Lucy added. "If Adeline is behind this entire thing, she has someone working for her—someone we can cut a deal with."

"This is where it gets tricky, Lucy. Elise is an unreliable witness. She's already lied to us. Harper was dead before she left the motel room. She flirted with the taxi driver. She went to another client and had sex with him. She admitted to accepting a substantial amount of money to take dirty pictures of Worthington. And, even knowing that whoever hired her gave her a lethal drug *and* tried to kill her, she hasn't given us a name. Plus, there's nothing that connects Elise to Adeline."

"Not yet, but we haven't been looking for that connection. But if it's there, we'll find it."

"I like your confidence, but not only do we need to find the connection, we need to make it stick. Circumstantial evidence isn't going to give us a warrant, not against a member of Congress, let alone an indictment. This case needs to be rock solid, and that means that not only do we need Elise Hansen and James Everett to tell us the truth, we need to break Mona Hill. She already admitted to sending Elise to James Everett. Which makes me think she also sent Elise to Harper Worthington, even if Elise said otherwise. She's the conduit and has absolutely no ties to Adeline—that we can find." Barry glanced at Lucy. "Are you going to have your A game when we interview her again?" Barry asked her.

"Of course."

He didn't say anything.

"Barry—I let her get under my skin once. It won't happen again."

He didn't say anything for a minute. Then, "I made some calls last night."

She knew what was coming. She didn't want to talk to Barry about her past. She didn't think he could know the details—it wasn't super secret knowledge that she'd been raped, but the circumstances surrounding her rape and how she killed her kidnapper *were* sealed. But because of her association with Rick Stockton and Hans Vigo—and the fact that her sister-in-law taught at Quantico—people had a lot of theories about her. Most wrong. Some close to the truth.

"Matt Slater and I went through Quantico together," Barry continued. "He told me about the prostitution ring you uncovered, the blackmail, the girls you saved."

"Do you not trust me?" she asked bluntly. "Is that why you're checking on my credentials?"

"It's not about trust."

"I beg to differ."

"I don't know you, and it's clear you have far more experience than most rookie FBI agents who didn't come from local law enforcement."

"I thought after working together for nearly a week that I've proven myself to you. And yet, you call the D.C. office for what? To dig up dirt? To find out if I'm going to fall apart in the middle of this investigation?"

"I don't know," he admitted.

"And what did Slater say? Because my partner and I solved that case, and we apprehended the killer and took down a corrupt lobbyist. People are alive because we did our job. That's all I'm trying to do here."

"Slater said you were protected from on high, but that you didn't need it because you were a good cop. But—because most people in D.C. know about your friendship with Rick Stockton among other high-ranking staff and would unfairly judge you by it—it was wise that you were assigned far away."

She didn't say anything.

Neither did Barry.

Maybe there was nothing else to say. She didn't like that Barry felt he had to check up on her. Especially after she'd thought they were working so well together.

Barry pulled into the parking lot at James Everett's development company. Lucy was about to get out of the car when Barry put his hand on her arm. "Slater also said that you took too many risks, were lucky to be alive, and your FBI file was thicker than most senior agents'—but unavailable without clearance from Rick Stockton himself, which he declined to give Slater when asked. That makes me suspicious."

"Let go," Lucy said quietly. Barry dropped his hand. She got out of the car and walked to the lobby, waiting for Barry to catch up.

He followed and didn't say another word about the conversation. Barry had reminded her once again that she would never escape her past.

Sometimes, she wondered why she even tried.

James Everett was clearly unhappy about seeing Barry and Lucy in his office Wednesday morning. So was his lawyer, Miriam Shaw.

"I've done all I can to help you," he said.

Barry took the lead. "We have a witness who said that

she took sexually explicit photos of you and turned them over to an individual who planned to blackmail you. Are you being blackmailed?"

Good lie, Lucy thought. The way Barry said it Lucy almost believed it. They were certain that's what happened, but they couldn't prove it. Yet.

Everett's face drained of color. "No!"

"I don't believe you, Mr. Everett."

Shaw bristled. "My client denies that anyone has blackmailed him. Is that the only reason you're here?"

"No. We are prepared to arrest Mr. Everett for solicitation and statutory rape."

"Since when does the FBI make arrests for solicitation?" the attorney asked coolly.

"United States Code eighteen, section one-five-nine-one clearly states that it's a federal crime to pay for sexual intercourse with a minor under the age of eighteen," Lucy said.

"I didn't," Everett said.

"Elise is sixteen," Lucy said.

"Bullshit," Everett said.

"James." His attorney placed a hand on his shoulder. Everett looked at his hands folded on his desk. Shaw said, "If you're going to go through with this travesty, I'll bring my client down to be arraigned, but he will not be spending any time in jail."

"Yes, he will," Barry said. "Unless he cooperates."

"I'll file charges of harassment."

"Go ahead," Barry said. "I will remind you that it's a crime to lie to a federal agent."

Everett's whole body sagged like air from a balloon. "This can't be happening," he said. "She said she was eighteen!"

Lucy said, "Her ID was a fake. Or did you even bother to check?"

"If my client is being blackmailed, then he's the victim," Shaw said.

"And we're willing to drop all charges if he cooperates," Barry said. "Who's blackmailing you, Mr. Everett?"

"I don't know!" he said with a half sob. "I haven't even seen the pictures. I—I got a voice recording Monday night. My voice. They sent a note that said to wait for instructions, to tell no one. I—I—" He glanced at his attorney. "I'm already helping the FBI on another matter."

Shaw stared at him, surprised. "*James.*"

"I couldn't tell anyone—they told me I couldn't, or they wouldn't give me immunity," Everett said. "But I told my FBI contact about the recording, and he didn't think it was important. He said everything would soon be resolved, and if the blackmailer contacted me again to let him know."

Lucy wondered if Logan Dunbar had that information before or after his meeting at the FBI office. If he had known, what else was he holding back from them? If he hadn't known then, why hadn't he informed Juan as soon as Everett told him? His lack of cooperation angered Lucy—she expected better from a colleague.

Barry said, "We know that you're a confidential informant for the FBI in the investigation of Adeline Reyes-Worthington."

Everett's eyes practically bulged out of his head. "No one is supposed to know!"

"San Antonio is our jurisdiction," Barry said, leaving it at that. "We need the voice recording. Now."

Everett hesitated, then opened his bottom desk drawer and pulled out a microrecorder.

Barry put on gloves and picked it up. He pressed play.

"You're late," Everett's voice said.

"I'm sorry. I'll make it up to you." It was a young female whom Lucy recognized as Elise. There were sounds of sex in the background—moaning and slapping—and it took a second for Lucy to recognize that Everett had a porn video on the television. Elise said, "You want me to do that to you?"

"I want a lot of things. How old are you?"

"How old do you want me to be?"

"Legal."

"I'm legal."

"You look younger."

There was silence for a long minute, except for the porn in the background, then the sound of rustling, then a glass being put firmly down on a table.

"I picked this hotel because the walls are thick, and I want to hear you. Understand?" Everett said.

"Yes. I need the money first."

Again, movement and noise. Paper. A drawer? Maybe not.

"What do you want me to call you?" Elise asked.

"Call me Daddy. And I'm going to spank you. Hard."

"Spank me, Daddy."

Lucy jumped when she heard the hard slap on flesh.

"All fours, little girl, I'm going to fuck you hard," Everett said on the tape. The sound of his hand slapping her echoed. "Tell me you want it hard."

"I want it hard, Daddy."

Barry shut the tape off. Lucy couldn't look at anyone. She felt dirty just listening to the tape. Memories threatened to flood her, violent memories. She couldn't go there. She had to control her emotions, control her feelings. Be the ice princess she'd been in college. Be the rock she'd been when she and Barry left the car twenty minutes ago. She felt every shield slide back into place. She first caught the lawyer's eye. Then Everett's. Every muscle tightened and froze.

Lucy said, "What did they say they wanted from you,

Mr. Everett?" Her voice was low and calm. Too calm. But that was the price to stave off the past.

"I don't know! I swear! They said to wait and they'd tell me. It's probably money. It's always about money, right?"

"We'll keep this. And if they contact you again, call me immediately," Barry said.

"What if they're keeping tabs on me? If they have my phone tapped? If it's someone I know?"

Barry wrote a number on the back of a business card. "This is a generic number, can't be traced to the FBI. Call it, and the switchboard will connect you with me wherever I am."

Everett stared at the number. "What about my other arrangement? I was promised immunity."

"Most FBI deals are for immunity for past crimes. Am I incorrect in assuming that extends to your arrangement?"

Everett didn't say anything.

"Do *you* understand?" Barry asked.

"Yes," Everett said quietly. "I understand completely."

CHAPTER THIRTY

Because Mona's profession required her to work nights, she had the luxury of sleeping in every morning. Her bedroom had blackout curtains that blocked any sunshine that threatened to creep in and disturb her beauty sleep. But rarely did she sleep past eleven in the morning, and Wednesday was no exception.

She stretched and swung her feet over the edge of her bed. It was quarter to eleven, and she had a full day ahead of her. She saw a message on her cell phone. It was from Tobias's contact, and she smiled.

We want it.

Of course they wanted the video. The woman was a federal agent. It was priceless, truly. From what she'd heard, Tobias's people had been looking for someone in the FBI to cultivate. This seven minutes would take little Ms. Lucy Kincaid down a peg or ten.

She showered, drank a cup of tea, and sat down at her computer. She made a mental list of everything she needed to do. First was to assign her girls—and boys—for the evening. A good business couldn't run on supplying only women for the particular needs of men. Some men liked men—and in conservative Texas, that meant discretion. The kind of discretion they paid handsomely for.

Her computer made an odd sound, like it was spinning, getting louder and louder. The screen was blue. Suddenly, white characters scrolled rapidly across the screen and smoke erupted from the hard drive. She jumped back. There was a spark and then the smell of burning metal.

Well, shit. She had everything on that computer, and it was only six months old. Thankfully, she had a complete backup, which saved her data wirelessly every night. She retrieved the backup drive from the closet and plugged it into her laptop in the kitchen.

First thing, order a new damn computer. That was under warranty, and if the dicks on the help desk thought they would make her pay, they had another think coming.

She turned on her laptop and at first nothing happened.

A cloud of suspicion washed over her. She reached over to pull the cable that connected her backup drive to the laptop, but smoke started coming from the laptop, and suddenly, the backup drive sparked and the plastic began to melt.

Someone was destroying her business.

"Don't move," a male voice said.

She turned and saw a man she didn't recognize in the doorway of her kitchen. He was six one, maybe six foot two, lean, with dark hair and blue eyes.

He parted his windbreaker and revealed a gun in a holster.

"You're not a cop."

"No, I'm not. But I have a deal to make."

She tilted her chin up defiantly. "I don't work with partners."

"And I have no intention of being your partner. But you'll want to listen."

She rose from the table. "There are two federal agents

outside. All I need to do is scream." Mona had been more than a little pissed off that Agents Crawford and Kincaid had sent two agents to watch her 24/7, but now she realized they might come in handy.

"I know. And I'll leave the way I came—through your basement."

How did this bastard know about her basement? It wasn't on the original plans for the building.

"If you alert them," the stranger continued, "I'll tell Darlene everything I know about you."

The blood drained from Mona's face and she sat heavily on the chair. The room was spinning. This was *not* happening. No one knew about Darlene. *No one.*

Sean watched as Mona began to panic. He picked up the small fire extinguisher he'd brought with him and put out the mini fire that the melted backup drive had started. He put the container down out of Mona's reach, and said, "Tell me everything about the people who want that video."

She was confused. "You want it, too? I'll sell to the highest bidder."

He itched to hit the woman, but he needed to control his temper. Beating up his punching bag had left his fists sore, and if she baited him he would misstep. He had to keep his emotions on complete lockdown. He put himself in Kane's shoes. He had to be as cold, as calculating, as shrewd as his brother.

"Let me explain something, Ms. Hill." He waited until she focused on him. "I know everything about you. I know you planted a fake death certificate at the Los Angeles County Registrar so that your sister would think you were dead and not be suspicious that a trust was set up to take care of her and her fatherless son. I know your mother was a drug addict and a prostitute who pimped you out, and would have pimped Darlene out if you hadn't intervened. I know that you are extremely smart and could have made your money legitimately—after tracking all your shell companies and bank accounts, even I was impressed. But instead, you choose to stay in the sex trade. To each his own, I suppose.

"But you crossed a line, and you do not want me as your enemy. I already destroyed your computers. And the archives in your basement?" Her eyes widened. "Gone." He snapped his fingers.

"How dare you involve yourself in my business," she said through clenched teeth.

"I don't give a shit about your business. I want the man who was going to buy that video."

She shook her head. "What's in it for me?"

He held up one of the photos that Renee had taken of Darlene and her son, just that morning. Mona couldn't prevent the full range of emotions that crossed her face, from rage to love to worry.

"I will take you down and then who will support your sister? Especially when she has to deal with the fallout of your criminal enterprise. Because not only have I traced your money, but I've traced every dime that's gone to your sister. The government will want it back. She'll lose her house. She'll lose the trust fund. She'll lose little Bobby's college fund. And she'll know that you supported her off the backs of women just like your pathetic mother."

He hadn't traced her money—he hadn't had time. He knew that he *could* do it, just like he'd tracked the businesses, but money and banking issues would take far more time to dig into.

But Sean was a very good liar.

"I will kill you," Mona whispered.

"Then my partner will go to the FBI with the evidence I've accumulated. And my partner will also go directly to Darlene with proof of everything you've done."

Her chin trembled but she didn't say anything.

"Who wants the video?"

She didn't say anything for a long minute. Sean saw the inner debate.

"You'll never survive," she finally said. "He's powerful. He'll beat you to a pulp and have his gangbangers cut off your dick and shove it down your throat."

"Who?"

"If I tell you, I'll have to run. He'll *know*. He knows everything."

Sean slammed his fist on the table. She jumped. "Name!"

"Promise me you won't go after my sister. She doesn't know anything."

"If you lie to me, I'll tell her everything. If you tell me the truth, I'll lose her file."

Through clenched teeth, Mona hissed, "Tobias."

CHAPTER THIRTY-ONE

Lucy decided that the best thing to do was to ignore her previous conversation with Barry about Rick Stockton and Matt Slater. She wished it had never happened. Fortunately, Barry seemed to agree because he didn't bring it up, either.

It was twelve thirty, and Tia had just sent them a message that the doctor was currently checking on Elise Hansen, but she should be released within an hour.

"Elise didn't tell us she'd recorded Everett," Lucy said, focusing on the case. That was where she and Barry worked best. She could never be friends with him, not anymore. That saddened her.

Never say never.

It wasn't likely.

"I noticed," Barry said.

"It's something I can push her on. She implied she took photos, but didn't say it outright. Not about Everett."

"If you're ready to go after her."

"I'm ready." She sounded defensive, which was the last thing she wanted. "Elise knew that Worthington was dead when she left the motel. She staged the scene to make it look like he'd received oral sex, but we know that he wasn't sexually aroused. Yet, less than an hour later, what did she sound like to you on the tape?"

"Like she was playing a part. Having fun."

"There are cruel people in this world," Lucy said. "But it takes an especially cold person to leave one man dead and then play sex games with another. To create an audio recording and, presumably, take pictures. But I'm wondering if those pictures even exist. Elise was vague, upset, and calculating all at the same time. Everett would have noticed being photographed, wouldn't he?" She didn't wait for an answer, and continued. "She didn't drug him—we saw him leave the hotel looking fine only hours after they had sex."

"She lied to us. Repeatedly."

"Whether out of fear of someone else, or fear that she was going to be caught, I'm not sure yet."

"Still, someone shot her."

"What is that expression? No honor among thieves? Maybe she actually told the truth, that she took Worthington's phone and they were angry about it. Or maybe she made a mistake we have yet to uncover. Maybe she wanted more money. Maybe whoever hired her didn't want a witness."

"I'm going with the latter. She's the only connection between Worthington and Everett. Someone gave her the curare to inject into Worthington. That's not a poison you can buy on the street."

"Mona Hill knows," Lucy said. "If we can't break Elise Hansen, we have to go back to Mona."

"We should be able to break her," Barry said. "Are you *really* up for this?"

Lucy had gone into this investigation thinking that Elise was the victim. That she'd been used and abused for years, ending up in a life of prostitution because that was all she knew. And maybe that was how it started. But turning to blackmail and murder? That she hadn't been disturbed about Harper Worthington dying haunted Lucy. Elise was concerned about her own freedom and culpability—and freely admitted that she thought she was giving him a knockout drug—but showed no remorse that he ended up dying from her actions.

Lucy had let her sympathy for victims of the sex trade overshadow her years of training in criminal psychology. She should have seen Elise Hansen for who she was at the beginning. She might not have known that the drug was lethal, but Elise was calculating and would say or do anything to get out of the mess she found herself in.

"I am definitely up for it."

Tia Mancini met Lucy and Barry at the hospital. "We're good to go," Tia said. "We can bring her to the station, interrogate her, then admit her into juvenile detention pending charges. We're going to put her in the medical wing because of her injuries, as well as for her own safety."

"I'd like five minutes alone with her," Lucy said.

Tia was suspicious. "Why?"

"I need her to know that *I* know she's a liar. I don't want to do it on the record. You can listen in."

Tia frowned. "I think I missed something."

Barry said, "We have a recording of her and James Everett, the john she was with after Worthington, and her tone and demeanor suggest that was having fun."

Tia grew angry. "Prostitutes are great actresses."

"What he means," Lucy said, "is that less than an hour after she left Harper Worthington dead—and forensics prove that he was dead before she left the room—she was cheerful and almost giddy while playing sex games with another john. And she had the wherewithal to record it. There's something going on with her, and I want her to

think about it on the drive over to detention. There's more
to it than her being afraid of whoever hired her."

"When I wanted you to play bad cop, Lucy, I wasn't expecting you to be such a hard-ass."

Lucy tried to ignore the comment, but it bothered her.
"A man was murdered, humiliated in his death, and she
won't tell us who hired her—even when we gave her all
the ways she could play the victim card. She needs to understand that we are serious. She tells us the truth, or she
goes to jail."

Tia frowned and looked like she wanted to argue, then
her phone rang. "It's the lab. I have to take it." She stepped
away.

"I guess you really are ready," Barry said.

"I know how to do the job," she said coolly.

"Lucy, I didn't mean anything by the conversation
earlier—"

She looked him in the eye. "Yes, you did. You don't
trust me and you called a friend to check me out. And then,
you wanted to make sure I knew about it. That's manipulative. I think you're a good cop, Barry. A really good cop
and I've learned a lot working with you this past week.
And I'm sincerely sorry that my diligence wasn't good
enough for you."

He wanted to respond, but couldn't because Tia came
back almost immediately. "That was Stu at the crime lab,"
she said. "The paper in Elise's pocket, the one with the instructions on where to meet, is special order." She looked
from Barry to Lucy. "It's ordered in bulk by the House of
Representatives for all district and capitol offices."

"Adeline Reyes-Worthington," Lucy said.

"One sheet of paper? Anyone could have taken it from
her office. A staff member. A constituent. Or it was
scrapped. There could be a half dozen explanations. There
was no letterhead on it, no other identifying marks to say

it came from *her* office. Which her attorney will shove down our throat. We need more."

"Her husband is dead. That should be enough to *talk* to the woman."

"Get Elise to tell us who hired her, and we go from there," Barry said. He ran his hand through his perfect hair, and it fell right back into place. "While you interview her, I'll call Juan. He needs to know about Everett, and about the paper."

Lucy and Tia went upstairs to Elise's room. She was sitting on the edge of her bed in clothes that weren't hers. She had on no makeup, and her bleached blond hair was brushed and pulled back with a rubber band, making her mousy brown roots stand out. She looked very young and very innocent. And sad. Lucy wondered if she was wrong about Elise. Maybe she'd been so victimized that she didn't even understand the seriousness of what she now faced.

Tia said, "Elise, we'll be bringing you down to SAPD headquarters for a formal questioning process, then you'll be transported to juvenile detention."

Elise frowned, her posture both defensive and defiant. "Why?"

"To keep you safe."

"They'll get to me anywhere." She sounded forlorn.

Tia said, "I'm going to wait downstairs for the van. I'll call you when it's here, Lucy, and you can escort Elise down." She caught Lucy's eye, almost as if to say, *Go easy.* But she'd tacitly agreed with Lucy's plan. Tia trusted her, and Lucy wasn't going to blow this opportunity.

Lucy closed the door. "Elise, I heard the sex tape you made with James Everett. It was sent to him as a precursor to blackmail. That makes you an accessory to blackmail. A very serious charge."

Elise tilted her chin up. "I didn't send it to him."

"But you recorded him without his consent. That tape was made an hour after you killed Harper Worthington."

"I *told* you, I didn't kill him. I didn't *mean* to kill him. It was an accident!"

"I don't know what to believe, Elise. I have a hard time reconciling what happened that night. I know how curare kills. He would have been alive, but completely immobile, for ten to thirty minutes. Yet, while he was suffering—or already dead—you pulled down his pants and sucked his penis."

Elise turned away. "I didn't." She had no anger in her voice.

"Then, you got a ride from someone—I think it was Mona Hill who took you to a much nicer hotel, where you went up to James Everett's room and gleefully played sex games, giggling and acting like a schoolgirl. Everett is a sick bastard, and I'm not giving him a pass on his disgusting behavior. But it takes a uniquely cold person to leave a dead man half-naked, then screw another john. You had thousands of dollars on you when you were shot. You can't tell me you needed the money. You're not even from San Antonio. My guess? You're originally from Nevada. I will find your parents, I will find out what happened to you there, who started you down this road where you now allow people who don't give a damn about you to use you like a pawn. You might think that you have the power because men want your body and will pay for it, but that's not power. That's hopelessness. The person who hired you—who gave you the poison to kill Harper Worthington—is the person who wanted you dead two nights ago. Why? Because you're a witness.

"You have two choices," Lucy continued, taking a step closer to Elise. The girl stared at her with a straight face, but her eyes were watering. Lucy didn't want to make her cry, but maybe getting her to fall apart would be what would give her the courage to finally talk. "You take Tia up on her offer to help you. Detective Mancini is one of the most dedicated and honest cops I know. She wants to help you get out of this life, to help you finish your education and get a job. And she can do it. That means you tell us everything—*everything*—including who hired you to drug Harper Worthington and why you came to San Antonio in the first place. You talk, you get a free pass if you join Tia's program. A second chance, which, at this point, I don't know if you deserve.

"Or you keep protecting the person who wants you dead. You will go to prison because we have enough on you to make sure of it."

Elise's bottom lip quivered. She glared at Lucy, tears rolling down her cheeks.

"Fuck you!" she screamed and threw a plastic cup half-filled with water at Lucy. It fell at her feet.

"It's your call, Elise." Lucy turned and walked out.

She walked down to the nurses' station and took a deep breath. She was shaking, but she didn't think she'd started shaking until she'd left the room. She'd hated doing that, but it was the only way she was going to get through to the girl. The girl wouldn't take kindness if it came from Mother Teresa herself, but a threat? That she understood completely.

"Good work," Barry said.

Lucy jumped. "I didn't know you were here."

"I listened in. You got to her."

"Let's hope so."

Tia called. "Van's here, at the south exit."

"I'm going to cuff her," Lucy said. "It'll send home the message that we mean business."

"You can't. She has her arm in a sling."

"I'll cuff her good hand to me," Lucy said. "And ride over with her. It'll send a psychological message that I'm sticking to her like glue until she talks."

Barry concurred. "It's a good idea."

Ten minutes later, Lucy walked out the south entrance with a very unhappy and agitated Elise handcuffed to Lucy's wrist. Tia met them at the automatic sliding doors. The SAPD transport van was parked in a loading zone twenty feet away.

"We're ready," Tia said, walking a step ahead of them toward the van. "And when—"

A shot rang out, followed by several more. A pain spread through Lucy's back and her vision wavered. She reacted immediately and turned her body to cover Elise while pushing her down at the same time. Tia fell on the sidewalk next to her. Lucy smelled blood. Hers or Tia's? Screams echoed. Someone was returning gunfire. From the corner of her eye, she saw Barry behind a pillar, gun out, shattered glass all around them. Lucy had her own gun out, but in her left hand because her right was cuffed to Elise. She could shoot with her weaker hand, but wasn't as accurate.

Then the gunfire stopped. There were shouts and cries and Lucy couldn't move.

"Kincaid!" Barry called.

She wanted to shout that she was okay, but she couldn't. She took in a deep, painful breath.

"Kincaid! Are you hit?"

"Vest," she said, breathless. "Tia."

She looked over at the sidewalk. Tia was lying there, bleeding. Unconscious.

God, no. Tia.

Barry took command. He motioned for the guards to secure the area. Two cops shielded Tia and helped a nurse and orderly pull her in through the doors.

"Elise, are you hit?" Lucy asked, breathless. She still found it hard to catch her breath and her back hurt. She prayed she was just bruised.

Elise didn't answer, but she was shaking, so that was a good sign, Lucy hoped.

Barry came over and said, "Holy shit, Kincaid. You're hit."

"No."

He reached down and touched her back. "You're wearing a vest. You were shot in the back. You would have been dead."

"Good thing I put on my vest this morning."

She didn't normally wear a vest on the job, unless there was a specific reason to. But because of Kane's visit last night and his warning to watch her back, she'd decided that for the time being, it would be a good idea.

"Did you get him?"

"There were two. I'm pretty sure I got one, but they were in a car and bolted. A drive-by. I have the make, model, and license, already put an APB out. Let's get you checked out."

"Elise," Lucy said. "Let's get up."

Elise was sobbing uncontrollably. "I did everything they wanted! Why do they want me dead? Why?"

"Who, Elise?" Lucy asked.

"Rob Garza. He's Adeline Reyes-Worthington's campaign manager." She took a deep breath through her sobs, then everything came out in a rush. "I—I came from Washington. Rob likes kinky stuff, that's how we met. Then he said he had a job for me in San Antonio, and since I was tired of Washington, I agreed. He gave me a fucking lot of money. Twice as much as you found. He gave me the syringe. He told me if I got caught, that no one would do anything because I'm an underage whore and you'd all feel sorry for me. But I didn't know what was in it! Everything else I said was true, I swear. I swear! I was just supposed to take pictures. That's it. Don't let him hurt me. Please, I'll do anything you want, don't let him hurt me."

She clung to Lucy like a toddler.

"I won't," Lucy said, looking straight at Barry. "He won't get to you again."

Elise was back in her hospital bed. Her stitches had split open and she'd broken her wrist when the fed had pushed her to the ground. They'd patched her up and given her a pain pill and told her to rest.

She closed her eyes. Inside, she was smiling.

That bitch had believed every word.

CHAPTER THIRTY-TWO

Sean sped through San Antonio toward the hospital as Kane's cell phone went directly to voice mail.

"Call me now, dammit!" He hung up and threw his phone on the seat. That was the sixth message he'd left for his brother since talking to Mona Hill.

This whole situation was fucked. How the hell could Tobias be involved in Harper Worthington's murder? What the hell was going on?

Flashes of hot and cold rushed through him. He couldn't tell the FBI how he'd gotten the information. He couldn't tell anyone, except Kane.

Calm down. Calm down. You know Lucy is okay.

It didn't matter that her vest stopped the bullet. She'd been shot while transporting the prostitute. All the pieces were rapidly falling together.

Mona Hill. A head prostitute who had a skill with money laundering. Probably made her money blackmailing businessmen, as well as by providing underage girls to perverts. Some men paid big money to order the exact sex toy they wanted.

Elise, the young hooker. Hired to incapacitate, blackmail, or kill Harper Worthington. Through Mona? Possibly.

Because Harper had figured out that his wife was using her position in Congress to not only line her own pockets, but to launder money for the cartels. It was all there, in the BLM audit, but Sean hadn't known exactly what he was looking at until he'd seen the tablet files that Harper had left behind in Dallas. Good thing, too—without that list of numbers, Sean would never have been able to put it together.

Adeline Reyes-Worthington. The FBI knew she was corrupt, but how long had it taken them to figure it out? Lucy said that the agent had been working the case for over a year. While Sean understood that the FBI needed solid evidence, he'd seen them go after other people in the white-collar world with far less than they had on Adeline. They were likely trying to reel in an even bigger fish . . . other members of Congress? Businessmen? So they kept the sting going for months, hoping to catch more in the net.

There was no doubt in his mind that if the FBI had told Harper Worthington when he'd met with them last month that they already had an operation in place, or if they'd taken Adeline down months ago, that Harper Worthington would still be alive.

But what connected Adeline Reyes-Worthington to Tobias? *Something* brought them together. If Adeline had hired Tobias to kill her husband, why not find an easier way to do it?

The problem was they knew little about Tobias. They knew he was running guns and drugs. They knew he was associated with Trejo and Sanchez—both of whom were dead. They knew he lived in Mexico . . . No, they *suspected* he lived in Mexico. He hadn't even been on Kane's radar until two months ago. No one knew what he looked like, no one knew how his operation worked, no one knew how far his tentacles spread.

Lucy. Tobias must have figured out that Lucy, not Brad, had seen him.

There was one person he could trust, other than Kane.

He had Brad Donnelly on speed dial. He didn't trust the DEA phones anymore, so when Brad answered Sean said, "I need to see you. University Hospital. ASAP."

Before Brad could ask why, Sean hung up. He parked but couldn't get in through the emergency room doors because they were blocked off by SAPD. He saw Juan walking briskly toward the entrance, his badge out. Sean ran up to him. Juan didn't say anything, but waved Sean in when he was cleared by SAPD.

"She's fine," Juan told Sean.

"I want to see her."

Juan nodded and they took the elevator up to the fourth floor. They stepped out into a sea of cops and federal agents. Barry was talking to the chief of police, and Juan immediately headed over there. "Milton, Detective Mancini is a tough woman. If anyone can pull through, it's her."

"Thank you, Juan. Agent Crawford, thank you for your efforts on scene. As I told your agent, Juan, this is an SAPD investigation. Tia is one of ours. But because she was working with your agents, we'll share everything. I hope you understand." Meaning, *We're not giving this up so don't pull any jurisdictional bullshit on me.*

"Of course," Juan said. "Any resources, any personnel you need, it's yours. I have Barry's report—anything come up in the last fifteen minutes?"

"We found the car, dumped under the freeway. It was stolen two miles from here less than an hour before the attack and the owner didn't even know it was gone. I have uniforms canvassing the area, plus looking at all traffic cams near where they abandoned the vehicle. We're processing it on scene to expedite evidence collection."

"This is the second attempt on Elise Hansen's life," Barry said. "SAPD has two guards on her, one outside her door, one at the staircase."

"And," the chief of police said, "there will be an officer at each entrance."

"And you're certain that she was the target?" Juan asked.

"We viewed the hospital security feed. It shows the vehicle waiting in the parking lot. The suspects aren't identifiable. As soon as the girl emerged from the doors and was clear of the pillars, they drove forward and started shooting. Tia was flanking street side, right in the line of fire. But we have no reason to believe that Tia was the target."

Sean asked, "Where was Lucy?"

"Excuse me?"

Juan said, "Chief Milton Turner, this is Sean Rogan, a civilian consultant."

The chief looked like he recognized Sean, but more likely it was the Rogan name. "Agent Kincaid had handcuffed herself to the prisoner and got her out of harm's way. We've reviewed the security tapes, and her quick thinking saved the girl's life."

"I want to see the tapes," Sean said.

Juan cleared his throat and changed the subject.

Sean walked away. He tried to call Lucy, but she didn't pick up her phone. He found a nurse. "Lucy Kincaid? She was one of the FBI agents on scene. She said she had a couple cuts being stitched."

"Are you with the FBI?"

"I'm her boyfriend."

"I'm sorry, only immediate family and law enforcement is entitled to information about a patient."

Sean ran both hands through his hair. He had been on

edge all morning, and it had only gotten worse. "I need to see her."

"I wish I could help, but it's hospital policy."

"It's a fucked policy!"

This was why he didn't follow rules. He should have hacked into the hospital computer and found her himself.

"You're going to have to leave."

"I'm not leaving."

"I'm calling security." She didn't need to call security, one of the SAPD officers came over to them.

"Sir, you're going to have to leave."

It took all of Sean's self-control to force himself to speak calmly. "I need to see Agent Kincaid now."

Barry Crawford walked over and showed his badge to the officer. "I'll take care of this." He escorted Sean down the hall, away from the skeptical nurse and the rest of the cops. "Lucy's okay, Sean. She's in x-ray right now."

Why x-ray? Was it more serious than Lucy had told him?

Barry took Sean into a small, empty office. He pulled out his cell phone and said, "I downloaded the security feed from the parking lot. Zach and our tech people are putting together every feed from the area, but this one will tell you what you need to know."

Sean didn't want to watch the feed, but he needed the minute to calm down. He saw Tia exit the building. Right behind her was Lucy, her right wrist cuffed to Elise's left wrist, because Elise's right arm was in a sling. They weren't in a protective formation—they hadn't expected trouble. The transport van was twenty feet down from the entrance. Almost immediately, Lucy's body lurched forward. She grabbed Elise, putting her body between Elise and the parking lot, and pushed her into the bushes against the building. Tia was shot twice, first in the torso, then in the leg. Barry was only two feet away, blocked by a pillar, firing back.

Sean grabbed the phone and played the beginning in slow motion.

The first shot hit Lucy in the back.

She went down with Elise, obscured by the hedge, and Tia pulled her gun but couldn't get a shot fired. She was blocking the shooters' target. If Tia hadn't been standing where she was, the bullet's trajectory would have hit Lucy as she started going down. The second bullet hit Tia's leg, which easily could have hit Lucy even though she was behind the hedge by that point.

"Lucy was the target," Sean said.

Barry frowned. "No. Elise was the target. They were shooting at Lucy to get to Elise."

Sean didn't say anything. He knew different.

"Where is she?"

"I know you're worried, but Lucy was wearing a vest. She acted quickly, did everything she was supposed to do. I talked to her. She's fine, but the doctor wanted an x-ray to make sure that there were no cracked or broken ribs. She *is* okay, Sean. As soon as the doctor clears her, she'll be out here. Give it a few more minutes. And stay away from the hospital staff—they're ready to toss you out."

"What else do you know, Barry?" Sean asked.

"I can't tell you that, Sean."

"I'll find out."

"I'm sure you will."

"Do you know who hired the call girl?"

"We have a solid suspect, but I'm not telling you who it is. He's most likely behind this hit. We have agents on their way to pick him up right now."

That means it wasn't Tobias. Because law enforcement had no idea who he was or where he was located.

"Wait here," Barry said. "I'll get you when Lucy is out of x-ray."

Barry left and Sean called Nate. "Nate, who's the suspect behind the shooting at the hospital? Crawford said agents had been sent out to arrest him, but he refused to tell me who."

"I'll tell you on one condition."

"I'm not going to go after him."

"Swear."

"I swear, Nate. I have some pieces to the puzzle, but I need this one. I suspect there's a connection between this case and what happened two months ago. When my brother was in Mexico."

Nate knew what had really happened down there, but Sean didn't completely trust FBI phones, so was discreet.

"How certain are you?"

"I wouldn't ask you if I wasn't almost positive."

"The girl confirmed that Rob Garza hired her to take dirty pictures of Worthington, and that he gave her the syringe. She swears she didn't know the drugs would kill him."

"She just gave him up?"

"No—it took being nearly killed twice to scare her into cooperating. Kenzie and two other agents are on their way to Garza's office right now. They'll bring him in for questioning, but I swear, Sean, if you retaliate, I can't protect you."

"I won't. Thanks, buddy."

Sean hung up and called Donnelly. "Where are you?"

"Trying to get into the hospital. It's a fucking zoo out here."

"I'm on the fourth floor. A private office, room E four-oh-four. Hurry."

Adeline had been trying to reach Tobias's people all day. Nothing. Nothing!

Her life was over. She was going to lose everything.

She straightened her spine. Never. She was too strong, too powerful to take this hit sitting down. She had plenty of money, plenty of resources.

She found Joseph Contreras in his small, tidy office off the kitchen. "You have to find Tobias, or someone! Tell them I'll pay him. Everything he thinks I owe. And more."

"I've tried, Adeline." Joseph looked pained and worried. "I'm concerned about you. I think we've underestimated this man."

"I don't know how! He was left with *nothing* two months ago. How could he do this to me?"

"Maybe he had a bigger network than we thought."

She didn't see how that could be, but there was no other logical explanation.

"Then we need to take a vacation," she said.

"Tonight?"

It was already afternoon. It would take time to liquidate money. There was plenty in her offshore accounts, but very little—since Jolene's lawyers had frozen all of Harper's assets pending distribution per his will—cash on hand.

"Tomorrow morning. We need to quickly and quietly drain my accounts."

"Should I call Rob?"

"No," she snapped. "I don't trust him. Even if he had nothing to do with bringing that whore to San Antonio, there's something strange about that whole situation. He screws her in D.C. and two months later she's here? Either Rob is playing both sides, or he's an idiot. No one can know what I'm planning. Don't use any of my phones. I don't trust the feds. Who do they think they are coming in here and treating me like a criminal? I'm an elected official! I'm their *boss*."

She paced, angry and nervous and scared. "Have everything ready by tomorrow and we'll leave, first thing in the morning." She froze. "You will come with me, right?"

Joseph smiled and rose from his desk. He was a tall man, with a hardened expression, but still very handsome. He'd been with her for nearly five years, and was the only one she could truly depend on.

He put his hands on her shoulders and kissed her lightly. "I am honored that you want me to join you. I promise, I'll make sure everything goes smoothly."

"You always do," she said, a bit breathless. They'd only slept together a couple of times, but each time had been a slice of heaven. "Do you want . . . ?" She left the thought open.

"Yes," he said, running his thumb over her lips. "But I have much work to do to make sure everything goes off without a hitch. In two nights, we'll be in Andorra. And then . . . we'll let nature take its inevitable course."

He was right, of course. She was just feeling a bit lost right now. And scared. "The guards are still here, right?"

"Of course, Adeline. I'll check in with them before I leave to take care of the business. They'll make sure you're safe. Don't leave the house. I won't be long."

Rob Garza had spent all yesterday and last night making calls, trying to figure out what the hell was going on. Elise Hansen was *his* contact. He'd been using her special services for the past nine months, had learned nasty bits of information about the people he worked with and for, in addition to having fun screwing the little whore. But who hired her to kill Harper? It had to have been Adeline . . . she must have found Elise after catching them in her office. She'd been so mad, but Rob ignored it because she was happy with the information Elise had uncovered. Yet . . . that was the one explanation. Adeline hired Elise to kill Harper because she no longer trusted Rob. Not only

hired her to kill Harper, but frame him. It wouldn't take
the feds long to track Elise down to D.C., and back to him.

And Adeline had the audacity to imply that it was *him*
who'd come up with this asinine plan? That *he'd* hired the
whore to kill Harper?

The backstabbing bitch.

Unless it really was Tobias—then they were both dead.

Elise Hansen was certainly capable of killing someone.
At times, she'd snuck up on him in his apartment in D.C.
The way she'd looked at him, she'd seemed to be just as
happy screwing him as stabbing him with a knife. But
she'd always come through. Always.

*How well do you really know her? You met her nine
months ago when you called for a girl who liked it
rough.*

He'd seen that she was smart, and he'd convinced her
to take photos with some of her clients. He'd read about a
lobbyist who'd blackmailed members of Congress by
making sex tapes with a prominent call girl. It was a great
scam—the lobbyist was caught only because she had too
many people in the know.

With Elise, it was just him and her.

Until Adeline walked in that day.

Except . . .

*The service you originally called. Are you that stupid,
Roberto?*

He winced at the sound of his ex-wife's voice bouncing
around in his head. They'd only been married for a year,
and while the sex had been amazing, Monica had enjoyed
demoralizing him and squashing his ego.

He had enough money to disappear. Get a new ID, a
new name, just . . . hide for a while. Someplace he wouldn't
stick out, like New York City. He'd get an apartment and
wait it out until the dust settled.

"Flight five-five-five to New York City is in preboarding. Would our first class customers please come to the red carpet?"

Rob picked up his overnight bag from the seat next to him. He ran into a well-dressed man of about forty in a dark gray suit and matching fedora. He looked familiar.

"Garza, isn't it?" the man said with a smile.

Play the game, play the game. He'd met thousands of people working for Adeline. That's why he was flying out of Dallas, to avoid people knowing who he was, but even here people in business or politics might know him.

"Yes, how are you?" He'd met him, but couldn't place him.

The man stuck out his hand. Rob took it, because not shaking it would be suspicious.

The familiar stranger put his other hand around Rob's and held it there for a moment. A sharp sting on the back of his hand had him trying to pull it away, but the man was stronger than he looked and held on.

He was no longer smiling.

The stranger leaned forward and said, "I heard you've been wanting to meet me."

"Tobias." His voice wasn't working right. His tongue was thick and his mouth was dry.

The man smiled. "It has been a pleasure doing business with you, Mr. Garza. But then you stole from me and thought you could take down my operation. Ironic, perhaps, because Marquez has always worked for me. You ran to him and he played his part perfectly. I got my money back—the money you and Adeline stole—and had all my detractors silenced in one beautiful slaughter. I'm going to tell you one more thing."

Tobias leaned closer, his grip stronger, and Rob's knees shook as his muscles painfully tightened. "I've had this planned for a lot longer than two months. You have a federal agent undercover on your campaign, and if I didn't kill you, you'd be in prison soon enough. But the feds were getting too close to how our agreement worked, and honestly? I never trusted you or Adeline not to talk if the FBI swooped in. I know when to walk away."

Tobias dropped his hand and disappeared into the crowd of travelers.

Rob couldn't talk. He couldn't move. He fell to his knees, unable to breathe. His muscles constricted. He was having a seizure.

I'm dying.

He collapsed onto the carpet as people buzzed around him, but he couldn't hear anything, and soon his vision faded to black.

CHAPTER THIRTY-THREE

Sean didn't tell Brad Donnelly everything he'd said and done to Mona Hill—Brad was still a federal agent—but he gave him enough of the highlights that Brad could fill in most of the information himself. The only thing he completely left out was the information about the video of Lucy. No one needed to know about that.

Brad sat down, his head in his hands. "Sean, you just put a big fucking target on your head."

"Like I care? His people shot Lucy in the back! That girl isn't the target, Lucy is. Or maybe both of them. But I can't tell Juan how I know this."

"Kane."

"I've been trying to reach him. He was at my house this morning, but hell if I know where he is now. I even called J.T.—Kane's partner—and said it was urgent. I've never done that before, so hopefully Kane gets the message."

"No, what I mean is we tell Juan and Sam that the intel came from Kane. We have to get a protection detail on Lucy."

"I'm her protection. She's not leaving my sight."

"Barry Crawford will love that," Brad snapped.

"You're not helping. I'm trusting you with this, Brad. It's not easy for me." He hoped he hadn't made a mistake clueing in the DEA agent.

Brad let out a long sigh. "Look, I have no doubt that you can keep her safe, but you're also a target, and if Tobias wants to take you both out, you won't be able to stop him. We have to get a detail on you both—maybe it'll draw him out. If we can get one of his people in custody, that gives us leverage."

"You do. Nicole Rollins."

Brad reddened. "She wants witness protection or fucking *immunity* and I'm not certain she knows much of anything. We can't give her a free pass."

Sean sat on the edge of the desk. "You're right. I'm sorry—I hate having Lucy in the crosshairs just for doing her job."

"It's more than her job," Brad said quietly. "You know that."

"No—we saved your ass because you're one of the good guys, and you'd have been dead and buried a thousand times over in the time it would take to cut through the bureaucratic bullshit. It may not be a job we get paid for, but it's our job nonetheless."

"Based on what Nicole told me—if I can believe her— Tobias orchestrated the murders of those nine people. What does that tell you?"

"He didn't trust Trejo's operation. Or he blamed them for what happened in Mexico."

Brad shook his head. "They weren't his people, Sean. That's all I can come up with. Tobias wasn't part of Trejo's group. But Tobias blamed Trejo for losing the guns, and Sanchez for not killing me."

"What do you mean by that? They tortured you."

"For no reason. It was fun for Sanchez. It was punishment because I'd fucked with him, tore him down in front of his *amigos*. Got his sister to turn against him. But Trejo was furious. He said something, I don't remember all of it, but something like, 'You were supposed to kill him.'"

"So Tobias blamed Sanchez because you're alive— maybe more because if he hadn't taken you to Mexico, we would never have gone down there. And they would never have lost the guns."

"Bingo."

"Tobias is cleaning house. Taking out the gang, going after Lucy. But how does this connect to Adeline Worthington and her husband?"

"Maybe it doesn't."

Sean shook his head. "Too many coincidences. It's all connected." He wished he could talk this out with Lucy, but Brad was going to have to do. "The girl, Elise Hansen, confessed that Rob Garza—Adeline Worthington's campaign manager—hired her to take pictures of Worthington, and then when she went to collect the rest of the money, he shot her. If Garza is responsible for her attack, the feds must think that Garza is behind the shooting here at the hospital."

"Does Garza have those kinds of connections? Since when does a political campaign manager go around killing people?"

"Fact: Mona Hill works for—or with—Tobias. Fact: Mona Hill sent Elise Hansen, the prostitute, to James Everett's hotel. Fact: Rob Garza sent Elise Hansen to Worthington. It reasons that Tobias is also connected to Rob Garza."

"And where does the congresswoman fit in? A pawn?"

"A co-conspirator. I'm not supposed to know this, but the FBI is already investigating her for political corruption."

"Then why kill her husband?"

"Because she doesn't know about the investigation, and Harper was digging into her finances and her abuse of power. HWI hired me to assist with the security and forensic audit. Though I haven't put all the pieces together, Harper found evidence in an audit that Adeline was using her position to create artificially high land values—when she wanted to sell, or when a friend wanted to sell—or artificially low land values when someone in her circle wanted to buy."

Brad stared at him, incredulous. "And no one figured this out?"

"We're talking about huge tracts of land, manipulating the environmental impact reports, causing delays or expediting processes. And isolated, these transactions appear perfectly normal. It's when you put them all together and identify the buyers and sellers, who benefits and who doesn't, it's clear that there's a major financial scam going on to defraud the government and defraud Adeline Worthington's opponents, as well as benefit her and her supporters.

"I've also been looking into her finances," Sean continued. "Not legally—so I can't give any of it to the FBI. But I can steer them in the right direction. She's been hiding money all over the world. If she wants to flee, she has the resources to do so."

"We have to tell Juan."

"I need to talk to Kane first."

"He'll give you cover?"

Sean nodded without hesitating. Kane would protect him just like he protected Lucy when he left her out of his report about what happened at the Trejo compound. Sean glanced at his watch. "Lucy should be done by now. How long do x-rays take?"

He stepped out of the office and into borderline chaos. The cops in the waiting area were all talking on phones or listening to Juan speak. Barry rushed by.

Sean grabbed him. "What happened? Is Tia okay?"

"She's still in surgery, still fighting," he said. He glanced at Brad, obviously surprised to see him. "I have to go."

"Where's Lucy?"

"I thought you knew she was done. She and I have to go."

"Not without me."

Barry turned to him. "Rogan, I don't know what your thing is, but your girlfriend is a federal agent and has a job to do."

"Lucy was the target."

"That's absurd."

Brad intervened. "Barry—an informant contacted me earlier, that's why I came here. There's some chatter that Tobias planned to take out a fed today. We assumed it was someone in the DEA, but when I heard about the shooting here, I realized that both Ryan Quiroz and Lucy were on the task force that took down Tobias's San Antonio operation. She could very well be a target."

Sean was surprised and pleased at how smoothly Brad blended the truth and the lies.

"And why are you here instead of your boss?"

"Because I'm an SSA, just like Juan Casilla," Brad snapped. "He's here, I'm here."

"We need to talk to Juan. This is all screwed up," Barry said.

Sean let Brad walk off with Barry to discuss the new information with Juan, and he called Lucy. She finally answered, her voice soft. "Hello? Sean?"

"Where are you?"

"I'm outside Tia's operating room. I needed to check on her."

"Where?"

"Second floor."

"I'll be right there."

Sean took the stairs down to the second floor. Lucy was

pacing in front of the nurses' station. Just seeing her made him breathe easier.

She saw him and her face showed everything he needed to see. He pulled her into his arms and hugged her. She winced, but when he tried to let go she held him close.

"Dear God, Lucy. If you hadn't put on that vest."

"Don't even think it."

"Are you okay?"

"I'm fine. A big bruise. No cracked ribs. I had the wind knocked out of me, that's it."

Sean touched a bandage on her arm. "What's this?"

"The bush I jumped into. Sharp branch. They sanitized it, gave me antibiotics, and glued the wound instead of putting in stitches."

He kissed her wrist. "We need to talk."

"Did Barry tell you?"

"He hasn't told me shit, Lucy. Completely keeping me in the dark. Brad and I think that Tobias is behind the hit, and you were the target, not the girl."

She shook her head. "No."

"Yes," he said emphatically. "I watched the video in slow motion. The first bullet hit you in the back. *You* were the target."

It was clear she didn't want to believe it. "I don't know . . ."

"I do. Tobias is neck-deep in this entire mess. I haven't put together all the pieces, but he's involved. Brad agrees." He couldn't tell Lucy how he knew, and he hated lying to her. He had to find a way to give her all the information without her knowing how he obtained it.

"It's Rob Garza," she said.

"I know—I talked to Nate after Barry cut me out of the loop. If Garza's involved with Harper Worthington's murder, it has to be because Tobias ordered it."

She frowned. "Why? It's his wife, Adeline. Garza is her campaign manager."

God help him, but he had to lie. "I got a cryptic message from Kane. I'm trying to reach him, but he's not available. Nicole Rollins told Brad that there was someone else dirty at the DEA. It's likely that someone in-house figured out that you were feeding Brad the information on Tobias, or one of the goons who escaped that night told Tobias you were there. Or hell, he could have been watching the entire time while Trejo's compound burned. I don't know how! All I know is that you're in danger."

"Garza's dead, Sean."

"What?"

"He collapsed at the Dallas airport. Had a ticket to New York City he bought today. Kenzie and a couple other agents were at Adeline's campaign headquarters with an arrest warrant when the call came in. They're now on their way to Dallas."

"Murder?"

"Most likely, but we don't have much to go on right now. Garza was seen shaking the hand of someone he appeared to know, the man walked away, and a few minutes later Garza collapsed and died. We're getting the security feeds, we'll find the guy. Airports have the best security in the country, his ID would have been checked, and we can compare his image to the security checkpoint. We'll know who he is."

Sean knew a half dozen ways to get around airport security, but he didn't say that to Lucy.

"But Elise has given a statement," Lucy continued, "and so far, everything she said is holding up. She was working in D.C. as a prostitute and met Garza first as a john. He offered her ten thousand dollars to come to San Antonio and take compromising pictures. She didn't know who or why until he sent her a photo of Harper Worthington and a location, plus a syringe that he said was ketamine in case Harper couldn't be seduced."

"Do you believe her?" Sean asked.

Lucy hesitated. "She's holding something back. I'll figure it out, and if I don't, I'll push her again. While the shooting the other night didn't seem to scare her much, today was another story. A lot spilled out right after, things I think she'd have rather kept to herself. She's calculating, but she's smart. I'll get the truth out of her, but it's going to take time."

"I know you will." He kissed her again. He wished he had asked Mona Hill more questions, specifically about this girl Elise Hansen. But it looked like Lucy and her people were learning what they needed to know.

"Barry was on his way down here—we're going to push Adeline tonight. We're waiting for approval from on high."

"Rick?"

"Probably. From what Barry said, when Juan called Agent Dunbar about bringing Adeline in, he went ballistic. So Juan went over his head."

"Good for Juan."

Lucy looked down at Sean's hands. "What happened?" She turned them over.

He looked down. His knuckles were scratched and there was a bruise on the top of his fist. "I was an idiot when I was working out this morning. Letting off steam with my punching bag. Nothing to worry about."

Barry, Brad, and Juan stepped off the elevator and approached Lucy and Sean. "Any word on Detective Mancini?" Juan asked.

"Still in surgery," Lucy said. "The bullet went in through her side, at an angle, caused a lot of damage. But there's plenty of blood on hand, and her captain is organizing a blood drive at SAPD if they need more."

Juan glanced at Sean. Sean couldn't read his expression, but Juan said to Lucy, "I'm sure Sean told you what Agent Donnelly learned today."

"Yes. I don't know how much to believe, sir," she said. "I'm sorry, Brad—but my witness pointed at Garza."

"And Garza is dead," Juan said. "We can't interrogate him. I can't discount the threat, considering all the fallout after Operation Heatwave. You were involved in the take-down, you and Ryan fingered Nicole Rollins, and you shut down the pipeline of boys they were using. If Tobias is behind this in any way, it's my duty to protect you."

"You can't take me off this case," Lucy said, her voice quivering. "We're so close to proving Adeline orchestrated her husband's murder."

"I'm not taking you off the case. Tobias is a terrorist, and I don't run from terrorists. Neither do you. But you're not stupid, Lucy. Brad's attached to your hip from the minute you leave your house until you return." Juan looked at Sean. "And I assume your home security is still the best."

"It is, but—"

"Sean, I've made my decision. I'll also be posting a unit on your house until we know what's going on, so don't give them a hard time. And I have two agents who will be following to make sure Barry and Lucy don't pick up a tail." He paused. "I don't have to tell you that Agent Donnelly is trained for this kind of detail."

"No, sir," Sean said. He wasn't happy. But he couldn't force himself into the investigation. He'd already crossed the line; he needed to step back and trust Donnelly to watch Lucy's back.

But he didn't have to like it.

"Good." Juan turned to Barry. "Dunbar is furious, but he's backing down. He's with the AUSA right now working on the case to present to the grand jury as soon as possible. AD Stockton said they have more than enough, but Dunbar had hints that Adeline was involved with a known criminal, a thug by the name of Javier Marquez. He wanted to develop that further, but he's going to have plenty on her. If we get her on murder or conspiracy to murder, she won't be given a slap on the wrist. And—she might turn on Marquez if given enough incentive. If she paid to have her husband killed, she's eligible for the death penalty. We can take that off the table."

Sean caught Brad's eye. He didn't dare say anything.

"Did you say Marquez?" Brad asked.

"Is he on your radar?"

"Yes, sir. We believe his gang took out nine people on Sunday night—the remainder of the Trejo/Sanchez gang. It's the case I've been working with Ryan."

"Are you positive?"

"Yes. The guns used in the slaughter were from the shipment stolen from the dead Marines six months ago. One of the shooters was shot during the attack and then executed by the gang. He has SAS gang tats on his arm. The San Antonio Saints swore allegiance to Marquez."

"What would a congresswoman be doing associating with a violent street gang?"

"That's the thing—Marquez likes to pretend he's a legitimate businessman. He's not running around the streets, but he has layers under him who are, like the SAS. We thought he might be making a move to take over since Sanchez is out of the picture." Brad glanced at Sean. "But," Brad added, "one of my informants believes that the hit on Sunday was sanctioned by Tobias."

Juan's jaw tightened. "Spill it, Donnelly. This informant of yours is Kane Rogan, isn't it?"

"Sir—"

"Don't. I've watched you and Sean exchanging signs for the last five minutes. I'm not an idiot, don't treat me like one."

"I wasn't—"

Juan cut him off again. "I don't suppose Kane Rogan would come in and discuss this with me?"

"Juan, it's true that Kane is a source, but it was Nicole Rollins who implied that Tobias was behind the hit," Brad said. "I talked to her yesterday morning."

Juan hesitated as he mulled over that information, then he turned to Barry. "Push the congresswoman. If she calls for a lawyer, fine. We'll bring her in officially tomorrow morning for questioning. If she confesses, arrest her."

"Yes, sir," Barry said.

"Go. Now."

Barry, Brad, and Lucy left. Sean itched to go with them, but Juan put his hand up.

"Do not say a word, Rogan," Juan said in a low voice. "I know the truth, just like I know you'll deny it with your last breath. This *Tobias* is after Lucy because she was in Mexico, not because she did a good job working on Operation Heatwave. She's in danger because you and your brother put her in danger. Without you and your resources, she would never have crossed the border. And because she has to lie about it, she's in even more danger."

Sean wasn't going to take the blame. The blame rested on the system that couldn't do anything to rescue a kidnapped federal agent or orphaned boys. "Donnelly would be dead. Those little boys would be dead. Some things are bigger than all of us."

"She was shot down there! And you know how I found out about it? Today. I went to see her while she was being stitched up, to make sure she was okay because she's my agent. And I saw the scar on her arm, still red and puckered. Fresh. Two months fresh. But even if I didn't recognize the healing process, I would have known because I've read her files. I know she's been shot before, and I know where. And she'd never been shot in that arm. So not only did a federal agent violate the law and risk an international incident, she was injured and her supervisor—*me*—wasn't even told."

Juan stepped forward and pressed a finger against Sean's chest.

"You poked the tiger, Sean. And the next time anything like this happens, the consequences will be a whole lot worse than two weeks' unpaid vacation."

"Juan—"

"Lucy is a good agent, Sean. A damn good agent. She has compassion and a rare skill set where she can see a crime scene through the eyes of a cop, a pathologist, a criminal, and a victim, all at the same time. Her analytical test scores were the highest among the last seven graduating classes at Quantico. I want her on my team.

"But she's a rookie. She's reckless. And like Donnelly, a maverick. She doesn't think things through. I've read her file. I know everything. *Everything*." He let that sink in for a moment. "But what I don't know is if you're good for her."

Juan started to walk away, then stopped and looked back at Sean. "I don't know what you or your family did for Rick Stockton, but he unconditionally vouches for you. I, however, don't trust you. Which means I can't fully trust Lucy, either. And I don't know if I can have someone I don't fully trust on my team."

Juan turned and walked away before Sean could respond.

Maybe Juan leaving was for the better. Because everything Sean wanted to say would only make the situation worse.

CHAPTER THIRTY-FOUR

Lucy gave Barry a partial apology while they were driving to Adeline's house. Brad was in the backseat and Barry hadn't spoken for five minutes.

"Sean is protective," she said by way of explanation. "It's his business. Security."

"It's not his business," Barry said.

"Rogan Caruso Kincaid specializes in protective services—corporate kidnappings, foreign kidnappings, hostage rescue, computer security. It's how he was raised." She paused. "We've been through a lot together. If he thinks the threat is viable, I have to take it seriously."

"Your own personal bodyguard," Barry mumbled.

"You're out of line, Crawford," Brad said from the backseat.

Lucy didn't want an argument. "If you got to know Sean, the way he thinks, how he assesses information, you'd realize he's an asset."

"He's not a cop," Barry said. "He has no jurisdiction and I don't care that he's consulted with the FBI in the past. It's a conflict of interest for him to consult on a case you're working."

"I can respect that opinion."

"You don't see it."

"I do, but—"

"There is no *but*. It's a conflict. The problem with bending the rules is that they become brittle. And more easily broken."

"Brad and Sean didn't get along at first," Lucy said, wanting desperately to mend these fences, "but they built a mutual respect."

"True," Brad said. "I thought Sean was a prick." He laughed, but Barry didn't crack a smile. "But when you talk about bending and breaking rules, Barry, remember this: if it weren't for Kane Rogan, I'd be dead."

Brad caught Lucy's eye in the rearview mirror.

"You don't owe Kane anything," Lucy said. "He did it because it was the right thing to do, not to be in your debt."

"I know," Brad said. "That's why it means even more."

Lucy glanced away. Brad had made it clear that he felt indebted to her, Sean, and Kane, but she didn't want that. She liked to think that anyone else, faced with the same information she had had at the time, would have made the exact same decision to go after Brad. Maybe it was naïve to think that—okay, she *knew* it was naïve to think that—but it helped her believe she was just like everyone else.

She changed the subject. "I'm having a difficult time reconciling something. If Garza was behind Harper Worthington's murder, why was he killed?"

"Assuming that he was," Barry said.

"I haven't seen the security tapes, but the witnesses were consistent and it's too much of a coincidence that he would drop dead while he was fleeing the state—at the same time federal agents were looking to arrest him. We were on to him, we had Elise in custody, he knew we were pushing Adeline—she must have called him after we showed her the picture of Elise yesterday morning. So he runs. That makes sense. But if someone killed him, that means Garza wasn't pulling the strings."

"Adeline Reyes-Worthington," Barry said. "You thought she was behind her husband's death from the beginning."

"I thought," Lucy clarified, "that she was lying. But taking out Garza . . . I don't know. He was her right hand, but she hires yet another person to take him out? When does it stop?"

"She still could have hired someone. Just like she had Garza bring in Elise from D.C. It was a smart move—except that they should have sent Elise out of town immediately. Or killed her. Keeping her around, with her connection to Mona Hill, it . . ." Barry's voice trailed off.

"You see it, too."

"See what?" Brad asked from the backseat.

"Bread crumbs," Barry mumbled.

"Exactly," Lucy said. "Elise's DNA and fingerprints were all over that motel room. Then she took Harper's phone and accidentally left it in James Everett's hotel room? When she realized she killed Harper, she didn't run away? Prostitutes are all about self-preservation, but instead, she met up with the guy who hired her and he tried to kill her."

"Now you've lost me," Barry said.

"Every piece of evidence has led us to Elise Hansen, and she gives us Garza on a silver platter."

"There's evidence—the stationery," Barry countered. "We worked hard for the information. She didn't give it up easily. It wasn't until after the second attempt to kill her."

"Except if Sean is right," Brad said, "Elise wasn't the target of today's shooting."

Lucy didn't comment because while Sean might be right, she didn't see how she could be the primary target. Maybe *one* of the targets.

She said, "I'm not saying that Garza wasn't involved; I'm saying that he was set up to take the fall. He's dead—point every finger at him as the ringmaster."

Brad said, "Someone tried to kill her the other night. If today was Tobias going after you, Monday was . . . Oh shit."

Lucy didn't realize the repercussions until Brad said his name.

"It's Tobias. From the very beginning," she said.

"What the hell was Adeline Reyes-Worthington into?" Brad said.

Barry was perplexed. "You think this drug dealer is behind this?"

"He's not a drug dealer," Brad said. "He's more than that. Until two months ago, no one knew who he was, he was just a name. But now . . ."

"His name got out because of what happened in Mexico," Lucy said. "We—you and Kane, I mean—outed him. Blew his anonymity, so to speak."

"And Kane stole two trucks' worth of his guns," Brad said. "And destroyed his San Antonio operation. Tobias then aligned himself with Marquez and had Marquez take out the rest of Sanchez/Trejo's failed gang. Almost as if . . . as if . . ."

"He had a temper tantrum," Lucy said.

"Why didn't he take the drugs?"

"Maybe he doesn't have a network to sell them. Operation Heatwave put a huge hole in his net. He's both purging and rebuilding."

"Where does Adeline Reyes-Worthington fit in?" Barry asked.

Brad said, "Political corruption. Buying and selling government land. Sean said—" He stopped.

Barry bristled. "You told Sean about the undercover operation?"

"Sean's the one who found the bug," Lucy said. "He knew it was a federal sting."

"And he tells the DEA."

"Barry—we're way beyond compartmentalizing this information," Lucy said.

No one spoke for a moment. Then Barry said, "If Adeline is as corrupt as Logan Dunbar seems to think, where did all the money go? And how does Tobias fit in?"

"I don't know," Lucy admitted. "But we're going to find out." She hesitated, then said, "Barry, I need you to give me a little leeway with her. I can flip her. But you have to trust me."

Barry didn't say anything for a minute. "All right," he finally said. "But watch my cues. If you step over the line, I'm going to rein you in."

"Where's all her security?" Lucy asked after they were buzzed in.

"It's getting dark. Maybe they're better at hiding at night."

Lucy closed her eyes. The hum of the car, the distant neigh of a horse. It was calm. Almost peaceful.

"No one is here," she said.

Barry looked around, but didn't say anything. He stopped the car and said, "Don't get out."

Barry called the patrol car that was stationed on the street outside for a report. "Any activity?"

"The house manager, Mr. Contreras, left at three this afternoon and returned at six. After, the rest of the staff left."

"How many?"

"There were two vehicles. I don't know how many were in each vehicle. At least two per vehicle."

"Thank you," Barry said.

Brad said, "I'll walk the grounds, make sure there's nothing off."

"Keep the channel open." Barry put in his earpiece and Brad did the same. They tested the signal, then Barry and Lucy went to the front door.

Joseph Contreras opened the door before they rang. "Adeline is in the den," he said. "She isn't feeling well and asked that you keep this visit short."

Contreras led the way to a small room near the entry. It was smaller and warmer than Adeline's office, with several chairs, built-in bookcases with history books and antique knick-knacks, and on one wall a map of Texas from before Texas became a state.

Adeline sat on a chair with her laptop, dressed in jeans and a simple blouse, her eyes rimmed red. "My campaign manager just died," she said. "I'm . . . having a difficult time. Can this wait until tomorrow? Or after the weekend? Harper's memorial is on Saturday."

"I'm sorry, this can't wait," Barry said. "We're here about Mr. Garza."

"How did you hear about his death?" Lucy asked.

"Airport security contacted me when they searched his identification and learned he worked for me. Why does that matter? Everyone I care about is dying."

"You mean murdered," Lucy said.

She blinked. "Harper was murdered. Security said that Rob collapsed at the airport."

"He was murdered at the airport," Lucy said. "When did you last speak to Mr. Garza?"

Adeline was struggling with her composure. "Yesterday," she said. "After lunch."

"Where were you?"

"Here. We were working . . ." Her voice trailed off and she didn't look at them.

"What did you discuss?"

"That's none of your business," she snapped. "It was campaign related."

"Did you discuss the girl I showed you a picture of yesterday? Her name is Elise Hansen."

"N-no," she said.

Lucy didn't believe her. Did this woman actually think that she was a believable liar?

"Were you aware that Rob Garza had hired Ms. Hansen for sex when he was in Washington?"

"No." She wasn't looking at Barry or Lucy, but at the bookshelf behind them. She was trying hard to keep it together.

Lucy continued to push. "Were you aware that Mr. Garza paid Ms. Hansen more than ten thousand dollars to come to San Antonio for the purpose of seducing your husband and taking pornographic photos?"

Adeline paled. "N-no. He wouldn't."

"Were you aware that Mr. Garza shot Ms. Hansen when she tried to collect the money?"

"God, no. No. That's not possible."

"We had an arrest warrant and were looking for Mr. Garza when he attempted to flee our jurisdiction by buying a ticket from Dallas to New York City. We believe he may have been trying to leave the country. But he was killed before he could board the plane by an unknown assailant. The Dallas FBI office in conjunction with Homeland Security is investigating his murder. But we're finding it hard to believe that you didn't know your campaign manager and chief consultant had your husband killed."

"I— That's not what happened. I had nothing to do with it. But—no. He couldn't be—but—" She stared at the wall behind them, not looking at either Barry or Lucy.

Lucy said, "Mrs. Worthington, do you know a man who goes by the name Tobias?"

Adeline started to shake. "Oh God. Oh God."

Barry glanced at Lucy and for a moment she thought that Barry was angry because she'd brought up Tobias, but his expression was one of total surprise.

He said to Adeline, "How do you know Tobias?"

"No. I mean, I've never met him, but . . ." She got up from her seat and walked to the bookshelf. She pushed in three books, and a hidden compartment opened. "Tobias thinks I took money from him. He killed Harper. I . . . I didn't think Rob had anything to do with it, but maybe . . ."

Adeline handed Barry an envelope.

"What is this?" he asked.

"Proof that I didn't kill my husband."

Barry first looked into the envelope, then he cautiously pulled out a single piece of paper. Lucy read over his shoulder.

> *Adeline ~*
> *I told you two months ago that if you changed allegiances, you would regret it. I want what you owe me. You have forty-eight hours, or you're next.*
> *I know you won't say anything to the police or FBI about this note, because I have enough evidence to bury you. Not only evidence of our arrangement, but proof that you had your husband killed.*
> *~ Tobias*

Barry took out a photo from the envelope. It was Harper Worthington half-naked in the motel room.

Lucy's stomach tightened. Elise Hansen must have taken this photo—and there was nothing sexual about it. It was obvious that the man was dead.

"You have to protect me," she said. "He'll kill me."

"What was your arrangement with Tobias?" Lucy asked.

She opened her mouth, then closed it. "I can't tell you that."

"This note says that he has proof that you had Harper killed."

"I didn't! He set it up. He's framing me! Rob must have been in on it, because that whore was his—" She stopped talking.

"You said you'd never seen Elise Hansen," Lucy said.

Adeline didn't say anything.

"We can't help you unless you tell us the truth," Barry said.

"The truth is that I don't know what he's talking about! But he must have thought I'd done something to him . . ." She seemed to realize that she wasn't making any sense and stopped talking. She took a deep breath and put her chin out. "I should have come to you first. I realize that now. I didn't know what to do."

Barry seemed stunned that she would think they were such idiots. Lucy wasn't. Lucy was angry and not a little bit worried. But she pushed her fear aside and said, "Tobias had your husband killed because you betrayed him. What specifically did you do for Tobias?"

"Nothing!"

"You're lying."

"How dare you," Adeline said. "I'm a member of Congress. I will have you fired, Agent Kincaid."

Barry said, "Mrs. Reyes-Worthington, I'd like you to come down to headquarters for further questioning."

"No."

"You're making this more difficult for yourself."

"I am not going to be treated like a criminal when I'm the victim."

"You're no victim," Lucy said.

"Get out of my house!" Adeline shouted.

Barry pulled out his phone. He said to Lucy, "Watch her," then left the room.

Adeline stared after Barry. "The audacity!"

Lucy glared at her. "Your husband was murdered because you were involved with a known criminal."

"Do not talk to me. I want a lawyer."

"Do you think this is a game? That you can give the right answer and pull a get-out-of-jail-free card? At a minimum, you're an accessory to murder. More likely, you're an accomplice." Lucy wanted to say more, but she bit her tongue. Barry hadn't brought up the political corruption or bribery charges, so she kept that to herself. But to Lucy, murder was worse. Murder was personal.

Adeline didn't budge. "You have no idea who you are up against."

Lucy refused to let Adeline bait her. She watched her closely and received a bit of satisfaction as the woman squirmed under her glare.

"There is no reason for Tobias to kill your husband except that Harper must have found something that connected to him instead of you," Lucy said, working her mind around what they knew versus what they suspected. "Tobias could care less about whether you're caught for doing something illegal, but there must be a paper trail that leads to Tobias, and he feared that Harper would find it. That's why he died. And you let it happen."

"I didn't! I didn't know!"

"But you knew that Harper was preoccupied. And you knew that you were involved in illegal activities with a gun runner."

Adeline's face completely drained and she sat down.

Lucy realized she was on to something. She sent Zach Charles a text message.

Dig into Adeline's finances—personal, campaign, corporate, anything—from mid-March through the present. See if there's anything odd or unusual. Ask Juan if you can use Sean for this.

She sent it before she could change her mind. She shouldn't bring Sean into it at all, but he had already analyzed Harper Worthington's business and financial records, so he was primed to dig into Adeline's. He'd see the connection—figure out what Harper had uncovered that had gotten him killed. Because the only reason for Tobias to have killed Harper was not just to scare Adeline or frame her, but because Harper knew something that could jeopardize Tobias.

"Who is Gary Ackerman?" Lucy asked. "Why did you get a restraining order against him seven years ago?"

Adeline didn't say anything.

"Did you know your husband was meeting with him?"

Again, no answer, but Adeline closed her eyes.

Lucy said quietly, "Do you know that Ackerman was murdered, too?"

"Dear God." Adeline put her head in her hands.

Barry walked back in. "Lucy." He jerked his head and she followed him into the hall.

Quietly, he said, "Juan passed me up to Naygrew. He listened to what just happened, and wants to get an arrest warrant. I wanted to bring her in now, but Naygrew thinks it puts the Bureau at risk."

"How?" Lucy would never understand politics.

"Because we have a lot of circumstantial evidence but nothing substantial. It's a big clusterfuck."

"And so she gets to go free?"

"No. Dunbar is going up in front of a grand jury tomorrow with the AUSA and they expect a multicharge indictment on bribery, abuse of power, political corruption, whatever they're calling it these days. She's not going to get a pass on murder. But we can't prove it at this point."

"She knows more."

"Which is why we're going to ask her to come in of her

own free will tomorrow morning to answer questions. If she refuses, we'll get a subpoena to compel her to answer. You need to work on Elise Hansen tonight."

"She lied to us. Multiple times."

"She's sixteen."

"I don't care. That photo . . ." Lucy shook her head. "Okay. I'll push Elise. Do what you need to do."

Barry walked back into the den, and Lucy followed.

"Mrs. Reyes-Worthington," Barry said, "I spoke to my boss, and he requests that you come to FBI headquarters tomorrow morning to answer additional questions regarding your husband's murder and what you knew about your campaign manager's activities."

"I don't know," Adeline said. "Can I think about it?"

"We can get a subpoena, if you would prefer. A subpoena would be part of the public record."

"Don't threaten me." Adeline's attitude had returned. "I can bring my lawyer, right? It's my right, of course I can bring him," Adeline answered her own question.

"Eight A.M."

"Fine," she snapped. "I'll be there."

CHAPTER THIRTY-FIVE

Sean drove to HWI after Juan Casilla chewed him out. It was the end of the day and most of the staff was gone, but Gregor Smith was still there.

As soon as Sean entered the building, Gregor greeted him. "Is it true about Adeline's campaign manager?"

"That he's dead or that he's a killer? Probably both."

Gregor led Sean up to his office. "Was Adeline involved?"

"I don't know," Sean said as they both sat down.

"I'm stunned. I don't know what to think. Why?"

"That's the million-dollar question. The FBI thinks that Harper found incriminating information about his wife's political corruption and that's why he was acting peculiar for the last month."

"Incriminating how?"

"She was on the Interior Committee. It oversees the Bureau of Land Management. She could have had inside information that would be profitable to her friends. Maybe Garza figured it out and decided to protect his boss. Maybe it was Garza who was sharing information." Sean paused. "Whatever was going on, she's certainly not innocent, even if she didn't have Harper killed."

"I got your report, I'm glad that our operation is clean—but I wanted to ask you about the BLM audit. You said that there was a problem, but didn't elaborate."

"I don't think that there is anything wrong with the files you have. I think that everything is going to match up fine for BLM. But I'd like to look at the records again and compare them with a document that Harper kept on a private tablet." Sean didn't tell Lucy he'd made a copy of the dates and parcel numbers. She'd shown the pages to him, but the FBI didn't have access to all the information. It would take them weeks to go through the files—because of manpower issues—and because Sean had access to HWI now, he could match them up in a few hours.

"Anything you need if it's going to help clear Harper's name."

"He's already cleared."

"The press leaked that he was with a prostitute."

"The FBI will issue a statement. It's clear that he was expecting to meet someone else, not a hooker."

Which was one thing that was bothering Sean, and if Lucy thought about it for one second she'd realize it, too. How did Garza find out about Harper's meetings with Gary Ackerman and why was he worried? How did he set up the meeting with Harper the night he was killed? Harper had thought he was meeting with Ackerman. It was an anomaly, and Sean didn't like it.

"They followed him," Sean said suddenly.

"Excuse me?"

"Sorry, I'm just working through something in my head. I think Harper was being followed. It's the only way his killer could have known he was meeting with the person who gave him information about the illegal land transactions."

"You've lost me. Are you talking about the BLM audit? Or something else?"

"Both. I can't explain right now, but if I can have access to Harper's office tonight, I'll tell you when I put it all together. Right now it's just a mess of numbers in my head."

"Go ahead—I'll be here until eight, but I've also put in twenty-four-hour security on your recommendation. An employee, not a service, as you suggested."

"Good. Loyalty decreases the chances of infiltration."

Sean left Gregor's office and went down the hall to Harper's suite, then through to his colleague's office where all the BLM files were. He didn't need the physical files, because Harper had already created a spreadsheet. Sean hadn't realized the importance of the spreadsheet until he saw the tablet files. Now it all made sense, but he had to merge the two data sets and then convince the FBI that they would match with Adeline's financials—without hacking further into Adeline's banking records to compare.

And, Sean thought as he quickly entered the data, if Adeline were smart, she'd do exactly what Mona Hill had done—create layers of shell companies to make finding the true source of the cash next to impossible. Maybe she *had* done it, but someone like Harper Worthington would be able to see the financial house of cards more easily than anyone else. Just like Sean.

Where did Tobias fit in?

Sean pushed that thought aside as he entered the data then created a calendar with the important dates—and realized that he needed names to go with each of these transactions. Fortunately, most counties had a database where you could look up basic property records if you had the parcel number. Sean plugged in the information. It was a painstaking process because he had to run each parcel number separately. But once he was done, he realized that each of the transactions was purchased by a variety of individuals all under the umbrella of a single entity. It didn't take him long to trace the entity to James Everett.

At least on paper.

The group, Texas Land Holding, was simply a pass-through account. Everett would buy and sell land, but the money involved didn't stay with TLH. It was moved immediately out—and tracking *that* would be impossible without banking records.

He'd already crossed into too many gray areas, but hacking into a financial institution would be clearly illegal, so he backed off.

Sean looked at the calendar. The last week of March stood out. Nine weeks ago. That was the week of Operation Heatwave, when Brad and Lucy had taken down the Trejo/Sanchez cartel and put themselves on Tobias's radar.

A whole bunch of transactions had occurred that week and the following week . . . and then nothing. Millions of dollars in land transactions, all with government land being bought or sold, occurred during a ten-day period, when during the previous seven years there were no more than two regional transactions a quarter.

Hadn't Lucy mentioned that James Everett had had a falling out with Adeline two months ago? Everett was working with the FBI, but there had been nothing in Agent Dunbar's statements that said they were investigating Adeline for money laundering.

Except they *were* investigating her for graft and corruption. They had sensed there was something else, which was why they hadn't indicted her for the shit she'd already done.

Had they only listened to Harper Worthington when he went to their office last month, he would be alive and the FBI would have had all this information. Some of the smartest financial wizards worked for the FBI—people even better with numbers than Sean, though he

wouldn't admit it. They would have put this together if
they only had the right information. But the process of
pulling together disparate and seemingly unconnected
data—that was not intuitive.

Harper had figured it out because he lived with Adeline and he was a brilliant accountant who specialized in
government audits.

Maybe Gary Ackerman, who had some wild conspiracy
theories, had told Harper a theory that made sense. Who
had reached out to whom?

And, dammit, where did Tobias fit in? The timing of
the sales was immediately after Operation Heatwave
ended, but what did it mean? How did Adeline connect to
Tobias?

Sean saved all the information he had to a flash drive,
sent another copy to himself, then sent a copy of the data
to a friend of his who happened to be an ASAC in Sacramento. Dean Hooper had once run the white-collar crimes
division out of national FBI headquarters. Normally,
he'd be the last person Sean would trust, considering
Sean's past criminal activities that *might* fall under the
purview of Hooper, but considering Kane had once saved
the life of Dean's wife, the Rogans had a clean slate with
the fed.

*Dean—One of my security cases has intersected
with one of the FBI's active investigations. I can't
legally dig any deeper, so I'm sending you what
I have. I have clearance from HWI to send all
pertinent data to the FBI that will help in the
ongoing investigation (I'll attach it so you have
documentation). I don't know the agent working
on your end—Logan Dunbar out of D.C.—and
you know how I feel about feds I don't know.*

Look at this—Money Laundering 101? If you

need an official report, contact RCK and jump
through the hoops.
   Best to Sonia.
   Sean

He shut everything down. It was after eight, but Gregor
Smith was still there. Sean bid him good-bye and walked
out. He was about to get into his car when he heard his
name.

Sean had his hand on his gun before he recognized
Kane's voice.

"Kane?"

"I would have been here sooner—I heard about the
shooting. Why aren't you sitting on her?"

"Because she's a trained agent."

"Bull-fucking-shit."

"Juan put Donnelly on her. Get in." Sean took the driver's seat and Kane slid in next to him. Sean pulled out.

"Where is she now?" Kane asked.

"She texted me that she was leaving the Worthington
house. It's about twenty minutes outside the city. Why? Is
she in immediate danger?"

"I need her to look at the security tapes from the Dallas airport."

"How did you get them?"

He didn't answer. Of course he wouldn't answer.

Sean sent Lucy a message.

When are you coming home?

He said to Kane, "It's Tobias, isn't it."

"He's good, Sean. He's damn good. I followed a trail
down to McAllen today and it was a fucking dead end. He
knows I'm following him, and tricked me."

"You're not easily tricked."

"I'm never tricked." He paused. "Rarely. I was real close yesterday before I saw you. He was here, in San Antonio, and my contact had verifiable intel. But when I got to McAllen, it was a trap. Now my contact is dead. They set him up. Tobias knows everything; he has people everywhere. I went through the black box that Trejo kept—there are files missing. I didn't realize it at the time, but Tobias must have pulled them before the kid stole the box."

"Which means he intentionally left some of the files, like the file on Nicole Rollins."

"Don't trust anyone, Sean. The DEA is not clean. There are at least two corrupt cops in SAPD. And I'm beginning to suspect someone in the FBI."

"Who?"

"I'm not telling you until I get something actionable."

"That's fucking bullshit, Lucy is there."

"Suck it up, little brother. If I'm wrong, and you slip up, you can kiss RCK's relationship with federal law enforcement good-bye, and that includes all the cover we've had for gray ops. I'm not putting us at risk because you want to play cave man."

"Fuck you." Sean remembered why he hated working with Kane. Until he'd moved to San Antonio, he'd only worked with him once in a blue moon. Now, it seemed they were working everything together.

"I'll tell you this—it's not Nate Dunning. He knows there's someone inside, and he's going to be my eyes and ears until we figure it out."

Sean's phone vibrated. He answered.

"Lucy."

"I'm heading to the hospital."

"Is Tia okay?"

"She's out of surgery and critical. That's all I know. I'm going to re-interview Elise Hansen."

"Why?"

"Some new information has come up."

"What?"

"Sean—I can't really talk about it."

"I don't care that Barry is in the car with you. Kane is with me. Something bigger is going on, and you're in the middle of it. I'm going to send you a security video that Kane found. Call me right back."

Sean hung up. "Give it to me."

Kane shook his head. "This is why I never fell in love." He pulled out his phone and pressed a few buttons.

"Your loss."

"I sent it to Lucy."

Less than thirty seconds later, Lucy called him back.

"I showed the picture to Brad," she said. Her voice was edgy, nervous. "It's Tobias. Did he kill Garza? Elise said that Garza is the one who shot her the other night, that he's the one who hired her in the first place."

"That may be the truth, but if it is, that means Garza was working for Tobias, and we know that Tobias likes to kill loose ends. You found the Garza connection, and Tobias figured he'd flip. He must have known something that Tobias didn't want made public. I found a connection between James Everett and Adeline Reyes-Worthington that implicates both of them in illegal land deals. I sent everything to Dean Hooper."

"Sean—"

"I didn't break any laws. But I don't know Dunbar from Adam, and I trust Hooper. If anyone has a problem with it, they can take it up with Hooper. You need to watch yourself, Lucy."

"Go to the hospital," Kane told him.

Sean made an illegal U-turn and headed to the hospital.

Sean said to Lucy, "Kane has information that Mona Hill was working with Tobias as well, through an intermediary. This bastard has his fingers in everything. Trust no one."

"If Mona Hill was working for Tobias, and Garza was working for Tobias . . . Oh, shit."

"What?"

"Elise. She's lied to us about a few things, but they didn't seem to be relevant lies. Now they are. She told us she took sexually explicit photos of her and Worthington for blackmail, but one of the photos she took was of him dead. And Tobias is the one who sent it to Adeline Reyes-Worthington, claiming that Adeline had his money."

"Where's Adeline now?"

"Home. We left about thirty minutes ago. We have agents on her house making sure she doesn't get the same idea that Garza had and try to leave."

Kane shook his head. "She's already dead."

Lucy said, "What did you say?"

"Kane thinks she's dead."

"We left her with her personal assistant and two agents."

"Call the agents, have them put eyes on her immediately," Sean said. "Tell them to bring her into protective custody. And tell them to be on high alert."

Joseph Contreras brought Adeline tea as soon as the three feds left.

He'd been itching to kill them, but the presence of Brad Donnelly threw a wrench in the mix. Donnelly knew who he was—not by this name, but he would certainly recognize him if he saw him. So Joseph stayed in his office and monitored the security cameras, watching Donnelly walk the grounds.

It had been far too close. If Donnelly had come to the door, Joseph wouldn't have been able to disappear.

"I don't want tea!" Adeline exclaimed.

"It will help you sleep. You've been through hell this week, Adeline."

Drink the damn tea, bitch.

"I don't want to sleep. We're leaving. Tonight."

"There are two federal agents in the driveway."

"Which is why I had you move Harper's car to the barn. We'll go out the back road. We'll be at the plane in less than an hour. It's very handy that you're a pilot, one of the many reasons I hired you. I'm already packed. I just need to get the cash from the safe, and my insurance package."

"Are you sure? Maybe you should cooperate with the FBI. They can protect you."

"Hardly. I'm not going to jail, Joseph! But Tobias will pay for this. He threatened me, recruited Garza, then probably killed him because that's what Tobias does, isn't it? He'll pay. I will use every dime to track him down and make him suffer. He created this problem in the first place—and I'm damn well not going to go to prison or die because of it."

She walked upstairs.

She certainly had bravado when no one else was around, Joseph thought.

He followed her up the stairs. If she wouldn't drink the tea, which would have been a far more peaceful death, he'd be perfectly content to make her suffer.

Unfortunately, he didn't have the time to prolong it. He suspected that Kincaid and Crawford would realize that they'd been manipulated.

Adeline started to type in the code to the safe. This was the one thing he needed her to do, because she was paranoid and changed the code every week. He needed the banking information.

"Why aren't you packing?" Adeline said before hitting the last two numbers.

"I'm packed."

The bell rang.

"Dammit! See who that is." The safe default beeped. "Now I have to wait five minutes."

He glanced at his phone and pulled up the security feed. Two federal agents, the two who had been in the car. Their guns were out. One moved around to the rear entrance.

How had the feds figured it out so soon? Were there only two agents?

He could handle two agents.

But he couldn't wait five minutes.

He reached out and grabbed Adeline.

"Joseph? What?"

He scowled. "You pathetic, greedy little bitch. I wish I had time to make you suffer—because I certainly know how."

Before she could respond, he jerked her body one way and her head the other. Her neck snapped.

"I never worked for you," he said.

The bell rang again.

Joseph ran down the stairs, then down into the basement. Behind the wine rack was a hidden door. Harper had closed it off because he was worried about home security when his daughter was little, but the door still worked—Joseph had made sure of it long ago. He grabbed his stash of guns next to the exit, slipped out into the side yard, and used the darkness to run to the barn. He picked up a secondary bag of supplies in one of the stalls, and tossed everything behind the seat of his truck, which he'd hidden in the barn instead of Adeline's Cadillac.

He sat behind the wheel and called Tobias.

"I couldn't get the codes from the safe. We'll need to use Everett."

"I've already put the plan in motion."

Through clenched teeth, Joseph said, "I told you to wait."

"You're not in charge. And obviously, I was right—Adeline wouldn't open the safe for you."

"The feds were knocking on the door. I had to break her neck."

"Finally. Damn, I hate that bitch."

Joseph wanted to break Tobias's neck. If he hadn't fucked up to begin with, they wouldn't have been in this mess. Though if Tobias hadn't fucked up two months ago, they might never have learned about the FBI sting. One silver lining in a cesspool of disasters.

"I'm going to base, you'd better not screw this up. We need that money if we're going to rebuild."

"I'm taking care of it."

"If anything happens to Elise, I'll kill you myself."

He hung up. Joseph had never wanted Elise and Tobias to work together. They were both dangerous on their own, but together they were reckless. It was like they fueled each other, each trying to outdo the other. But he'd promised that he would protect both of them, no matter what.

Thank God they weren't *his* family.

CHAPTER THIRTY-SIX

"Who is Mona Hill and what information do I have about her?" Kane asked Sean after he hung up with Lucy.

Sean told him the truth. He told Kane everything, including that Hill had Lucy's rape tape.

"You should have killed her," Kane said. "She now knows where you're vulnerable. Another reason why I have no attachments."

Sean had thought the same thing—not that he shouldn't love Lucy, but that he should have killed Mona Hill. But he wasn't Kane, and killing someone was always the last choice on his list. He was hedging his bets that Mona's affection for her sister would keep her far away from him and Lucy. "I know where she's vulnerable."

"The difference is she's ruthless and will take out innocents. You won't. She'll figure that out eventually."

Sean ignored the comment.

"It makes sense now," Sean said. "Adeline has been laundering money for Tobias, and two months ago—when we raided Trejo's compound—something changed in their relationship and she backed off. There was a shitload of transactions right before and after we found the guns, and nothing for the last two months. James Everett was talking to the feds, Harper Worthington started investigating his wife, and Garza came up with the plan to use his pet hooker to kill Worthington."

"Garza was a pawn," Kane said. "It was all Tobias. And if James Everett was talking to the feds, I'm betting he's dead, too."

"They need Everett," Sean said. "The escrow accounts are controlled by Adeline and Everett. The Texas Land Holding group."

"So he might not be dead now," Kane said dryly. "Give Tobias a few minutes to torture the money out of him."

Kane was certainly in a shitty mood, but it probably had something to do with his informant being killed.

Sean's phone rang. "It's Hooper," he told Kane, then answered on speaker. "Dean, it's Sean—Kane's with me. You got the files?"

"Explain."

"Exactly what I said—I was hired to do a forensic audit on a government contractor who'd been murdered, and my case collided with Lucy's investigation, which collided with an undercover political corruption case. I can't legally access those accounts, but my gut tells me Adeline Reyes-Worthington was laundering money by overpaying for properties she or her landholding group owned. Basically, buying from herself, but it doesn't look that way on paper."

"You're right, but there's more here than that. It's going to take me a while to sift through the scam—this account is flagged, and it's active right now."

"You mean someone's moving money?"

"Yes."

"Let me have access, Dean. I need to find out where that person is physically located."

Hooper hesitated.

"We don't have time to go through channels," Sean said. "I'm not bullshitting you, lives are at stake."

Kane spoke. "Hooper, it's Kane. This is connected to Tobias."

"Are you positive?"

"Yes. They took out one of my informants today and set a trap for me, but I got out."

"You always do." Dean paused a moment, typing on his computer. "Okay, Sean, you're on, but you have to understand—once the money is gone, it's going to be ten times harder to trace."

"I don't want to fund that bastard any more than you do."

Sean pulled over and told Kane to drive. He ran around to the passenger side, pulled out his small laptop, and started a trace on one of the accounts. "The bastard already has over a million dollars. I can slow down his network, but I need to be on site to redirect the money without tipping anyone off."

"What are you going to do?"

"I'm setting up another escrow account and when I get access to his actual network, I can make it look like he's transferring money to the offshore account that I'm assuming Tobias controls, but it'll actually be going to an escrow account that Dean Hooper controls."

"How much is there total?" Kane asked.

"Twenty, give or take."

"*Twenty million?*"

Sean nodded, typing rapidly. "I got him. Everett's office." Sean typed the address into his modified GPS system. "Floor it. I've slowed him down, but it's not going to take him long. If it was me, I would already have all the money."

Lucy was furious, and in a rare burst of anger she took it out on the cop who was supposed to be guarding Elise Hansen. "How did she just *walk out*?"

"I'm sorry, Agent Kincaid. She complained of chest pains and the doctor thought she might have internal injuries from the fall. He took her to get an MRI. I waited outside the room, and only just learned that no doctor had ordered an MRI."

"Did you check his badge? Check his ID?"

"Lucy," Brad said, and put his hand on her.

She brushed it off. "I should have figured it out earlier."

"How?" Brad said. "We had no reason to think—"

Lucy cut him off. "It was that damn photo Tobias gave to Adeline. It wasn't a sex shot—it was proof of the kill." She involuntarily shivered, then locked down her emotions. She was too angry and too upset to be any good to anyone. She had to think like Elise.

"She's cold, calculating. She's a sixteen-year-old sociopath."

"Okay, but—"

She barely heard Brad. "She's so methodical that she lured in a grown man in physically good condition, killed him with a poison. Not just any poison, but one that would cause him intense pain as he died. She watched him die."

"You don't know that," Brad said.

"She did. I'm certain of it. Then she took off his pants and made it appear as if they'd had oral sex."

"You're grossing me out, Lucy, and I don't get easily grossed out."

"She may have spit on him. It doesn't matter. But she *wanted* her DNA on him." Lucy paced. "Either she doesn't understand forensics or she didn't care what the final report would show, only that the initial report supported the scene she was setting. She left her DNA . . . Why?"

"She wanted to be found," Brad suggested.

"Her prints weren't in the system, the chances that her DNA would be are next to nothing."

"I don't know, but—"

Lucy snapped her fingers and stopped walking. "She wanted us to be looking for her. As soon as we started asking the right questions—when we found the phone and linked Everett to Mona Hill, she gave us Garza on a platter."

"You mean she shot herself?"

"No—she must have a partner. Whoever drove her from the motel to the hotel. I thought it was Mona Hill. Maybe it is . . . It's ballsy, because gunshots are unpredictable. The individual would have to be an outstanding sharpshooter. But I'll bet she was standing still when she was shot—less chance of killing her accidentally."

Lucy continued. "But Tobias killed Garza, and Tobias sent the photo of Harper to Adeline and said he wanted his money. Why frame either of them?"

"Maybe he killed Harper Worthington as a threat. The letter gave her forty-eight hours."

"And she didn't pay, so Elise was the sacrifice. Maybe. To give us a witness to point to Garza. Because Garza and Elise had a connection in D.C. It's convoluted, but it holds together." Lucy frowned. "Then why kill Garza?"

"Because he knew something?"

"Or maybe because he was working with Adeline and Tobias makes a point to take out everyone in an organization. We have to find Elise." She looked around. "Where's Barry? How long does it take to get security tapes?"

As if on cue, Barry stepped off the elevator and strode down the hall. He showed Lucy footage of Elise in her hospital gown being wheeled into an MRI room by a man in a white coat. They couldn't see his face well, but he wasn't old—maybe twenty-five. Young to be a doctor. "We found her gown and IV drip in the MRI room, and then, about ten minutes before we arrived, this was captured at the main entrance."

Elise was walking out arm in arm with the same man. Lucy could tell based on his height and gait.

"We know him," Lucy said. "That's the witness who said she'd run to his car while being shot at."

"Peter Rabb," Barry said. "I've already sent SAPD to his address and put a BOLO out on his car." Barry looked at his watch. "They have a twenty-two-minute head start."

Lucy's phone rang. It was Juan. "Hello, sir," she said, surprised he'd called her and not Barry.

"The two agents we had sitting on Adeline's house said that you'd called and ordered them to check on her."

"Yes, sir, I did. I'm sorry, I should have gone through Barry, but he was on the phone and—"

"Adeline Reyes-Worthington is dead. Joseph Contreras is gone. There was a door in the basement that went into a side garden, and they believe he used that to escape."

"He'd worked for her for years. Are you certain he killed her?"

"I sent an ERT unit to process the entire house. Her neck was broken, there was no struggle. The agents searched the house, but there's no sign of Contreras."

"Adeline was our only lead—no, James Everett. Adeline and Everett were in business together, he was being blackmailed by Elise. With Adeline gone, Everett is the only one who knows where the money is. We need to find Everett immediately—he's the next target. And considering he's been giving information to the FBI—"

Juan interrupted. "Understood. Get to his house. He has a wife and two children. I'll call SAPD and send backup." He hung up.

"Tobias is cleaning up. Whatever this game was," Brad said, "He's starting over."

"Not until he gets his money," Lucy said. She hoped. If he didn't care about the money, then the Everett family was already dead.

They rushed out of the hospital and Barry called headquarters for Everett's home address. He sped out of the parking lot and toward James Everett's Alamo Heights home. Because it was nearly nine on Wednesday night, the streets were relatively clear.

"What makes Tobias tick?" Lucy wondered out loud. Elise was a killer—she understood killers better than drug dealers or gun runners.

"Power," Brad said. "A man like Tobias lives on his reputation, which is built on power and fear. If his enemies see that he let Adeline get away with keeping money that belonged to him, that emboldens his opposition. So he has to take a stand. Kill her husband. Pressure her."

"And when she didn't cave—oh, no." Lucy realized Adeline's mistake. "If Contreras is working for Tobias, he knew that Adeline was talking to us, and once we got her into FBI headquarters, she might tell us everything. So he killed her and ran."

"He must have planned it from the beginning," Brad said. "Tobias is not spontaneous."

"He put Contreras in her organization to keep an eye on her. For years."

"Or he recruited Contreras," Barry suggested.

"True," Brad said. "Either way, he must have figured out the FBI had an undercover operation. He had access to everything—her house, her finances, her friends, her campaign information."

"What if," Lucy said, "Contreras became suspicious of Harper? Contreras lived in the house. What if he saw the change in Harper's demeanor? But he took it more seriously than Adeline and had him followed. He could have known he'd gone to the FBI in May. What if they thought Harper was the FBI informant? And didn't know about Dunbar's operation?"

Barry nodded. "At first I didn't see where you were

going with this, but now it makes sense. If they suspected Harper was working with the FBI, they would follow him, and that's how they found out about Gary Ackerman. Harper needed someone he trusted, and the only person he could be certain wasn't involved in Adeline's criminal enterprise was an old friend from school with a loyalty to their mutual friend Roy Travertine."

"So Ackerman helped Harper put together the details. Because of Ackerman's work with Travertine, he'd know more about campaigns and campaign finance law than Harper, but Harper knew about money and numbers, and together they figured out what Adeline was doing."

"It still doesn't explain why Harper flew into San Antonio just to meet with Ackerman."

"If Tobias knew about Ackerman and Harper, he could have figured out how they were communicating and sent Harper a message to meet. We know they met in different places each time," Lucy said. "Ackerman was paranoid, so the request for a spontaneous meeting might not have seemed odd to Harper."

When they pulled up in front of Everett's house, the lights were on and an SAPD police car was parked out front. The three of them got out of the car. Barry showed his badge and introduced them.

"We checked on the family. There're three people inside, Mrs. Everett and her two children, a teenage boy and a young girl."

"Where's her husband?"

"Mrs. Everett said he was working late."

"Can you stay out here and watch the house? One of Mr. Everett's associates was murdered, and we have reason to believe the killer may be after Mr. Everett," Barry said.

"Yes, sir."

Barry stepped away from the police car and said to Brad and Lucy, "We need to go to his office."

"I want to check on the family first. Mrs. Everett might know more than she told the police," Lucy said.

"You think she's part of it, too?"

"I'm not making any assumptions. But we need to talk to her, find out what she knows."

"Go ahead. I'll call Juan and send a couple of agents to Everett's office, then check the perimeter, make sure the house is secure."

Lucy and Brad walked up the path to the front porch. Security lighting around the house showed neatly trimmed bushes and trees. The house itself was a two-story brick structure on a large double lot, but it had a cookie-cutter feel to it and looked like most of the other two-story brick houses in the area. Lucy loved the custom house Sean had found for them; it was unlike any other in their neighborhood.

She knocked on the door. A moment later, a woman answered.

"Yes?"

She showed her badge and Brad flashed his. "I'm FBI Special Agent Lucy Kincaid. This is Agent Brad Donnelly. We're looking for Mrs. Everett."

"That's me," she said. "The police were already here." She looked over Lucy's shoulder. "Oh, they still are." She frowned. "I just spoke to my husband, and he said he'll be home soon. Now I'm getting worried."

The woman in front of her had short, stylish brown hair and blue eyes. She was taller than Lucy's five feet eight inches, and looked about thirty. She was certainly not Mrs. James Everett—not the woman Lucy had seen in the photograph in Everett's office.

She would have walked away then, except there were

two children in the house. That meant they were in danger.

"There's no reason to be alarmed," Lucy said. "Would you mind if we came in and sat with you until your husband returns?"

"Why?" she asked.

"We need to talk to him."

"Why does the FBI need to talk to my husband? What's wrong?"

The woman was a good actress. Lucy would take her down now, except she wasn't confident that there wasn't someone else in the house with her. Until she knew the children were safe, Lucy had to go along with this charade.

"Ma'am, we understand your concern," Brad said, taking Lucy's cue, "but I can assure you that we're only here to help."

"Thank you, but I think it's best if you wait outside."

Lucy put her foot inside the door. "Mrs. Everett, where are your children?"

"Upstairs. Sleeping, of course. It's after nine."

"I'd like to check on their well-being."

That stumped her. She recovered quickly, and said, "What on earth for? I'm not going to have you wake up my kids."

Brad said, "Mrs. Everett, there's been a verifiable threat against your husband and we're here to check on you and the children. Other agents are checking on your husband at his work."

She stared at them, as if searching her mind for an answer.

There was a distinct cough from the dining room, which Lucy could only partly see from her vantage point. She put her hand on her gun.

The fake Mrs. Everett pushed the door all the way open.

Now Lucy could see that the boy—about twelve or thirteen—was tied to one of the dining room chairs. He was the kid from the family photo in James Everett's office.

A familiar man stood behind him, a gun aimed at the back of the kid's head. It only took Lucy a second to remember where she'd seen him.

"Peter Rabb," Lucy said.

"Hands up, step in and close the door. Or he's dead, then the girl will follow."

Lucy didn't see the younger daughter. She couldn't assume that there were only two hostage takers.

Lucy stepped in.

"You too, Donnelly," Peter said.

As soon as they'd stepped inside, the woman shut and bolted the door.

"Move apart. Hands up."

Lucy moved toward the dining room. Brad didn't budge.

"Joyce, disarm first Donnelly, then Kincaid. His gun, his phone, check for other weapons."

Joyce complied. She was definitely scared of Peter, but she wasn't a complete novice. She found all their weapons and put them on the dining table in front of Peter.

"Where's Mrs. Everett and her daughter?" Lucy asked.

"They are none of your concern," Peter said.

Lucy stared at the boy. He was scared out of his mind, but he kept glancing at the large, curving split staircase that branched off the foyer.

Either a third bad guy was upstairs with the other two hostages, or the girls were restrained.

"Are they okay?" Lucy asked.

"For now," Peter said. "Agent Donnelly, your reputation precedes you. Not so tough, really, not in person. Please have a seat."

"I'll stand," he said through clenched teeth.

"Sit." Peter motioned to one of the dining chairs. "Now."

Slowly, Brad sat.

"Joyce, take those cuffs," he gestured to where she'd put them on the table, "and put them on Agent Donnelly."

The woman complied as if she were used to taking orders.

"Peter," Lucy said, "you now have two federal agents as hostages. Let the Everett family go."

He laughed. "Right. Sure. You don't have the control here. No one is leaving until I get the call. Understood?" He glanced at the grandfather clock in the corner. "Quarter after nine. It shouldn't be much longer." He smiled. "But this really is a coup. Both of you here together."

"You work for Tobias." Lucy needed to keep him talking. Not just to learn information, but to buy time. Barry would soon figure out that something was wrong. And when the agents arrived at Everett's office, they would know he was under duress.

Peter didn't say anything, so Lucy asked, "Where's Elise?"

"Not here."

"Is she with Everett?"

Peter didn't answer. A thump came from upstairs. He frowned and said, "Joyce, check on them."

Joyce picked up one of the guns and went upstairs.

That told Lucy there was no one with the mom and daughter. Just Joyce and Peter.

Peter hadn't told her to sit down, so she remained standing in the middle of the foyer. She caught the Everett boy's eye and tried to reassure him, but he was shaking.

Peter pulled out a phone. He sent a text message, probably to Elise or Tobias announcing that he had Lucy and Brad at gunpoint.

This was just getting better and better.

Joyce returned a minute later. "They're fine," she said.

"What made the noise?" Peter asked.

"The headboard against the wall," Joyce said. "I triple-checked them. I swear."

Lucy was trying to assess Peter. She thought back to when she'd met him at the hospital, when he came in asking about Elise's welfare, like a good citizen. In hindsight, he'd been too interested, hanging on every word. He wasn't the leader—he was smart, but not like Elise. He wasn't as shrewd or calculating. She made a judgment call and said, "Peter, Elise isn't coming back for you."

"She's not coming back at all," he said. "Do you think she's stupid? She said you'd come here to check on the family as soon as she disappeared from the hospital. I don't know how she knew it, but she was right." Peter glowed like a proud lover. Did he think that Elise actually cared about him?

Lucy was surprised as well. Such a deduction showed not only intelligence, but keen psychological interpretation. Far beyond a normal sixteen-year-old.

But nothing about Elise Hansen was normal.

"She didn't know about him, however," Peter said, glaring at Brad.

"What I meant to say is, as soon as Elise gets what she wants, she's going to disappear and you'll be left here with five hostages."

"You know shit." He glanced at the clock.

He was definitely waiting for something. Probably for Elise to call. Then he would either kill them all and disappear, or tie them up and disappear.

Except Elise wasn't going to call. Elise was using Peter Rabb just like she'd used Robert Garza and James Everett and even Mona Hill. Lucy understood her much better now—and her growing knowledge terrified her.

"Peter," Lucy said, "let the boy go."

"Sure," he said.

Lucy almost breathed easier.

Then Peter burst out in laughter. "When pigs fly."

CHAPTER THIRTY-SEVEN

Elise Hansen sat in the chair and played with the knife. She was ambidextrous, which helped, but she preferred her right hand. But it would be a while before she'd be able to use her arm, and she didn't even have mobility with the broken wrist.

It sucked.

But if she wanted, she could still throw the knife at the fat sniveling perverted asswipe and pierce his heart.

When he was done transferring the money.

She yawned. "It's been forty minutes, dumbass. Are you fucking with us? Because if you are, I'll call Pete and he'll kill your boy."

"Don't. Please. I'm doing everything you want."

The turd was sweating. Seeing him sweat and squirm and beg had been fun at the beginning, but now she just wanted to be done with him.

She looked over her shoulder. "Jay? How much do we have?"

"Three point one million."

She sighed and leaned forward. Her body was sore from when the fed had knocked her down, "saving" her life. And Toby was mad that Elise hadn't known she was wearing a vest! How was she supposed to know? Was she supposed to feel her up? *Right.* And even if she *had* known, how was she supposed to get that tidbit of information to the idiots Toby had hired to kill the bitch? Why didn't they shoot her in the head? She didn't have a bulletproof *skull.*

"Jimmy," she said. "You're being slow. Which makes me think you're fucking with me."

"I'm not! I swear. Come see. The network is slow. I don't know why, it's just taking a long time for every command. I don't know what else to do. I've tried everything."

"Maybe if Pete fucks your wife? I can have him Face-Time you while he tears her up. That would be fun. Maybe that would motivate you. Naw, it would probably just turn you on. *Especially* if I have Pete spank her."

"Please don't hurt my family."

"Oh, no, Daddy, I wouldn't think of it. Spank me, Daddy. *Harder.*" She laughed. Oh, *damn,* she was having fun. "Jay, make sure *Daddy* isn't lying to us."

She watched as Toby's right-hand goon walked behind the desk. He pressed the gun to Everett's temple and looked at the screen. "It's going, Elise. Forty-seven percent."

"This is the fourth account! Don't you guys have broadband or a T3 connection or something? Are you in the fucking stone age of the Internet?"

Everett was shaking. "They could be updating the system. Or doing maintenance or . . . I don't know, I don't know!" he sobbed.

Her phone vibrated and she saw that she had a text from Pete. Shit, that guy was needy. She'd told him to do *one thing* and this was the third time he'd texted her. But she looked, because she wasn't stupid. If there was a problem, she needed to know about it.

She pulled her phone from her pocket and read the message. "Oh, shit! I don't fucking believe it. Toby is going to be thrilled."

Jay gave her an odd look. She rolled her eyes. She didn't care what the goon thought. She called Toby.

"Hey, big brother, I have some in-ter-est-ing news."

"Everett is dead and we have my money."

"*Our* money," she corrected. "Almost as good. Your two favorite federal agents showed up at Everett's place. They're disarmed and tied up, waiting for us."

"Kincaid and Crawford?"

"Kincaid and *Donnelly*."

"Are you sure?"

"Pete just texted me."

"I don't trust him."

"He's harmless."

"He's an idiot."

"True. So? Can he shoot them? Gut them? Maim them? Rape them? Cut their fingers off? Hey, I can get Donnelly's dick for you. Box it up with a pretty bow."

"Shut *up*."

She laughed.

"Something's wrong."

She stopped laughing. She liked playing games, but Toby had the best instincts of anyone she knew, even herself. And *she* was pretty damn magnificent.

"Get out."

"What?"

"It shouldn't be taking this long. He's stalling, or the feds are already there. How much do we have?"

She looked over at Jay. "Toby wants to know how much we have."

Jay looked at his tablet. "Three point three."

She repeated the number. Toby swore a blue streak, and she held the phone away from her ear.

"Elise, dammit! Are you there?"

"Sorry. Dropped the phone." She winked at Jay. "You were saying?"

"Do exactly what I say," Toby said in a low voice. "Tell Jay to stay until we reach ten mill, then kill Everett and disappear. But you need to leave now."

"What about the agents? I don't like Kincaid. She looked at me funny. I think she's psychic or something."

"There's no such thing as psychics."

"Yeah, well, she was suspicious."

"Tell Pete to kill them all."

"Are you sure?

"Do what I say or I *will* kill you, Elise. You've been pushing me this week."

"I'll kill you first," she said in a singsong voice. "Stop, Toby. You know I love you more than anyone in the whole wide world." She winked at Jay. "You're my *big brother.*"

"Then start listening to me, little girl!"

"Hey, I'm moving. You don't have to be such a bully." She kissed the phone and hung up.

"Jay, come here."

The big lug lumbered over. She stood on her tippy toes and whispered, "The boss says when we get to ten mill, you know what to do."

Jay nodded.

She loved stupid hunks.

She kissed him, because she knew he hated it when she did that, then she turned to Everett. "Good-bye, Jimmy."

"Please. My family. Don't hurt them."

"They're better off without you." She didn't say that they, too, were going to be dead, because then he might not finish giving her brother back his money.

Well, *their* money, because they were family.

Sean heard every word Elise said.

He and Kane were in the office adjoining Everett's. Sean had hooked up his own computer to the network and was slowing everything down, while simultaneously trans-

ferring the money to a different account than what was
being shown to Everett and the goon watching him. He estimated that Everett had transferred just over two million
dollars to Tobias before Sean set up the account to siphon
off the funds. Now every transaction went directly to an
FBI-controlled account. He kept the transfer moving
slowly because there was no doubt in his mind that Elise
would kill Everett as soon as he was finished.

Kane had drilled a small hole in the wall and inserted
a camera so they had eyes in the room. They also had
ears because Sean had a microphone attached to that
camera.

He whispered, "They have Lucy. I have to go."

"No," Kane said. "Do your job."

"Fuck you."

Kane glared at him. "SWAT ETA is less than five minutes. I can't do what you do."

"I don't care about the money."

"You stay here. I'll go."

Lucy was the love of his life; if anything happened to
her he would never forgive himself. Or Kane.

"I'm trained for this," Sean said.

"*I* trained you," Kane said. "We can both save Lucy, but
only *you* can do this." He waved his hand at the computer.
"Now do it."

He left before Sean could argue with him anymore.

Sean could barely focus. He closed his eyes and breathed
deeply, then stared at the computer, the numbers rapidly
scrolling in front of him. Tobias's people thought they'd
only received three point three million, but nearly eight
million had gone through, out of nineteen different accounts. Sean had diverted the difference into the escrow
he'd set up, but he didn't like Tobias and his people having
any money. They could do a lot of damage.

It was just Sean on-site until the FBI SWAT team

arrived. He sent Leo Proctor, the FBI SWAT team leader, another message, updating him on the status of Everett and the money transfer, plus the fact that Elise was getting ready to bolt.

But he couldn't just let that little bitch go.

He launched an app he'd written and accessed all phones within range. He had to turn on her GPS before she left the building. He found Elise's phone on the network through the wireless function, then mirrored her chip on his phone.

Everett changed escrow accounts. Sean hesitated.

"See? It's going faster now," Everett said next door.

"Good," Elise said. "Toodles!"

He heard the door in Everett's office open. He manually typed in computer code that would turn on her GPS. Even if she'd disabled it, there was a factory setting that allowed the company to blind track their customers. Sean hacked into it and programmed his phone to track Elise.

Then she was gone, and the twentieth escrow account was already drained. Shit! Everett switched to another account, and Sean siphoned off more of the funds than previously, but sent false data to Everett's system so he'd think he had more money.

Sean had to stay on top of the computer transactions. As soon as Everett changed escrow accounts, Sean had to piggyback on the new transaction or lose it.

It had been next to impossible for Sean to let Elise walk out of the building. But Kane was right—the more money Tobias had, the more damage he could do.

That woman was a psycho.

Every passing minute felt like an hour. Proctor finally sent him a message that they had arrived.

Sean informed him of the change, that Elise had left but Jay was holding a gun on Everett, and Lucy and Brad were being held hostage at Everett's house, along with the Everett family.

> *Kane is on his way—if he's not already there. Give*
> *your people a heads up.*

He heard nothing from Proctor for a minute. Everett switched accounts and started blubbering next door.

"This is the last one," Everett said. "There were twenty-four, I swear."

"There's supposed to be twenty million. Where's the rest?" Jay said.

"I don't know! The computer says you should have all the money."

"My bank says I don't."

Jay. He was Mona Hill's contact. The one to whom she'd sent the ten-second video of Lucy chained up and about to be raped.

Sean wanted to beat the bastard senseless.

He had to control the rage. He wasn't an angry person. He'd always been fun loving. Carefree.

Not always. He'd been extremely angry when his parents had died.

And then when he'd been expelled from Stanford because he'd hacked into the computer network and exposed one of the professors as a pedophile.

And then when he'd been at MIT and learned someone was stealing the pensions from retirees.

And when he found the foster kids locked up, malnourished, beaten—and some of them dead—in an old Mexican prison.

Yes, he had rage because he hated bullies. He hated people who preyed on the weak and innocent. Who stole money from old people and abused children. But he didn't just have angry feelings about these bullies, he acted.

Because if he didn't, who would? The FBI couldn't stop these people, not all of them. The FBI had known about Lucy's rapist after the bastard raped and killed one of their own agents, but couldn't find him for *five years.* Had they done their job right the first time, Lucy would never have been kidnapped and raped.

And that bastard Jay would never have seen her suffer. Even a ten-second clip was ten seconds too many.

Jay was talking too low for Sean to hear. Sean shut down the network completely to buy more time.

He sent Proctor a message.

Now or never—I shut down the network to stall, but Jay just realized that they're missing seventeen mill.

Sean closed down his laptop and stuffed it in his bag. He walked over to the peephole and saw Everett frantically typing on his computer.

"I'll shut down, then bring everything back up."

Jay grabbed Everett by the collar and hauled him out of the seat. "Who did you tell? Did you call the police?"

"No! No, I swear, don't hurt me. Don't hurt my family."

"Too late for that."

Jay pressed a button on his phone. A text message? A sign to Elise? Or Tobias?

"We're going," Jay said.

"Just don't hurt my—"

Jay hit him on the head.

"Shut. Up."

Sean sent Proctor a message saying that Jay was on the move with Everett.

He's holding a .45 and has another weapon under his jacket.

Almost immediately, Proctor responded:

We're in place. Stay where you are.

Sean complied because there was no way he wanted to get killed today.

Jay left the office and then there was silence. For a long, long minute, total silence.

Suddenly, bright lights flooded the building from outside. A bullhorn bellowed, "FBI! Freeze! Drop the weapon or we will shoot."

There was movement outside, but Sean couldn't see anything through the closed blinds.

A single rifle shot echoed, then there was commotion.

But it was only the one shot. They'd taken out Jay, who was their only link to Tobias.

Sean looked at his phone and saw that Elise was in a vehicle, her signal moving too fast to be on foot.

Jay wasn't their *only* link.

"Rogan!" a voice called out.

Sean opened the door to the office where he was hiding. Leo Proctor, in full SWAT gear, came down the wide office corridor, flanked by a team of six. He told the men to fan out and search the building.

"He's dead. He refused to comply, and we couldn't let him leave with the hostage."

"You get no complaints from me."

"Casilla wants a full report."

"He's going to have to wait. This isn't over. They have Lucy."

"Casilla knows that Lucy and Donnelly are hostages. We have a team there. Our top hostage negotiator is already on scene."

"I'm not going to the house," Sean said, though that's

exactly what he wanted to do. "Elise Hansen is on the move. I'm tracking her."

"Shit, Rogan, you can't—"

"And how long until you get someone in place to track her?"

Proctor spoke into his mic. "Dunning, Quiroz, meet me at base stat."

"Thank you."

"Don't thank me. You're going to turn everything over to Quiroz. It's up to him if you get a ride-a-long."

Two minutes later, Sean was showing Ryan and Nate how the GPS tracker worked, and where Elise was. He made up a bunch of technical jargon to make it sound far more complicated than it actually was. Ryan said, "Just come with us, but don't do anything stupid."

"No, sir," Sean said with a straight face.

Nate sighed, but only Sean heard him. He caught Nate's eye and stared. Nate understood. He didn't say a word.

Ryan grabbed one of the FBI SUVs and Sean navigated from the passenger seat.

Elise was only a few miles away, but she was going in a familiar direction.

"I know where she's going," Sean said. "She's going to Mona Hill's place."

"Who's Mona Hill?" Nate asked.

"She runs a prostitution ring, but she's also one of the people Elise hooked up with when she arrived in San Antonio. She doesn't know the area well, so it stands to reason she'll go to the one place where she's comfortable."

"You'd think she'd be running," Ryan said.

"Maybe she's picking up something. Like money." Or killing Mona Hill, another loose end.

"How certain are you?" Nate asked.

"Ninety percent."

"I know a faster way. I think we can beat her there," Nate said.

"Give it to me," Ryan said.

Nate navigated and Sean considered what he was going to do if Mona Hill ratted him out.

He would have to cross that bridge if and when he came to it. He still had the trump card about her sister, and he would use it.

"Kane learned that Mona Hill has a connection to Tobias," Sean added. "A connection that isn't solely through Elise. I just want you both to be prepared."

"Your brother has been around a lot lately," Ryan said. "Your point?"

"What's really going on?"

"You know as much as I do," Sean said. *Almost*.

"Somehow I doubt that."

"Kane doesn't tell me everything." Which was true.

"Turn left, then a quick right into the alley," Nate said from the back. "This brings us right across from her property."

Ryan did as Nate directed, then cut off the lights.

The apartments were all dark.

"Where is Elise?" Ryan asked.

"Less than a mile."

"Let's go in and wait. Rogan, stay. I'm not joking." Ryan handed him an earpiece. "You be our eyes, let us know what she does when she gets here."

Sean bristled, but he stayed in the SUV.

Ryan and Nate, both in black SWAT gear, left the SUV and ran across the street. They blended into the tall hedges that surrounded the dark property, then the building blocked them from Sean's view.

Sean waited for Elise. A Jeep drove up and slammed on the brakes in front of the apartment complex. Elise got out of the passenger seat and headed toward Mona Hill's unit.

"She's coming your way," Sean said over the com. "There's someone else in the car."

"Stay put," Ryan said over the com. "That's an order."

Sean didn't take orders from Ryan or anyone. But he waited.

The driver got out. It was Mona Hill. She stood next to the Jeep waiting for Elise to return.

This was fucked.

Sean slipped out of the SUV and, using other parked cars as a shield, approached the Jeep. He muted the com so Ryan couldn't hear what he was saying.

"Mona."

She jumped. Fear flashed over her face, then anger. "Get the fuck out of here. You're lucky they're giving me a second chance."

"Run."

"I can't."

"Do they know about your sister?"

Her eyes widened. "No! God, no."

"Then go. Disappear. You're good at that."

"They'll find me. You don't know these people like I do."

"Mona, I'm not telling you again. Leave. I will stop them."

"You can't."

"Don't underestimate me."

There was a loud crash from the apartment and Mona jumped. Over the com, Ryan ordered Nate to go right.

"Now," Sean told her.

Mona jumped back in the Jeep and sped off. Sean ran back to the SUV but stood to the side. He unmuted the com.

"The Jeep just left without her," he said. "Elise is cutting across the lawn running after it." Elise had a bag over her shoulder that she hadn't had before.

Nate came from behind the building and tackled the girl. She went down on her bad arm with a scream. He got up and secured her.

Ryan asked through the com, "Did you see who the driver was?"

"No," Sean lied. "He didn't get out of the car."

"Plates?"

"No, sorry."

Nate said, "Suspect is secured."

They approached the SUV. Sean handed Ryan back the earpiece.

"Can you please drop me off at Everett's house before you take her in? Kane isn't responding to my messages, and neither is Crawford."

"It's because your lover is dead, and no one wants to tell you," Elise said with a bloodied-nose smirk. "Go ahead, check my phone."

Nate pulled it out of her pocket and looked at the history. He didn't say anything.

Sean grabbed the phone from Nate. Ten minutes ago, at 9:50 P.M., Elise had sent Peter a message.

Kill them all and disappear.

Ryan pushed Sean back before he could hit the girl. "Lucy is fine," Ryan said.

But he didn't know that. No one did.

CHAPTER THIRTY-EIGHT

The grandfather clock chimed 10:00 P.M.

"There's police everywhere," Joyce said.

"Get away from the fucking windows," Peter ordered.

Joyce cowered and sat on the floor, her back against the wall.

When the police cars and unmarked vehicles began to arrive, Peter had told Joyce to handcuff Lucy. She should have expected it, but she'd hoped that she'd have more mobility.

The phone had been ringing on and off for the last twenty minutes.

"You need to answer the phone," Lucy said when it started ringing again.

"So they can stall? I know how this works." But he was worried. He hadn't planned on being caught. What criminal did?

Elise Hansen. She'd planned on being caught. It was a game to her.

But she'd also planned on escaping. Perhaps the shooting at the hospital this morning had been the first escape attempt. Or maybe Kane and Sean were right, and it had been an attempt on Lucy's life.

Or both.

The phone stopped ringing.

Peter had barely moved. The boy, still bound and gagged, sagged in the chair. He might have fallen asleep, or just felt defeated. There had been no more sounds from upstairs. Lucy wished she could find out if the mother and daughter were okay.

Peter kept looking at his phone. A message had come in a few minutes before, and Peter seemed to be waiting for something else.

"Joyce, go upstairs and get the mom and girl. We'll kill these two, then take the kids hostage. They won't shoot us with kids."

"We can't go out there!" Joyce exclaimed. "This wasn't supposed to happen. You said there was a plan."

"Elise had a plan," Lucy said. "Her plan was to leave you here holding the bag. She has the money, and she didn't come for you."

"Shut up," he said. "Go, Joyce! Get them!"

Joyce ran up the stairs. The phone rang again.

"Answer it, Peter," Lucy said, her voice calm and reasonable. "You need to tell them that everyone is fine."

He shook his head.

"Elise is a sociopath," Lucy said. "She only cares about herself. You know that, don't you? How long have you known her? A few weeks?"

"You have no idea who Elise is."

"Tell me. Tell me how you see her."

"She's fucking smart. She's not scared of anything."

"How did you meet?"

"I worked for—" He stopped as Joyce ran back down the stairs.

"They're gone."

"What the hell?"

"They're not where I left them!"

"Did you let them go? I tied them up, I know they were secure."

"No! I swear—"

"You had a soft spot for the girls. You bitch—"

"I didn't touch them!"

SWAT must have found a way in through the attic or a second-floor window. She caught Brad's eye and he gave her a little nod. He thought the same thing. Good. Two safe, one to go.

"They're going to kill us. They're going to kill us!" Joyce screamed.

Peter shot Joyce in the head. Lucy jerked involuntarily and almost caused the chair to tip over. Joyce crumpled to the tile floor, blood pooling around her head. Lucy stared at the body. She hadn't expected him to kill his partner. She shook her head to clear it.

Focus, Lucy. Focus on Peter. Get him to lower his guard. Just for a minute.

The phone rang again.

"Answer it," Lucy said, "or they'll swarm in and you'll be dead." She glanced at Brad again. He caught Lucy's eye, then blinked once and refocused his gaze toward the ceiling.

She discreetly looked upstairs. There was the curving staircase, a landing, and then the hall disappeared to the right and left. She saw the tip of a sniper rifle aimed in the direction of Peter. But there was no clear shot from that angle.

"I need to think! How can I think with all that noise?" He pulled the boy up from his seat and held the gun on his neck. The boy sagged, his eyes on the dead body. Peter held him up.

"Don't look at her," Lucy told the kid. "Look at me."

The boy averted his eyes from the body to Lucy. They

were glassy with terror and resignation that he was going
to die. No child should witness murder.

She wanted to offer a trade, her for the boy, but the way
Peter was acting, he would think it was a trick. He wouldn't
do anything she said. Lucy looked at Brad. He'd been hit
a couple of times, but the injuries were minor. Fortunately,
he'd kept his mouth shut for the most part. Peter definitely
had an issue with male authority, which was probably
why he responded so strongly to Elise's powerful female
presence.

"You'll walk in front of us, Agent Kincaid," Peter said.
"Open the doors for me. Stay close. But make no mistake
about it, I will shoot this kid if you do anything different
from what I say. We're going to walk out, get into the closest car, and drive."

"I can't drive cuffed."

"You'll manage."

He pushed the kid forward. Lucy backed away toward
the front door and gauged the angle of the sniper to Peter.

Two more feet. Two more feet.

"Peter, think this through," she said.

"What do you think I am, stupid? I'm not stupid!" He
aimed his gun at Brad. "One down, one to go," he said.

A shot came from the stairway above, taking off the top
of Peter Rabb's head. He collapsed and the boy fell down,
covered in Peter's blood.

Lucy rushed over to the boy, and even though she was
cuffed, she shielded him with her body. "It's okay, it's
okay," she said over and over. She looked over at Brad. He
was unharmed. Peter hadn't gotten a shot off.

SWAT swarmed in from upstairs, the front, and the
back. Someone helped Lucy up and took the boy outside.
She felt the cuffs being released from her wrists, and another officer uncuffed Brad.

Sean ran in, followed by Kane. Sean pulled Lucy into his arms and held her. "Elise told him to kill you. I thought he had."

"I'm fine. I'm fine," she repeated.

They stood there for a moment. When Lucy opened her eyes again, Kane was gone.

Maybe he hadn't even been there.

Lucy bolted upright in bed.

The clock said it was 6:10 A.M., but she'd been sound asleep. Something had jolted her awake, and it wasn't a nightmare.

Sean sat up. "Luce—what's wrong."

"I don't know. I thought I felt something, like an earthquake."

"There's not many earthquakes in Texas." He kissed her, and gently pushed her back down on the bed. "You got my heart racing." He kissed her again, then he frowned. "You're shaking. Are you sure you didn't have a nightmare? Lucy?"

"No, it's just—"

Sirens rang throughout the city. They were far away, but there were a lot of them. They both got out of bed and quickly dressed in the clothes that were lying around. Sean turned on the television to the local news and Lucy picked up her phone. She was about to call FBI headquarters when her cell phone rang.

"It's Brad," she said and put him on speaker. "Brad?"

"You're okay?"

"Yes, what happened?"

"I know why they left the drugs at the shooting. There was a bomb inside. Tobias just blew up the DEA evidence locker. I don't know how many guards were inside. At least two, but it's shift change. Not to mention the desk sergeant.

Do you know how many cases are still pending? It's a total clusterfuck."

"How'd you know? It just happened."

"I'm in the office—as soon as I heard the explosion, I
knew. I had to make sure you and Sean were okay. It's my
fault."

"It's not your fault, Brad."

"There was a specific reason for them to plant the
bomb," Sean said. "It couldn't have been just to cause
havoc."

"Why not?" Lucy said. "Tobias seems to live to cause
problems for the DEA. Wait—I thought SAPD had the
case."

"They did, until ATF took it over. We share office space
with ATF's field office, and—"

"And an evidence locker," Sean said. "Maybe SAPD
was the target."

"No. It was us—most drug cases fall under the DEA.
With that much heroin on scene we would have normally
been the lead. And even if we weren't, we work closely
with SAPD on all major drug busts."

"I'm sorry, Brad. Don't blame yourself," Lucy said.
"You couldn't have known."

Brad didn't seem to hear her. "I have to go," he said.
"Sam's talking to Juan now, they're going to sweep all evidence lockers, police stations, the FBI office, you name
it. It was a fucking Trojan horse. There could be more."

"Call us later," Sean said.

"Tell your brother. He needs to be extra careful." Brad
hung up.

Lucy said, "I need to talk to Elise."

Sean looked pained. "No."

"Sean, I can do this."

"But that girl—"

"I know exactly what she is. I'll be okay." She kissed him. "I have you to come home to."

Elise was in solitary and it took Lucy two hours of waiting before they brought her to the interview room. Without her makeup, she looked younger than her sixteen years. But her eyes were old. Old and calculating.

Elise hadn't talked, and they knew nothing about her that they hadn't already known. Elise had called Tobias her "big brother" but Lucy was skeptical. Tobias was at least forty. Elise was sixteen. More likely that he was her father—if they were related at all.

"I knew you'd come and see me," Elise said.

"Tell me why your brother set a bomb in the DEA evidence locker."

Elise's eyes sparkled. "I thought I heard the big boom. Toby is so fucking smart."

"What case did he want to destroy?"

Elise smiled and bit her lip. She stared at Lucy and raised an eyebrow. "All of them," she whispered. She tilted her chin up, as if daring Lucy to question her.

"He's too smart for that." Lucy's heart was pounding, but she kept her voice flat and even. She hadn't been trained to deal with sociopaths like Elise Hansen. Lucy had faced many killers, some as cold and confident as Elise. But none of them had been sixteen. None of them had been so elusive. Without knowing who Elise was in the past made it twice as difficult to understand her now.

"You think you're smarter than we are?" Elise grinned. "We had you going all week."

"Did your brother have those eight gang members killed—and a child—just to disguise the C-4 as heroin?"

Elise didn't answer. She attempted to look bored, but it was clear she was enjoying this conversation. She certainly wasn't scared. While intellectually Lucy knew that Elise had lied to them and manipulated them throughout the entire investigation, this moment was the first time she believed it.

The revelation chilled her all the way to her soul.

She said, "There was no guarantee that it wouldn't have been discovered before he set it off."

"But. It. Wasn't." Elise leaned forward as if she were going to share a secret. "I know what you want. You want to fix me."

Lucy raised an eyebrow. "No, actually, I don't. Some people are permanently broken. Like Humpty Dumpty, no one can put you back together."

"Hmm. Maybe you're smarter than I gave you credit for. But I'm not broken. I'm exactly the way I want to be. I won't be in here long."

One of the more philosophical arguments in criminal psychology was whether psychopaths were born or created through their environment. Most experts believed that sociopaths were born—individuals with no innate ability to form attachments or feel empathy toward others—but not all sociopaths turned into psychopaths. Were psychopaths—those with a predisposition to cruelty—curable? Were psychopaths created because of chemical imbalances in the brain? Were they created by their environment? Or were they mistakes of nature?

Lucy and her brother Dillon had argued about the subject many times. Dillon believed that some people were born cruel. Lucy believed that environment played a bigger role in the formation of a psychopath. Maybe they were both right, and both wrong.

Two things were clear to Lucy as she and Elise stared, each of them assessing the other. Elise was most certainly a sociopath. And there was no doubt in Lucy's mind that Elise had been cold, cunning, and cruel from the moment she had her first complex thought. Her environment might have expedited her journey from sociopath to psychopath, but it was a road Elise Hansen had always traveled.

Lucy said, "The evidence in your case wasn't in DEA storage, if you were wondering."

"I'm sure it's not," Elise said with a fake yawn. "I get a trial by jury. Never underestimate me. Or Toby. We always win."

Lucy leaned forward. "Not this time. We have most of his money. We caught on to your game early enough to trick you, and we diverted the money into an FBI account. If you think your brother is going to be able to buy or bribe you out of jail, think again."

Elise seemed amused. "We'll see about that."

Lucy said, "I will be testifying against you. If you think you're good on the stand? You've never seen me."

"You won't."

"Don't count on it. I'm looking forward to the day I can tell the court exactly what you are."

"You won't, because you'll be dead."

A chill ran down Lucy's spine at Elise's matter-of-fact tone, but she kept her expression impassive as she rose from the chair. "You don't scare me. You're a calculating, street-smart, manipulative sociopath. You talk a good game, but I won. And I will find Tobias. He will pay for his crimes. You *can* count on that."

She turned and walked out. Before she closed the door, Elise said, "It ain't over until the fat lady sings."

Lucy shut the door firmly. Stood there, took a deep breath. She was shaking. Damn, had Elise seen it? She hoped not. She hoped she'd kept her fear locked down while facing that monster.

Brad was waiting for her in the observation room. "I didn't know you were here," she said.

"I got your message late. Hoped I could talk you out of it." He rubbed her arm. "You okay?"

She nodded. "Fine." But her voice was clipped and tense.

"You shouldn't have gone in there. Just like me facing Nicole might not have been the smartest move. Nicole knows how I'll react and pushes all my buttons. Elise is . . . different. She's intuitive, and not in a good way. She wanted to scare you."

"I know," Lucy said. "I had to face her and show I wasn't intimidated."

"I think you did."

"I don't think she cares. She has a hundred little plans she's working on, and we need to warn the warden that she's dangerous. We need a psych evaluation immediately, and not just any court-appointed shrink. I'm going to talk to the AUSA about getting my brother Dillon appointed. He's an expert witness, consults with the FBI all the time, and he won't be snowed by her."

And she wanted to see her brother. All of them. She wanted her family. For years she'd detached from her family because when they looked at her, they saw her as a victim. It hurt, and she couldn't explain it to them or to herself. She'd brought them back into her life one by one. First Jack, then Dillon, then Patrick . . . and with Sean by her side, she realized she could face anything. Family made her stronger.

What kind of family had created Elise Hansen?

Brad and Lucy walked out of the observation room and through the maze of security in order to retrieve their weapons from the desk sergeant.

"What's going on with Worthington's estate?" Brad asked. "Between the congresswoman's money laundering and Harper's murder, I figure it's a mess."

"Logan Dunbar, the agent from D.C., is staying for a week or two to process the evidence found in her house and office. There was a file in her safe that is coded, but Dunbar thinks it's proof of her money laundering, and once they figure it out, it will lead to Tobias. Barry is working with Dunbar and the AUSA on the case and any other indictments."

"You don't sound optimistic."

"I'm angry, Brad. Harper Worthington is dead because he tried to do the right thing. First he came to us—the FBI—and we turned him away. So he investigated his own wife. Mona Hill, part of this conspiracy from the beginning, has disappeared. Maybe she's dead, but the way Tobias works he would have left her to be found—not just for us, but to keep his own people in line. Nicole Rollins is still working on a plea agreement and I really believe she could have stopped all of this—but we'll never know. A little boy was shot to death because his parents were gangbangers, and that just doesn't seem right. As if just because of his birth, he was condemned. And that girl—" Lucy stopped and took a deep breath. "I promised myself I wouldn't let her get under my skin."

"What we do isn't easy," Brad said.

"No one promised it would be. Thanks for letting me vent." Lucy wanted to go home and disappear in the pool house with Sean. No phones. No computers. Just the two of them. While she was still angry with Barry for talking to people about her behind her back, she owed him big for reminding her that she had a life outside of the job.

"We have one thing we didn't have before," Brad said.

"What?" She thought back on her conversation with Elise but didn't know what Brad was referring to.

"She admitted to knowing about the bomb, about the entire plan. Conspiracy. Every crime we can charge to Tobias, we can charge to her."

"You think she can sway a jury?"

"No. We'll both see to that."

She hoped he was right. But she was never going to underestimate Elise Hansen.

CHAPTER THIRTY-NINE

One Week Later

Lucy stared at the tiny baby through the glass. Her nephew, John Patrick Thomas.

He was beautiful. Perfect. John Patrick was the future, the hope of the current generation.

She and Sean had flown in Sean's Cessna and landed in San Diego only an hour ago. Now, John Patrick was twelve hours old and had already made a huge impact on the Kincaid family. He wasn't the first grandchild—or nephew. That had been Justin, twenty-six years ago. Lucy's nephew who had been her best friend for the first seven years of her life . . . until he'd been murdered.

Nelia had been young when she had had Justin—only twenty—but with the seven Kincaid children, Lucy was surprised—and sad—that there hadn't been another grandchild born for twenty-six years. She looked at the newborn and couldn't help but wonder if he would be the only one.

But it wouldn't matter. He would be well loved.

Her hand went to her hollow stomach. She wondered how it would feel to grow a little human inside her. But she would never know. The emptiness filled her, overwhelming her with a grief she didn't understand.

"Lucy." Sean came up behind her and put his hands on her shoulders. "Why are you crying? Is everything okay with Johnny?"

"Yes," she managed to say. "It's just me."

She turned to face him. He needed to know what she was thinking, how she felt. She'd kept this pain locked up for so long . . . she didn't know what to say. "I can't have one."

"I know that, sweetheart." He touched her face. "Don't cry. Please don't cry."

That made the tears fall faster. "It's . . . hard. I didn't realize I've been in mourning for so long. When I saw Molly two months ago, saw you rock her, when you smiled down at that beautiful baby . . . my heart swelled because you will make an amazing dad. You glowed with her, Sean. I'd never seen you like that before. And I . . . I can't give you that. We can't have a half Lucy, half Sean. It . . . it hurts so much. M-m-more than I ever thought it would."

He held her tightly, so tightly she almost couldn't breathe. He didn't say it would be okay, because they both knew it wouldn't. She would survive, because that was what she did. But the pain of a loss—the grief for something she could never have—would haunt her. And because Sean loved her, it would haunt him, too. And she hated that. She didn't want him to feel this same loss. But she held on tighter because he gave her the strength, and the will, to love.

"I love you, Lucy," he whispered. "Forever."

Sean had bought the engagement ring months ago, before they'd moved in together. He'd planned on proposing over Christmas, but so much had been going on, the time didn't seem right. Then he thought of proposing over Lucy's birthday, but Jack and his wife, Megan, had made a surprise trip to San Antonio.

But Sean should have done it long ago.

The pain on Lucy's face when she looked at John Patrick had nearly broken Sean. He didn't know how to make her feel better. He didn't know how to make her feel whole again. Because to him, Lucy was exactly who she was supposed to be. He would have done anything to turn back time and stop the brutality of what had happened to her, but he didn't understand why she thought he'd love her any less. Because whether or not she could conceive a child played no part in the enormity of his feelings. It was Lucy and him. It had to be Lucy and him, forever.

He would spend his entire life making sure she knew she was well loved.

Though originally they were supposed to stay with Connor, one of Lucy's brothers, and his wife, Julia, Sean had told Connor they wouldn't be coming. Instead, Sean called in a favor from a friend and took Lucy to a beach house up the coast in Mission Beach. She slept in the car and didn't even notice that they missed the turnoff to Connor's place.

It was late, and Sean managed to get Lucy inside without a lot of questions. It helped that she was exhausted.

"Is Connor already in bed? Should we say hello?" she asked.

"We'll talk to him tomorrow," Sean said, and ushered her into the master suite.

Lucy yawned. "I haven't been here in so long I don't even remember this. Wait—they must have moved. They weren't this close to the beach before."

Sean kissed her and helped her undress. He put her in bed and covered her up. "Sleep, princess."

"I guess I'm tired."

He kissed her.

"I love you, Sean."

She was asleep before he could get the words out.

"I love you, too, Lucy," he whispered and held her close to his chest. It was a long time before he, too, slept.

Lucy woke up to the sound of ocean waves. The bed was soft, with a thick down comforter. Sun streamed through high windows over the bed, but when she opened her eyes, she saw a wall of windows overlooking the ocean.

This was *not* her brother's house.

She sat up and stared. The view was spectacular. It made her realize how much she missed living near the ocean. She liked San Antonio, but her heart belonged to the Pacific Ocean.

She looked around, but Sean wasn't there. Their overnight bags were on the floor by the door. She got up, grabbed a thin bathrobe, and went to find Sean.

The smell of breakfast filled the air. Not only bacon and eggs and fresh coffee and orange juice, but more. She followed her nose to the kitchen, where Sean had a huge buffet of food lined up. He was wearing a chef's apron.

"Is my whole family coming here? How long do I have to get ready?" She looked around. "Where are we?"

Sean smiled and kissed her as he put a plate of fresh fruit and a pitcher of orange juice on the buffet. "Just us."

She stared at the feast, dumbfounded. "We can't eat all this."

"Who cares? I didn't know what you'd want to eat, so I made a little of everything."

"So my family isn't coming?"

"Nope."

"Why aren't we at Connor's?"

"I wanted you all to myself. At least for today."

"Where are we?"

"My friend Hank—you haven't met him, but we were roommates before I was expelled from Stanford. He owns this house. He lives in Seattle, owns a major computer gaming company, comes here only a couple times a year. I traded for this weekend."

"Traded what?" she asked warily.

"My services. Though my services are worth far more than one weekend at his beach house."

Lucy couldn't keep the grin off her face as she looked around the large, open floor plan and the expansive deck that jutted out over the sand. "I don't know. I think it's a pretty fair trade."

"Then you have no idea how much money I make." Sean kissed her again. "Dish up, we're going to eat outside."

Lucy was almost giddy. She piled far too much food on the plate and took it and a cup of coffee outside to where Sean had set up a table with flowers, seashells, and a bottle of champagne that looked expensive.

"Champagne in the morning?"

"You can add orange juice and call it a mimosa," he said. "Start eating. I'll be right back."

He left for a minute and Lucy stared at the ocean. She could stay here for a week. A month. Suddenly, the idea of going back to work made her sad. She wanted *this*. Time alone with Sean. In this small piece of paradise. Didn't they deserve it?

Barry Crawford was right—she needed to learn how to better turn off the job. Sean loved her for who she was, but they both deserved more down time, alone time, *peace*. She no longer felt that taking time off was a waste. Or, as she had in the past, that her off time gave her too much time to think about her mistakes, her past, and the pain in her life. That's why she'd worked so hard in college, that's why she'd had multiple internships—she'd never wanted a minute to relax. School, work and sleep, that had been her life for years.

No longer. She could now sit quietly and listen to the

ocean and not panic that she should be doing something else. She nibbled on a strawberry, her favorite fruit.

Sean returned with his own plate of food. He'd left the apron inside. He poured two glasses of champagne and added just a little orange juice to the top. He held up his glass. "To us."

She smiled and clinked her glass to his. "To you. You make everything better."

"For the rest of my life, I hope."

"Sean, you always do. When I see you, I know I'm okay. You're a tether to all that is good in me." She paused. "Last week, after that awful day when Barry said he couldn't trust me and I had to listen to that sex tape and Tia was shot . . . I reverted back to my old self. Cold. Icy. I felt it happen, as if it were a physical change. I couldn't stop it if I wanted to, but I got through the day. I didn't think it would go away.

"Then I came home and you were there. I saw you, and all those layers just melted away. Because of you. Only you."

Sean took her glass from her and put it on the table next to his. He held her hands. He kissed them. "I was going to take you out to dinner tonight, on the pier, and watch the sunset."

She smiled. "You still can. I think I might be motivated to get up in, oh, nine or ten hours."

"I thought it would be romantic watching the sun go down."

"It is, because you're with me."

"But I realized this morning when I watched you sleep that sunsets are an ending, and we are just beginning. So instead of tonight, I want to do this now." He reached behind the vase of wildflowers and pulled out a small, velvet bag.

"You're shaking," Lucy said.

Sean didn't say anything. He was never at a loss for words. She looked into his deep blue eyes and saw tears.

"What's wrong?" she said.

"Nothing. I just love you so much." He turned her hand over and poured a ring into it. "I want to marry you. I've wanted to almost since the day we met. I would have proposed on New Year's, but with everything that was going on . . ." His voice cracked. "You changed my life, Lucy. You gave me purpose and hope and love. I don't want to be your boyfriend anymore. I want to be your husband."

Lucy stared at the ring. It was both simple and exquisite, neither too big nor too small, a solitary, round, brilliant cut diamond. It sparkled as she tilted her hand. She tried to speak, but couldn't. She slipped it on her left ring finger. She rarely wore jewelry, but it fit perfectly. It looked like it belonged.

Because they belonged together.

She rose from her seat, walked around the small table, and sat in Sean's lap. "I love you so much." She kissed him.

His hands tightened around her back. He was still shaking, even as they kissed.

She whispered. "You didn't think I would say no, did you?"

"You haven't said yes."

She smiled at him and played with his hair. "You've always been able to read my mind."

"Say it. It would make me feel better."

"Yes, Sean. I will marry you."

He grinned and kissed her all over her face and neck until she laughed. He leaned her back, stared at her, his dimples showing, his eyes mischievous and full of love.

"I knew you'd say yes."

EPILOGUE

Nicole Rollins shuffled into the near-empty courtroom, feet shackled and hands cuffed in front of her.

Brad was there, her former partner. Of course he was, the noble, tragic hero. Driven by duty and honor, uncorruptible.

And Samantha Archer, her former boss. Sitting there looking like an ice princess, her long hair wound tightly up behind her head, as tight as her ass. If Brad had her position, this deal would never have been made, because Brad would have killed her. At a minimum he would have pounded the walls of the DOJ until they listened. But Sam, like so many women in high positions, didn't like to rock the boat. It wasn't that they were worse than their male counterparts, it was that they didn't want to be seen as a bitch or a ball-breaker. The deal hadn't been easy, but in the end, Nicole knew that Sam would give in just to get the name of the other traitor in the DEA.

Like Nicole would ever tell them.

Nicole's attorney, two AUSAs, the bailiff, the court reporter, and the judge.

Wholly unnecessary because she'd already signed the deal. She'd played her part perfectly. She knew they'd never give her witness protection, but they had agreed to give her a fake identity and transfer her to a federal prison in New England. She'd made them jump through hoops, telling them how terrified she was she'd be killed, that she already had a price on her head.

She was such a good actress. Because she certainly wouldn't be around to fulfill her end of the bargain.

She sat at the table and waited while the AUSA read out all the charges and stipulations. What she'd agreed to do, what they would do, yada yada yada. *Boring.*

And then came the fun part.

"Will the defendant please rise."

She stood.

"Do you understand the charges that have been brought before this court?"

"Yes, your honor."

"And you have agreed to waive your trial by jury and enter a guilty plea?"

"Yes, your honor."

"I need you to affirm that you are guilty of all charges as set forth in the document."

"I am guilty, your honor."

The violence was only beginning. And when Nicole was done, Brad would suffer. He might be the only one she would decide to let live. Because when everyone else he cared about and worked with was dead, he'd know it was because he couldn't stop her.

A thrill ran through her spine. She almost smiled.

"In exchange for your plea and cooperation with the AUSA, you accept being transferred to an undisclosed federal penitentiary under an undisclosed name, where you will serve twenty years with no opportunity for parole?"

"I do."

"Would you like to say anything to the court?"

"May I say something to my former boss?"

"Yes," the judge said.

Nicole turned slowly, her chains rattling. She looked at Brad and Sam, her face as impassive as she could make it. "I'm sorry," she said as contritely as she could muster. "I wish things had been different." Different, absolutely. She wished that Brad Donnelly had actually died when he was supposed to.

"I am ashamed," she said, "and humbled that this court and the US Attorney have allowed me to help in any way I can, as penance for the atrocities I've committed. I only hope that you can one day forgive me."

She stared at Brad. He didn't react. She winked, then turned to face the judge, her head down.

"The court will stipulate to the agreement between these two parties. Ms. Rollins, you'll be transported next week to this court to answer questions that the AUSA has prepared regarding the known criminal named Tobias, his alleged sister known as Elise Hansen, all their associates, the explosion at the evidence locker, and reveal the identity of other compromised agents and employees of which you are aware. On Friday, you'll be transported to federal prison, where you will serve out the remainder of your sentence."

"Thank you, your honor."

She glanced back over her shoulder. Brad wasn't there.

Nicole almost smiled. He wouldn't be able to stop the storm that was coming. The violence would rain down on him and everyone he cared about. And she'd let him live through it all, because he would suffer more knowing he couldn't stop her.

She could hardly wait for next week.

Brad Donnelly thought it was over, that this was the end for her. She wished she could see his face when he learned the truth.

Today was only the beginning.

Dear Reader:

Characters usually come to writers as either fully formed individuals or works in progress. Maxine Revere came to me almost fully formed.

It's sort of a funny story how Max came about. In 2010 I was interviewing literary agents. I shared this idea I had, a series focusing on an investigative reporter named Max Revere who traveled the country solving cold cases. The first book would solve a murder from his past, the crime that had set him on his journalistic path. Dan Conaway at Writers House was enthusiastic about the concept and the character, but asked, "What if Max was Maxine?"

As soon as he said that, not only did I realize Dan was going to be my new agent, but Max also blossomed to life. I'd had this idea for two years, but it wasn't until I got over the idea that Max was a guy that her character evolved. And Maxine Revere was born.

Notorious begins the series with Max going back—to her hometown, to her roots, to ultimately

*face the tragedy of her best friend's murder
thirteen years ago, which paved the road she's
since traveled. Home is the beginning for all of us;
for Max it was also an ending.*

*A few months ago, my editor asked me to write a
prequel to* Notorious, *a short story that gives a
snapshot of who Max is and why she does what she
does. Why does she care about cold cases? Why did
she agree to host a cable crime show when she
doesn't like working for anyone but herself? Why
would she drop everything to look for a missing
college student, when she has no ties to the community he disappeared from and no relationship with
his family?*

*While I love writing short stories, my idea of
"short" usually falls in the novella range, and this
story is no exception. I'm grateful that my editor told
me I could tell the story any way I wanted, and I
hope you enjoy reading* Maximum Exposure *as
much as I enjoyed writing it. And, mostly, I hope you
like Maxine Revere as much as I do.*

*Happy reading,
Allison Brennan*

CHAPTER ONE

Investigative reporter Maxine Revere couldn't explain what drew her toward a particular investigation. She couldn't articulate why she wasn't interested in a cold case across the city, but would jump on a cross-country flight to pursue an even colder case.

She appreciated the fact that she didn't have to explain herself to anyone.

Independently wealthy, she could pursue any lead that caught her attention. For her news articles, she'd conduct a preliminary investigation to decide if she wanted to spend the time solving the case, then write a proposal and send it to one of three editors she liked to work with. They'd give her the flexibility and the credentials to follow through, and she'd submit her report when she was done. Sometimes—most of the time—she went ahead with the full investigation even before anyone wanted the story. For her books, she immersed herself in the community with the people who were affected, hoping not only to tell the story of the crime—victims, survivors, perpetrators—but also to understand everyone involved.

She couldn't imagine doing anything else with her life. Because of the success of her true crime books and the popularity of her in-depth reports, she received hundreds of letters every month from families and friends of victims who wanted her to look into a violent crime, most often a disappearance or a homicide. Letters from killers claiming they were innocent rarely appealed to her, nor did the claims of innocence by loved ones who believed—or wanted to believe—that their mother/husband/boyfriend/daughter/friend was railroaded by the system.

Though she couldn't explain to anyone else why she was going to Colorado to investigate the disappearance of Scott Sheldon from his college campus, as soon as she read the letter from his mother, she knew she *was* going.

First, she called Scott's mother, Adele Sheldon. She rarely pursued an investigation without the blessing of one of the family members. In this case, Adele was both surprised and relieved that Max had called her. Max listened to the mother talk about her son and his disappearance, repeating most of the information from the letter, but adding an important detail: search and rescue had only last week actively started to look for his body. Adele gave her the contact information of a detective in Colorado Springs, someone at the park service, the head of campus police, and Scott's former college roommate. It was a good start.

Max made contact with the detective, who wasn't helpful, because both the college and the campground Scott went missing from were out of her jurisdiction. The campus security chief didn't take her call—supposedly out of the office—but Max left her contact information. She briefly spoke to the head of the park service search team, Chuck Pence, who confirmed the pertinent details. She wanted to talk to him further when she arrived in Colorado Springs. Max read all newspaper and online reports on Scott's disappearance, but there wasn't much written.

After the preliminary research, Max called Adele again

to confirm that Scott's mother still wanted her help. The woman sobbed.

"Y-yes," she said. She took a deep, audible breath. "I need to know what happened to my son. I need the truth."

Truth. Most people thought they were strong enough for the truth, but sometimes they resented Max for digging into their life, their family, their friends. Max always believed the truth was better than not knowing, and not everyone concurred with her philosophy.

"It might not be what you think, Mrs. Sheldon. We might learn things about your son you wished you didn't know."

"I don't care," she said. "Not knowing what happened, not having his body to bury, is worse than anything you might learn. My son was a good boy. Smart. Shy. Trusting. He never forgot my birthday; he cared deeply for his sister, Ashley. I love him. I want to say good-bye. Maybe you don't understand."

She understood exactly how Mrs. Sheldon felt. Max hadn't lost a child, but she'd lost people close to her.

She said, "I'll be there."

Max booked a flight without checking her calendar. When she looked at her schedule the next morning, she saw that she was supposed to have lunch with Ben Lawson.

Max dialed his number, glad that this time she had a legitimate excuse to cancel. She'd canceled on her old college friend twice already. The first time, he'd been understanding; the second, he was irritated.

Third time? He would be irate.

"Don't you dare cancel on me," he said before she could even get a soothing *hello, how are you?* out of her mouth.

"It's work, Ben."

"It's *always* work."

"I'm a busy woman."

"You're an *impossible* woman. We're having lunch."

"My flight leaves at three, I need to be in a cab by twelve forty-five."

"Meet me right now."

"I need to pack."

"You're not canceling on me again, Maxie."

"Do *not* call me that, Benji."

He let out an exasperated sigh. "I need to talk to you about something. It's important."

"Everything with you is important." Ben always had something going on. He worked in film, had done something out in L.A. for a few years after he graduated from Columbia, and now worked for a television station here in New York City. Max had no idea what he actually did, only that he had three phones and never stopped talking.

"I'm serious, Max. Please."

Ben never said please. Now Max was curious. "Eleven thirty, same place."

"I'll change the reservation. Thank you." He hung up quickly, as if she might change her mind.

She stared at the phone. A please *and* a thank you? Now she was not only interested, but suspicious, too.

She didn't have much time before she had to meet Ben. She packed a large suitcase plus her overnight bag, which should be enough for the four or five days she planned to be in Colorado Springs. If she decided to stay longer, she'd ask her neighbors—who took care of her place during her frequent travels—to ship out anything she might need.

Max left her luggage with her doorman so she didn't have to lug it to the restaurant. She lived in TriBeCa, on Greenwich Street, and Ben lived on the Upper West Side. That he would come all the way down here to have lunch at the Tribeca Grill was partly because of the good food, but mostly because he wanted something from her. Ben was a schmoozer and glad-hander, but he was also busy and selfish. He expected people to come to him.

But Ben knew Max; she liked her neighborhood. It was certainly in his favor that he'd made reservations at one of her favorite restaurants. Someone who didn't know her might think that Ben was manipulating her, but when it came to her old friend, she supposed she allowed him to do it. He'd never been able to convince her to do anything she really didn't want to do, but he did have an uncanny ability to see through her bullshit. She admired that.

Ben was already at the restaurant when she arrived. She eyed her old friend before he spotted her. Ben hadn't changed. He was tall and slim, with an intensity about him, as if everything were either critical or top secret, and she'd always wondered why he hadn't gone into politics. He had that Teflon coating that seemed so perfect for politicians and car salesmen, but he combined it with the boyish charm of a high school quarterback. When Max wanted to irritate him, she'd call him "Ken" because he had that too-perfect, polished smile to go with his WASP appearance.

He spotted her almost immediately, which wasn't hard, because she was tall with dark red hair. He looked relieved, as if he'd feared she might not show.

"I said I'd be here." She gave him a light kiss. She and Ben had never had a romantic relationship—the thought made her want to laugh out loud. In fact, they weren't naturally friends. Ben and her college roommate, Karen Richardson, had been close, and Karen's death their senior year ended up bringing Ben and Max closer. Ironic, perhaps, because Karen had once told Max that her life would be perfect if her two best friends actually *liked* each other.

Max wouldn't say that she *liked* Ben, but she respected

him—and for her, respect was more important than the emotions involved in liking or disliking anyone.

Ben said, "You've been avoiding me."

"Not well enough." She stared pointedly at her watch. "I'm walking out of here at twelve forty. My car service is picking me up at my apartment at twelve forty-five."

"Then order."

She laughed and leaned back as Ben looked over the menu.

"What?" he said.

"No small talk, no how have you been?"

"You hate small talk."

"That never stopped you before when you want something."

The waiter came over and they ordered. Max added a glass of pinot grigio and Ben stuck with iced tea.

"I have a fantastic opportunity for you." He ran a hand through his dark blond hair, which fell immediately back into place across his forehead. His dark eyes were bright with excitement. "Your own television show."

Max stared at him. "A television show," she said flatly.

"*Your* television show."

"No."

"You didn't listen to my pitch."

"I don't need to listen to your pitch."

"Yes, you do. I don't think you understand what an amazing idea this is. It'll be like a news magazine, but better. We'll be integrating all communications media—television, a Web site, podcasts, social media, print. It's cable, more flexibility, more edge. Multiple venues will get your reports out to more people."

The excitement in Ben's voice grew as he spoke. Max was grateful her wine arrived.

"I like my job," she said after sipping her drink.

"You don't have a job."

She snapped her fingers. "Exactly. I investigate the cases I want, write the articles I want, do what I want. Do you sense the theme?"

"You do what you want because you're rich."

"You make being rich sound like it's a bad thing." She sipped her wine and assessed Ben over the rim of her stemware. "You're not exactly collecting welfare, Mr. Lawson, grandson of Tobias Lawson the Third, the self-made and successful businessman who owns half of Boston."

Her attempt at getting under his skin failed. He said, "You're scared."

She laughed again. "Ben, you know me well enough to know I don't scare easily."

"Not by anything out there—" He waved his hand loosely toward the quaint cobblestone intersection. "—but by change. You're not even thirty, but you're an old stick-in-the-mud, as my grandmother would say."

"Then let me stick in the mud *here* and leave me alone. I don't want a television show."

"Your books are doing fine, but you only write one every two or three years. Newspaper readership is way down, and they're still scrambling to get their online component growing. You pay for your own research, your trips, your investigations. If you had a television show, production would pay all that."

"Because, like you said, I'm rich. If I want to spend my money investigating a cold case in Small Town, USA, I can. If I sell the article, great. If not, I don't care." Except she did. She cared because if she couldn't find anyone interested, the story wouldn't get the exposure it deserved. But that had nothing to do with television.

As if she hadn't spoken, he continued. "Cable television is not the crazy aunt in the attic anymore."

She arched an eyebrow. "Is that even a saying?"

"We'll have an entire *team* working for *you.* I would be your producer—"

"Hell no—"

"And you would have a say in what cases we cover."

"Say? I would have *a say?* My answer was no at the beginning, and now it's 'over my dead body.'"

"I don't accept that."

Their food arrived but neither of them picked up a fork. Usually, Ben amused or annoyed her; today he was pissing her off. "Ben, we've known each other for ten years. Have you ever in your wildest dreams imagined me taking orders from anybody?"

"You wouldn't. You'd be the boss."

"It doesn't sound like it."

He sighed, played with his food. "Max, without you, there is no show. *You* are the show."

"I don't want to be the show."

"You're blunt, you're beautiful, you have an uncanny ability to see through people's bullshit and get them to spill their secrets. In two years, I can make *Maximum Exposure* the top news show on the network and the top investigative show on cable television." He held up his fingers in a V. "Two years!"

"You're calling it *Maximum Exposure?*" Unbelievable. "That's a play off my name, isn't it?"

"It's perfect. You expose the truth. The good and the bad. You're honest. You're driven. You already have a name because of your books, you have a platform. Not just a platform, but stage presence. I've watched every interview you've ever done on television, and—"

"What?" she interrupted. "Why would you do that?"

"I'm a news junkie. You know that. And because of Karen . . ." For a second, he hesitated, and she saw the young college boy that he'd once been. Then the producer

Ben Lawson was back. "I follow crime. You're a natural. The camera loves you, even if you're in the middle of a swamp with gnats swarming your head."

"You saw that?" She hadn't thought that feed, when she found three boys dead in a Louisiana swamp, was picked up by any station other than the local Baton Rouge affiliate.

"This is the natural next step for you. Or are you going to be satisfied running around the country solving crimes like Nancy Drew on steroids?"

"Now you're being insulting."

"You're good, dammit! You're wasting your talent."

Max stabbed a fork into her salad and stuffed the mix of chicken and lettuce into her mouth before she let loose on Ben. He was right, she was blunt—so much so that she could go for his jugular right now, and just say good-bye to their odd and unnatural friendship.

She didn't want a television show. She didn't want a staff, didn't want to report to anyone or have anyone report to her. She liked her life just the way it was. It was comfortable. She could fly off to Colorado Springs to investigate the disappearance of a college student that may or may not have involved foul play, and not worry that she was going to say or do something that would screw with ratings and cost people their jobs.

She liked being the only one she was responsible for. She liked her freedom. She *needed* her space. And Ben, of all people, should understand that.

The word "no" was on the tip of her tongue, when Ben said, "Don't say yes now."

"I wasn't going to." But she smiled. She couldn't help it. Ben had that way about him, making her crazy one minute and laughing the next.

"Think about it, Max. I'll email you my proposal, the

one I used to sell the idea to Robert and Catherine Crossman, and maybe it'll explain things better than I have."

"You explained things well enough," she said.

"Go on your trip. Read my proposal. And tell me yes when you come back."

The smile disappeared. "Don't be cocky. I don't want to do this."

"Yes, you do." He visibly relaxed. "We have ten minutes before you have to leave to catch your plane. Tell me about this trek to Colorado Springs. Who, what, why, when, where, how."

"College student Scott Sheldon, missing for six months after walking away while on a camping trip with friends."

"Dead?"

"Probably."

He stared at her. "You're going because of Karen."

"No, I'm not." But there was some truth to his observation. Karen disappeared while she and Max had gone to Miami for a wild spring break their senior year. She was definitely dead—the police had found evidence of a violent death with an extensive amount of blood—but her body was never found. Max had spent a year of her life searching for answers, and still no one knew what happened beyond a theory that couldn't be proved. And a killer had walked away.

She swirled her wine in her glass, but didn't drink. "Scott's mother wrote to me. She doesn't know what happened to him. If I can find out—well, she might be able to sleep better."

Adele Sheldon had said, *I need to know what happened to my son. I need the truth.*

Max was good at uncovering the truth. Not everyone appreciated it; not everyone was truly strong enough to handle it. But Adele Sheldon was a grieving mother with no body to bury. She accepted that her son was dead, had told Max that if he were alive, she'd know in her heart. *I'm in limbo, Ms. Revere. I want to bury his body.*

Ben didn't say anything for a minute. He leaned back, a sad and wistful expression on his handsome face. She wished she had something to say, something cutting or witty, but her mind was blank. They were both thinking about Karen, a girl they'd loved, and Scott Sheldon, a boy they didn't know. All hostility she'd felt toward Ben for his ridiculous idea to give her a television show dissolved.

"What happened to the kid?" Ben asked.

"I won't know until I talk to his friends or find his body."

"You're searching for his body?"

"That's the plan."

He leaned forward. "This would be a great report for your television show."

"I don't have a television show," she said, glaring at him again.

He smiled, picked up *her* wineglass, and drained it. "Not yet."

CHAPTER TWO

Max woke up at 4:30 A.M. in a luxurious suite of the Broadmoor resort in Colorado Springs, cursing Ben for her uneasy sleep. Seeing him and talking about Karen had brought up all the memories, failures, and frustration of that year in Miami after Karen disappeared. Max often had insomnia—she fell to sleep easily enough, but if she woke at two or three in the morning, it was rare she could go back to sleep.

She'd stayed at the Broadmoor many times in the past; it was one of her favorite resorts. The executive suite had a fireplace, balcony and breathtaking view of the snow-covered mountains. Max appreciated quality accommodations, and didn't mind paying for them. She pulled herself out of bed and decided to wake up with strong coffee and a bubble bath.

Ten minutes later, she sighed as she sank into the hot, scented water. She sipped the sweetened coffee and closed her eyes.

When she should have been relaxing in the deep tub, her thoughts instead went back to Miami, back to when she was twenty-two and enjoying spring break with her best friend and roommate. Columbia had hooked them up their freshman year and it should have been hate at first sight—Karen was everything Max was not. Karen was short, Max was tall; Karen was chatty, Max was reserved; Karen was a slob, Max was neat. Blond hair to red hair; brown eyes to blue; middle-class family to wealthy family.

Yet, somehow, they worked. It was books, Max believed—they both loved books, both were lit majors, and they had the same sense of humor. Better, Karen didn't lie. She was as blunt and straightforward as Max, and Max ended up trusting Karen more than she did anyone.

She'd needed Karen at a time in her life when everyone she'd known and grown up with proved to be untrustworthy. Her friends, her ex-boyfriend, her family. Max had wanted to be far from home, moving from California to New York, and she didn't look back. Max didn't want to care for anyone except herself. She understood—because she had always been honest with herself—that the reason she didn't want any close friends was because she had abandonment issues. First her mother dumped her on her rich grandparents' doorstep and walked away, sending her sporadic postcards that had ended abruptly when she was sixteen; then nine years later, her friend Lindy was killed the week of their high school graduation. She didn't want to get attached to anyone it would hurt her to lose.

But Karen was the type of girl who latched on and didn't let go. When Max was irritated with her, she called Karen a parasite, impossible to get rid of. But now, more than ten years after they'd met, Max knew Karen was exactly what she'd needed to reconnect with the flawed but compelling human race.

Karen wasn't perfect. She was a flirt. She drank too much. She slept with the wrong guys and got her heart broken more times in their first year of college than Max had in her lifetime. They needed each other—Karen to bring Max down off her pedestal and enjoy living again, and Max to protect Karen from herself.

But in the end, she couldn't protect Karen. Karen had disappeared, and though Max and law enforcement knew she was dead, they'd never found her body, nor brought her killer to justice.

The one time Karen lied to her had proved fatal.

Max sighed and stretched. The water had cooled uncomfortably, so she quickly finished her coffee, pulled the drain, and rinsed off under a hot stream of water through the dual jets. She dressed in layers, since the early spring morning was cold, then dried her thick hair and put on make-up while drinking another cup of coffee.

Finally, she felt ready to start the day.

She called room service for breakfast and more coffee. She didn't like to eat in her hotel room, but she couldn't bring her desk down to the restaurant and she had work to do.

After room service left, she ate a blueberry scone and reviewed her e-mail. While on the flight yesterday, she'd planned her day, but Max preferred to remain flexible when starting an investigation. She had the basics of the case, but it wasn't as cut-and-dried as she'd have liked.

First, there were jurisdictional issues. The college was in the county, not the city of Colorado Springs. The campsite where Scott Sheldon had disappeared was in a national park, putting the location under the federal government. The National Park Service rangers were responsible for the initial search and rescue, but they had a joint operation with the county and adjoining cities. Adele Sheldon had told her she filed the missing persons report with the college and with Colorado Springs PD, and Detective Amelia Horn was her contact. Why CSPD? Neither the college nor the campsite was in the city. Who was really in charge? Detective Horn had nothing to add when Max spoke to her, pointing out that CSPD *wasn't* in charge.

Max pulled out a trifold board she'd created last night and set it up on the credenza. The time line was clear, even though it made no sense.

Last Halloween Eve, nearly six months ago, was a Friday. Scott Sheldon told his roommate that he was going camping with three friends—Tom Keller, Arthur Cowan, and Carlos Ibarra. They planned to be back Sunday morning.

According to the statements by Scott's three friends, they'd been drinking and joking Friday night. At some point, Scott got angry—no one claimed to know exactly what set him off—and he grabbed his backpack and left. When he didn't return, they assumed he was sleeping in the truck, which was parked an hour's hike from the campsite.

The next morning, Scott still hadn't returned. The weather turned from overcast to rain, and Keller, Cowan, and Ibarra returned to the truck. When they didn't find Scott, they looked for him in the area, but the rain came down hard and heavy. They left—there was nothing in the notes saying that they went back to the campus on Saturday, but that was implied. It snowed late Saturday night and the boys said they trekked back to the campsite Sunday morning and looked for Scott. They didn't call the rangers, they didn't alert campus security, *nothing*, until Sunday afternoon.

That was the part of the story that set off Max's instincts. Why had it taken them so long to tell anyone that Scott was missing? Why did campus security wait until Monday morning to notify the park service? By that point, the storm was so severe, they could search for only a few hours each day. By the end of the week, the roads to that area of the mountain were impassable.

There was no doubt in her mind that Scott Sheldon had died on that mountain, but the question was how and when. The fact that he was missing for nearly forty-eight hours before the three boys had alerted *anyone* told Max they were lying about something.

She reviewed her notes until eight, when she called Chuck Pence with the park service. He was based in Colorado Springs, near the police station, but Pence was on the search and rescue staff and had led the effort to find Scott. His specialty was working with tracking dogs.

He wasn't there, and the staff said he was already in the field. Max left a message and reviewed her schedule. She'd wanted to talk to Pence first for more background on the search and what, if anything, they'd found that hadn't made it in the official files, but that would have to wait. She considered talking to Detective Horn again, but after their phone conversation, Max suspected it would be a waste of time. If she learned anything new, she'd talk to the police. She'd go to the college first and talk to Scott's roommate, then track down the others.

While she drove the thirty minutes to the Cheyenne College campus, she got two calls, which she sent to voice mail. The first from Ben. She wasn't going to talk to him about the television show until after this case, and she was already thinking of more ways she could tell him no—since the blunt no she'd already given him didn't work. The second call came from her editor. Max didn't have anything good to tell her, and Emma was going to be disappointed.

Max had written four true crime novels, the first about Karen's disappearance and the subsequent investigation. The latest book was coming out this summer, and Emma wanted another proposal. But Max didn't have a case that excited her. She read the crime blotters, tracked the news—there were a lot of interesting cases, some even more interesting than Scott Sheldon's disappearance. But nothing jumped out at her as thrilling enough to invest several months of her life into research and interviews, then another six to nine months verifying facts and writing the book. Writing the last book had nearly gutted Max. She'd investigated claims of elder abuse in a Miami facility and uncovered a ten-year reign of terror by the director she had dubbed the Wicked Nurse of Miami. Not very creative, and her editor had cut all but two references to the nickname from the book, but it was still the way Max thought of the bitch who seemed to take pleasure in making sick, old people suffer.

She didn't want to go through that again, not yet. She briefly considered the Scott Sheldon case, and maybe there was something here that would warrant a full-length book, but Max didn't see it yet. She first needed to talk to the people involved—maybe shining a new light on the matter would get them to talk—or slip up, if they were harboring a violent secret.

It was nine when she arrived in the visitors' parking lot. The campus was small, at least by Max's standards—three thousand undergraduates, half of whom commuted to the campus, and an even smaller graduate program. A typical liberal arts college, where students predominately majored in the humanities and arts, though there was a new earth science building and a recent influx of students majoring in environmental science and conservation. Not a surprise, considering the campus was in the Rocky Mountains.

The grounds may have been modest, but they spread out and up the mountainside, with tree-lined cement trails winding around the perimeter. A quad, of sorts, was built around a possibly natural waterfall, which filled a small lake. A stream meandered out, and judging from the marks in its banks, it was lower than it had been in the past. Still, the campus seemed like a rather idyllic place. No towering redwoods and pines as in California and much of the Rocky Mountains, but this place still had the fresh clean air and crisp cold Max loved.

She used to go skiing all the time—in far colder weather than this. She still skied when she could, but more and more she spent her hours investigating or planning an investigation. This was the first winter she hadn't spent time at her cousin's resort in Vail. Too many cold cases had grabbed her interest, and she'd also been finishing the book about the Wicked Nurse of Miami.

Her work—vocation, really—consumed her, and taking time off to have fun just hadn't seemed important after the tragedies she immersed herself in. And as her editor, who was probably her closest friend in New York, had told her, Max was a workaholic.

Max had downloaded a campus map, but each path was well marked with signs and arrows directing her. She was looking for Rock Creek dorm, where Scott Sheldon had lived for the two months before his disappearance. His roommate had been Ian Stanhope, an environmental science major from Denver. Scott had been an environmental science major as well—and in fact, Scott and Ian seemed to have lived parallel lives.

Both were strong but not straight-A students; both were at Cheyenne on partial merit scholarships. Both had one younger sibling—Scott, a sister; Ian, a brother—and parents who divorced while the boys were in junior high school. Had they become close friends or bitter enemies? Sometimes, similarities made you hate a person because they highlighted—often unintentionally—your own flaws.

She didn't have a sense of who they were as people,

only who they were on paper. Scott hadn't been involved with athletics; Ian was on the baseball team for the college, a D-III school. Through social media, it appeared that Ian had many friends, lots of direct and indirect connections to college, his high school, and Denver. Scott's profile had been taken down, probably by his mother or sister, but his mother told her that he'd been soft-spoken and reserved, with only a few friends growing up.

How few? Had he made friends during his two months at Cheyenne before he disappeared? Was he homesick? Did he like college? Were his grades okay or was he struggling? Was there a girlfriend his mother didn't know about? Ex-girlfriend? His mother said he didn't have a history of depression, but a family might miss that, especially if the depressed person tried to keep it from them. Or if the onset was sudden. These were all things she would find out.

She knocked on Ian Stanhope's door again and considered that he might not be there. Classes, socializing, studying.

A small guy came out of the room next door, backpack over his shoulder. "If you're looking for Ian, he's probably at the gym if he doesn't have class."

"Can you point me in the right direction?"

"South exit, right, and follow the signs to Cougar Stadium."

Max followed the directions and less than five minutes later was standing in the lobby of a rather impressive athletics facility for a small college. The gym portion was well equipped with several weight machines, treadmills, and an area for free weights. It was clean and bordered on two sides by windows, which looked out into trees. Half the machines were being used.

She referred to a photo of Ian, then looked around. She spotted him working with free weights. Ian watched her approach, a mixture of apprehension and pleasure in his expression.

"Ian Stanhope?" she asked.

"That's me." He grinned and wiped his sweaty face with his shirt. He was a good looking nineteen-year-old with blond hair that fell into his eyes. That he didn't push it away bothered Max. Could he even see through the mess?

"I'm Maxine Revere." She handed him her business card. "I need a minute of your time."

"Why would a reporter want to talk to me?" he said, a half smile still on his face.

"Do you have a class?"

"Not until noon."

"Great."

He looked from her to her card. "You're from New York."

"Yes."

He lost his smile and didn't move. He tossed his head, moving his clump of overgrown hair to the side. "What do you want to talk to me about?"

"I'm looking into Scott Sheldon's disappearance, from last October. You were his roommate."

"I wasn't on the camping trip."

"I promise, I won't take too much of your time."

He mumbled, "I have class."

"At noon, right? We'll be done before then."

Usually, for Max, the direct approach worked best. She didn't like playing games or manipulating people into talking to her. But sometimes, she needed a gentle touch. She couldn't tell if he was more upset or worried, but something was up with him.

She said, "How about if I give you twenty minutes to shower and change, and I'll meet you at the student union?

Coffee, brunch. My treat." There was always the chance he would bail, but she knew where to find him.

"Is something wrong?"

"Other than your roommate has been missing for six months?"

"I mean, no other reporters have been around here asking about Scott. Like, ever."

"I specialize in cold cases. Twenty minutes enough time?"

"Yeah—the quad has a food court," he said. "I'll meet you there. The student union is just vending machines. Gross stuff, really."

She walked out, noting that Ian watched her before he disappeared through the locker room doors.

She'd definitely thrown him off, but she didn't know why. Ian hadn't been part of the foursome who'd gone camping, so what did he have to worry about? Unless he knew something he hadn't told the police.

While she waited, Max checked her e-mail and text messages. Ben had sent her a message asking if she'd read his proposal. She didn't respond. The truth was she *had* read it on the plane—and she still wanted to say no. The proposal was outstanding, and he'd addressed all her concerns, even though she hadn't told him what they were. He even resolved issues she wouldn't have thought to question, as if he'd known she'd come up with problems on the fly.

Ultimately, she had to decide if this was what she wanted to do with her life—or at least the next few years. Right now, she was very comfortable. She liked what she did; she liked her freedom.

It didn't take long before Ian strode purposefully to her table and sat down. He had combed his hair back, so it wasn't falling in his eyes as much. She smiled, pushed her papers back in a folder, and sipped her coffee. "What can I get you?"

He put a water bottle in front of him. "I can't eat right after I work out. But thanks." Ian looked around the quad sheepishly, as if he didn't want anyone to see him talking with her. "I don't understand why a reporter is interested in Scott," he said.

"I specialize in cold cases. My Web site lists the articles and books I've written."

His eyes widened. "You're writing a book about Scott?"

"Not a book, an article. I spoke to his mother, Adele Sheldon, and she asked me to look into his disappearance."

"Oh." He stared down at his hands, not meeting her eyes. "I met Ms. Sheldon when we moved in. Her and Scott's sister, Ashley. And then when she came to get his things. It was—uncomfortable. I felt bad."

I felt bad. "Bad" didn't cut it. Max had been much closer to Karen than Ian had been to Scott; the pain and rage she'd allowed to simmer were a dark fuel that drove her for the year after Karen disappeared. But Karen was not Scott; Max was not Ian.

"I understand that you didn't know Scott before you became roommates."

He shook his head. "We got paired up by the school. Same major, and like me, he's neat. Some of the guys in my dorm—well, they're slobs. I didn't want a slob. So we got along."

"I read the police reports. You told Detective Horn that Scott was quiet, you never saw him do drugs or drink, that he kept to himself. Is that accurate?"

Ian nodded. "He wasn't a bad guy once you got to know him."

That was an odd comment. "But before someone got to know him? Did other people not like Scott?"

"No, of course not." He frowned, drank some water.

"Ian, no one's perfect."

He shrugged. "No one had a problem with him."

Max switched focus. "You told police that he went camping with friends on Friday, October thirtieth. He didn't return with the others, but you didn't contact campus police."

"It's not my fault he got lost!"

"I didn't say it was your fault." She assessed him. He was upset, but why? "You didn't go on the trip, did you?"

"No. I feel bad about the whole thing. I mean, if I thought I was supposed to call the police when he didn't come back, I would have. I didn't know the guys he went with, not well. Scott was—he was a little strange, okay? But one-on-one, he was cool, we got along. Not best friends or anything, but okay. He just hung out with different people."

"Can you give me some names?"

"Don't you have the police report? I'm sure they all talked to the police. He didn't have a lot of friends."

"Tom Keller, Arthur Cowan, Carlos Ibarra," Max read from her notes, though she knew the names by heart. "Did he know any of them before?"

"Before what?"

"From high school, his hometown."

"I don't think so."

"What about you?"

"No. I didn't like Scott's friends. I don't even think Scott liked them much, but they hung together."

"What I don't understand is why no one contacted campus police immediately. Why they waited for so long."

He reddened. "You're talking about me."

"Should I be?"

"I should have called, okay? But I didn't think about it."

"Even after the storm Saturday night and Sunday."

"I just— Look, I've felt like shit since I found out he wandered off and died on that mountain. I wish I could have changed it, but you weren't there, you don't know what I was thinking."

"Then tell me."

He wanted to talk about it. She could see it in his eyes. He was torturing himself over something.

"Look, I didn't think. Scott was out, I had a girl in, I figured he was hanging with his friends. We're in college. It's not like we keep tabs on each other. He said they were going camping for the weekend. When the storm hit, I thought he and the others might have gotten stuck getting out. But I didn't think anyone was in danger. I figured if they were in trouble, someone else would have known about it." His knuckles were white as he gripped the table. "I didn't know Scott had gotten lost until Monday morning when campus security came by looking for him."

Max could see it. A nineteen-year-old boy, on his own for the first time. Probably didn't even think Scott was his responsibility. Maybe the instinct would have developed over the year; maybe not. But one thing was certain: Ian Stanhope felt guilty about his inaction.

But did Ian's inaction cost Scott Sheldon his life? Any more so than that of the boys he went camping with? Max didn't see that. It was the other three who should have done something, said something, sooner.

"Do you know why the other three didn't tell anyone on Saturday that Scott was lost? Do you know why they waited so long?"

"You'll have to ask them."

"Do you know where I can find them?"

"You found me."

"Because you were Scott's roommate."

He shifted uncomfortably. He looked like a man, but he wasn't, and his boyish uncertainty shone through. "I didn't like Scott's friends. They were all weird, like him."

"Weird how?"

"I don't know."

"Not jocks?" she suggested.

"Not *anything*. Like, put a dozen loners together and you have a dozen loners in the same room. They weren't like a team, or a group, or even in the same major, or what."

"So you haven't seen any of them in the last six months."

"One of the guys, Tom Keller, is in my math class. But we don't meet today. Tomorrow at ten. Pike Hall, if you want to stake it out."

"I'm here today."

It took him a good minute before he said, "Jess Sanchez. She was a friend of Scott's, she's okay. She's the only one who seemed to be worried about Scott at the time, anyway."

"You weren't?"

"Look, I said Scott was weird. Honestly? I thought he'd show up Monday and be all, like, why were you so worried? I'm really sorry about everything, but I don't know what I could have done different."

Max considered that. If she and Karen hadn't become close friends while they were roommates, would Max have worried if Karen was out all weekend? Probably not. She might even have been relieved to have the room to herself.

"I'll talk to Jess," Max said. "Where can I find her?"

"She works at the bookstore on campus. You can't miss her. She wears all black, has a nose ring, and is tiny.

She looks like a freak, but like I said, she was the most normal out of all of them."

Ian left and Max read over the police report again.

Jess Sanchez hadn't been one of the group that Scott went camping with and Scott's mother hadn't said anything about a girlfriend. Was Jess a friend or something more? Why hadn't she contacted campus police if she was worried, as Ian implied?

Time to find out.

CHAPTER THREE

Ian's description of Jess Sanchez was accurate. She was indeed tiny in every way—barely five feet tall, not even one hundred pounds. Black hair, brown eyes, naturally tan skin, a nose stud, and multiple piercings in her small ears. She looked more American Indian than Hispanic as her name suggested. She agreed to talk to Max after Max told her she was a reporter writing about Scott Sheldon's disappearance, but her tone was indifferent. She told the guy she was working with that she'd be back in ten minutes; then they stepped outside.

"It's freezing," Jess complained as she zipped up her coat and pulled a cap over her short hair.

"Is there a lounge where we can sit?" It was cold, but the sky was so clear, it looked like it would shatter.

"I'm fine. So why are you here after nearly six months? No one cared when he got lost."

"No one?"

She rolled her eyes. "Right. Search and rescue. Too dangerous, they said, to look for him in the storm. So Scott's probably dead because it was too cold for everyone else." She shoved her hands into her pockets and walked briskly. Fortunately, her legs were short and Max easily kept up with her.

"Jess, search and rescue did everything they could with the information they had. And, like you, I don't think Scott survived."

The girl stopped walking. Her cheeks were bright from the cold. "I didn't say that."

"Let's look at the possibilities: One, Scott ran away, voluntarily disappearing. There's no evidence to support that. Two, Scott stomped off in anger like his friends said, and has built a shelter and survived for six months. Or three, Scott died on that mountain before anyone started looking for him."

Jess frowned, but didn't say anything. Max continued. "There's no evidence that Scott ran away or that he survived. I'm pretty certain he's dead, and so is search and rescue. Even his mother, and parents are the most likely to believe that their child found some way to survive the unsurvivable. But I think there's more to what happened that weekend than what your friends told the police."

"*My* friends?"

"Tom Keller, Carlos Ibarra, and Arthur Cowan."

"They're not *my* friends."

Max raised an eyebrow. "No?"

"Art and Carlos *used* to be. But not anymore." She averted her eyes, and the anger in her voice went down a notch.

"Why?" Max asked bluntly.

She shrugged, still didn't look Max in the eye.

"Because of what happened with Scott?"

"No." Jess was being evasive.

"What do you think happened?"

"I don't know."

Maybe not, but she knew *something*.

"I have to go back to work." Jess turned abruptly and headed back the way they'd come.

Max followed. "Jess, I'm not leaving until I find the truth. Scott's family deserves to know what happened. They deserve to bury a body, don't you think?"

Jess stopped walking. She stared straight ahead, not facing Max. "I wasn't on the camping trip. I don't know what happened. I just—"

"What?"

"I just don't think what they said happened did. But if it didn't, they're not going to say anything about it now, so we'll never know the truth."

She spoke fast, but Max understood. Jess thought her friends—her former friends—had lied.

"Tell me what *you* think."

"I can't. I mean, I don't know what to think! Look, I really have to go." She opened the door to the bookstore.

"Where can I find them?" Max asked her.

"Art and Carlos are on the top floor of Canyon Hall. Room four-twelve. Tom's in the same dorm, but I don't know his room."

Jess closed the door on her. Max decided to let her go—for now. She'd be back to push Jess after the guilt and suspicion had had time to do their job.

Max almost smiled. She hadn't even been here a day, and already her suspicions were proved right—meaning, she wasn't the only one who thought what happened the weekend Scott disappeared was odd. Time to track down Scott's so-called friends and dig for the truth.

No one answered when Max knocked on room 412. She considered her options.

She could search their room, but there were a lot of people going in and out. And if Cowan and Ibarra returned and found her inside, she might have a difficult time getting them to talk to her. Not to mention that being kicked off campus would make it harder to uncover the truth.

She walked down the staircase and passed three girls who were chatting about a party in another dorm. They'd heard about it on Twitter.

Max snapped her fingers. *Social media.* These were college kids; they made a career out of telling the world where they were and what they were doing.

She leaned against a wall on the first floor, just inside the main entrance, and pulled out her phone. She opened her social media app and found Arthur Cowan's social profiles through his affiliation with Cheyenne College. Once she found Cowan, she found Tom Keller through a common association. Arthur and his roommate, Carlos Ibarra, had privacy settings on their accounts, so she couldn't see their status reports or pictures, but Tom posted publicly—apparently everything he did when he did it.

Tom had been tweeting for the past hour from his English class about how bored he was, and it took Max only a few minutes to learn he was in Edwin C. Becker Hall. While walking across the campus, she pulled up his social media photos and found a recent likeness. She also found photos of Cowan and Ibarra and now could pick them out in a crowd.

She asked a passing student what classroom Mr. Thurston taught in, and was directed to the second floor of Becker Hall.

Max leaned against the wall outside Thurston's class and thought about how to approach Keller. He seemed to have found his wild side in college. Numerous photos showed him visibly intoxicated at parties. Didn't these kids know that everything they posted on the Internet was permanent? Max supposed a future employer might overlook a few drunken college parties, but Tom was going to have to grow up.

She could use that.

The English class was over at 12:10, so Max had a few minutes to dig into Keller. There wasn't much more than what she'd found on his social media pages. He was interested in video games, drinking, girls, and not much else. There was also something missing.

She scrolled back through his photos as far back as they went—nearly three years—and there were no pictures taken while camping, fishing, or hiking. If fact, he appeared to have no interest in camping. Odd, considering where he went to college.

It might not mean anything, but she felt the twinge she got when information didn't fit. She wished she could scour the pages of Cowan and Ibarra. She was able to scroll through their friends—Jess Sanchez was in both lists. Would Jess let Max use her log-in to access their pages? Max would definitely ask.

Students began to exit the class a few minutes before it was officially over. Keller was one of the first kids out, and Max immediately followed him. He was a tall and gangly kid, not quite beefy enough to fill out his frame. He slouched slightly, as if he'd grown early and never been comfortable with his height.

"Tom," she called out when they were at the base of the stairs.

He turned and spotted her, gave her an obvious look up and down. "You're not in my class," he said with a flirty grin. "Unless you're the new teaching assistant."

"Maxine Revere, reporter." She handed him her card. "Let's talk."

He stared at her card, his brows pulled together. "Reporter?"

"Scott Sheldon."

He handed back her card. "I need to go."

"I have a few questions."

He brushed past her. "I have nothing to say."

"Why? If what you said happened is true, why don't you want to talk about it?"

He turned and stared, his eyes narrow. "*If?* What's your deal? What do you mean, 'if'? I told everyone what happened. Why do you care?"

"Scott is classified as a missing person. Were you aware that the rangers are still looking for his body? When they find him, they'll know what happened."

The kid, already white, paled even more. "They know what happened because we told them what happened. You have no right to harass me."

Keller's voice rose, squeaky and worried. Others in the hall looked over, overtly curious. Max didn't care. She wasn't the one with something to hide.

"I'm not harassing you, Tom."

"I don't have to talk to you."

He bumped into a group of students in his haste to get away from her. He scowled at them, then pushed open the double doors and hurried outside into the steadily falling drizzle.

Something was definitely up.

Max went back to the bookstore to talk to Jess about her social media password, and Jess told her she couldn't talk.

"When do you get off?" Max asked.

"Two thirty. I really don't want to get involved."

"You already are, and I think you know that." But Max could wait if it would encourage Jess to cooperate. She said, "I'll be back in two hours. Just to talk, okay?"

"Whatev," Jess said, and went to ring up a student.

Max went outside and frowned at the wet sky. If she was here on campus until three or later, she wouldn't have time to visit the campsite. Tomorrow, she'd do it first thing.

She located the campus security office on the map and walked briskly to the small building west of the main administration wing. By the time she arrived, her coat and hair were more than a little damp.

The office was dry, warm, and set up like a police bull pen with a front desk separated by a low partition and ten or twelve desks, each backing to another. Four of the desks were currently occupied. The receptionist smiled. "May I help you?"

She handed the woman her card. "I called two days ago, but no one returned my call."

The receptionist returned Max's card. "You can go to the administration building and talk to the public affairs director."

"I need to speak with the head of security."

"Is it a security matter?"

"Yes."

It was, after all, a matter of how they conducted their security operations.

"You're not a student."

"No."

"You'll have to speak to the public affairs director. I can't help you."

Max wanted to push, but she assessed the receptionist as well as the security officers who were giving her the eye. The eye that told her they were suspicious of outsiders.

"What is the public affairs director's name?" Max asked. She had the information in her notes, but she hadn't planned on speaking to public affairs unless as a last resort.

This was a last resort.

The receptionist typed rapidly. "Stephanie Adair," she

said. She wrote the name and phone number on a notepad. "If you go to the administration building, the front desk will be able to help you."

All polite, now that she knew Max was leaving.

Max would return. She had questions, and if they didn't answer them, the *no comment* she recorded would speak volumes.

Max left for the administration building next door, wondering if they were that rigid with all reporters, or just the reporter who said she was looking into Scott Sheldon's disappearance. Was the receptionist the person she'd first spoken with? Why hadn't she given her Adair's name on the phone? Had she been briefed on the case and told to divert any future calls—or visits—to the media rep?

She went inside and asked for Stephanie Adair. She was directed to an office on the second floor. The girl at the desk was young, likely a college student, and immediately called Ms. Adair when Max asked for her.

"Ms. Adair said she'll be a couple minutes, if you'd like to wait."

Like most everything at Cheyenne College, the administration building was modern, more like an office building than a college. Two empty cubicles filled the room behind the student receptionist, stacks of paper and a computer on each. Lots of plants and a picture window looking out onto the quad made the office appear bigger and brighter.

A couple minutes turned into ten before Ms. Adair stepped out of the door behind the receptionist. She, too, looked young enough to be a college student, but she was dressed better and wore quite a bit of makeup.

She smiled and extended her hand. "I'm so sorry to keep you waiting, Ms. Revere. You caught me on a phone call, and I have a lunch meeting. But if you'd like to walk with me, I'll see what I can help with."

"Thank you," Max said automatically, though she had the feeling Adair was trying to get rid of her.

Adair walked briskly down the hall toward the main staircase. "What can I help you with?" she asked.

"I'm investigating the Scott Sheldon disappearance."

Adair sounded perplexed. "Scott Sheldon? I don't know who that is. Should I?"

"He was a student who disappeared last October while camping with three other students."

"Oh, yes, I heard about that. I only started in this position in January."

Great. She was new. But that might actually help Max. "I'd like to speak to the security chief about the matter. According to the police files, that would be Frank Hansen, and he's still on staff."

"Yes, Chief Hansen is still here. Policy is that any press inquiries about the college, faculty or students go through my office."

"I have questions, you shouldn't have to play the delivery girl. If you could simply grant permission—"

Adair stopped at the bottom of the staircase which opened into the wide lobby. "If you e-mail me your questions, I'll talk to Chief Hansen and get them answered."

"It would be better if we talked face-to-face. You're welcome to be there."

Adair smiled. She looked pleasant, but she was being hard-nosed. "No, that's not possible. But I promise, I'll get your questions answered quickly." She handed Max her business card. "My email and phone number are on the card."

Max didn't like the answer, but she wasn't going to get a concession out of Adair. Max slipped the card into her purse and forced out, "Thank you."

"I'll walk you to the parking lot."

"I have other things to do."

"Oh, I'm sorry, but since you're not a student or faculty or guest of either, you need to be cleared by the administration building and given a pass before you're permitted to be on campus. Security reasons. I'm sure you understand." Adair smiled, too brightly, and led the way to the parking lot.

"And how do I do that?" Max asked.

"The front desk can direct you to the visitors' office."

Max turned and went back into the building, leaving Adair staring after her, confused.

Let her be confused. Max had more questions, and she wasn't leaving until she had answers.

CHAPTER FOUR

By the time Max was done jumping through the hoops necessary to get a one-day visitor's pass, it was close to two thirty. Max returned to the bookstore and waited under a dripping tree for Jess to get off work. As soon as the petite girl walked out, she rolled her eyes.

"I have a three-o'clock class."

"I'll walk with you."

"What do you want?" she said. Her voice was almost a whine.

"I'd like your Facebook password."

"What?" She shot her a slanted gaze. "You're insane."

"I went through Tom Keller's profile because it was public, but Arthur and Carlos have private pages. I noted that you were on their friends lists. Therefore, if I can use your account, I can see what they've posted."

"Why?"

"Because they lied. I don't know why or what about, but they weren't being completely honest about what happened on the mountain when Scott disappeared."

"They wouldn't hurt him," Jess said, defiant.

Max hesitated. "That's a bit of a leap. Did they have a reason to hurt Scott?"

"No," she mumbled.

"Mrs. Sheldon needs to know what happened to her son. I think search and rescue has been looking in the wrong place. They would have found him by now."

"Not if he got lost. Maybe they are looking in the wrong place, but only because Scott got lost," she repeated.

"I won't tell anyone you let me use your account."

"What are you looking for?"

"I don't know yet. Just snooping right now." She was trying to lighten the mood, but Jess didn't smile.

"All right. Whatever." She stopped walking and tore a piece of paper out of one of her notebooks. She scribbled down an e-mail address and password. "I'm changing my password when I get out of my class," she said. She was going for an angry tone, but it came out sad. "Just—if you find out what happened, what *really* happened, would you let me know?"

"I promise."

Max watched Jess walk off, then turned and followed the signs to the library. The building was too warm, but right now Max needed the heat—her hair was wet, and while her coat kept her torso dry, her jeans were uncomfortably damp. She went to the restroom and brushed her hair, then pinned it up to keep the strands out of her face. Then she went out to the main room and planted herself at a table near windows that looked out at the Rocky Mountains towering high above the campus. While she loved Columbia and thrived in a city, Max also appreciated the peace that this small college enjoyed. It reminded her that maybe she needed a vacation.

Right. Because you relax so well.

Most of her vacations became working vacations.

Max pulled out her iPad and logged in to Jess's Facebook account. Jess seemed to be pretty typical in her usage—she logged in nearly every day, posted funny pictures, photos of her friends, a lot of posts about events at the bookstore and rallies on campus. Most of the pages she followed were indie music bands, heavy on alternative music.

She clicked through to Arthur Cowan's page. He wasn't a social media nut like his friend Tom Keller, but he posted consistently. His interests were rather eclectic—but it was clear he spent a lot of time in the outdoors. He had pictures posted of him and friends skiing, and based on the level of difficulty of the slopes, he had experience.

She scrolled through his pictures, many of them outdoors with small groups of friends, mostly including Carlos. Few, if any, with Tom. He had a lot of people he was friends with on Facebook, but few comments on his posts—almost all from Carlos, his younger brother who was in junior high, and someone from his English class who posted odd snippets of apparent humor that Max didn't quite understand. From the few comments over the past year along with the photos, Max put together a clear portrait of Arthur Cowan: he was a prankster, and while some people found him hilarious, most thought his jokes were in poor taste. At least a dozen posts were people telling him he did something "not cool" and Arthur would tell them to lighten up or that it was just a joke.

He was athletic, but seemed to participate only in individual sports like skiing. Carlos and Arthur had gone to high school together, and seemed to be inseparable. Three months ago, several people ragged on him for writing profanity on a kid's face with permanent marker, because the kid was the first to pass out drinking at a party.

Max flipped over to Carlos Ibarra's page. He hadn't posted anything for three weeks, and his last post was a photo of him and Arthur during spring break in Los Angeles. They were on the beach. That photo had become his avatar. Carlos had even fewer friends than Arthur, and as Max looked at the history between them, it became clear that Carlos and Arthur were joined at the hip. They did everything together, they both majored in business, they shared a dorm room. Arthur was clearly the dominant personality.

She frowned. What did all this tell her? Absolutely nothing.

Not nothing, Max. There's a pattern here. One of these things is not like the other.

Tom. He wasn't part of Arthur and Carlos's two-man clique. He was a year younger—Scott's age. He tried too hard to make friends, as evidenced by his constant parties and incessant posting and poor attempts at humor. No one consistently popped up on his page. He was awkward and a bit nerdy, drank because it was social and he thought he could make friends. Max had known kids like him in college—the ones who were the life of the party, but mostly because people laughed at them.

How had Tom Keller hooked up with Arthur and Carlos? Why had the four of them gone camping?

Tom was the weak link. Carlos and Arthur were longtime friends; Tom wasn't part of their clique. If Max could get him to talk to her about that weekend, then maybe the truth would come out.

Max was about to log out of Jess's account when another thought occurred to her. Jess hadn't been social with these boys since Scott disappeared, at least publicly, but it was clear she'd known them. Max clicked over to Jess's private messages. She didn't want to invade her privacy more than necessary, so she skimmed the names until she found one familiar.

Scott Sheldon.

Even though his account was deleted, the messages he'd sent to Jess were archived on her page. Reading them, it was clear that they were friends and might have liked each other more, but both talked around it. That would fit with Scott's shy reputation.

Thursday night, before he left on the camping trip, Scott had sent Jess a message.

S: Why are you mad that I'm going camping with the guys?

J: Since when did Art and Carlos become "the guys"? Art's a jackass. I told you that last week.

S: It's not easy for me to make friends. Ian thinks I'm a nerd, and all he talks about is baseball. I played baseball one year, when I was 9. I was the worst player on the team and once, when I tried to catch a fly ball, it hit my forehead and I passed out. I don't fit in anywhere, and Art is nice to me.

J: Scott, you'll find your niche. We're friends, right? Art is only nice because he wants something.

S: It's just for the weekend. I'll call you when I get back, okay?

J: Whatever.

Jess was irritated with Scott. She'd followed up that conversation with a message Sunday morning.

Are you around? The weather sucks, call me, I want to make sure you got back okay.

Max scrolled further and found a thread between Art and Jess more than a year ago. She immediately realized that Jess and Art had dated a few times, and Jess called it off.

A: Why are you so mad at me?

J: You're an asshole, and if you don't know why I'm mad, go fuck yourself.

A: Come on, it was a joke. Can't you take a joke?

J: It wasn't a joke to anyone but you and Carlos. I'm done.

A: Well screw you, you have no sense of humor.

Max copied and pasted both threads of messages. She wanted to ask Jess about this, but the girl was still in class. Max checked Tom's social media hive, and he hadn't posted anything since she confronted him outside his English class. Mr. Social Animal had gone silent.

More than a little interesting.

She went back to Art's page and looked through the photos that were posted immediately prior to the camping trip. Scott was in a few, mostly from a party the weekend before. Jess was in a few of the group shots with Scott, and so was Tom.

On the day they left, there were some photos posted to Art's page via his phone from the interior of Carlos's four-wheel drive. Another photo of Art, Tom, and Scott at the campsite holding beers. Then nothing else from the trip.

That seemed . . . odd for someone who documented his life on social media. She went back to Tom's page, and he hadn't posted anything after 4 P.M. that day. His last tweet was:

Going camping! Haha. #nointernet #techwithdrawal

If there was no Internet, when had they posted the picture from the campsite?

She looked at the information. It was posted Saturday morning, at 8:35 A.M.

Sometimes, there was a weak cellular connection and it could take an unusually long time to upload a picture, but that should drain the phone battery. They could have brought extra phone batteries or a portable charger. Anything was possible. Still, something seemed . . . weird. Not that they were drinking at 8:35 A.M., but because that picture, based on the sun and quality of light was obviously taken in the late afternoon. That was confirmed by the tag Art had added:

Me and buds, last camping trip of the season. We have plenty of beer and food! Haha.

She downloaded the picture. There was information embedded in most photos uploaded from a mobile device. She didn't remember how to access it, but when she got back to the Broadmoor she'd call a friend who would do it for her.

Max packed up, slipped on her coat, which had nearly dried, wrapped her scarf around her neck, and walked outside. The light, steady rain continued. Great. She should have retrieved her umbrella earlier.

She headed straight for Canyon Hall and up to the fourth floor. She listened outside room 412. People were talking inside, though she couldn't make out specific words. She knocked loudly. A few seconds later, the door opened.

Arthur Cowan was a lot shorter than she'd thought—about her height of five foot ten. He stared at her—first her face, then his eyes dipped down to her breasts, which were covered by her coat, then back to her face. "Hell-o," he said.

"That's the reporter," a voice came from the room. Max couldn't see Tom Keller, but it sounded like his whine.

"Maxine Revere," she said, and held out her card.

Art frowned. "We have nothing to say to you." He started to close the door.

Max put her boot in the opening. "You don't know my questions."

"Tom says you're writing an article about Scott. That you think we lied."

"Tom," Max said, pushing open the door and stepping into the dorm room. "That's not what I said."

The room was a mess, and she thought about Ian's comment about not wanting to live with a slob. The main room had two small couches and reeked of stale food and beer. Two open doors led to bedrooms, which were equally messy. There was so much clothing and paper scattered in one room, she couldn't see the floor.

"Hey," Art said when she brushed past him. "We didn't invite you in."

She said, "What really happened on that camping trip? Don't you think that Scott's family deserves the truth?"

"I'm calling campus security," Art said. But it was Carlos who pulled his phone from his pocket.

She had to talk fast. The papers she signed to get the visitor's pass included a whole slew of rules, including an admonition not to harass students. Some people might think that questions were a form of harassment, and since she'd already tipped her hand to Stephanie Adair, she didn't want to be removed from campus now.

"To confirm the time line, based on your statements to the police, you three, with Scott Sheldon, went to a known campground approximately an hour's drive from here. When you arrived, you decided to hike two miles to another campground, less popular but still on the map. Friday night, even though it was forty degrees and dipped down to subzero temperatures before sunrise, Scott walked off, angry, because of an argument. To quote Art, 'It was just a stupid disagreement.'"

She looked at the boys in turn. Tom stared at his feet, Carlos stared at Art, and Art stared at her.

She continued. "When Scott didn't return Saturday morning, you went back to the truck and didn't find him there. But instead of looking for him, or notifying the rangers' station, you left. In fact, you didn't notify anyone that Scott was missing until Sunday."

"There was a storm," Tom began. "We—"

"Shut up," Art said, sneering at Tom. "Don't talk to her." He stepped toward Max. "Get out."

If he thought he was intimidating, he was wrong. Max had gone up against far more intimidating men—and women—than Arthur Cowan.

"The storm didn't really turn bad until Saturday afternoon. You could have called the rangers' station, told them Scott was missing. They would have gone up there and looked for him until dark. Yet you waited until Sunday morning to inform campus security." She eyed the boys carefully: Art, red with anger; Carlos, still focused on Art, concerned; Tom, pale and twitchy. "After that, it's campus security who's at fault for not contacting the rangers until late on Sunday."

"It's not our fault he left," Tom said.

"Shut the fuck up, Tom!"

Art took a step toward her. She wasn't scared of the kid, but he was certainly hot under the collar. "Get out of my room. Now."

"Your reaction tells me you're a liar, Arthur. I will prove it."

He pushed her. She took a step back, raised an eyebrow. "Touch me again, and I *will* put you down, little man."

His eyes narrowed and he fisted his hands. Carlos stepped up. "Hey, Art, campus security is on their way."

"Get out!" Art screamed at her. This time, he kept his hands to himself.

Art was a powder keg. She glanced at Tom before she turned to leave. The kid was pale. She definitely needed to talk to him again, alone.

She opened the door. Art's eyes filled with hate and fear. A big temper problem. Known as a prankster. Maybe he took out his anger through cruel jokes.

Maybe one of his pranks turned deadly. She mulled that idea over in her head. Something to dig into, and Jess Sanchez was the best resource.

She left the dorm with the intention of hunting down

Jess and pushing her about her past relationship with Art and asking her about the types of pranks he played—the ones that went beyond writing on his drunk friends. But as soon as she left the dorm room, she was confronted by two campus security officers.

"Ma'am, visitors need to check in with the administration."

She showed them her visitor's pass. "Were either of you on duty the weekend that Scott Sheldon disappeared?"

"You'll have to speak to the chancellor, ma'am."

"I should instead speak with your security chief."

"I'm sorry, we're not authorized to talk with the press. All press inquiries must go through the communications director." He paused. "But you know that."

"I do. I spoke to her earlier and she helped me get this visitor's pass." Which was true. Adair did direct her to the appropriate office to obtain it. "Thank you for your help."

She turned to head to the bookstore, hoping that the staff there would point her to Jess Sanchez's dorm. The taller officer said, "Ma'am, we've had a complaint that you were harassing three of our students. Your visitor's pass has been canceled, and we need to ask you to leave. If you would like to return, you'll need to check in with the administration."

She considered her options. She really wanted to talk to Jess, but she also wanted to investigate the picture she'd downloaded. She didn't want Art to figure out that she'd spoken to Jess, either. He might scare her into being silent. She seemed like a tough girl, but under the surface had been skittish. And fearful of Art.

"I'm leaving," she told the security officers. They escorted her to her car. She turned and thanked them. "You can tell your boss I'll be back with more questions."

She got into her car and saw the campus cops standing in the rain, watching her drive off.

Her phone rang. She'd forgotten to set up the Bluetooth in the rental, so pulled over to the side, right by the main entrance to the campus. She answered the unfamiliar number.

"Ms. Revere? This is Chuck Pence from the park service. I head up search and rescue. I got your message."

"I'm in town and would like to talk to you about the search for Scott Sheldon's body."

"You're in Colorado?"

"Yes, just leaving Cheyenne College right now after an enlightening conversation with Scott's friends. Do you have time to meet? I can come by your office now."

"I'm still on the road. I can meet you somewhere in two hours."

That would be close to six. "I'm staying at the Broadmoor. I'll meet you in the main lobby at six."

"I'll be the man with the dog."

She smiled and hung up. With a final glance at the Cheyenne College sign, Max pulled back onto the road and headed for her hotel. She would most certainly return.

CHAPTER FIVE

Max's friends had often criticized her that she was prone to judgment. She assessed people quickly, and experience had proved that her initial opinion was generally accurate. Even with her college roommate, Max had been dead-on with her assessment—which included the fact that Karen had a big, fat, trusting heart. Max was drawn to that, maybe because she found it so difficult to trust anyone.

Chuck Pence walked in promptly at six with a beautiful golden retriever. But it wasn't just the dog that identified Pence to Max; it was also his no-nonsense manner and his no-nonsense voice, which Max remembered from their phone conversations.

Pence had the sharp eyes of a cop, but with a focused calm Max didn't often see in the police she worked with. His movements were minimal, suggesting both confidence and military or police training. His dog, which wore a service collar, was young, not much more than a puppy—maybe two years. That the dog obeyed the subtle commands of its owner told Max more about Chuck than anything else.

Quiet. Focused. Sharp. Max suspected he preferred dogs to people and probably didn't like crowds.

She already liked him.

She approached Chuck with a smile. "Mr. Pence, I'm Maxine Revere. Thank you for meeting with me." She surveyed the lounge.

"Trixie is a service dog," Pence said. "She can stay."

"There are heat lamps outside. It would afford more privacy."

"Lead the way."

She opened the terrace doors that led to the outdoor lounge. A few other brave souls were enjoying the crisp evening under heat lamps. The intermittent rain from the afternoon had cleared up; moonlight lit the high clouds. She found a table away from the doors.

The hostess approached with a smile. "May I get you and your guest anything, Ms. Revere?"

"Pinot grigio for me." She turned to Pence. "You?"

"Coffee," he said. "Black."

The hostess left and Max leaned back. Pence didn't. She began.

"First, thank you for coming out here. I would have been happy to meet with you tomorrow at your office."

"I'll be in the field tomorrow," he said. "You said you wanted to discuss the Scott Sheldon disappearance." He looked her in the eye. "I hope you're not here to give his mother false hope that he might be alive. It's been nearly six months, much of it in subzero overnight temperatures."

"I suspect, as you do, that he's dead. And has been since the weekend he disappeared. But I read the police reports and today spoke to some of the people involved, plus a girl who knew him and the three boys he went camping with. Something is off about their story, and I want the truth. Scott's mother deserves to know what really happened."

Chuck didn't say anything as the hostess delivered their beverages. Max sipped her wine. She was in no rush.

"What makes you think that anything other than what's been said happened?"

He didn't have an accusatory or suspicious tone. Matter-of-fact with a hint of curiosity.

"I can't point to one specific reason why I think that the boys are lying. It's more a big picture feeling I get." She paused, not for the first time wondering if her past and everything that had happened with Karen were clouding her judgment. And, not for the first time, she dismissed her worries.

I need to know what happened to my son. I need the truth.

"Adele Sheldon wrote to me after your office started looking again for Scott's body. She convinced me that Scott wasn't the type of person to put himself in danger. She has questions that haven't been answered. He didn't hike or camp, and—"

"And that makes him that much more likely not to understand the dangers of wandering off."

Max gave Chuck a nod. "It also makes me wonder why he agreed to go camping that weekend with three boys he barely knew. He had no relationship with the kids before college. None of the kids was his roommate. They had some equipment, but not the type of gear seasoned campers would take in this climate."

"I agree with you on the latter point, but I've been doing this for years. If I had a nickel for every camper who went up unprepared . . ." His voice trailed off. "What else? They were college students, irresponsible. Frankly, I'd call them stupid, and their stupidity got one of their friends killed."

"That's the thing—I don't think they were friends."

Max continued. "Jess Sanchez, who works in the

bookstore, was a friend of Scott's. She let me access her social media pages. She's Facebook friends with all three boys. I looked through each photo archive, and there were no photos of Scott with any of them except for one." She knew she was about to tread on dangerous ground here—but since there was no criminal investigation into Scott's disappearance, and the picture had been posted publicly, she figured she was warranted. "I downloaded a photo taken at the campsite. However, it was uploaded the morning *after* it was taken. I sent it to a friend of mine in New York who can get the GPS data off the photo, when and where it was uploaded."

"What is that going to tell you?"

"I don't know yet, but in the police reports, the boys claimed they had no cellular reception at the campground, yet they also claim they didn't leave until noon on Saturday. They must have uploaded it elsewhere. Then, on Twitter I found tweets from Tom Keller—who can't seem to go ten minutes without telling the world something trivial about himself—sent Saturday. Mostly innocuous stuff, but again, no cell coverage, so where was he when he was tweeting?"

Chuck said, "I have a daughter in college. I'm moderately tech savvy, and if I understand my social media, there's the option of setting tweets and posts in the future, and it's automatic, correct?"

"Yes. But the content didn't appear to be preplanned, they were responses to other tweets. So my conclusion was that either they weren't at the campground they said they were at, or they weren't at the campground at all."

Max let that information sink in. She drained her wine and put the glass aside.

Then she added, "Jess tried to talk Scott out of going. I learned after I talked to her that she had been in a relationship with Arthur Cowan last year, but hasn't spoken to him—at least publicly or through social media—since Scott disappeared. I plan to talk to her soon, but campus police ran me off this afternoon."

"Some cops don't like reporters," he said.

"That wasn't it—trust me, I know when a cop doesn't like me because of my job." She smiled. Sometimes, it was fun playing with law enforcement, getting them riled up. But usually, she tried to be professional. "I cornered the boys in their dorm room, and they called security because I asked hard questions they refused to answer. They're lying," she said, not for the first time. "I'm going to prove it."

"Your observations are interesting, but I still don't understand what you're getting at. Unless you're saying that my team is looking in the wrong place."

"Maybe," she said. "I'd like to go up with you tomorrow."

"I planned to go today, but we had to call it off when a child went missing. We found her, thank God. She could have died tonight the way she was dressed. It may be April, but it still gets damn cold in the higher elevations. There's one more quadrant that needs to be searched. At oh-eight-hundred." He sipped his coffee.

She thought she might have to do a harder sell, but he seemed amicable to including her. "It bothers me that they waited twenty-four hours before telling campus police, and then the campus police waited until Monday morning before contacting the park service."

"You and I read the same reports, Ms. Revere. And as I said, college boys can be brainless. But even if my team had been told Saturday night when the boys got back to campus, we couldn't have gone up there. It was the first big storm of the season, came in earlier than anyone thought. Even me, and I'm pretty good about predicting storms." He shrugged. "It was a tragedy, and those boys are going to have to live with this for the rest of their lives."

It was hard for Max to explain her gut, what her instincts said, but she tried. "I think there was something else going on that weekend, something that put Scott in danger. And—" She stopped. What more could she say without treading into conjecture?

"And the only proof you have that the boys are lying is your gut."

She wanted to say she had more than that, but she couldn't. "I would call it . . . circumstantial evidence. The photo. The fact they weren't close friends. That Arthur Cowan is an expert skier and should have known better about weather conditions, or at a minimum alerted the ranger station the same night Scott disappeared. That they all acted suspicious when I asked questions. Nervous."

He tilted his head and smiled. "Most college boys would be nervous when a beautiful, intelligent woman questions them."

She laughed. "I hardly think that was the reason. Certainly not for Arthur Cowan, who was belligerent and threatening. If you need credentials, I can give you references, people in law enforcement and others who can vouch for me."

"Ms. Revere," he said, "why are you so far from home? You have no ties to Colorado or Colorado Springs. The Sheldons aren't longtime family friends, are they?" She shook her head. "So why do you care?"

What did she tell him? That she didn't know why she'd flown two thousand miles on her own dime to find out what had happened to Scott? That wasn't completely true. Did she share a half truth? That Adele Sheldon's letter pulled her heartstrings? Stirred her curiosity? She couldn't stop thinking about him, or shake the deep belief that she could uncover the truth.

But lying wasn't something that came natural to her. Too many people in her life had lied—either to her face or by omission. She spoke the truth, but kept it simple.

"My best friend disappeared when we were in college," she said. "Her body was never found. I know she's dead, just like my instincts tell me Scott Sheldon is dead. Except with Karen, there was evidence that she'd been murdered." She paused, wished she had ordered a second glass of wine, but she sent the hostess away with a look ten minutes ago. "Her family still suffers with the unknown. I visit them every year, and the pain—it's never left. But they still harbor an ounce of hope. That hope is trumped by the pain they feel with her loss—not the loss specifically anymore, but the *not knowing*. When I heard about this case, when I talked to Adele—I think I can help her find peace. I don't want her living with the unknown, like Karen's family. If Adele knows what happened, she can grieve and be there for her daughter."

Karen's sister had lived in the shadow of Karen's disappearance for the past seven years. Laura would have graduated from college last year if her life hadn't been turned upside down. As it was, she barely graduated from high school, never went to college, was in and out of rehab. Scott's sister wasn't Laura, but Max had seen firsthand how the pain of grieving parents forever marked the surviving children.

"Do you have the proper clothes and footwear for a prolonged search?" Chuck asked.

"Yes."

He nodded. "Be at ranger headquarters by oh-eight-hundred, properly geared up. Like I said, there's one more grid to search. If Scott's body is up there, Trixie will find him."

At the sound of her name, the golden retriever perked her ears up. She stood as her master rose. "Thanks for the coffee."

"Would you like to stay for dinner?"

"Thank you, but I'm already late getting home. My wife is a patient woman, but I need to get back."

CHAPTER SIX

On Wednesday morning, Max arrived at the ranger headquarters at quarter to eight. The morning was cold but completely clear, and the weather report had said it would warm to the fifties.

Chuck introduced her to Tim and Ann Callow, volunteers with search and rescue. They were both lifelong residents of the area and had been part of the initial search team. Older than Chuck, but both appeared fit.

"Chuck told us you're a reporter from New York," Ann said, overtly curious. "Sounds fascinating."

"You won't catch me dead in a city like that," Tim said with a grin.

"I'm a city girl at heart," Max said. "Though I enjoy the mountains. My cousin owns a ski resort in Vail, and I try to visit every year."

They chatted as they loaded up the four-wheel-drive truck and Chuck checked provisions. Chuck drove and asked Max, who sat in the passenger seat, "Is that a map of the search area?"

"Partly—I printed it from the park service Web site

and marked it up based on the information I learned from the police reports. They parked here—" She put her finger on the map, then traced it south. "—and camped here."

"We've been focusing on the area between the campground and where they parked. The witnesses said he walked toward the car. But at night, he may have inadvertently left the trail. We've covered every area between, but now that we have had warmer weather, Trixie can be of more use. She's still young, not fully trained, but our last cadaver dog died."

From the backseat, Ann said, "We owned Mickie, Trixie's mother. She died six months ago, cancer. We still have the two male dogs from her last litter. Chuck took Trixie, and the other two bitches went to friends of ours in Denver who are training them for their own unit."

"Trixie is a great dog," Chuck said, "but training takes time. She's smart, though. Smartest dog I've had, and I've had plenty."

Max absently reached back and scratched Trixie behind the ears. She loved dogs, and the only thing she regretted about her career—and all the travel it entailed— was that she couldn't have her own pup. But it wouldn't be fair to the animal to be alone so much, or left with neighbors when Max was out of town.

While she petted Trixie with one hand, she marked off on her map where Chuck said they'd searched. "Why didn't you search south of the camp?"

"Like I said, we focused north and east because of the terrain and where the truck was parked. We also covered a mile perimeter from the campsite during the initial search. We had more than a dozen people the three days after we were notified—though we only had a couple hours each day where we could be out."

"So the perimeter was defined based on information those three boys from Cheyenne gave you."

He hesitated. "You sound suspicious."

"I am."

"Do you think Scott was murdered?"

"No," she said immediately, but then she wondered. "It would explain a lot, but at the same time, eventually the body will be discovered, and if it's clear he was murdered, a more thorough investigation would put those three under more scrutiny. But intent to kill is not the same thing as being responsible for a death. What if there was an accident and some reason the boys didn't want to admit to it?"

"Like if they had been drinking? Doing drugs?"

She nodded. "Maybe. Scott dies and they fear getting in trouble, so they leave him and make up a story about how he left without them."

"One of my first encounters with a corpse was finding a pair of young lovers who'd dropped acid about a hundred miles north of here. They hadn't brought any provisions, no sleeping bags. They were so wasted, they wandered off and we found them buried in leaves. Died of exposure in below-freezing temperatures. Even in the summer, it gets really cold at the higher elevations when the sun goes down."

Tim said, "Ann and I were up here during the initial search. Chuck and his team covered more ground than anyone thought possible, considering the storm. If there was an accident, it wasn't at the campground."

That validated Max's theory. "Maybe," she said cautiously, not wanting to offend the three, "you were searching in the wrong place."

Chuck turned off the winding paved road onto a well-packed dirt and gravel road. Any remaining snow was deep in crevices and under trees, where little sunlight reached, but it looked like spring was fully blooming in the Rocky Mountains. They bounced around in the cab more than Max's stomach liked, so she put her map away and focused on the terrain.

About a mile later, Chuck pulled over in a clearing. There were deep rivets from other vehicles that had come and gone, and several marked paths. "This is where the boys parked," he said. "It's a two-mile hike to the campground. We've covered everything around this area both six months ago and this past week."

Max stretched her legs and brought out her map again. "This is the trail map that's downloadable from the National Park Service Web site," she said. She pointed to an area southeast of the campground. "What's over here? This looks like a marked path."

Chuck studied it, nodded. "It leads to an abandoned Boy Scout camp."

"It also looks like a direct route to the highway."

"It's not—it's treacherous, and the trail is impassable in winter." But he studied the printout that Max had brought. "I can see why the route appears direct. But why would he go that way?"

"The question is, why would the others lie about the direction he took?"

Chuck considered for a long minute. "Ann, Tim, can you take this quadrant?" He pointed to a section west of the campground. "It's the only area we haven't covered in the last week. I'm going to take Trixie to follow Ms. Revere's hunch about this trail."

"No problem," Tim said. He checked his watch. "It'll take four hours, give or take."

"We'll meet back here, at the truck, at one thirty," Chuck said. "Unless any of us find something. We'll use the emergency band, keep the chatter to a minimum."

"Be safe," Ann said. She and her husband left, each with their own backpack and radio.

They walked down the trail that led to the campground. It took them thirty minutes, walking at a brisk pace, but the trail was relatively flat, making it easy. Trixie stayed with them until they reached the acre-size campground. Max looked around. There were two fire pits, neither of which had been used for months, if not years. The snow had completely melted, but there were some remnants in shaded areas. The clearing was nearly perfectly round, the west bordered by huge boulders that, when scaled, would likely reveal an amazing view. The rest of the clearing was framed by trees. To the west, they were spindly; to the east, thicker and taller as they went down the mountainside. They were still below the tree line and seemed to be in the middle of nowhere, but less than two miles from where campers could park. From far in the distance came the sound of running water.

"Peaceful," Max said. "But when I was researching, there appear to be more popular—and populated—places to camp."

"Many," he agreed. "This is off the beaten path, so to speak. But it's on the map, so it's not unusual to have people come here. Because of the old Boy Scout camp, there're visitors who like to hike the area."

"Is that camp still viable?"

"It closed seven, eight years ago. It's accessible only via a bridge over a narrow canyon, and it was destroyed one winter. There's a newer camp a few miles north, and the local troop decided not to rebuild the bridge. You can still reach the camp, but it's a long trek." He hesitated. "If Scott went that way, it's treacherous with steep drops."

Chuck didn't have to elaborate. Max could easily picture a scenario where Scott died of injuries he sustained while trying to find his way out of the forest.

Chuck let Trixie off her lead and gave her a command. The golden retriever delighted in her freedom and raced ahead, down a narrow, overgrown path. They followed. Less than fifty yards off the campground, the trail was covered with slushy snow while also dipping steeply down. Max couldn't see Trixie anymore.

The temperature also dropped dramatically as the canopy of towering pine covered them.

"This is going to sound like a dumb question, but will Trixie just keep going until she finds something?"

"She'll come back every five to ten minutes and get a confirmation from me to continue." As if on cue, Max heard a rustling, and then Trixie appeared at a point where the trail seemed to disappear. Chuck gave her a hand signal, and the dog ran off again.

Chuck said, "This isn't much of a trail at all, and if he went this way, I can easily see how he'd get lost. Some hikers like to go back to the scouting camp, but with the bridge out, most avoid it."

"Could Scott and his friends have found it?"

"Yes, but why wouldn't they have told us that was where they'd been?"

Max could think of a half dozen reasons, none of them innocent. An accident, murder, violence, drugs, drinking—any number of things. She'd become so jaded over the years that she wasn't surprised at what people said or did to each other. Her instincts told her that those three boys had lied to the police about *something;* whether they were capable of murder was another question.

"Watch your step," he said. "There's a stream that cuts through up ahead. It shouldn't be too wide yet, but with the melting snow, it's going to be running and the ground's slick. We cut off the search there, since there was no evidence he'd gone this way."

They turned another sharp curve, and a stream came fast down the mountain in a twenty-foot waterfall and went under the path. A makeshift bridge had been built over it—but it didn't look stable.

"One of the scout troops did that," Chuck said. "Probably safe, but step over it if you can." He went first, then held his hand out for Max. She took it and stepped over. Trixie showed her head, Chuck signaled her, and the dog ran off again.

The vast beauty of the mountains could turn to a nightmare—in the dark, in the winter, during a storm. Scott was out here, alone. Angry. Scared. Had he really walked off? Gotten lost? Why? It didn't make sense, knowing what she did about him.

They continued on, more than a half mile past the stream. They'd already been walking for an hour. The only sounds were dripping water, birds, a faint rustle of leaves. There was no wind, no voices, no traffic.

Max could handle only so much silence before she started getting nervous. Chuck was ten feet in front of her because the path was too narrow for them to walk side by side. "If—" she began when Trixie barked.

The steady barking cut through the subtle sounds of the forest. Max slipped and fell on her ass. "Shit," she muttered.

Chuck turned, smiled, and offered her a hand again, which she gratefully took. He pulled her up with strength she wouldn't have expected from his trim frame. "Trixie found something."

"Could it be an animal?"

"She knows the difference. And if there was a threat, she has a different bark."

They continued down the path, an even steeper embankment than before, but Max managed to keep her balance by holding on to the tree trunks as she went. Then the path leveled out. "The old scout camp is through there." He pointed straight ahead. "You can see where the bridge collapsed."

At first Max didn't see; then it was clear that it had been a rope bridge. Thick ropes were tied to a tree trunk on either side of a steep cavern that looked at least a hundred feet deep and twenty feet across. An echo of rushing water came up from the depths.

Max never considered that she was afraid of heights, but it would take a lot of cajoling for her to take a rope bridge over that cavern.

Trixie's steady barking came from the right. Away from the scouting camp.

They turned and walked steeply up a trail twenty yards before they found Trixie standing, her head facing into a grove of trees. Chuck called her back with a whistle, and she immediately came to him and stopped barking. He gave her a scratch and a treat, then some water.

Max tried to be patient, but it didn't come naturally. She inched forward, and Chuck followed.

Just off the trail, a black sleeping bag was bunched up against a tree, partly buried in leaves and dirt. There was some snow that hadn't melted, but as they approached, the ground was soft and muddy.

At first, Max didn't see anything other than the dark bag. Then she saw the fingers of a hand, barely exposed through the opening.

"Stay here," Chuck told her. He walked over, bracing himself against the tree trunk to keep from sliding down the slick mud. He pulled back the top of the sleeping bag and peered inside. A foul stench hit Max, and Trixie whimpered, then lay down with her head on her paws. If a dog could look sad, Trixie was miserable.

Max squatted down and scratched her behind the ears. "You're a good girl, Trixie," she said. Her voice cracked.

Scott Sheldon was most certainly dead, his body remarkably preserved in the cold climate.

"Well, shit," Chuck said. "You always hope they ran off with their girlfriend."

He knelt to inspect the body. "No obvious signs of injury. No visible blood—if there was blood, I suspect the animals would have found him long ago."

"Their statements were identical," Max said, anger rising. "They claimed that they were hanging out at the campsite, drinking beer, and joking around. Scott got mad and stomped off toward where they'd parked, two miles away. At night. But on the map, where they parked was in the opposite direction from this trail. So either they lied about the direction—"

"Or were too drugged up to notice," Chuck suggested, and Max agreed that it was a possibility.

"Or," she continued, "they lied about him leaving in the first place."

"Before you jump to conclusions, Ms. Revere, let's see what the coroner has to say. She's a fine doctor. If there was foul play, she'll figure it out." He pulled out his radio and contacted Tim and Ann. "Tim? Go back to the truck and retrieve the gurney and body bag. Meet us at the campground. We'll lead you to the body."

CHAPTER SEVEN

"What happened?" Adele Sheldon asked Max.

Max was in her room at the Broadmoor, sitting at her desk. She didn't know what to say—a first for her.

"Detective Horn called me," Adele said, a hitch in her voice. "I knew he was dead, I knew it, but . . . ," Her voice trailed off on a sob.

"Would you like me to drive down and see you?" It was almost a two-hour drive. She didn't want to go tonight, but she would, for Scott's mother.

"No, I want you to find out what happened. You were there. You saw him."

"We need to wait for the autopsy results."

"That's what the detective said." Adele took a deep breath, worked to control her emotions. Max let her; she didn't need to rush this. "I wanted him to be alive, but I knew in my heart that he wasn't. I'm his mother; I think I've always known."

"Though we can't be sure until after the tests, there were no visible injuries." To preserve evidence, Chuck and Tim had bagged Scott's body while still in the sleeping bag. They examined him for visible head and chest wounds, but there were none.

"Did he suffer?" she asked, her voice small.

"It doesn't appear so." Max didn't know what to say, so she said what she thought was accurate. What might give Adele a modicum of comfort. "If he died of exposure, he most likely fell asleep and then just didn't wake up."

Adele didn't say anything. She probably knew that dying of exposure wasn't as peaceful as Max implied. But would it help anyone to know if Scott had been in pain?

"I'm sorry, Adele."

"It's okay. Why did it take you to find him? They would never have found him if you didn't light a fire under them."

"We don't know that. I spent the day with Chuck Pence, the head of search and rescue. He looked as long as he could after Scott's disappearance, but we found your son in a different area than where they initially focused."

"I don't understand what you mean."

"They had time against them last fall. The storm was getting worse, and they concentrated on the area between the camp and where the boys had parked their truck. Scott was found on the opposite side of the mountain, nearly two miles southeast of the campground; they parked two miles north of the camp. I suspect that Chuck and his team would have found Scott in the next couple of days. I met them; they weren't going to give up. I just— made it go faster." She didn't mention at this point that it had been her suggestion to check the other trail, because that really didn't matter—not to Adele. It would matter when Max talked to the three boys who left Scott alone on that mountain.

"Are you leaving?" Adele asked.

Max had thought about it. She didn't know why seeing Scott Sheldon's thawing body had disturbed her so much. She'd viewed an autopsy before, seen crime scene photos, once researched a child abuse case that left a little girl in a coma. That small, unconscious body had unnerved Max on multiple levels.

But this—she'd never seen a body so exposed. So . . . vulnerable. So *dead*. An autopsy was clinical and scientific. She could separate the procedure from the person. Crime scene photos were two dimensional, violent and grotesque, but again, she could view them as a reporter and not with undue emotion.

But Scott . . . he was right there, and had been for nearly six months. In his sleeping bag, suggesting he knew he couldn't get back to the campground where his friends had pitched a tent. He'd curled up against the tree, in his sleeping bag, and died. Had he known? Had he thought he would wake up in the morning and find his way back? She'd already checked—the average temperature in Colorado Springs that night was fifteen degrees. Chuck told her that would mean in the mountains where the boys had camped it would have been even colder, likely below zero. Scott's sleeping bag wasn't designed for subzero temperatures.

Had he wandered around and gotten lost? Why?

"I'm going to wait until the autopsy results come in, talk to the detective, then talk to the boys again."

"Do you think—something else happened?"

"I don't know, Adele. I think—" Max didn't want to share her theories with Adele. Not until she had proof. "I'm not sure that the entire story has been told."

"Call me. I—I'm going to have a funeral for him. Detective Horn said a few days and I should be able to . . ." Again, her voice trailed off.

"Let me know about it. If I'm still here, I'll come."

"Thank you. Thank you." Adele hung up and Max was relieved. The grief of parents twisted her stomach in knots. She had a headache—she hadn't eaten since breakfast. She wasn't hungry, but knew she needed to eat something or she wouldn't be able to sleep. Especially when she couldn't get Scott Sheldon's dead body out of her mind.

She made a reservation at the Tavern, her favorite restaurant at the Broadmoor. She'd been to the resort many times in the past—it was one of her favorite places to relax—only this time, she didn't feel relaxed.

Chuck called her cell phone as she was leaving for dinner. "I wanted to see how you're doing. You were very quiet during the drive back."

"It's been a long day," she said. "I'm dining at the Tavern, if you'd like to join me."

He didn't commit. "I'll see."

"You know where I am," she said, and hung up. She didn't want small talk; she didn't really want to talk at all.

The restaurant was across the courtyard from the main building. She stepped out into pouring rain. The doorman handed her a complimentary umbrella, and she smiled her thanks, but had no energy to talk. Her thoughts were filled with images of Scott Sheldon dying alone—buried in snow, pounded with rain, covered with layers of mulch. Her melancholy turned to anger. There was no reason he should have died on that mountain.

She was seated immediately and ordered a crab cake appetizer and wine before she looked at the menu. The wine, thankfully, arrived first.

She stared at the fire across the room, sipped her wine, and tried to force her mind to go blank. It was something she had a hard time doing, turning off her thoughts. Either her mind had to be working or her body—preferably both. But today all she felt was cold, even in the warm restaurant and wearing her favorite cashmere sweater and snug wool slacks. She shouldn't be cold, but even the hot shower after she returned from the mountain hadn't warmed her.

The loss hit her. What had Scott been thinking those hours he lay in the cheap nylon sleeping bag? Had he known he was dying? How long did he stay there, too cold to move, too cold to call out? Was he disoriented? Severe hypothermia lowered the body temperature so much that victims got confused, often hallucinating and wandering, their heart rate dropping, their major organs slowly shutting down. Did it take a couple hours? All night? He would have lost consciousness before he died, but the hours leading up to that would have been full of fear and pain.

A miserable way to die.

But was there any good way to die?

By all accounts, Karen had been stabbed to death—how else could she have lost so much blood? Did she die faster than Scott, and did that make it some sort of blessing? Or was it more painful, more fearful? Did it matter? They were both young people, in college, with their lives ahead of them, and they were dead. One violently, and one by the stupidity of others.

Whether it was malicious or not remained to be seen.

Her crab cakes came and the waitress asked if she wanted to order dinner. "Not now," Max said. "Another glass of wine, please."

She nibbled on the crab cakes and watched as Chuck Pence crossed in front of the fire and sat across from her.

"Where's Trixie?" Max asked.

"Home. Finding a body, even though she's trained for it, is disturbing for her as well as us. My wife knows how to soothe her."

"Have a drink with me," Max said as the waitress came with her second glass.

He said to the waitress, "Scotch, neat."

"Do you have a preference?"

"No," he said.

"Top shelf, single malt," Max told the waitress. "Thank you."

"Reporting must pay well," Chuck said.

"Not particularly."

"Detective Horn told me you're also a writer. Books."

"True crime." She didn't feel the need to share more of her history with Chuck. "I'm sorry I was abrupt on the phone." Apologies didn't come easy to her, but she had been snippy, and Chuck had been helpful. "I appreciate that you took me out with you and the Callows today."

"I wish there could have been a better outcome."

"We both knew the outcome."

"That doesn't make it any easier."

They sat in silence while the waitress brought Chuck's Scotch. He sniffed, sipped, nodded. "Thank you."

"Did you get the preliminary autopsy report?" Max was familiar enough with the process to know they wouldn't get a final report until the exam and all tests came back.

"The autopsy is scheduled for tomorrow morning. Amelia said she'd call me when she knew anything." He paused, sipped some more. "She doesn't usually do that, but she knows this has been bothering me. And she suspects I'll inform you."

"Why doesn't she call me?"

"She's uncomfortable talking to the press."

"She talked to me on the phone the other day."

"Curiosity."

"And you? You deal with the press all the time?"

"Never. But you don't strike me as a typical reporter."

"I'll take that as a compliment."

"I did learn something at the coroner's office. The visual exam of the body shows no external cause of death. There were some scrapes on his arms consistent with tree branches or falling and skinning his arm, but other than that, no visible wounds. X-rays showed a fracture in his left fibula. He probably could have walked on it, but it would have been painful. Because the body was frozen for so long, and based on average temperature for the area over the last six months, the coroner hopes to get a good tox screen, see if he was on drugs. Alcohol will be next to impossible to find—it breaks down in the system in a matter of hours, but it also speeds up hypothermia."

"If he was found Saturday, would he have survived?"

"I can't answer that. He was in apparent good health, he should have been able to survive, though he'd have had extreme hypothermia. By the second night, I would put his chance of survival—given what he was wearing and the sleeping bag—at less than twenty percent. If he'd fallen in the creek we crossed to find him, that would have lowered his body temperature dramatically and he wouldn't have survived even more moderate temperatures than what he had. Without those answers, I can't speculate."

He paused, sipped his Scotch. "You're suggesting that had the boys informed the rangers on Saturday that he was missing, we could have found him."

"Yes."

He let out a long, slow sigh. "I don't know."

"We found him in a different area than you originally looked."

"Correct."

Max nodded.

"I don't know what you're thinking, Ms. Revere, but you're thinking."

"Max. My friends call me Max." He was right; she was thinking. "What if they deliberately misled search and rescue?"

"Playing devil's advocate, why? There's no physical trauma. No signs of abuse, no bruising, minor scrapes consistent with the environment."

"If something else happened—maybe drug related,

maybe something Scott knew—something that, if he were found alive, he would get the others in trouble."

"That's a mighty big leap, unsupported by any evidence."

"There's plenty of evidence," she said bitterly. "It's a matter of how we look at it. Is Detective Horn going to talk to them?"

"Not until after the autopsy report comes back."

"They'll have plenty of time to synchronize their stories."

"I think it would be best if you stayed in the background. Amelia is a good cop. If there's something there, she'll find it."

"She told me on the phone that there was no evidence of foul play then, and if there's no physical evidence now, there's not going to be an investigation. It's not like I'm impeding an official police inquiry. I can get Tom Keller to confess. He's the weak link."

"Confess to what?"

She stared Chuck in the eye. "The truth."

Max rarely found herself drunk, but she was tipsy when she walked back to her hotel room. She hoped the alcohol would help her sleep, but suspected it would more likely contribute to vivid and disturbing dreams. She drank water while checking her e-mail. Her editor—she filed it away to respond to later. Ben, again nagging her about the television show. She e-mailed him back.

If you keep nagging me, I will block your e-mails and never return a phone call. I'll let you know when I make my decision.

There were several other messages she ignored or deleted, and then she saw the note from her computer genius in New York, Grant Malone.

I analyzed the image you forwarded. It was uploaded

at 8:39 a.m. local time on October 31. The image was uploaded via Wi-Fi, the code was also embedded in the image. I've attached the GPS location and verification of the Wi-Fi code.

She clicked on the attachment. The photo had been uploaded from a hotel off the interstate that was nowhere near the campground. In fact, they were thirty-seven miles away, in a warm hotel room while Scott Sheldon died a slow and painful death, cold and alone.

CHAPTER EIGHT

When Max woke Thursday morning, she planned to go directly to the college campus and confront Tom Keller with the evidence, compel him to tell her the truth. But she needed more evidence than a photo she'd downloaded from the Internet. It convinced her, and it might convince Tom to talk, but Arthur Cowan was a wily bastard, and Max needed something irrefutable. Something else to sway Tom Keller that telling the truth was his only choice.

She doubted anyone at the hotel would remember three college boys after six months, but she might be able to convince one of the staff members to look up information for her. It was worth a shot.

And if they wouldn't do it out of the kindness of their hearts, Max had enough cash to convince them. It had worked in the past.

The hotel was twenty-five minutes north of Colorado Springs, outside the city limits and off the interstate—the same road they used before turning up the mountain to get to the campground. On the drive, Max called the campus bookstore to talk to Jess, but learned she didn't work Thursdays. Max couldn't convince the person who answered to give her Jess's cell phone number or her dorm room, and while Max couldn't blame them for protecting Jess's privacy, it was frustrating. She gave the person her contact information and said that it was urgent Jess contact her.

Urgent might be an overstatement, but Max had an idea, and Jess was her best bet to put it in action.

Then she called Chuck Pence, but he didn't answer. She left a message on his voice mail. She considered calling Detective Horn, but feared the cop would tell her to stay out of it. Max had no plans to do that. Better to ask for forgiveness than permission, Karen had always said. Max never agreed with her . . . until she became a freelance reporter. Asking for permission rarely worked.

Plus, she'd been in jail before, and it was no fun.

The embedded photo information identified not only the hotel's Wi-Fi, but also narrowed the location to the south wing. It wasn't until she parked in the guest lot that she realized she didn't have a plan that didn't involve bribery. Not everyone could be bribed. But she was here, she wasn't going to stop now.

She walked in and assessed the lobby. It wasn't a five-star hotel, but it wasn't a dive, either.

It was ten in the morning and the building was relatively quiet. She had three options—concierge, reception, or find the manager. There were two people at the reception counter, so Max picked the concierge, an older man in a well-cut suit. His nameplate read ANDERSON.

She approached with a confident smile and handed him her business card. "Maxine Revere. I'm following up on information about three guests who stayed here last October thirtieth. I'm hoping you can help me."

"We don't give out guest information, hotel policy."

"I completely understand, Mr. Anderson. I don't need personal information. I have the names of the guests, I would simply like to confirm that they were in fact guests on that night. Even a verbal confirmation would be sufficient."

She discreetly slid over a fifty-dollar bill.

He barely glanced at it, but his expression darkened. Dammit, she'd blown it. She rarely read people wrong; she thought for sure he would cave.

"I cannot help you, Ms. Revere, and if you persist, I will call security."

Jerk. She forced herself to smile and walked away, taking her fifty with her.

She could feel Mr. Anderson's eyes boring into her back, so she turned into the lounge. Fortunately, it was open. She wasn't much of a morning drinker, but right now she was out of options. She needed a backup plan, and that meant sitting down to think. It didn't help that she hadn't slept well last night, odd dreams of searching for Karen intermingled with finding Scott's body. Only, she found Karen—bloodied and staring at her as if everything were her fault.

Why didn't you do something?

Why indeed. Max couldn't save Karen from her bad choices. She hadn't even been able to prove who had killed her. But she wasn't going to give up finding out why Keller, Ibarra, and Cowan left Scott to die.

During her restless sleep, Max had come up with a theory. Arthur Cowan was the joker, and from what she'd seen on his social media pages, he could be cruel. What if he was still infatuated with Jess, but Jess wanted nothing to do with him? And then he thought Jess and Scott were together? Would he play a "prank" on Scott, leave him on the mountain? And if so, why hadn't Tom Keller or Carlos Ibarra stopped Art from doing it? Why hadn't they told someone sooner? Was Carlos so loyal to Art, and Tom so desperate to make friends, that they would do anything he wanted?

All the evidence—circumstantial though it was—told Max they'd left Scott Sheldon at that campsite, by himself, all night. And Scott must have thought they wouldn't come back, so he tried to get out on his own.

Why, dammit? There has to be a reason!

The bartender, a fit, attractive, forty-year-old black guy wearing slacks and a button-down white shirt, approached her with the clichéd line: "What's your poison?"

"Be honest. How are your Bloody Marys?"

He smiled, revealing perfect teeth. Max had always appreciated a nice smile. "The best in Colorado. I prepare my own mix fresh every morning."

"I want the good vodka, but make it weak."

He dipped his head and mixed her drink. She watched his fluid, sure movements. He set it in front of her and she read his name tag: JOHANN. "Why do you look so glum, pretty lady?"

She wasn't in the mood to flirt, so instead said bluntly, "I couldn't bribe your concierge."

Johann laughed, and his next words to her held a hint of an accent she couldn't immediately place. "Sugar, you should have asked me."

She slid over the fifty she was going to give to Mr. Anderson. "Keep it. You can't help me."

"Try me."

She sipped the Bloody Mary. Nodded appreciatively. "You're right. Best in Colorado. Better than my cousin's five-star Vail resort."

"I know."

"You know the resort?"

He winked. "I just know I'm the best."

She laughed and felt the tension washing away. "Six months ago, three college students stayed here. I know it, I have a photo they took elsewhere but uploaded through your hotel Wi-Fi. But I need to confirm it."

"Aw, yes, our guest privacy. Wouldn't you expect a hotel to respect your privacy?"

"It depends."

"Depends?"

"I'm a reporter. Sometimes I want people to find me."

"Did they drink?"

"Probably. But they were nineteen and twenty."

"Did you have a fake ID when you were nineteen or twenty?"

"No," she answered truthfully. Then she smiled. "But my college roommate did."

He slid over a napkin and pen. He didn't have to tell her to write down the names. She put them down—including Scott Sheldon. He didn't look, but took the napkin and walked to the end of the bar, into a small office she hadn't noticed until he stepped in and the light flickered on.

She wasn't going to hold out hope, and instead enjoyed her drink. Already, a plan began to form. She knew Tom Keller was the weak link, but she'd also learned from Ian Stanhope, Scott's roommate, that he and Tom shared a class together. If she could catch up with Ian, she could convince him to reach out to Tom. She'd play on the roommate's guilt if she had to. She'd present the evidence to Tom—the photo would have to be enough. Max could spin the story, watch his reaction, play off it, until Tom broke down.

Johann returned and Max said, "Thank you for the delicious drink. It helped—I have a plan."

He smiled. "I can tell you—though I can't give you a copy—that the third name on your list signed for a room service charge that included a bucket of Corona. Our buckets come in four or eight; he signed for the eight bucket."

Her heart thudded. She had them.

"How long do you keep the records?"

"One year."

She drained her Bloody Mary and left the fifty on the bar. "Thank you, Johann. That's just what I needed."

Max drove toward the police station to give Detective Horn all the information she had and ask what she was going to do about it. If Max were the cop, she'd haul all three of those boys into the police station and question them until they admitted they killed Scott Sheldon. At this point, Max didn't think it was an accident. Maybe they hadn't *intended* for Scott to die, but their callous actions resulted in his death. Manslaughter at a minimum, and maybe even second-degree murder.

If *premeditated*? That would put this crime on a whole other field.

Her phone rang; it was Chuck Pence.

"You have news?" she asked.

"Officially, cause of death was hypothermia. Scott's organs shut down. The coroner is sending tissue and blood samples for further analysis, particularly drug screenings, but right now the preliminary cause of death is accidental."

"It wasn't an accident!" Max pounded her fist on the wheel of her SUV.

Chuck remained silent. Max needed to control her temper. This case had gotten under her skin, and it wasn't Chuck's fault. "Chuck," she said, "I have proof that Arthur, Carlos, and Tom left Scott at the campsite then drove to a hotel where they stayed the night."

"Proof?"

"That photo I mentioned to you last night—my guy in New York pulled out the GPS of where and when it was uploaded. At a hotel, Saturday morning. The photo was tagged with the hotel's Wi-Fi and GPS location. It's a fingerprint. I spoke to the bartender and he pulled records from the night of October thirtieth—Carlos Ibarra ordered a bucket of eight Coronas. The night they were supposed to be at the campground."

"The hotel just gave you that information?"

"I asked nicely."

"You should tell Detective Horn. I'm not a cop, Max."

"But you agree with me."

"You can't know that it wasn't an accident."

"If they left Scott Sheldon alone on that mountain with no means of getting home, except on foot, they are responsible for his death."

"He should have been able to survive the night," Chuck said. "We found his backpack and tent near the body. He never set it up; had he, he may have survived."

"You don't know that! And hypothermia causes delusions and poor judgment. And just yesterday you said if he'd fallen in the creek and gotten wet that hypothermia could happen faster. He may not have had the mental capacity to pitch the tent or consider that he *was* suffering. And if they were drinking, that speeds everything up, right?"

"There's no indication that anyone forced him to drink."

"Scott Sheldon is not to blame for his death," Max said. "That's like saying a woman wearing a short skirt is to blame for her rape."

"That's unfair," Chuck snapped.

Maybe it was, but it was also true. "If those boys had not left the mountain, Scott would be alive. They played a cruel joke on him, and he ended up dead."

"Good luck in convincing Amelia. You're going to need a lot more than a photograph." He hung up.

Max took a deep breath, but it didn't make her feel any calmer. She hadn't wanted to antagonize Chuck—she liked the guy—but didn't he see what she saw?

Horn hadn't impressed her as someone who saw the possibilities of the situation. Max needed something more, something that would convince the police that there was a criminal case to pursue, that three selfish college students had led another student to his death.

She drove past Colorado Springs and continued south, to Cheyenne College.

It was nearly noon when she walked into the bookstore. Jess wasn't there. She approached the long-haired guy behind the counter. "I'm looking for Jess," Max said.

"She doesn't work today."

"I called earlier. Maxine Revere. Did she get my message?"

"Like I said, she doesn't work today, and I'm not her personal message service."

"Do you know where I might find her?"

He sighed dramatically. "I'm not supposed to give out information about students."

Max didn't want to line this jerk's pockets, but she'd paid bigger assholes for information. She slid over a twenty.

"Music theory, Stevenson Hall."

She didn't bother to say thank you, and strode over the Stevenson Hall.

By the time she arrived, students were streaming from the building, some carrying instruments, others with the typical backpack or messenger bag. Her height was an advantage, and she stood on a small, decorative bridge that gave her a better vantage point. The gray sky suited her mood.

Max had to convince Jess that her theory was solid. The girl already suspected something went wrong that weekend, even if she didn't say anything at the time. Maybe Jess didn't realize she knew something important, or maybe she did but she was too scared to talk.

As the crowd thinned to a trickle, Max grew increasingly discouraged, fearing she'd missed Jess. Then she saw the petite sophomore walking with her head down, her messenger bag slung over her shoulder.

"Jess."

The girl barely looked at her. "Go away."

"I can prove they killed Scott."

Jess stopped, and looked at Max. Tears filled her dark eyes. "Wh-what?"

"They left him on the mountain. I don't know if it was supposed to be a joke, or if they intended to kill him, but it was malicious and they need to be held accountable."

"How do you know?"

"I have a photo uploaded to Facebook Saturday morning from a hotel, not from the campground. And Carlos Ibarra signed for a bucket of beer Friday night. I think you know why they didn't like Scott, why they would pull such a cruel joke that ended up getting him killed. Tell me, Jess. Scott deserves for the truth to be told."

Jess stood there shivering, but made no move to go inside. "I—I didn't know."

"I was with search and rescue when they found Scott's body yesterday."

Her eyes widened. "You found him?"

"Huddled in a sleeping bag under a tree. He died there, cold and alone, while Art, Carlos, and Tom were partying it up in a hotel."

Her lip quivered.

"Why did you stop talking to Art after Scott disappeared?" When Jess didn't say anything, Max pushed. "You dated him last year."

"Not for long. He's an asshole." Jess took a deep breath; then everything poured out. "His pranks are mean. He told me he found a kitten behind his dorm, then held up this paper bag and threw it in the pond at the quad. I jumped in and it wasn't a kitten in the bag, it was a rock, and he stood there and laughed at me. Tried to convince me that it was just a joke, that he would never hurt an animal, but I didn't believe him. I broke up with him and he spread nasty rumors about me. He doesn't have many friends, except Carlos. I don't know why people believed him, but you know how people are."

"Were you and Scott involved?"

"No—maybe we could have been. But we were just friends. I told him not to go camping with Art, that he and Carlos couldn't be trusted. Once, when Art and I were making out in his dorm room, Carlos jumped out of the closet and they laughed at me. Art had my shirt off, it was so humiliating. I should have broken up with him then, but I believed him when he said he didn't know. It was only later—" She looked away.

Max reached out and squeezed her arm. "Jess, this isn't your fault. Art is a bully and enjoys hurting people."

Max added, "Did Art think that you and Scott were involved?"

She shrugged. "But he's never hurt anyone. His pranks are just mean."

"Hurting people doesn't mean physically hurting them. But this time, with Scott, he went too far. Help me prove it."

"He'll never admit it."

"He doesn't have to. I need you to get Tom Keller to meet you in your room."

"Tom's just like them—maybe not mean, but he tries so hard to get people to like him."

Max could work with that. "Please, Jess." Max was out of options. If Jess didn't agree to help, Max would have to turn over what she had to Detective Horn, and she didn't think it was enough. Max could think of a half dozen ways the boys could explain away why they were in the hotel, and without proof that they maliciously left Scott Sheldon to die, they'd get away with it.

Just like Karen's killer got away with murder, because her body had never been found and he had a damn good lawyer.

"You really think they left him up there? By himself?"

"I do."

Jess looked at her feet. "All right. I'll call Tom."

CHAPTER NINE

Max sat with Jess in her dorm room, an awkward silence between them. "Jess, is there anything else you want to tell me?"

She'd been biting her nails ever since she got off the phone with Tom. "I shouldn't get involved."

"Someone has to stand up for what's right." In all the investigations Max had covered, too often people had turned their back on someone who needed help. Or, were blinded by the evil in another. And just as often, Max had met people who did help, who went out of their way to care for those who couldn't care for themselves. People who recognized evil for what it was and did something to stop it. "Do you really think Art will stop being cruel? Do you think he'll learn any lesson from this, other than he got away with it?"

"It had to be an accident."

"That's what you want to believe," Max said. And maybe it was. Maybe Art didn't want Scott dead, but that didn't mean he wasn't culpable in his death.

Something Tom had said when she first talked to him came back to her.

It's not our fault he left.

The comment could be taken in two ways. Either he left because he was mad, or left the campground before they returned for him. What if Scott didn't think they would return? What if they gave him the impression that they wouldn't? And when the weather turned, he might have thought he had no other choice but to try to find his way out on foot.

Jess jumped when there was a knock on the door. Max got up to answer it.

It was Tom. He saw her and turned to leave.

Max grabbed his arm and pulled him into the room. "You're not going until you tell me the truth."

Tom looked at Jess. "What's going on?"

"You killed Scott!"

Max winced. Going for the jugular wouldn't get them answers.

"Is that what she told you? That's not true!"

Max closed the door so they wouldn't attract an audience.

"You went along with one of Art's stupid jokes, didn't you?" Jess said. "I thought you were better than that. I thought you were Scott's friend. That's what *he* thought."

"I was! I liked Scott! He just wandered off. We didn't know what to do."

Max said, "Tom, I know what happened, and I can prove it. You, Art, and Carlos went to the campground with Scott. But you left him there. Maybe you were having a few beers, and thought it would be fun to play a joke. He goes to pee against a tree and you all leave. Or he falls asleep by the fire, and you sneak off. Whatever you did, he was alone, and you, Carlos, and Art drove thirty-seven miles to the interstate, checked into a hotel, and ordered Corona beer from room service."

He stared at her, obviously stunned that she knew. "Then," she said, "Art posted a photo of you, Carlos, and

Scott at the campsite. Only, he didn't realize that whenever you upload a photo through a mobile device, it logs
certain information. In this case, the GPS and time *where*
you uploaded it. Eight thirty-nine Saturday morning—
through the hotel's Wi-Fi, with the GPS putting you at the
hotel that morning. The same morning you said you woke
up at the campground and Scott was still not back.

"What I think—and jump in if I'm wrong—is that you
went back there Saturday morning and Scott wasn't there.
You may or may not have looked for him; probably called
for him a few times. But it was raining, and it was cold.
You went back to the college late, then tried to find him
again Sunday morning. But it was snowing and either you
pretended to look, or you didn't even go all the way to the
campsite. You didn't tell the campus police until Sunday
that Scott was missing."

Tom was so pale, Max knew she had pegged the truth.
"Had you contacted search and rescue Saturday morning, when you first realized Scott wasn't where you'd left
him, Scott would have survived."

Jess gasped.

Tom was trembling. "No. It wasn't like that, not exactly."

"Then how was it?"

"I can't—"

"Fine. Don't tell me. You'll be talking to the police
very soon. I'm meeting with Detective Horn to give her
all the evidence I uncovered, in addition to a signed statement by the bartender that Carlos Ibarra's credit card was
used on a hotel charge the night you told police that you
were camping in the mountains."

She had no qualms about lying. She was pretty sure
the police would be able to get a statement from the bartender. They could also get a warrant for the hotel guest
records.

"I—I—I didn't want to. It was just a joke, we didn't know it was going to snow. We didn't know he wouldn't be there. If he'd stayed, we would have brought him back."

"But he didn't stay. He was scared, lonely, didn't know you were going to return. Probably mad, too. He broke his leg, couldn't move. We found his body yesterday. Two miles from the campsite, in the opposite direction from the entrance. He broke his leg because you and Art and Carlos left him up there alone with an inadequate sleeping bag."

"I'm s-so sorry." He bit his lip and stared at Jess. "Jess, I didn't mean to hurt anyone."

"Tell that to his mother," Max said.

"It was an accident. I didn't want Scott to get hurt. I didn't want to stay out all night, just a couple hours, but—"

"Was it Art's idea? Or Carlos?"

"Art. It was his idea."

Jess interjected, "And you didn't have the balls to stand up to him? To tell him he was being a jerk?"

"I—I couldn't. Art, well, I—I—," Tom stuttered, unable to finish his thought.

Jess started to cry. "Art's mean and spiteful and he makes you feel like anything that goes wrong is your fault. I know. Oh God, this just sucks. Scott was a good guy."

"I will get Scott justice," Max said. To Tom, "If you confess, the police will go easy on you. Just remember— if you continue to lie, you'll only get yourself into deeper trouble."

She waited until Tom left, then picked up her iPad, which was sitting on Jess's bed. She stopped recording. "Thank you, Jess."

"I—I didn't believe you."

"Yes, you did, otherwise you wouldn't have gone out on a limb to set this up." Max put her iPad in her bag and said, "Stay away from Art and Carlos. Tom isn't going to be able to keep this conversation secret, and I don't want you to get hurt."

"I'm okay," Jess said.

"Art lost his temper with me when I confronted him Tuesday. He pushed me. He's a hothead. If he has a weapon, or uses his weight to bully you—"

"I'll stay away from him," Jess said. "I don't have classes tomorrow. I think I'll go visit my mom."

"Good idea. You have my numbers. Call me if you have any questions. And if Art harasses you, call the police."

Jess walked Max to the door. "Thank you. I—I didn't think anyone really cared what happened to Scott, but you do."

Max left the dorm room and walked through the campus to where she'd parked her car. She got in and called Detective Horn. It took several minutes before she could finally get her on the phone. "Detective, Maxine Revere."

"I remember. Chuck told me you put yourself in the middle of this investigation."

"You mean there's an investigation?"

"You know what I mean."

"There's an investigation now. I have evidence that Arthur Cowan played a prank on Scott Sheldon and left him in the mountains without any way to get back to the campus or phone for help. Carlos Ibarra and Tom Keller were complicit. They stayed in a hotel that night. I'll bring everything to you—"

"I already talked to Chuck. There's hardly enough evidence to counter what they've told us."

"Tom Keller confirmed everything. It was Cowan's idea and Tom went along with it because Cowan intimidated him."

Detective Horn didn't say anything for a long minute. "Bring me what you have," she finally said. "I'll see if there's anything here. But even if the boys left Scott up on that mountain on purpose, there may not be a crime here."

"Why the hell not?" Max said, then cringed. Being confrontational at this juncture wasn't going to help her get in the detective's good graces.

"I said I would look at what you have, but I'm not happy about any of this. A kid is still dead, and no one can bring him back."

Max stared at her phone. The detective had hung up on her.

Max tossed her phone on the passenger seat and pulled out of the parking lot. She mentally wrote a few possible headlines.

POLICE REFUSE TO SEEK JUSTICE

STUDENTS WHO LEFT COLLEGE BOY TO DIE ON MOUNTAIN WALK AWAY FREE AND CLEAR

DELAY IN NOTIFYING SEARCH AND RESCUE LEADS COLLEGE BOY TO DIE OF EXPOSURE

None of them were good. She'd leave the headline to her editor, but she already had half the story written in her head. She wanted to highlight Scott Sheldon's life, his innocence, his trust, his stolen future. She wanted to highlight the failure of a system that didn't have a clear process to deal with missing students. She wanted to expose the three boys—particularly Arthur Cowan—for their culpability in the death of a peer.

Max had never been religious, but she'd read Bible stories, and one that always stuck with her was the Good Samaritan. That someone would stop and help another, who was obviously ill and in pain, even though it wasn't expected of him—resonated with Max. It pained Max that others would walk by and not give the ailing person the time of day, avoiding them, *ignoring* them. And too many people had looked the other way with the disappearance of Scott Sheldon. The boys who left him on the mountain. Tom Keller, who knew he'd done wrong but kept the secret. Ian Stanhope, Scott's roommate, who didn't think it was his responsibility to look out for his roommate. The campus police, who waited too long to notify the ranger station. Even the detective, who didn't think there had been a crime.

Someone had to stand for Scott.

Maybe because Max was hot under the collar, or maybe because she was preoccupied, trying to come up with a perfect headline for her article, she didn't notice that the car behind her was gaining until it was right on her tail. She glanced in her rearview mirror in time to see the large truck a second before it rammed her. She couldn't see the driver, it happened so quickly.

Her head hit the steering wheel even though her seat belt locked. She couldn't maintain control of her car around the bend.

Thoughts flitted in and out of her mind so fast, she barely acknowledged them. First, that she was in trouble. Then, that when she died she might finally find out exactly what had happened to Karen. Then her survival instinct kicked into high gear as she fought the urge to brake and instead sharply turned the wheel to avoid hitting a thick tree head-on.

The SUV spun twice, and didn't flip over. The air bags didn't deploy, maybe because there was no front-end collision. She rolled to a stop.

Her heart raced as she sat in the car, in the middle of the road, her hands gripped tight around the steering wheel.

She couldn't move. She wanted to. She wanted to get out of the damn car and walk—no, run—after the truck that hit her. She looked around, but didn't see it. Hit and run. Dammit, someone had rear-ended her and left. She was shaking, and she didn't want to be scared. She refused to be scared. Her breathing was shaky. She focused on slowing her heart rate, taking long, deep breaths.

She hadn't noticed another car pull over until the driver tapped on her window. "Ma'am? Are you okay, ma'am?"

She tried to nod. Her neck was stiff. But nothing felt broken. She took a deep breath. Her chest hurt where the seat belt dug into her skin.

But she was alive. She was alive and scared, and that made her angry.

"Ma'am?"

She slowly put the SUV in park. The engine wasn't on, probably stalled out or broken. With shaking hands, she fumbled with the door latch and finally opened it.

"Ma'am, my wife called 911. Help is on the way."

"Thank . . . you."

He put his hand on her shoulder. "Don't try to get up. I got the other driver's license plate. The police will find him."

"Good Samaritan," she mumbled. Her head hurt.

"You're bleeding," he said.

She touched her forehead and came back with a little blood. "I'm okay," she said. But she didn't try to stand. Her knees still felt weak, and her head was fuzzy.

And then she thought: Had someone hit her on purpose?

CHAPTER TEN

Max took advantage of all the resort amenities that weekend, relaxing for the first time since before she took the elder abuse case in Florida. Had she really started that over a year ago? She might even stay here until her cousin's wedding next weekend, when she had to face her family back in California. If she did, she could attend Scott's memorial service on Wednesday evening.

She didn't relax easily, but swimming in the heated pool, soaking in the spa, and being pampered with massages—she finally felt the tension and stress from the tragedies and the car accident disappear.

The truck that hit her was registered to Carlos Ibarra. He had an alibi for the time of the collision—he was in class. Police questioned Arthur Cowan and Tom Keller, but both denied driving the truck. Police found it abandoned several miles from the accident. There were no prints at all in the cab, suggesting it had been wiped clean.

There was no doubt in Max's mind that Arthur Cowan had rammed her, but there was no proof, either.

She had to let it go.

She didn't want to.

When Chuck Pence called Monday afternoon, she

invited him for a celebratory drink. "Bring your wife, and Trixie." Max would enjoy the company, both human and canine.

"I'll see," he'd said, and agreed to meet her at four.

She was sipping her wine on the outside terrace when she saw Chuck step out with Trixie. The woman on his arm was not his wife, however; it was Detective Amelia Horn. Immediately Max knew something was wrong.

She watched them approach her table. The cop wasn't looking at her, but Chuck was. His long face hung even longer.

Max leaned back and scratched Trixie while motioning for Chuck and Horn to sit down. The attentive waitress approached. Horn asked for water only. Chuck, a beer.

Max sipped her wine and waited for one of them to tell her what in their case was messed up.

It was Chuck who spoke. "Amelia asked me to come with her to explain the situation."

Max waited. Inside she was heating up; she knew what was coming before either of them said anything. But still, she waited, a vision of the calm she didn't feel.

"It was supposed to be a joke, like Tom Keller told you last week," Chuck said. "They didn't mean for anyone to get hurt."

"Drunk drivers don't mean to kill anyone, but they still get prosecuted when they hit someone while driving drunk."

"It's not the same thing," Horn said.

"They left him on the mountain in below-freezing temperatures with a small tent and sleeping bag that were insufficient for the weather."

"Had Scott stayed at the campground, he would have survived," Horn said.

"So it's Scott's fault that he's dead? You'll tell that to his mother?"

"I already spoke to Mrs. Sheldon. She understands. I explained that while the D.A. wasn't filing criminal charges, she was welcome to file a wrongful death case in a civil court. But she doesn't want to press charges."

Max felt sucker-punched. "You sugar-coated it. Arthur Cowan is a bully who's an expert skier and would have known that conditions could turn at any time."

"They all admitted to what they did, that they went back up Saturday morning, looked for him, couldn't find him, panicked when the storm got worse."

"And waiting until Sunday to tell campus police? And campus police waiting until Monday to tell the rangers' office so a search party could be sent out?"

"It's a tragedy for everyone. The D.A. has already cut a deal. They pleaded guilty to a misdemeanor charge of reckless endangerment and one year probation."

"That's unacceptable," Max said.

"I don't believe you're a lawyer, or a cop, or have any say in what the D.A. does or does not do."

"This is bullshit," Max said. "Scott Sheldon is dead because of those three, who were sleeping in a warm hotel room while Scott died alone in the woods. Where's the justice?"

"If this went to trial, their lives would be ruined, and the D.A. wasn't confident he'd get a conviction. Their story was emotionally compelling, and Cowan already has a lawyer."

"Of course he does." Max had seen all this coming, but she thought *something* good would have come from the truth.

Adele Sheldon has a body to bury. She knows what happened to her son. That's why you did this, Maxine. You came here for the truth, and that's what you found.

But right now, the truth wasn't enough.

"I didn't have to come here and tell you any of this," Horn said, and stood. "Our hands are tied."

"They lied to you. They lied to everyone."

"I'm sorry."

"And Carlos's truck being used to run me off the road?"

"Look, I understand why you're upset, and I would be, too. I pushed. But there's no proof that Arthur Cowan was driving. None. No security camera, no witnesses. You didn't see the driver. The witness who helped you didn't see the driver. It could have been Tom Keller, or anyone else. We pushed both of them; neither budged."

The waitress came with the water and the beer. Max stared at Trixie, who lay both alert and peaceful next to Chuck.

"Then there's nothing more to say," Max said. Not now, at any rate. But she'd been working on the article all weekend. She would expose to the public everything that had happened to Scott Sheldon, and who was responsible.

"I'm sorry," Horn repeated, then left.

"I tried," Chuck said quietly. "But without physical evidence, and all three sticking to the same story, it wasn't possible to get the D.A. to change his mind. He didn't even want to put up a plea deal, but Amelia convinced him that a misdemeanor and probation were better than nothing."

"It's not fair."

God, she hated the feeling and couldn't believe she'd said it out loud. She damn well knew life wasn't fair. Her life had been a roller coaster for twenty-nine years. Was it fair that her mother had walked out on her, dumping her with her older grandparents? Was it fair that her college roommate was murdered and no one could prove who'd killed her? Was it fair that Scott Sheldon died the subject of a cruel joke?

Fairness had nothing to do with living. Max believed in the truth, believed that all truth was knowledge, and with that knowledge, justice would prevail.

Nowhere in that was there *fairness.*

She and Chuck sat drinking in silence.

Truth. The truth could be told. Because truth was a different brand of justice.

Max called Ben first thing Tuesday morning.

"I'll be back in New York next week. I sent you changes to your proposal."

"You'll do the show?"

"If you agree to my changes."

"Yes."

"You don't know what they are."

"I don't care."

She smiled, genuinely smiled, for the first time in days. "Yes, you will."

"Okay, give me the basics."

"I want creative control. I want to decide what cases I investigate and air. I liked your Web site idea, the short articles, the snippets around the country—we need to expand that."

"Did something happen in Colorado?"

For someone so self-absorbed, Ben had a knack for getting to the truth. She had to admire the trait.

"This case—a group of college kids left another student in the middle of nowhere as a prank. He died, they got off with probation. As if Scott Sheldon's life isn't worth the cost of a minimal sentence."

"What do you hope to accomplish, Max?"

"Shine a light on the cruelty of human nature, how the selfish choices of a group of kids resulted in the accidental death of another, how their lies and misdirection resulted in a mother not knowing what happened to her son for six months. Six months of the unknown. Of fear and worry. The emotional turmoil the callous actions of youth created in a family."

"Okay."

"Okay?" She expected him to argue with her, that the story wouldn't be "sexy" enough or big enough for a cable news show.

"I trust you, Max. I know you'll put the right angle, the right spin on it. But it won't fill up the forty-four minutes we need for the show."

"I can—"

"Hold it. This is my job, making this work. A theme— those left behind. Friends and families of missing persons. I'll find three other cases you can interview, and we'll use your Colorado case as the positive, of persistence in finding the truth." He paused. "You'll have to talk about Karen."

"No."

"You wrote a book about it, it's a perfect lead-in for the show. You're the best person to understand how these families feel. Max, trust me on this—I'm not going to sensationalize Karen's disappearance. It's a hook. You know it. And I've read your book a half dozen times. You had a call to action—if anyone knows anything, they need to come forward. We can do the same call to action on this show. We'll find cases like Scott Sheldon, and call people to come forward."

She liked the idea. She really liked it. If she worked on cold cases, the chances were that most of these people were dead. But closure—that would help the survivors.

"Find a runaway," she said. "Someone who might come home if they knew their family ached for them."

"I knew you had a knack for this."

"I'm not doing a weekly show. I wouldn't be able to do these cases justice."

"Semimonthly."

"Monthly."

"Max—"

"But I liked your proposal about integrating with a Web page and current cases. We can do more of that if I'm not investigating a cold case every week, which takes time."

"You'll have a staff."

"Monthly."

"Fine."

"You gave in too easily."

"I actually pitched the show as a monthly program. I tweaked the proposal to give you something to negotiate away."

She laughed. Maybe Ben did know her better than she thought.

"Send me the contract when you have it drafted."

"It's already drafted. I'm sure you'll have changes."

"I'm sure you're right. I'll read it on the plane. I'm going to a wedding this weekend."

"You're not going to regret this, Max. This show is going to be huge. I promise."

But Max wasn't sure. If it wasn't successful, all that would be hurt was her own ego. But what would happen to her life if she and Ben made *Maximum Exposure* a success? Would she ever have time to work the cold cases she wanted? Would she regret giving up some of the control over her stories? Would people recognize her? One of the benefits of being an investigative journalist was that she was, basically, anonymous. People might look at her because she was tall or attractive or well dressed, but she wasn't famous.

This was cable, she reminded herself. Small beans. Maybe no one would watch it.

She said to Ben, "I'll see you in New York."

Six Weeks Later

Max stood in the doorway of her new corner office on the eighteenth floor of a state-of-the-art building on the Avenue of the Americas.

"It's small," Ben said, "but the view is great."

It was, and Max certainly couldn't complain. She would have preferred an older building with character, but the television studio needed technology and amenities that the larger buildings provided—including dishes on the roof to send and receive satellite transmissions.

She'd met the Crossmans and liked them a lot—more than she thought she would. Particularly Catherine, who had a sense of humor to go along with her sense of style.

"I'm going to work from home sometimes." Often.

"That's not a problem, but you need your own space here. I have a list of assistants for you to interview. I selected the top three from a large pool of applicants. I know you like to support the university, so I made sure they were all Columbia graduates. We also have an internship program with the college."

"Good." Maybe she and Ben would get along after all. "What's wrong?"

She walked around to her new desk. There was nothing on it, but that would change. She sat in the chair. Comfortable, but it would need to be broken in. "Nothing's wrong."

"I have some news you might like." He pulled a letter from his pocket.

It was from Cheyenne College, the office of Stephanie

Adair, addressed to Ben Lawson, Producer, *Maximum Exposure*.

"What?"

"Just read it."

She did, and she smiled. "They fired the chief of campus security."

"And implemented new security protocols related to when and how they report crimes or potential crimes to the local authorities."

"Good." She nodded as she scanned the letter a second time. "Good."

"It won't bring Scott Sheldon back."

"No."

But maybe the new procedures would prevent another mother from suffering the same grief as Adele Sheldon.

It would never be a perfect world. But keeping a bright light on the truth, exposing lies, highlighting evil, holding people accountable for their actions—or their inactions—would help.

"We're scheduled to tape in one hour. You should get down to makeup and get ready."

"Just give me five minutes."

Ben left, and Max walked over to the window, looked out, and took a deep breath.

Today was the first day of the rest of her life, but she would never forget those who'd died. Not Scott Sheldon, not Karen Richardson, and not her best friend from high school, Lindy Ames. A case that was still unsolved, and probably always would be.

NO GOOD DEE...

Read on for an excerpt from Allison Brennan's next book

NO GOOD DEED

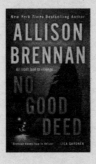

Available in November 2015 from St. Martin's Paperbacks

CHAPTER ONE

Nicole Rollins had always been a meticulous planner. She had contingencies for almost every possible scenario, which was why she'd been able to fool the DEA for fifteen years. People were mostly predictable, and mostly fools.

Even though being arrested wasn't in her master plan, she had a contingency, and the minute she was arraigned, the clock started ticking. Her people knew what to do and when to do it. The timeline, by necessity, had to be fluid, but when she was ready, she gave the signal and the countdown began. Nothing was left to chance, because she only had one shot at escaping and she had to get it right.

And if she got it wrong? She'd go out big and take as many of those motherfuckers with her as possible.

But she wasn't going to get it wrong.

Today marked the end of her old life. Cliché, but true. Nicole sat patiently in the back of the federal van, her face blank. Bored. Defeated.

Boredom and defeat were the furthest things from her mind. Anticipation flowed hot through her veins.

Her feet were shackled and locked to a bolt on the floor. Her hands were cuffed in front of her and attached to a chain around her waist. She wore an orange jumpsuit—

she despised orange, it made her skin appear sallow—and her blond hair was now cut short, without concern for style.

She kind of liked the short hair. After a trim, it would fun and sassy. She needed a little fun in her life after being in jail for ten weeks. She'd have to dye it darker, maybe add a few highlights, enough of an appearance change until she could hook up with a plastic surgeon she knew in Monterrey, Mexico. He was so good he'd be able to change the shape of her face and eyes just enough that the feds would be hard-pressed to identify her.

Two armed guards sat in the back, one with his back to the front of the truck, the other directly across from her. Another guard drove, and a fourth was in the passenger seat. A steel-reinforced door with a bullet-proof window separated the cab from the back. Closed-circuit cameras showed the rear compartment to the guards up front. They were being recorded, but there was no live camera feed. She didn't care—within thirty minutes, she'd be dead or gone, and how it happened would be irrelevant.

Two federal SUVs escorted the van, front and back. This was the third time Nicole had been transported from the jail to the federal courthouse. The first two times were uneventful, but necessary so her team could adjust last-minute details. Last Monday, she went to the courthouse to give the Assistant United States Attorney a juicy morsel to exploit. On Thursday, it was to review documentation and sign the plea agreement. After the explosion at the DEA's evidence locker ten days ago, the AUSA was more than happy to have a valuable source of information.

The angry, defeated look on Brad Donnelly's face as he watched her in the courtroom had thrilled her to no end. She won, he lost.

He had far, far more to lose before she was done with him and the people he worked for.

Today, they were taking her back to the courthouse to spill her guts. Third transport, it had become routine. She'd already agreed to the plea deal, so now it was just a matter of talking. Everything she knew about Tobias, his operation, the gun and drug trades, the money-laundering arrangement he'd had with the now-dead bitch congresswoman—she had all week to unburden herself, to make good on her promise before being transported to a federal prison far from Texas.

She wasn't going to say a word. She'd be free or dead before she ever made it to court.

Nicole was used to stakeouts and long periods of waiting; she remained calm. Very calm. An alert dream state.

Waiting.

Waiting.

Nicole smiled deep inside, so deep that her blue eyes remained blank and her mouth a thin, straight line. Her plan was nearly foolproof. She had contingencies on top of her contingencies, which was why the DEA had never known she was the most dangerous fox in their henhouse.

The transport van slowed as they approached a red light, after the lead SUV drove through the intersection. The guards glanced at the cross traffic. There were supposed to be no stops on the short, ten-minute drive from the jail to the federal courthouse. The lead car had a sensor that turned red lights green so they wouldn't even have to slow down.

Full stop meant trouble.

They stopped. A school bus was coming through the intersection, they couldn't risk a collision.

Nicole couldn't see the bus from the back of the van, but she knew it was there.

She didn't smile. She didn't react at all.

But she'd been ready for a very long time. Her heart

pounded in her chest, adrenaline surging in anticipation. And still, she remained motionless.

If Brad Donnelly had been in charge of the operation, he would have changed the route and time at the last minute—it was his M.O. But Nicole took the gamble when she planned her escape that the AUSA would follow standard protocols for a cooperating prisoner, and that Samantha Archer wouldn't even tell Donnelly the where or when because he'd been so angry about the plea agreement. That was one of those factors that Nicole couldn't control—who said what to whom, and if what they said would matter. But Sam Archer was predictable, and if she *had* told Brad about the transport, she wouldn't let him anywhere near it. One reason Nicole had pushed him so hard earlier—both when she was his partner and after her arrest—was to keep him on the edge. Sam Archer got nervous when Brad was in maverick mode. She much preferred to work with cops who took direct orders without question.

And Nicole's gamble worked.

It also helped that she'd stacked the deck, so to speak, by having someone on the inside to ensure that the AUSA didn't deviate from protocol. And if they did deviate? She had another plan, though that would have resulted in a higher body count.

This time, she didn't need it.

The guard sitting directly in front of her spoke into his radio. "Report."

The passenger said, "Traffic stop."

The guard was suspicious. Too smart for his own good. He said, "It's supposed to be green all the way."

"The lead car is holding up across the intersection, we have the tail car, nothing out of the ordinary."

The guard said, "Run it."

"Pedestrians. A school bus."

Nicole smiled and closed her eyes.

The school bus full of children rolled into the intersection and stopped, blocking the transport van.

"Shit," the driver said. He radioed immediately. "Alpha-One, we have a situation. Code Yellow."

The lead SUV responded. "Back up, re-route parallel to the north."

"Negative," Alpha-Two responded. "Civilian vehicles behind us, no way to turn around without exiting the vehicle and directing traffic."

Alpha-One said, "Code Red, be alert. Back-up en route."

The school bus didn't move. Three masked men emerged with fully-automatic weapons and opened fire on the front of the transport van.

The windshield was bullet-proof, but enough pressure from high-caliber weapons and even bullet-proof glass breaks.

In less than ten seconds both cops in the cab were dead.

It had been Nicole's idea to use the school bus. No cop would return fire when her crew was shielded by innocent kids.

The guards in the back of the transport van had their guns out—one aimed at Nicole, one aimed at the rear door. The smart guard who'd sensed a problem before the problem occurred, reported through the open mic, "Two officers down! We're under attack. Three shooters minimum, possible hostile driver, multiple hostages in the bus."

There was no response.

"Alpha-One, this is Zeta-One. I repeat, officers down. Under attack. Hostages in bus. Confirm."

Silence.

"Alpha-Two! Are you there?"

Silence.

One of the two masked men climbed up the front of the truck, through the broken glass, and extracted keys from one of the dead guards. The other men guarded the area.

"You'll never get away with this," the smart guard told Nicole. "They'll hunt you down like a rabid dog."

She didn't say a word, just stared at him.

He turned his gun on her. "I die, you die."

"And then all those children die," she whispered.

His face fell. She smiled. Just a small smile, but her excitement was growing and she couldn't contain her glee.

Sirens roared from seemingly every direction, coming closer.

"Open the door," Nicole said.

The armored transport van had to be unlocked from the outside, but opened from the inside. Her team could get in because they had the right tools, but it would take longer.

Time was critical.

"Officer, if you do not open the door in ten seconds, my people will start killing those children, one by one, until you do."

"Don't do it, Isaac," the second guard said.

"Seven seconds. I'm not bluffing."

The smart guard, Isaac, was torn. She saw it in his eyes. This was the type of dilemma they'd been trained for, even when the threat was rare. Did you let a prisoner go to save innocent lives? It was a fair trade, as far as Nicole was concerned. But in training, you never gave in to terrorists. In the textbooks, there were hard and fast rules. All criminals were terrorists. Do not negotiate with terrorists.

"Four seconds."

Isaac glanced out the front and saw a fourth gunman come out of the bus holding a child in front of him.

But children . . . that was a wild card. You can train for it, but until you were in a situation with the barrel of a gun at the back of a child's head, you really didn't know what you would do.

Isaac got up and turned the knob. The click told her it was open.

"Put the gun down and you'll be spared," she said.

"Don't do it! They'll kill us both!"

She looked Isaac in the eye. "I'm not lying."

The door opened, and Isaac put his gun down and his hands up.

The other guard didn't. He didn't get a shot off before a bullet pierced his skull.

One of the masked men quickly unlocked Nicole's shackles. She picked up the gun that Isaac had dropped. "No one will believe it, but Isaac, sleep well because you will save those kids."

"Will?" he said through clenched teeth.

"Time?" she asked one of her men.

"Eight fifty-four and thirty seconds. Thirty-one, thirty-two—"

Nicole cut him off and turned back to Isaac. "You have five minutes, twenty-ish seconds to get those kids off the bus before the bomb goes off. And if you are wondering? There really is a bomb. And it really will go off at nine a.m."

Nicole ran alongside her rescuers. The police would be closing in fast, but they had an escape route already in place. A car idled in the alleyway off the main street, and Nicole and the others jumped in. The other two men who'd stayed with the bus had their own escape route.

The driver glanced at Nicole. "You cut your hair."

She touched Joseph's face. "It'll grow back."

"I like it."

She smiled as Joseph sped away. She pulled a gun, watch, and cell phone from the glove compartment box. They didn't get too comfortable. They didn't talk. They listened to the police band as Joseph traversed through downtown San Antonio. It didn't take long for Isaac the smart guard to alert authorities to the bomb threat.

It was no idle threat.

She glanced at her watch, her stomach tingling with anticipation. She stripped off the jumpsuit and pulled on the simple black dress that Joseph tossed her.

They were almost to Amistad Park when she heard the explosion in the distance.

Distractions always worked.

The explosion was the cue for the helicopter to land. It had been painted to look like a news chopper. She and Joseph got out of the car and ran across the soccer field to where the chopper had landed. The men in the back jumped into the front seats and drove off to dump the vehicle and pick up something clean. Less than three minutes after the explosion, Nicole and Joseph were strapped in the helicopter, lifting off from the grass.

Joseph leaned over and kissed her hard on the lips, then held her face in his hands and looked at her. He didn't have to say anything—couldn't over the sound of the blades whirling above them—but his eyes said everything.

She was loved. And she was free.